PRECESSION
Pisces – Aquarius – Capricorn

Also by Derryl Flynn

THE ALBION
SCRAPYARD BLUES

PRECESSION
Pisces – Aquarius – Capricorn

by Derryl Flynn

First published in 2025 by Grinning Bandit Books
http://grinningbandit.webnode.com

Copyright © Derryl Flynn 2025

Cover design by Derryl Flynn

First published by Grinning Bandit Books in 2025

Copyright © Derryl Flynn 2025

'Precession' is the copyright of Derryl Flynn, 2025.

This is a piece of fiction and any characters or names that relate to any persons, robots, supercomputers, aliens, or wind spirits, living or dead, is purely coincidental.

All reasonable efforts have been made to contact copyright holders for material that may have been cited, referenced, or paraphrased within these pages. Acknowledgements and sources can be found at the back of the book.

All rights reserved.
No part of this book may be reproduced or transmitted in any form or by any means, electronic, digital or mechanical, without permission in writing from the copyright owner.

ISBN 978-1036928193

DEDICATION

To all the brave souls who stood in the parks and refused the three-dart-finish.

Contents

PART 1 – AEON OF THE FISH — 1
East of Lashka Gah, Helmand province, Afghanistan, 2012 — 3
Camp Bastion, Helmand Province — 8
Leeds, England 1993 — 11
1994 — 16
1995 — 23
Summer 1995 — 28
1996 – 1997 — 44
1997 – 2001 — 52
Camp Bastion – 2012 — 63

PART 2 – AEON OF THE WATER BEARER — 67
Carver Garrison, Essex — 72
The City Within a City — 72
It's Grim Up North — 96
Kersha — 110
Ampleforth — 121
Ruston Parva — 138
Percival Snodgrass — 157
The Twelve Apostles — 169
A Meeting of Minds — 174
Reunions — 191
Good Vibrations — 219
Healing The Past — 224
The Aquarians — 244

PART 3 – AEON OF THE GOAT — 249
Brigantia, North Isle — 251
Down from Catterick — 254
Sanctuary — 259
An Education — 264
Further Education — 275
Amun's Story — 282
Redemption – Deception — 290
Glaston — 299
Expecting to Fly — 308
The Hawks Fly Home — 327

Acknowledgements — 334
About the author — 335

Crazy Horse,
we hear what you say
One Earth, one Mother
One does not sell the Earth the people walk upon
We are the land
How do we sell our Mother?
How do we sell the stars?
How do we sell the air?
Crazy Horse,
we hear what you say
Today is now at end
Praying Smoke touches the clouds
On a day when Death didn't die
Real world time Tricks Shadows lie
Red, White, Perception, Deception
Predator tries civilizing us
But the Tribes will not go without return
Genetic light from the other side
A song from the Heart
Our Hearts to give
The Wild Age, the Glory Days live
Crazy Horse,
we hear what you say
One Earth, one Mother.

We are
The Seventh Generation

>	John Trudell

"The simple step of a courageous individual
Is not to take part in the lie.
One word of truth outweighs the world"

>	Aleksander Solzhenitsyn

"It is possible to believe that all the human mind has ever
accomplished is but the dream before the awakening"

>	H G Wells

Part 1 – Aeon of the Fish

East of Lashka Gah, Helmand province, Afghanistan, 2012

My name is Andrew Sarvent, Surgeon Lieutenant Commander serving with 3 Commando Brigade Royal Marines. I was a newly qualified general practitioner when I deployed here. I'm still only twenty-eight years old, but I've seen death at close quarters many times now. I've also seen it in different styles, if you can call the frighteningly fascinating declension to necrosis and mortification a style. Dealing with death on a daily basis has become part of my job, something, given my career choice, you would have thought would be part of the remit, anticipated and accepted; and I did, but never like this. To witness the macabre theatre of a dying man's bewildered reflection of a life terminal as he acts out the final moments of his ultimate scene, while that old clichéd notion of death, the hooded figure with scythe scenario waits at my shoulder with its slow, creeping reach and cold hand of clay. Or when the grim reaper tires of games and flicks the switch, snuffs the candle. Step on an IED: consciousness to oblivion in a microsecond. Death so shockingly instant. This is what I guess I mean by style. I suppose different people living alongside death think, cope, and deal with it in different ways. I can't help but wonder about death and its many manifestations. Death guided by fate and destiny, or random and arbitrary; who are we to tell? Death for cause; death without reason, the effect remains the same for those it takes and for those it leaves behind. Grief unimagined. Souls scoured hollow. Emotions wrung out to dry. Maybe this is what happens inside your head when you're halfway through your second tour of duty in this Godforsaken place. Or maybe it's just because of the person I've become.

Sometimes it's easy to see what a smile betrays; at other times it isn't. With certain soldiers of the ANA the latter nearly always applies. In the case of the young squaddie sat opposite me it's the former. Fear. Fear of the unknown; his unsure, nervous grin reeks of it. I hope my return smile and nod have all the confidence and reassurance they're delivered with without betraying the uncertainty that lies behind them. I glance over at my MEDEVAC team; they're

PRECESSION

both going through their own personal rituals; they've been here before. Reidy is going through his kit, checking and re-checking. Sergeant Farris is staring into space, seemingly oblivious to his surroundings. He's in the zone. In a few moments time we'll all be shaking hands with death.

Captain Towler taps me on the shoulder and signals me ready. The look in his eyes is like an invitation to death. He lowers his goggles over them. I nod to my two paramedics, Farris snaps alert in an instant as the Chinook hits earth and the deep breath I inhale enters my lungs in a series of shudders. Captain Towler's barked orders to his men are lost in the dakka-dakka din of the rotors as we spill out into a whipped-up swirling storm of orange-grey dust. In front of me his men fan out and disappear into the tornado. I grit my teeth and run aimlessly. Clear of the rotor wash I hear the shout, '*medic!*' Sixty metres to my left a guy is knelt over a casualty. He frantically waves us over. I take a quick glance behind to check my team is with me and we crouch-sprint as fast as our equipment will let us. To our right, the twisted remains of a Jackal, flipped onto its back and still burning. The heat hits us with a diesel and cordite kiss, and behind us we hear the crack and whine of small arms fire. I reach the casualty almost on my belly. Both his lower limbs have gone. He's semi-conscious, calm and quiet apart from an occasional dull moan. The section medic has applied tourniquets in a frantic effort to stop the bleeding. I glance up at him; he's only young, twenty at most. His whole body is shaking involuntarily – shock.

'Are you okay?'

'. . . Sir,' he gives me a bewildered nod. At least he's noticed my rank, which is a good sign.

'IM?'

'Plasma, morphine.'

'Good man.' I need to establish triage quickly. 'How many more casualties?'

'One – two,' he says confused.

'Let's go.' I urge him on. One of my guys takes over and we move off. After only a few metres the young squaddie stops dead in his tracks confronted by a severed arm, its hand grotesquely reaching up to us out of the dirt as if pleading for some sort of deliverance. Other bloodied bits of body parts lie scattered around us, a human jigsaw. The kid, trying to hide his horror, looks sideways at me for some sort of guidance. There's nothing we can do here except to pick

PISCES

up the pieces. *T4,* I mutter to myself. It's a non-priority body bag job. Close by I see the third casualty, just off the road as it falls away into a ditch. I scurry over but before I get to him, I hear the urgent shouts of, *'Incoming!'* We hit the road and press ourselves into the dirt as the whoosh of an RPG flies over our heads and lands with a loud crump into the earth about eighty metres in front of us. From behind the cover of a Ridgeback and a couple of Snatch Vixens, I hear the rattle of LMGs and the *whoomp* of a mortar as the remainder of the ambushed patrol along with Captain Towler's men return fire in the general direction of the attack. We were supposed to have the protection of an Apache, but up to now I'd neither seen nor heard it. I'm on my feet as soon as the fallout debris from the RPG has subsided, and I scramble down beside the casualty, silently praying that someone has locked in the co-ordinates and has called in an air strike. This guy has caught the blast in the lower abdomen, directly underneath his Osprey CBA. I lift my goggles and try to wipe stinging sweat out of my eyes but only succeed in sticking sand and grit to them. I unzip my bag. Method ends up a frantic rummage. In my haste a glove tears. I rip it off cursing and slinging the shredded latex to one side. Procedure takes a back seat as I cut away at fragged bits of blood-soaked combat vest that have fallen into the gaping hole that had been his stomach. In the near distance I hear rounds pinging off armoured steel. I take a quick glance back at the upturned smouldering Jackal and back to this poor bloke's terrible injuries. It must have been one hell of an IED to do this amount of damage.

'Sarvo . . .?'

I look up in surprise. The badly wounded soldier has just opened his eyes and called me by a nickname I hadn't heard in years. '. . . Is that you?' He asks it almost casually. 'What the fuck are you doin' here?'

I'd hardly looked at the face beneath the helmet. Now he's conscious, leering at me just like he used to. The shock, the circumstance, and the recognition all collide in a microsecond. Inside me, lactic acid and adrenalin surge. The scene freezes surreally. 'Harper?' I manage in a cracked whisper.

'Lance Corporal Harper, chor - took yer advice - did summat wi' me life - joined up . . .' He pauses and grins. It hides a grimace. '. . . Now look what Terry's gone an' done – fuckin' ragheads.'

'Don't worry mate. We'll have you patched up and back at Bastion in no time,' I try and reassure him while avoiding his eyes.

PRECESSION

His abdomen is a mess, and he is haemorrhaging badly. He needs a miracle, and my experience tells me he isn't going to get one. I try and stay detached, remain professional, but it's almost impossible. My thumping heart is trying to vacate my chest, while my head tries to stay rational in a swirling sea of irrationality. As if these circumstances aren't horrific enough. I sense the reaper close by. Death plays its ace – *Deal with this one, you fucker* – This guy was my childhood best friend.

'Are you in pain?' I ask while tapping air pockets out of a hypo.

'Can't feel a fuckin' fing, charver - but me lug 'oles are ringin' - fink me eardrums are bust.'

Least of your worries, mate, I say to myself, plunging the needle into his thigh. Over my radio I hear the flight lieutenant's voice come over in crackling waves. He's not happy. Out here the Chinook is a big target and a sitting duck. Where is the air cover? All at once our collective prayers are answered. Overhead I hear the roar of a Tornado and moments later two loud crumps as a couple of Paveways are dropped onto the Taliban compound half a mile away. Breathing space. I send the young squaddie back to help stretcher the first casualty. My colleague Corporal Reid drops in beside us and puts in a temporary IV.

'Could do wiv a ciggi, chor . . .' Harper manages just as the diamorphine takes hold and he slowly closes his eyes. We tape him up and carefully lift him onto a litter, ruefully watching the field bandages change colour. Overhead, the Tornado makes another pass and sends what sounds like a Sidewinder into the insurgent compound. A percussion wave of noise and heat washes over us. I radio in two T1's and a T4 and we evacuate. By the time we reach the Chinook, the Apache arrives on the scene, banking sharply over our heads, completing a recce before letting loose a couple of rockets into the Taliban position. We take to the air, leaving Captain Towler and the rest of the patrol to mop up. Our farewell is a shower of anti-missile chaff, just in case any of the enemy had escaped the attentions of the Tornado and Apache. We hook up our two survivors and make them as comfortable as possible. I radio in code vampire for extra blood to be on standby. The relief of escaping that hellhole is tempered by the certainty that my old mate isn't going to make it. His vitals are weak, and deep down I know no matter how much stuff we pump into him we won't be able to save his life. The other guy, - I glance over at Reidy who gives me a reassuring nod - well, he won't ever walk again, that's certain but it looks like he's earned himself a one way back to Brize Norton. I look at them both and unashamedly wish it the other way round.

'Where's me ciggie, charver?' rasps Harper as he regains consciousness, much to Corporal Reid's amazement. We'd put enough morphine in him to quieten a horse.

'You can't smoke inside these things, Harper, lad,' I tell him. 'You can light up once we get back to Bastion.'

'Hands off cocks - on socks.' He grins up at me before closing his eyes again. I smile to myself. It was the line from *Kes* he always used to come out with. - They were the last words he spoke.

PRECESSION

Camp Bastion, Helmand Province

I scrub hard at my red stained skin like a man possessed. This is the angry phase, where the fatuity of it all hits home. I've seen men self-harm when they go through this bit. Psychologically it has something to do with survival guilt, coming home from a patrol when a mate hasn't. I silently curse this cause to hell, this act of sophistry that is no cause at all, this human made mire borne of lies, deceit and duplicity.

Fatigue finally takes over from anger and I buttress my hands against the cool tiled wall of the shower. My head follows, and in a frisk like position I allow the cascading water to caress my weary limbs as I watch the last of Darren Harper's dissipated blood swirl away with the sweat and the soap.

Darren Harper – Darren Harper, Harper – Darren Harper. I mouth the name to myself mantra fashion, over and over; just two words travelling merry-go-round in my head. Their very nuance slowly becoming abstract, the joined-up letters not even resembling a name anymore, let alone someone I knew.

I climb into clean fatigues and prepare for the task I detest. I can cope with removing shattered limbs and patching up gaping wounds. It's my job; it's what I've been trained to do. But this bit, the bureaucracy of death, the wrapping up of another wasted life, I hate. I stare at the death certificate, pen poised, hovering; ready to sign, seal and deliver one more statistic into the annals of bullshit history. Darren Harper – Fuck.

I sling the pen on the fold-up table that's supposed to resemble a desk and take a slug from the bottle of Jack Daniels that's acting as my crutch this evening. I silently salute our friends from across the Atlantic for their magniloquent philanthropy, although, more than likely, this latest batch of Southern hospitality had been purloined from the American store of plenty by some beleaguered, disgruntled, disenchanted team of British Borrowers. The Borrowers: that's what the Yanks called us, the third world army. Funny, but painfully true. Mercifully, much of the jibe was directed at our leaders and politicians and not the boys they fought alongside. Anyway, we had our own take on the ways of our illustrious allies and their amusingly blinkered view of the world. Politics aside, I was thankful of this bottle, this passport to temporary oblivion that someone had thoughtfully set down in front of me during the sobering aftermath of today's events.

Another two casualties just came in. Another IED. SMO Lieutenant Commander Naylor said he'd deal with it even though officially he was off duty. Off duty, that's a laugh. In reality, there's no such thing here at Camp Bastion. The job's twenty-four-seven and you grab respite from dealing with the torn flesh and broken bodies when you can.

Corporal McAllister appears out of a mess of scurrying personnel. Amidst a background of organised chaos, he drops the dreaded brown envelope onto the desk in front of me. I stare at it blankly. It contains Darren Harper's personal effects.

'Sorry sir,' he says shuffling awkwardly from foot to foot. 'I understand you knew him.'

I offer a solemn nod in confirmation.

'Sorry sir,' he repeats, knowing full well the words won't offer too much comfort, but I thank him anyway before dismissing him back to his grim duties. In the distance someone screams. Someone else barks out orders. I watch him walk away and merge with the madness in his green, crimson spattered theatre gown.

With a heavy sigh I push the envelope to one side, leaving the job of listing personal effects until last and scan the forms that need filling out: Lance Corporal Darren Harper. 3rd. Battalion The Rifles. Age: 28. Cause of death: Injuries sustained: Location of death: I fill in the details in between slugs of bourbon, just to numb the emotions. I take my time.

I get myself outside half the contents of the bottle before I feel ready to make an inventory of the stuff inside the envelope. I spread the contents out on the table and take a deep breath. I've seen it all before. Most of it is what your regular squaddie would carry about him, but there are two items apart that manage to stiffen me sober. One is a well-worn colour snap of a woman and two boys. I hold it closer to the desk lamp to get a better look. I feel like I should know her, the face seems familiar, but a name won't come to mind. I assume her to be his wife or partner, mid to late twenties, bobbed brunette hair. A robust, healthy-looking lass, maybe a touch overweight but smiling happy. The kids: one a toddler, no more than two. The elder: four or five; cheeky little grin; number two cropped

PRECESSION

head; a dead ringer for his dad. I hold the photo at arm's length in a shaky grip and try and put a freeze on my lips and chin that have started to tremble. Having carefully placed the photograph back in the envelope I pick up the other item that held a special interest for me. It was a sterling silver chain on which hung a pendant of a hawk in flight. I had one just like it, although I hadn't seen mine in years. It was more than likely tucked away in some old tobacco tin amongst the other collected artefacts of my youth, gathering dust in the attic of my parent's house, but I was sure I still had it. I hold this symbol of the most unlikely of childhood friendships in the palm of my hand and gently rub a thumb over the worn, tarnished metal. Like some bereaved Aladdin coaxing the genie out for one last time I wish him back. And slowly, yet inevitably the events that took place earlier today outside Lashka Gah begin to hit home. Despite the anaesthesia of the Jack Daniels, when the adrenaline created by trying to save lives under fire subsides, the reality hits you like a punch to the solar plexus. Shock manifests itself in different ways. I'm a doctor; I've seen it many times. But I'm still human. My eyes begin to sting with fatigue and the rest of it. Even when they fill with water the stinging won't go away. Memories start to flood my senses. Yes, I'm still human – barely.

PISCES

Leeds, England 1993

I never knew what hit me, and I didn't see it coming, but it hurt. I'd only felt pain like that once before, when I was six, walking in the park with my mum and a ball some older lads were playing with hit me full in the face and knocked me off my feet. The pain felt the same, but it wasn't a ball that hit me this time, although I still saw stars, or flashes of bright light that you describe as stars, and I still ended up on my back looking up to the heavens with all the wind knocked out of me.

A fuzzy circle of sneering faces appeared above me silhouetted against the bright blue September sky. A couple of the faces jeered down at me, and I took three or four sly kicks to my ribs and buttocks. I scrambled to my feet, but before I caught my balance I was knocked sideways again. The jeering crowd parted as I fell. On my way back down something warm and wet sprayed from my nose, and I fleetingly caught sight of a couple of kids using my new brown leather satchel as a football. On my hands and knees, I gingerly felt up at the now throbbing source of pain and caught a handful of red. It dropped through my fingers in thick blobs and merged with the black asphalt, while regular drips from my bust nose caught up, adding to the ever-widening damp patch. I felt dizzy and sick.

'Fuckin' hell, he bleeds a lot, don't he?' were the first coherent words I heard.

'I hardly touched the soft twat,' someone sneered.

'Aww, look what you've done to him, Briggsy, yer rotten get,' piped up a girl from the crowd.

'See if yer can knock him out, Briggsy,' encouraged another kid.

'I'll knock *you* out in a minute, yer pleb,' said a menacing voice I assumed belonged to Briggsy, whoever he was. I made to get to my feet again, but a knee in the back kept me down on all fours.

'Lerrim up now Briggsy, yer big bully, you've gone an' brok his nose,' pleaded the girl.

'Who asked you, yer slag? Keep yer snek out.'

A pair of manky looking trainers suddenly appeared in front of me attached to a pair of filthy, black pants that were fraying at the bottom. 'What's goin' on?' asked the voice they belonged to.

PRECESSION

'Briggsy's gone an' smashed him in his face an' brok' his nose,' repeated the girl.

'Who is he?'

'Dunno, he looks like a posh kid.'

'What yer hit him for, Briggsy?' demanded the scruffy kid.

'What's it to do wi' you, yer Gypo?' Briggsy dismissed him with a snarl of contempt.

'Don't call *me* a gypo.'

'Thy *is* a gypo. Wanna mek summat of it?'

'Say it again, yer fat cunt.'

'Gypo . . .'

I felt the scruffy kid make a lunge, and I took a whack to the side of my head as he did so, but I suddenly felt free of the knee that was in my back and pinning me down, so I took the opportunity to scramble to my feet and quickly distance myself from the now scuffling pair.

"ere y'are mate. Are yer alright? Yer new bag's a bit scratched.'

The girl had retrieved my satchel and was holding it out for me with a sympathetic look as I continued to try and stem the flow of blood from my nose.

'Satchel,' I blubbered, blowing bubbles of red.

'Eh?'

'It's a satchel.'

The look of sympathy turned to one of incomprehension, so I offered her a muffled thank you and took it from her. She wasn't a pretty girl. In fact, she also looked a bit of a scruff. She had a uniform on of sorts, but it was too big for her, even though she was far from skinny. It looked like a hand-me-down. Her hair was shoulder length, dark and greasy-lank. She was staring at me, fascinated, like I was from another planet.

'What school have *you* come from, then?'

'St. Botolphs.'

She continued with her look of incomprehension and added a slight curl of the lip. I looked down at what was my clean white handkerchief that didn't have much white on it anymore.

'You're not from round 'ere, are yer?'

I looked at her and the three or four other kids that were still milling around gawping at me with a curiousness that was tinged with contempt. Here I was, first day at a new school in my new, clean uniform that didn't look too new or clean any more, clutching my new scuffed and scratched leather satchel in one hand and trying to stem the flow of blood with the other. No one else had satchels. No one else had new uniforms or shoes that had been polished. She had stated the obvious.

'No,' I said. 'No, I'm not.'

Alongside the pain I had a mix of feelings, like I was the star attraction at some freak show, or a wounded animal being surrounded and stalked by a pack of braying hyenas. Nearby, the one they called Briggsy and the scruffy kid were squared up in a push and shove stand-off, hurling insults and obscenities, goading, daring one another. Briggsy was bigger, both in height and weight, but the scruffy kid had a hardness about him, wiry but mean. I had an urge to move away, find a corner and lick my wounds, but my feet wouldn't budge, and I stayed rooted to the spot.

'Teacher!' I heard someone hiss loudly, and in an instant the pack of hyenas had evaporated into the Serengeti of the playground. Even Briggsy and the scruffy kid had sloped away amidst glowered threats and promises. By the time the teacher arrived I was stood all alone, still rooted to the spot with my head back, red rag stuck to my face, looking up at the blue sky once again.

'What's been going on here?' she demanded.

'Nothing, Miss – tripped and fell, bust my nose.' I lied.

My mum and dad were great parents, lovely people, but at that moment I hated them. I hated my dad for having got himself transferred up here. I hated mum for making me wear a brand-new uniform, and buying me a satchel, complete with pens, pencils, ruler, compass and the rest of it. She lived in a time warp. Who had satchels these days? Worst of all, everyone thought I was a posh kid, which was far from the truth. Mum and dad were working class, but they were hard working. Dad was an engineer who had to move to this place because of his job. Mum was a company bookkeeper. We weren't poor but we certainly weren't posh. We came to Leeds at the start of the summer, and all the Middle schools of choice were full, even though they were in our catchment area. This one wasn't even on our list, let alone in our area. It served two of the roughest estates in the city. We would be appealing.

PRECESSION

At break I found myself a quiet spot in a shady corner, hopefully out of harm's way and observed the chaotic buzz of excited kids on the first day of a new term from a safe distance. I gingerly touched my nose, which, thankfully, had stopped bleeding but was still grazed. The school nurse assured me it wasn't broken, although there was noticeable swelling. I still don't have a clue what that Briggsy character hit me with.

'Hey up, 'ere yer are, mush. I've been lookin' all over for yer. How's yer neb?'

The scruffy kid appeared quickly from around the corner of the building and in no time was up in my face. I instinctively backed away.

'It's ok,' I said eventually, 'a bit sore.'

He nodded and grinned, and for the first time I saw him up close. Along with the knackered trainers and the fraying black pants he wore a grubby navy sweatshirt that roughly approximated the school's colours. The only neatness I could detect in his whole appearance was the number two cropped hair. He continued to grin.

'Er, thanks for what you did this morning,' I said just for something to say.

'Ah, that's alrate,' he smiled dismissively. 'I hate that bastard anyway.'

'Who is he?'

'Briggsy? – He's just a nobody who thinks he's somebody. Reckons he's gonna be cock o' this school, but he's wrong. 'ere, want one o' these?' He delved into a pocket and came out with a handful of blackjacks and fruit salads. I thanked him and took a fruit salad. 'Tek some more,' he urged. 'Go on, I nicked a shitload from t'shop this mornin'. I took a couple more. He un-wrapped three or four blackjacks shoving them in his mouth together and pretty soon he was grinning liquorice as we chewed in silence for the next few minutes.

'What's yer name, mush?' he asked eventually.

'Andrew.'

'Andrew?' He pulled a face and curled a lip. 'An-drew?' He looked at me to see if I was serious. I nodded apologetically. 'What's yer last name?'

'Sarvent.'

He looked at me blankly.

'Sar-vent,' I repeated like I was talking to a deaf person.

PISCES

'Where do you live?'

'Roundhay.'

'Roundhay,' he said raising an eyebrow. 'Bit posh up there innit?'

'No,' I countered defensively, 'just normal.'

We looked at each other with the recognition that our perceptions of normal were light years apart.

'What's your name?' I asked, although I wasn't half as interested as he had been.

'Harper – Daz Harper. People just call me Harper.'

'Where do you live?'

'Gipton.' He said it like the word carried great significance, waiting for some sort of reaction that would normally come from the very mentioning of the place. I had never heard of it, and I quickly got the feeling that it wasn't a place I would be in a hurry to get to know.

I'm saved from having to strain the conversation further by the bell, signalling end of break.

'See yer around, Sarvo, an' remember, if that cunt bovvers yer again just give us a shout, yeh?'

I gave him a vague nod before he disappeared back around the corner as quickly as he had appeared. I looked down at the two fruit salads that had started to turn sticky in my hand. I thought about the manky pocket they came from and quickly threw them in a nearby bin.

I trudged back to class still silently cursing my parents. The last thing I needed was protection from some chav from Gipton. The first thing I needed was a successful appeal.

PRECESSION

1994

My parents appealed. They appealed three times. By the time the third appeal had failed I was already into the last term of my first year and was past caring. During that period I had somehow managed to avoid any more nosebleeds, and thankfully, the satchel had been assigned to a cupboard under the stairs.

I hadn't been accepted by all and sundry. I was still referred to as the posh kid, but I had a new best friend. His name was Darren Harper. How it came about, to this day I'm still not too sure, but it did. The origins of such an unlikely friendship are hard to pin down, and I'm not about to start analysing the chemistry of its beginnings now. It could have been something to do with a willingness to share a seemingly never-ending supply of purloined confectionary in return for exclusive use of a Gameboy, but it was more than that.

I didn't seek out his company or companionship at first, in fact I actively avoided it, but there was something about his persistence, the physical and if necessary violent removal of anyone else who inadvertently sat next to me in class, the permanent in-your-face inane grin, and the constant seduction of surreptitious under-the-desk penny sweets. It had all started with a reluctant, anything-to-keep-the-peace, kind of tolerance and had somehow led to me thinking of him as a mate – my only mate. I had even got used to the permanent odour of what smelled like wet dog and foist that would emanate from his person and permeate anything within a five-metre radius. I guessed that he didn't care to wash too often, and I later learned that the bath at home was what one of his older brothers used to grow cannabis plants in, although at the time I didn't have a clue what cannabis was.

Harper had plenty of other chav mates, but his relationship with them was more about violent one-upmanship and who could skank who the most. Nearly all my class were world and streetwise. The stuff they seemed to know made my nine-year old naivety shine out like a Belisha Beacon. That's all we were, nine- and ten-year-olds, but most of them spoke and acted like adults, albeit nasty, child-like adults. They knew all about things they shouldn't have and yet knew nothing about what I held important or fascinating. The act of

PISCES

growing up according to their age seemed to have passed them by.

School was boring for all of us. For them, because they appeared to have the attention span of goldfish. For me, because what the teachers were trying to impart was nothing short of remedial and so I simply switched off.

Like a lot of the kids in my class Harper wasn't a regular patron. He would often go missing for days, even weeks on end, and during such times I would be left to the mercy and persecution of Briggsy and his ilk. I actively tried to stay out of trouble but was quietly determined not to allow anyone get the better of my vulnerability whenever my minder wasn't around. At some point I knew I had to stand on my own two feet, and when one break time I found myself surrounded by Briggsy and a couple of his hyena mates attempting to tax me for my Gameboy, I knew that time had come.

My dad had enrolled me for Taekwondo classes when we first came to Leeds. I took to the ancient Korean martial art like a fish to water and during the school year had quickly progressed through the first ten junior rankings known as *geup* and was already on my first dan. Briggsy was a big lad, but he was also a bit of a lard-arse, a monster-muncher. He was far from fit, as I had observed on many a PE lesson. I figured if I could stay light on my feet, take on the ringleader, I might just be able to make a monkey out of the fat boy, and then maybe the rest of his droogies would back off and leave me in peace.

Briggsy had his hand out, palm up, beckoning with his fingers. 'Hand it over, yer little puff,' he demanded with a leer.

I was backed against a wall, which is where I didn't want to be. I edged myself slowly away so that I had some manoeuvring space behind me. Briggsy and his little team followed me in a menacing semi-circle.

'Give – if yer know what's good for yer.'

I went as if to comply. I put a hand into the inside pocket of my blazer and slowly brought it back out as a fist. I took up a poomse, planted a stance and centred my gravity. With my eyes I beckoned him towards my outstretched arm. This seemed to confuse him a little as even Briggsy would have known I wouldn't be able to conceal a whole gameboy within my fist. He approached cautiously, the leer never once leaving his big ugly mush. He grabbed my wrist and roughly twisted my arm so my hand faced upwards.

'Open up,' he demanded.

PRECESSION

I slowly released my fist, revealing nothing but an empty palm. This confused him some more, so as the cogs whirred and before he could become enraged at my messing about, I deftly twisted out of his grip, grabbed *his* wrist and pulled him towards me all in one swift movement. He came easy, all off balance and I planted my right spear-hand into his liver meridian, one of the major and vulnerable pressure points. It was the first time I had executed jiapsul and it was textbook. Briggsy turned to stone for a second or two and his eyes glazed over before collapsing like a sack o' spuds. That would have been enough to keep him quiet for a while, but I had to show his lieutenants that I meant business. As he dropped to his knees I finished him off with a sokuto, a side kick to the chest, a move I would have loved to have delivered to the side of his head, but which my discipline strictly forbids. I performed taeguek il jang and returned to choom-bi, the ready position, while Briggsy's mates performed guppy shapes and visibly shrank before my eyes.

"kin hell, posh kid knows kung-fu,' one of them managed to utter. I retained choom-bi and stared hard at the pair who had started to back away, said nothing. 'He knows kung-fu,' the kid repeated in awe. Beyond striking distance, he decided to make a run for it. His mate, quickly realising he was now on his own, soon followed hot on his heels. 'He knows kung-fu,' I heard him shout one last time, to no one in particular, as they both disappeared round a corner.

When they were out of sight I relaxed my stance. The bully who had given me the little silver scar on the bridge of my nose a year earlier lay on his side in a crumpled heap. He made no sound, but as the bulk of his dishevelled form rhythmically rose and fell, I could tell he was still breathing.

Word soon got round that the posh kid was no longer a pushover and from then on in I was generally left alone. Don't get me wrong, over the next two years it wasn't all plain sailing. There were plenty of other kids ready and eager to take on the deposed Briggsy's mantle, but together Harper and I were usually afforded a healthy respect and given our space, and I rarely had to resort to martial arts again.

There weren't many kids on our street, and the few that were went to better schools and appeared even more nerdy than I was. At home I was surrounded by plenty of stuff to occupy my time with, and I'd always been content in my self-imposed isolation, so, making friends with the aloof type who went to school in the back of daddy's

PISCES

Volvo was never at the top of my agenda.

'You know you're quite welcome to bring a school friend home for tea anytime if you like, love,' mum said casually over breakfast one morning. Up to then Harper and I had never seen each other outside of school; we lived miles apart, and I could tell that my antisocial tendencies had begun to worry mum slightly.

'Ok,' I said as casually as she had offered, but remember thinking at the time – *fine Mum, you asked for it. I bet you don't offer twice.*

§

'Did your mum say it was ok then?' I asked as we stood waiting for the bus.

'What?'

'You staying at mine for tea.'

'What's it got to do wiv her?'

'Haven't you even asked her?'

'Why would I?'

I shrugged. 'Won't she wonder where you are; won't she have made you some tea?'

Harper looked at me like I was talking soft. 'Don't talk soft,' he said snapping off a large chunk of cherry liquorice between his teeth and offering me the rest. I refused with a shake of the head knowing that mum would have made an extra special effort with whatever she put before us and would be upset if she didn't see clean plates.

By the time we turned onto my avenue Harper had devoured all manner of cheap sweets. 'You won't want your tea,' I said, sounding like my mother.

'Course I will, I'll eat owt, me,' he said popping in a pink coloured flying saucer.

It was obvious his mum never cooked for him. He relied on a get what you can, when you can, any which way you can regime wherever sustenance was concerned and never mind the quality.

'I've never been up here before,' said Harper, eyeing up the eclectic mix of Edwardian and pre-war dwellings. 'This is where our Frankie comes robbin'.'

He picked up a stone and flung it at an unsuspecting tabby sat sunning itself on a fence. I gave him a look of reprehension and immediately felt even more like my mother.

PRECESSION

'Don't like moggies,' he spat. 'Like dogs, can't fuckin' stand moggies.'

I had been unsure if all this had been such a good idea, now I was beginning to feel certain.

I'll never forget the look on mum's face when she opened the door to us. Wiping her hands down her apron, the beaming, welcoming smile soon morphed into a fixed grimace that did its best but ultimately failed to retain smile status.

'Oh – oh,' she said hanging on to the door that I thought any minute now might be shut back in our faces. We both looked at her blankly. Harper was still chewing on something.

'Mum, this is Harper. Harper, this is mum,' I said flatly. He gave her a vague nod of the head.

'Oh – oh,' she said again just about gaining enough time to compose herself before stepping to one side to allow us in, albeit reluctantly. Eyes bulging, she gave me a *what-the-fuck* look as we stepped by. I gave her a smile and politely enquired as to what time tea would be ready. She said we had a half hour window. Before we went upstairs, she reminded us to take our shoes off, which in hindsight wasn't such a good idea as she would be out with the Glade for the rest of the evening. We trudged off up to my room, Harper with the big toe of his right foot sticking conspicuously out of the end of his smelly sock. Afterwards Mum asked why he wore odd shoes. I told her it was because apparently you can't nick trainers in pairs.

I suppose when you've got stuff you take it a bit for granted. I never felt privileged in any way, nor had I ever felt deprived. I'd not much thought about it really, but I guess most of the things I ever asked for I tended to get without too much bother. Harper surveyed my room in silent wonderment, his eyes flitting sharply in all directions, his hands wanting to touch, poke and probe everything at once. I followed him around the room, amused at his giddiness. I watched him lift two of my precisely placed Mutant Ninja Turtles off a shelf, Leonardo and Michelangelo. I laughed to myself as I watched him make them do battle, making what he thought were all the appropriate martial art noises. He quickly moved on to my model Porches and Ferraris while I carefully placed the discarded turtles back to their original positions. Next came Dad's old vintage Dinky and Matchbox toys that he'd lovingly looked after as a kid and proudly handed down. By the time he'd moved on to my Airfix kits

PISCES

I'd begun to get a little nervy.

'Don't touch that!' I shouted as he made a move for my pride and joy, The Ark Royal.

'Chill out, Sarvo, I aren't gonna brek it.'

I formed a barrier between him and the labour of love that took me months to complete. 'It's not a toy,' I explained. 'You're not supposed to touch it.'

'What's it for, then?'

'It's a model; you're just supposed to look at it.'

He pulled a face like I was crackers and moved onto something else. The more precious I became, the more bored he got. He ended up looking through my telescope.

"kin 'ell, yer can see rate into that house,' he exclaimed.

'It's for looking at stars,' I said.

'What, yer mean you've never looked at women gerrin' undressed?' he asked incredulous.

'No,' I said shocked and embarrassed.

'Bollocks you haven't,' he said disbelieving.

'Stars and birds, Harper, that's all. We're not all perverts like you.'

'Wow, look at this bird,' he shouted suddenly all exited.

'Piss off, now. Stop messing about.'

'No, serious,' he said all seriously. 'It's a beauty. It's got wings all black an' blue like a Maggie, burrit in't a Maggie.'

'Here, let's have a look.' I edged him away from the telescope and peered through the eyepiece. 'It's a jay.'

'No, it in't.'

I looked at him like the moron he was. 'It's a bloody jay,' I told him with authority.

'How do *you* know?'

I tutted at him and walked over to the bookshelf, pulled out my Ladybird book of British Birds and opened it at the colour plate of The Jay. 'That is a bloody jay, my friend,' I said stabbing a finger at the page. 'And I'll have money on it.'

Harper looked at the illustration, then back to the telescope. He did this two more times before he seemed convinced. 'Yer rate, it is,' he said at last. 'I've never seen owt like it.' He seemed genuinely thrilled.

'You're lucky,' I said. 'It's not often you see a jay, 'specially round here.'

PRECESSION

With its characteristic screech, Harper watched the bird swoop down from the oak tree and gather a vole or something up in its claws from the garden opposite and carry it away all in one swift movement. He was enraptured.

I watched him eagerly leaf through the book with his grubby fingers. He struggled to read the sections on any bird that caught his interest, so I read them for him. He reminded me of Billy Casper from the film Kes. I hoped he would wash his hands before tea.

Mum had made a chicken plate pie with mashed potato, broccoli and gravy. Dad was working late, so Mum and I watched fascinated as Harper noisily wolfed down the contents on his plate with lighting speed, minimal chewing, the food hardly touched the sides, his earlier unhealthy intake of sweets having no effect whatsoever on his appetite. He sat bored and impatient while we finished ours. The broccoli remained untouched.

'Alrate that, missus – ta,' he said as mum gathered up the plates. 'Not rate keen on them little trees.'

'You mean the Broccoli?' said Mum.

'Whatever.'

'Have you ever tried it?'

'Nah.'

Mum continued to look bewildered, right up to when she served the home-made baked rice pudding out of its Pyrex dish. Harper eyed it suspiciously. He'd only ever seen rice pudding out of a tin.

After tea I dug out the Kes video. He said he'd never seen it before. We sat and watched it in almost total silence; the only sound being our occasional sucks and slurps as we devoured a seemingly endless Harper supply of sugary kola kubes. His concentration was unfamiliarly intense. I'd never seen him so still and quiet.

I'll never know if it was that chance encounter with the jay or the revelation of the Ken Loach film that triggered the passion, or whether he was born with an obsession of all things feathered, or if his ornithological bent stayed with him until his dying day, but for the next six years or so it would remain as the hub of our unlikely friendship, the universal centre for many a crazy adventure as we journeyed our rocky way toward youth and adolescence.

PISCES

1995

Stalagmites, stalactites – when you'd seen one dark, dank cave you'd seen 'em all, announced Harper, but maybe not quite as articulately, after he'd been ordered back to the bus for trying to knock the wig off an ancient limestone formation known as 'The Judge' with some carefully aimed rocks. He didn't seem to care that this curious phenomenon had taken thousands of years to form its peculiar shape; he was simply bored. Trouble was, he'd gone and spoiled it for himself, as the next stop on this rare school outing was a falconry centre just outside Settle.

'Let him off sir, he won't do it again I promise,' I pleaded on his behalf.

'If he can't be trusted in the presence of inanimate objects, I'm certainly not going to trust him in front of live ones,' stated Mr. Dyson defiantly.

'He didn't mean it sir, he gets bored easily, that's all.'

Dyson looked down at me askance. 'Is that supposed to provide some sort of excuse for that kind of behaviour, Sarvent – hmm?'

'But he loves birds, sir. He's been waiting for this bit for ages. It wouldn't be fair to take it away from him now.'

'Well, he should have thought of that, shouldn't he? Cause and effect, Sarvent, consequences and all that – hmm?' He ushered the last of the kids off the bus, all except the banished Harper who was sat at the back looking hard done by.

'Aww, don't be tight sir; I'll look after him. I'll make sure he won't do anything daft, honest I will.'

'That's quite a responsibility you're placing on yourself, young man,' he said and pondered for a while. He looked at the hapless Harper, then back to me, no doubt wondering what misdemeanours he would undertake if left to his own devices all alone on the bus. 'Very well, I'll take you at your word – but God help the pair of you if he so much as steps one foot out of line, is that understood?'

'Aww thanks sir. He'll be as good as gold, I promise.' I gave Harper a grin and a come on with a nod of the head and he was at my side in an instant. 'Say you're sorry,' I hissed out the corner of my mouth, followed by a kick to a shin when he was hesitant.

PRECESSION

'Sorry fer chuckin' stones, sir,' he mumbled. 'I won't do it again.'

'A week's detention for you both if I get one whiff of trouble; is that clear?' We both confirmed in unison that it was. 'Now go on, catch up with the others.'

Harper was like a dog with two cocks in that place. When the guides spoke about the different species of bird on show he hung on their every word. I'd never seen his attention held for so long. He asked question after question, never giving the other kids, who waited patiently with their hands up, a look in. He was the first in line with glove and jesses for the flight demonstrations and was reluctant to let anyone else have a go. Black kite, Griffon vulture, Harris hawk, Golden eagle, he loved them all, but the bird that left him dumbstruck was the spellbinding Peregrine falcon. The speed and velocity at which it came onto the glove and took the meat was awesome. As the rest of us all gasped in amazement Harper turned to me with his familiar grin and a sparkle in his eyes that I'd never seen before or since – priceless.

It hadn't been such a good idea to allow him into the gift shop. He was like a magpie. Anything that glittered caught his attention and I had to have eyes in the back of my head to prevent him from spoiling it for us both. I tried hard to explain that anything sold in the shop went towards the upkeep of the birds, and that nicking stuff wouldn't be doing them any favours, but he found it hard to grasp the concept. Anything on show was fair game as far as he was concerned. If they were daft enough to leave stuff within arm's reach that was their look out.

The shop was only small, and it didn't take many bodies to fill it. Over a sea of heads and a mess of hustling bustling kids I could see Dyson hovering, trying to keep a beady eye on us. Harper was fingering a piece of cheap jewellery, a pendant of a hawk in flight attached to a silver chain. It was fastened to a padded card and there were more of them hanging from a rack. £9.99 read the price tag – made in Taiwan – was written in small print on the back of the card.

'I'm havin' this,' he hissed, looking around furtively.

'No, don't,' I hissed back. 'You'll get us done.'

I tried to take the thing from him without drawing Dyson's attention, but he was too quick for me.

'I'm havin' it,' he growled and gave me a look like a dog protecting a bone.

'Please, Harper,' I pleaded. 'Don't nick it.'

PISCES

'Fuck off,' he said nastily. 'What's it to you anyway?'
'I'll buy it for you,' I blurted.
'Yer what?'
'I'll buy it for you if you want it that badly.'
He looked at me like I was crazy.
'Piss off,' he said eventually. 'You an't gorra tenner.'
'I have,' I said. 'That's exactly what I've got.'
'Where from?' he asked, his eyes narrowing suspiciously.
'It's mine, I told him truthfully. 'Pocket money what I've saved.'
'Bollocks!'
'Honest – look.' I reached into the back pocket of my pants and pulled out the folded note. He looked at it wide eyed. Pocket money to him was an unknown concept. Pocket money that had accrued to a tenner wasn't even a concept.

'Jeeesus,' he purred.

'Come on,' I said, holding out my other hand in an effort to coax the contraband from behind his back. 'You can have it. I can afford it.'

Harper hesitantly handed it over, looking at me levelly as if any minute I was about to skank him, still not certain if I was serious and not entirely barmy. I took it from him and joined the small queue at the counter. Dyson sidled over and clicked a finger by way of demanding a look at my potential purchase. I handed it to him, and he fingered it, turning it over and around on its flat card before handing it back with a sneer.

'More money than sense, lad – more money than sense.'

Before we were back on the bus, Harper had discarded the packaging and was wearing the thing around his neck with great pride. As I recall, he was so pleased with himself and the pendant that I never even got a thank you from him, and by the time we got back to school I knew why.

He pulled me to one side behind a corner of the PE block and fished inside one of his bottomless pockets. With his Harper grin he pulled out a flat card to which was attached a sterling silver chain and a pendant of a hawk in flight identical to the one I'd bought that was still sitting around his grubby neck. He just couldn't resist.

'Harper, you divot!'

'There yer go, chor,' he beamed, thrusting the stolen item at me. 'One good turn deserves anuvver.'

I backed off disgusted, like he was handing me a turd.

PRECESSION

'I don't want it, you tea leaf,' I spat at him.

He looked at me uncomprehending, a look that slowly turned to hurt.

'It's different when I bring yer sweets, innitt?' he muttered. 'Don't bovver yer then, does it?'

He had a point, but I dismissed his argument with a noise of contempt that told him I still held the moral ground.

'I fought it'd be cool for us both to have one,' he said in a sulky tone. 'Fuckin' fing weren't werf a tenner anyway. At least now we've got two for us dosh.'

'*My* dosh,' I corrected him.

'Yeah, okay,' he said still acting all hurt. 'Fuck it,' he said finally. 'If yer don't wan' it I'll flog it for a quid or summat.' He looked up at me with puppy dog eyes. 'I fought we was mates is all. I fought it'd be cool, like bruvvers or summat.'

Harper started to bend and misshape the piece of card that the chain was attached to, and I began to feel like shit. He was good at making me feel shit.

'Why do you always. . .' I began. '...Why can't you just. . .' He looked up at me with those eyes again. '. . . Aww, forget it.'

I reluctantly took the thing from him and tried to re-shape the card. His face turned from morose to happy in an instant.

'Purrit on then,' he enthused. I did as I was told and stood there like a lemon waiting for his approval. 'Cushty,' he purred and offered me a fist. 'Just like bruvvers, chor.' We clashed knuckles and my mate was content. I was just glad he didn't produce a knife and demand that we seal it in blood.

The following weekend I persuaded Mum and Dad to take a drive up into The Dales and we do the whole show at the falconry centre once again.

Walking round the gift shop I found the benevolent box, and when my parents weren't looking, I slipped a tenner into it, the very last of my savings, but at least from then on in I was able to wear my symbol of friendship with a clear conscience.

For the rest of that year Harper became bird obsessed. And he never once removed the pendant from around his neck; he even admitted to sleeping in it. His sole mission in life now was to own a bird, just like Billy Casper in the film. I thought it was just a phase, something that would cool in him once the visit to the falconry centre had become a distant memory, but I was wrong. His resolve to obtain

PISCES

a hawk of some description became stronger day by day, and he told me he'd even started to build an aviary on his granddad's allotment in readiness.

§

'Do you still wanna be a vet when you grow up?' Harper asked me while I tried to dodge salvos of paper missiles. It was the last day of term, and everyone was giddy.

'Yeah, among other things,' I shouted above the classroom din. 'Not decided for definite – why?'

'I've got you yer first job, charver,' he said, taking careful aim with a missile of his own and with that twinkle in his eye.

The following six weeks would form the sharpest learning curve of my childhood. In fact, it was a time I would start to leave my childhood behind forever. I would soon discover a different world, full of different rules, where the very word took on an ambiguous definition. What I would see, hear and do would help shape the person I would become, the man I am today, for good or bad, better or worse – it would be an eventful summer.

PRECESSION

Summer 1995

I stepped off the bus onto the noisy and busy main drag that was Harehills Lane. It was the start of the six-week summer holidays, and it was as hot as hell. I took in a reluctant lungful of diesel fumes from the engine of the double-decker as it pulled itself and its shadow away from the kerb leaving me on the pavement in the glaring heat. Mum had offered to drop me off, but I had become sick of being nannied around. All the other kids in my class were fiercely independent, maybe because they had to be, they didn't have a choice. I had decided I had to be more like them, more like Harper who sometimes left me shocked and red faced at the things he knew and talked about, the stuff he'd done. I was eleven now, as I had to keep reminding my cloying, overprotective parents, and I felt a desperate need to stand on my own two feet and shake off some of that naivety that had become an embarrassing millstone around my neck.

Harper had this uncanny knack of appearing as if from nowhere, emerging from the shadows and taking you by surprise. And, as if on cue, he did just that: tapping me lightly on a shoulder before moving swiftly and silently to one side so that I turned and saw no one. I revolved three-sixty before I clocked his familiar inane grin.

"sup, charver?' he said by way of greeting while handing me a stick of Juicy Fruit. 'Warm, innit?'

I opened my mouth to say something, but he was already on the move, stepping out onto the busy road, oblivious to the traffic.

'C'mon, mush,' he shouted. 'Can't wait to show yer.'

I rolled up the gum and stuck it in my mouth to the background noise of horns and squealing tyres and decided to wait for a gap in the road rather than get myself maimed or killed. I still had no idea what sort of surprise he had in store for me but if his recklessness coupled with the giddiness he was displaying was anything to go by it had to be something good. And, as ever, it was that particular glint in his eye, that bouncy effervescent state of optimism tinged with a faint whiff of mischief that intrigued just enough for me to want me to keep that unlikeliest of friendships alive.

I watched him waiting impatiently on the other side of the road hopping from foot to foot like he had worms or wanted to pee badly, in his baggy trackie bottoms and a dull grey Leeds United shirt that used to be white, and was at least two sizes too big for him, which left me surmising that he'd more than likely acquired it from someone's washing line.

When I eventually reached the other side of the road, he announced that he had to nip to the chemist. I followed him to escape the heat of the sun. Inside was quiet and cooler. I took in the curious mix of clean antiseptic, barley sugar, and Dr. Scholl product aromas as Harper deftly slipped a roll of surgical bandage, Elastoplast and a bottle of cough medicine into his pockets from the exposed shelves before making his way to the pharmacy counter. He handed a prescription to a woman in a white coat. She took a moment to scrutinise the crumpled piece of paper. She turned it backwards and forwards in her hand, all the while casting suspicious looks in Harper's direction. Eventually she went into the back, which was the cue for Harper to grab a couple of packets of throat lozenges from the display on the counter in front of him. He stuffed them into the pockets of his already bulging trackie bottoms. After a while, a man in a matching white coat, greying beard and thick, black-framed glasses came to the counter.

'Whose signature's this?' he demanded.

'Dr. Mutvali's,' said Harper.'

'This isn't Dr. Mutvali's signature,' the man said, holding up the script.

'It is,' said Harper confidently. 'It's got his surgery stamp on it.'

'That's as maybe, but Dr. Mutvali did not issue this prescription. Where did you get it from?' Harper gave a careless shrug.

'Who's the Methadone for?'

'Me sister.'

'What's her name?'

'It sez there on that bit o' paper.'

'If this is for your sister, she should know that she has to come for it in person and that she has to take it in the presence of a pharmacist.'

'Ah, but she's poorly, so she's sent me for it.'

The bloke with the beard and the glasses and the white coat looked at the woman in the white coat. They both raised their eyebrows.

'Wait there,' said the man before disappearing out the back. The

PRECESSION

woman folded her arms and glared. Harper started whistling nonchalantly and out of tune. I stood there like a lemon, clueless as to what was going on.

We must have stood like that for at least five minutes until an elderly lady came in and asked where they kept the Sure-Shields. The woman in the white coat unfolded her arms and came from behind the counter to assist the old dear. While they were preoccupied, I watched wide-eyed as Harper slinkily edged his way around the back of the counter, putting a finger to his lips to make sure I kept quiet. He inched his way towards the door that led into the back of the chemists and slowly pushed it open a few inches before peering in.

The assistant turned and caught him in the act.

'Hey!'

I jumped out of my skin and Harper made a dash for it.

'Leg it!' he shouted, hurtling past me and nearly knocking the bemused old lady and the packet of laxative she was holding for six. 'The bastard's callin' the feds!'

I scrambled after him, out of the door and up the street at a pace, not daring to glance over my shoulder to see if we were being pursued. Sweat, confusion, panic and annoyance; what the hell was I doing knocking about with this idiot?

We put a fair distance between us and the chemists before Harper slowed down to a rate I could catch my breath in order to bollock him.

'What was all that about, you knobhead?'

He turned, grinning and panting in my face. 'These.' He dipped into a pocket and pulled out a roll of paper tied round with a rubber band.

'What are they?'

'Scripts.'

'Where the fuck did you get them from?'

'Ask no questions . . .' he said tapping the side of his nose.

'What, you're forging prescriptions? Are you crackers?'

'I could mek a fortune wiv these.'

'How?'

'Drugs to order, charver. Go mad for 'em on t'estate.'

'You have to be eighteen to get prescriptions.'

'Yeah, well I din't know that, did I?'

I shook my head at his stupidity. 'So, what're you gonna do with 'em now?'

PISCES

'Flog 'em to our Frankie,' he said, stuffing them back in a pocket. 'He'll mek use of 'em.'

I remember a voice inside my head telling me to stop, turn around and catch the next bus back to Roundhay, but for some inexplicable reason I didn't. The kid was trouble with a big T, I knew that for sure, and I knew that keeping his company for the next six weeks could potentially land me in big bother, but, like iron filings to a magnet, I stuck with him and we continued on our way despite the growing sensation of foreboding that had started to creep up my body and mix with the sweaty, sticky state I was in. I never really did fathom why someone like Harper would ever want to be mates with somebody like me, or why somebody like me would want to be buddies with someone like him, and on that sweltering July day as we ventured further into the guts of Gipton estate I knew it would be a question I would pose to myself more than once.

'What's up with your sister?'

'Nowt.'

I looked at him puzzled.

'Oh, yer mean the Mefadone - Our Shirley's a skaghead,' he said as a matter of fact.

This was to be the beginning of my *real* education.

'What's a skaghead? What's Methadone?'

Harper flicked a stone into the air and whacked it first time with a stick he had found. The stone sailed through the air and pinged off a car bonnet parked up the road. With a satisfied nod he turned to me and grinned.

'Why did you nick all that stuff from the chemists?' I asked trying to divert his attention away from this new and potentially catastrophic pastime.

Failing to repeat the stick and stone trick a second time, he turned to me and pulled a face. 'You don't half ask some daft questions, Sarvo,' he said irritated. He tried to connect with a stone for the third time, but his stick beat the air in a mad swish and the stone feel to the ground at his feet. 'I swiped the froat sweets 'cos they was right in front o' me goin', "nick me, nick me". The uvver stuff - you'll see why soon enough.'

'Tell me now,' I demanded, 'I don't like surprises, especially your kind o' surprises.'

PRECESSION

'You'll like this one,' he insisted. 'I promise you'll like this one.'
I looked at him full of dubiety.
'Honest to God, Sarvo. On me Mam's life, you'll like this one – trust me.'
I didn't.
We continued on our way, Harper rattling his stick across some railings, jabbering on about this, that and nothing, fending off my "daft questions" whenever I could get a word in edgeways. When he ran out of railings, he used the stick to torment a snarling Pit Bull Terrier that had raced up a garden path at us as we passed. He jabbed his stick at the beast through the gaps in the wooden gate that thankfully separated us from the increasingly demented animal. From a safe distance I watched appalled as Harper swore insults at the dog that had begun to froth at the mouth.
'Pack it in yer little bastard, go on, piss off before I set it on yer,' screamed a woman bounding down the garden path towards us.
Harper withdrew his stick and backed away slightly. 'I'll fuckin' geld it if it comes near me.'
'It'll eat you fer breakfast, yer little shit.'
She was a big woman, and she quivered when she moved. Her greasy hair was scraped back off her face, revealing parrot-perch sized earrings. She wore a grubby, black-cropped singlet that showed off her ample bingo-wing arms that were adorned with crude tattoos and an equatorial gut complete with belly button piercing, but the flimsy spandex top was fighting a losing battle trying to contain her huge breasts. Elastic-waisted pedal pushers and fluffy coral-coloured slippers completed the picture. I couldn't decide who was scarier, her or the dog.
Harper and the woman traded threats and insults on an equal footing; he showed no respect for age or gender. When he called her a fat cunt and threatened to poke *her* with his stick she came to the gate and began untying the twine that held it closed from the gatepost. The dog was going mental. Harper brought the stick crashing down about her hands as she desperately tried to release the crazed canine. This only made her more determined. Face turning purple, she screamed foul-mouthed obscenities at him, and the gate began to move. Harper flung the stick at her trying to buy us a few precious seconds, and soon we were legging it again, only this time I'd stolen a few yards on him. We tore down the street like Olympic sprinters. In the background I could hear dog feet scraping for

purchase on pavement and a manic, howling bark of a warning as it started in hot pursuit. On Harper's direction we doglegged down a snicket that was dead ended by a tall wall. He scaled it like he was superhuman. Straddling the top, he leaned down to me offering a hand. I took a leap of faith, and as I caught his grip, I felt a tearing of cloth. My feet and free hand scrambled frantically up the rough Yorkshire stone. With my heart crashing against my chest, I joined him at the top of the wall and looked back to see the mad mutt savaging a good third of what had been my left trouser leg.

Pissing himself with laughter, Harper dropped down the other side of the wall onto some wasteland. I followed him. I wasn't laughing.

'Look at my strides, you fuckin' idiot – my mum'll kill me.' I stood up to see raggy material flapping around a bare leg. This only set him off some more; rolling around in the dirt holding his stomach while I, beginning to resemble more a native of Gipton at every turn, stood there scowling.

We walked. I'd stopped speaking. At regular intervals he would convulse, wiping away tears with the back of a filthy hand. We came across a load of discarded ceramic toilet bowls that Harper proceeded to smash to bits with half-mackies and any other form of rock he could lay his hands on. He looked at me with that gleam in his eye and couldn't understand why I wasn't joining in the destructive fun. Harper knew how to enjoy himself, and some. And it wouldn't be long before I learned how and why he'd developed his particularly nihilistic brand of escapism.

By the time we turned onto Harper's street, and in addition to the Chemist and Pit Bull incidents, we'd been harassed and threatened by a gang of kids on BMXs, chased yet again by an equally feral pack of stray dogs, witnessed a bloke in a string vest beating up his screaming wife on their doorstep, and seen the aftermath of a mugging outside a post office where some poor old bloke had been relieved of his freshly collected pension. All these things happened as a matter of course for Harper; nothing seemed to make him flinch. I had been in his company and part of his violent and frightening world for little over an hour.

'Handin' out any freebies today girls?' Harper shouted to a couple of mini skirted young women click-clacking their way on high heels across the street.

'Aye, come back when yer balls have dropped,' one of them

PRECESSION

shouted back.

"ere, my nads are down by me knees an' I'm hung like a fuckin' donkey,' he yelled at the top of his voice.

'We don't do animals,' said one.

'Unless the price is right,' added the other, prompting a spontaneous burst of cackling as they continued on their way.

'Slags!' he dismissed them before doing a double take at my open-mouthed status. 'What?'

'How do you gerraway with that?'

He gave me the incredulous look. 'They're a pair o'tarts, on the game - anyway I've had both of 'em,' he added thinking there was no end to my innocence and that I just might be stupid enough to believe anything he said. I thought he was having me on but with Harper you could never be too sure.

'Where the fuck have you been, yer little cunt?' growled Frankie Harper, stepping out of a heavily laden, rusting old Transit van and carrying a large cardboard box. He had sweat patches underneath the arms of his t-shirt where tattooed muscle was trying to burst out. This was one of Harper's brothers, a mean and nasty piece of work who looked nothing like his younger sibling apart from the obligatory number two cropped head. 'Who's this?' he added without waiting for an answer to his first question.

'Me mate, Sarvo.'

'What the fuck's up with his strides?' he asked his younger brother as if I was incapable of answering for myself, making me feel even more like the alien I was.

'He let a dog have 'em.'

'Here, tek this.' Frankie threw the box at him and Harper proceeded to stagger up the path towards the house. 'Wait there, raggy arse,' he turned to me and commanded, 'there's one for thee as well.'

Frankie had just come back from a 'fags and booze' cruise to Calais, and after half-an-hour of enforced labour we were both sweating and knackered. Van empty and with every bit of spare space of the council house packed tight with black market goods, Harper stood in the cramped hallway with his hand out in anticipation.

"sup wi' thee?' growled Frankie.

'Wages,' demanded Harper.

PISCES

Frankie stuck his fag in his gob and reached into a pocket. With lightning speed, he brought up his other hand and gave Harper a resounding crack around the head. I winced.

'Cheeky twat,' said Frankie and marched out of the house.

In the filthy bathroom I peed into a toilet without seat or lid. In the bath to my right grew a forest of, what I thought at the time, were tomato plants, although they smelled nothing like the tomato plants my dad grew in his greenhouse and showed no sign of bearing fruit – of the red variety, anyhow.

After discarding my shredded pants and climbing into a spare pair of Harper's filthy joggers I eased my way down past the boxes of cigarettes and beer that were piled high on the carpet-less staircase to be met by what I could only describe as the dirtiest looking living thing I had ever seen working its way up the steps towards me. It was a baby, barely a year old, not even a toddler, wearing only a dishevelled paper nappy. It grunted and gurgled, scaling the bare wooden treads and using the teetering, precarious mountain of boxes as support. I froze.

'Harperrr!' I called, still rooted to the spot, not knowing what to do. He appeared at the bottom of the stairs, and I just pointed, horrified. He tutted, roughly snatched up the kid, and marched off muttering and cursing.

"ere, look after yer brat, yer lazy cow, an' change its nappy; it fuckin' stinks.'

I continued down the stairs and knocked my head on the smell. I concurred.

An argument ensued, becoming raucous and shrill as more female voices joined in. As the decibels rose, the baby started to scream, and a dog began to bark.

It would be some time later, after he had decided to fill me in on some of the more sordid and seedy details surrounding his so-called family and the upheavals of his life thus far, before I began to understand what being Darren Harper was all about. Meanwhile, I stood there, the soles of my trainers acting like Velcro on the sticky carpet of what could laughingly be described as a living room, witnessing bedlam while a look of bemusement became fixed to my face and a sensation of disgust coursed through my body.

Shirley Connett was a heroin addict. She had been systematically raped and abused by her stepdad from an early age. When she was seventeen, she bore him a son. By then she'd already turned to

PRECESSION

narcotics, and the child was taken into care. Now she sat dishevelled and unkempt in an armchair that looked to have been dragged in off a council dump, her vacant stare only interrupted by nervous bouts of nail biting and frantic puffs on a cigarette.

Marie Harper was sixteen but looked three years younger. She was the mother of thirteen-month-old Ryan who was crawling and bawling around the filthy floor with the contents of his overflowing Pamper threatening to escape. George Harper, stepdad of Shirley, was also the biological father to both Marie and little Ryan alike. George liked to keep it in the family – in more ways than one.

George Harper's depravity seemingly knew no bounds. As well as incest the alcoholic degenerate would try his hand at most perversions. And his party piece usually took place after closing time on a Sunday afternoon, where he would drunkenly gather his petrified brood into the front room and, under the threat of physical violence, had them regularly witness the sickening spectacle of him on his knees fucking the family Alsatian while *Songs of Praise* played away on the telly.

Now I knew my mate was fond of telling tall tales and was prone to exaggerating but in this instance the mix of fear and hate in his eyes when he related this was for real. At the time it was hard for my inexperienced, relatively innocent mind to conjure up this sick picture of pure evil. As an adult and having witnessed hell at close quarters many times now, the thought of George Harper and the things he put that family through still makes me shudder.

Marie Harper sat at the other end of the room, trading vicious expletives with her younger brother, totally oblivious to the attention seeking cries of her baby who was now struggling to get back on his feet because of the extra weight of his over laden, soggy nappy.

From my wide-eyed observations I'd sussed that a good percentage of Gipton females were big women and Harper's mum was no exception. You couldn't slide a razor blade between the sink, her and the cluttered unit at the other side of the tiny galley kitchen in which she was stood issuing a bollocking to her son who was now taking a large swig from a plastic bottle of coke, seemingly oblivious to the tirade directed at him. She wore a black cotton bell-tent shapeless dress. Her knees and legs were heavily veined, puffed and swollen. Too much flesh creased her ankles, and her feet were trying to burst out of manky looking slippers that didn't fit. She was freakishly overweight and was obviously finding it hard to breathe as she continued to bawl out her youngest, gasping and rasping in between pulling fag smoke deep into her labouring lungs.

Completing this Addams style family of in-breeds were Jimmy Connett and Carl Harper. Along with George, both were off the scene. George and Jimmy were respectively doing time in Armley and Strangeways. Jimmy had taken a machete to his stepdad one Saturday night outside The Delvers pub and was currently serving nine years for attempted murder and GBH. George Harper's nefarious deeds came out at the trial, and he too was doing a stretch for various acts of profligacy, including bestiality. Carl Harper was off the scene for a different reason. The second youngest of the Harper clan was decapitated in a joy riding incident in which he was the driver of a stolen car. Harper didn't like to talk about him. Oh, and there was the dog, not Sheba, the poor nervous German shepherd bitch who had developed the twitchy habit of forever glancing behind her when she heard a male adult voice. She had mercifully died a while back. Buster, the Staffordshire bull terrier was the new and thankfully unmolested addition to the Harper family. He had recently mastered the knack of opening the fridge door with snout and paw and devouring anything he found within, which usually was never that much. On this occasion his luck was in, and before anyone could stop him, he had snaffled a whole one-pound pack of margarine and had eaten it, wrapper and all. He had promptly regurgitated the yellow mess and was now busy eating the slimy pile off the kitchen floor for a second time. Buster, it seems, was the only Harper who could be bothered to clean up after them.

'He's your dog, gerrim outta my sight an' tek him for a fuckin' walk, will yer?' screamed Harper's mum. Harper necked some coke and belched out loud.

'I can't, we're on a mission. I can't tek him where we're goin,' he bawled back at his mother.

'You're off buggerin' about wi' that bird again. Aren't yer?'

I shot a glance at my mate. All at once he looked crestfallen.

'Aww, you've gone an' fuckin' spoiled it now, yer big fat cow. It wa' gonna be a surprise.' He slammed the plastic bottle of coke hard down onto the already sticky looking kitchen unit. Brown fizz erupted up and over the sides, cascading over the unit and onto the kitchen floor. Happily distracted by this, Buster now had a drink to go with his sicked-up butter.

'Don't you fuckin' swear at me, yer stroppy little twat!' Mrs H

PRECESSION

screeched after us as Harper marched out of the house in an almighty huff, dragging me along in his wake.

'You've got a bird,' I exclaimed excitedly, doing my best to put the scene of squalor I'd just witnessed to the back of my mind, and all the while trying to match his stride as he stormed down the garden path. 'What is it?'

'Wait an' see,' he chuntered, still annoyed at having his bonfire pissed on.

I was quickly beginning to learn that all life didn't exist on a level playing field. Society was made up of strata, and I realised that the layer Harper inhabited bumped its way somewhere along the bottom. But I was soon to discover that this particular social class felt neither inferior nor subservient to any other. To say this place was lawless wouldn't be exactly true. Successive generations of Gipton and Harehills natives grew up with their own, unwritten laws; laws of the jungle maybe, but this was urban jungle, a parallel universe where convention and statute book law didn't apply. Justice via shooter and baseball bat prevailed here. It was a land of no-go, social depravity and state dependency supplemented by a thriving black-market economy. The back of a barely street legal transit van was the Gipton stock-market trading floor where any commodity could be had at a price, from drugs to designer gear. Pan-crack entrepreneurs fought for survival in a shaky hierarchical kingdom held sway by transient extortionists and mad men. And at the very bottom, scrambling around in the mire, twentieth century Fagins fenced for modern day Dodgers of which Darren Harper was just one of whose numbers were legion.

'Nah then, bugger lugs, how's tha doin'?' Tommy Watts didn't resemble Dickens's Victorian Yid, but his game was just the same.

'Alrate,' replied Harper.

'Has tha got owt for me?' he asked, climbing out the back of his van. It was becoming a familiar sight.

'Aye, these. . .' Harper reached into his back pocket and produced the paper roll.

'What are they?'

'Blank scripts, surgery stamped an' all.'

Tommy Watts: lanky haired, badly tattooed, pock-marked, pot-bellied, forty-odd year old, pulled a face, picked his nose, scratched his knackers and let out a forced puff of bad breath all in one movement. 'Can't move them, young 'un, they'll be numbered an' registered.'

'Junkies round here aren't smart enough to suss that.'

'How many yer got?'

'A dozen.'

Tommy stroked his whiskers ponderously in the best dealer tradition. 'You'll be gerrin me a bad reputation, young Harper,' he said eventually. 'Tell yer what I'll do . . .' Dipping into a cardboard box in the back of the van, he emerged holding what looked like a plastic CD case. '. . . I'll let yer have half a dozen o' these.'

'What, six CD's? – Fuck off!' said Harper contemptuously.

'Hey, don't gerron yer high-horse, charver; these aren't CD's.'

'What are they then?'

'These, my friend are the future.' He opened the case and held the shiny disk up to the sun where a prism of rainbow colours danced along its surface.

Harper glanced at me then raised his eyes to the heavens with a sigh in anticipation of some Tommy Watt bullshit.

'These little babies'll mek video obsolete inside six months.'

'Come again?'

'Out of date – Defunct,' I interrupted and explained for Harper's benefit.

'Go to the top of the class that man,' said Tommy, acknowledging my presence for the first time.

'Yer still an't told me what the fuck it is,' said Harper getting evermore impatient.

'It's called a DVD.'

'Digital Video Disc,' I qualified.

'Err, right again fella. Bit of a know-it-all, your mate, innee?' Tommy made an aside to Harper while cocking his head in my direction.

'There's no bullshitting this kid, Tommy,' warned Harper.

'I thought they weren't out until later on this year,' I said suspiciously.

Tommy stared at me through eyes that had become slits. 'Ahh, once more your assumption is correct, young man. These what I have here are the very latest prototypes, direct from Japan; first in the country; special assignment.' He held the disc aloft, wagging it triumphantly.

'Remind me warrit does again,' said Harper unimpressed.

'I've told yer – same as a video only a thousand times better.'

PRECESSION

'What's on 'em then?'
'Films.'
'What films?'
'Dunno, it's all in Japanese . . .'

Having established that Tommy's little items of ground-breaking technology were neither use nor ornament seeing as how the machines required to play them on weren't even on the market yet, Harper started haggling over the stolen prescriptions in hard cash, pitching in at twenty quid and eventually coming away with a fiver.

'I thought you were gonna flog 'em to your Frankie,' I reminded him as we were on our way once again.

'That skankin' cunt's gerrin nowt off me no more.' Harper hawked up a coke-tinged lurgi from the back of his throat and flegged the brown pellet of spittle contemptuously onto the pavement.

We headed down a dusty path overrun with weed and summer growth. Insects buzzed and whined, going about their daily routines, and Harper swished merrily away at grass and shrub with a newly acquired stick. The path opened up onto a large but haphazard spread of allotments; some tended and in use, others abandoned or neglected. Pens of geese and ducks protested our presence, while clutches of bantam hens clucked and pecked the dry earth oblivious to our passing. Pigeon fanciers in sweaty vest tops rattled cans of corn, enticing circling squadrons of homers back to their lofts, and all the while my senses were being assaulted by the sickly-sweet smell of manure fed cabbages and cauliflower reeking in regimented rows.

Tucked away in what at first appeared to be a dilapidated, unused corner, was a scrubby patch of land shielded by a bank of hawthorne hiding an ancient looking greenhouse and a clumsily constructed mess of wood and chicken wire. The greenhouse appeared to be bursting from floor to roof with what had become a familiar looking plant, the rich emerald foliage of which was pressed up hard against every square inch of glass. A rich, pungent aroma permeated the immediate surroundings. The pallet wood and wire contraption next to it was, of course, Harper's aviary.

You had to look twice, but next to an old, upturned tin bath on top of which rested a half-drunk bottle of Bell's sat an old man, positively ancient, dressed in an equally looking ancient suit of the de-mob variety, flat cap so weathered and worn it actually had a sheen to it. He sat stock-still, walking stick propped out in front of him. Snow-white whiskers grew out of a weather beaten, parched-like-leather face. And the reason you had to look twice was because the old bloke didn't flinch. He just sat there statue like, blending in with his surroundings like he'd become a part of them, like some ancient sage guarding the gateway to the eighth wonder of the world. On closer inspection you could just detect a slight move of the lips as he chewed serenely on a sprig of hawthorne, but apart from that, nothing, not a nod or raised eyebrow to our sudden appearance. I was unnerved.

'Who the hell is that?' I whispered harshly out the corner of my mouth.

Harper looked up and about as though he didn't know who I was talking about. 'Oh, you mean him,' he said totally disinterested. 'That's me granddad, or at least I fink he is,' he added as an afterthought.

'What, you don't know your own bloody granddad?' I asked disbelieving, but still in a whisper.

'Well, I don't know, do I? I've never had owt to do with him. I fink he has summat to do wi' me mam.'

'You mean he's your mum's dad?'

'Yeah, could be.'

I pulled my incredulous face once again. Harper returned it with a *what-the fuck-does-it-matter* look. He went and stood in front of the old bloke.

'Hey, old fella,' he shouted, 'are you me granddad, or what then?'
Nothing.

'See,' he said looking back at me with a shrug. He peered down into the old lad's sedentary features. 'You're a silly old bastard, aren't yer?' he shouted condescendingly.

'Is he deaf?'

'Fuck knows – silly old cunt,' he left as a parting shot and went over to unlock the aviary.

As I turned to follow with a bemused shrug, the old man let out a resounding fart. I turned quickly in his direction. His face hadn't slipped an inch.

Harper unbolted the rickety wooden door and turned to me with his *be-ready-to-be-amazed* look. The early afternoon light flooded into the enclosed part of the aviary, while sunbeams cut through gaps in the poorly constructed pallet wood illuminating dust and creating a spotlight effect on what was meant to be Harper's surprise. I took a

PRECESSION

breath and held it. Subtle hues of brown held my gaze: Tawny-tan to orange accessorised in flecks of chestnut and white, and a bright mustard-yellow cere. It was a young Harris hawk, and just like in the film, it was a Colin Welland moment.

'Well, what d'yer fink?' beamed Harper while I stood there marvelling.

'It's a beaut,' I whispered reverentially. 'Where did you get it?'

'Oh, - I know people.' He dismissed the question, like it was none of my concern. I didn't push it.

'How old is it?'

'About five monfs, I fink.'

'She's gorgeous.'

'How d'yer know it's a she?'

'If it's only five months it's too big for a male.'

Harper nodded in deference to my ornithological knowledge.

'What you gonna call her?'

'No names; it's a hunter, not a pet.' And, at that moment, as if by savagely agreeing with her keeper, the bird let out a raucous scream as was peculiar to the species. (Later, I would name her Beauty, after her Binomial name *Parabuteo uncinctus*, but I never uttered it in front of Harper). As Beauty continued to notify us of her presence, I couldn't help noticing something wasn't right. Her left wing spread and flapped wildly in a spectacular show of buff coated plumage, while the right one jerked about in a futile effort.

'What's up with her wing?' I asked as my initial excitement evaporated.

'Not sure, I fink it's broken.'

'Fuckin' hell, Harper, you can't keep a bird with a broken wing.'

'That's why you're here, charver,' he said, emptying his pockets onto an old set of drawers, that judging by the dried blood stains, he used as a fresh meat chopping board.

'What?' I said, suspiciously eyeing the crepe dressing, Elastoplast and the rest of the items he'd nicked from the chemists.

'You can make her better,' he stated assuredly, 'you're the man.'

'Bollocks,' I sent the assuredness back at him. 'I've never set a broken wing before.'

'All vets have got to start somewhere,' he said looking me straight in the eye while offering me a throat lozenge.

Harper's misplaced faith, and his powers of persuasion, found me reluctantly soaking balls of cotton wool with cough medicine, and placing them in a plastic bag. He hooded the screaming bird while I prepared the crepe bandage and cut strips of Elastoplast.

'I don't like this,' I said gingerly sniffing the ether-like aroma emanating from the bag of cotton wool. 'What if we kill it?'

'It's just to keep it quiet while we splint the wing, we don't have to knock it out.'

I shook my head, I wasn't happy.

'You're never gonna be a fuckin' vet if you're squeamish,' he said snatching the bag from my grasp.

Thus, Harper became my anaesthetist, and I shakily performed my first act of healing.

Come the end of the holidays Beauty's wing was fully mended and we soon had her flying low over the endless rows of smelly veg, glove to glove. Although she was secured on the end of a creance line, poultry keepers and pigeon fanciers, growing evermore nervous, formed a posse and told us to 'bugger off'. It was just as well. If we were ever going to be serious about this, we would need to broaden our horizons and have to think about letting her fly free. It was around this time that I had decided I no longer wanted to be a vet. Suddenly, I had higher aspirations. I don't remember how or why I came to that decision, but I had firmly set my stall out – I was going to be a doctor.

PRECESSION

1996 – 1997

Harper and I became self-taught falconers. I read the books and passed on the knowledge; he became the expert. Over the next few years we co-owned several raptors, including a buzzard, a goshawk, two more Harris hawks and even a beautiful eagle owl that didn't do much; he was just good to look at.

My old man bought us all the necessary gear and made sure we did things the right way. He sacrificed most of his spare time to take us up on the moors, and over time we learned to man the birds via swivel and leash, creance line and lure. But the moment Beauty flew free from the glove for the first time was still the best ever.

It was the end of autumn, the last of the leaves had been swept from the trees, and the air was keen, blowing in short, sharp gusts that stung the eyes and made your nose run. High up on the moor, looking down on the town of Ilkley, sporadic flurries of sleet gave portent of what was to come, heralding the onset of winter. The clouds above scurried along in shades of grey, but they remained high, and a weak sun did its best to steal through the gaps making shadows race along the purple heather undulating seamlessly with the contours of the land – perfect.

Harper, dressed in total disregard and without deference to the seasons, stood a few yards away with the bird on his arm while Dad and I wrapped up to the nines, hands in pockets and shoulders hunched, watched in anticipation. He slowly undid the hood with the help of his teeth and free hand then held her at arm's length expectantly. She glanced around, nervously taking in the surroundings. She looked at Harper as if seeking his guidance. She opened her beak, but her feeble cry was taken with the wind. For what seemed like an age they stood stock-still staring at each other. Will she, won't she? Would she come back? My heart was pounding away in my chest. A breeze caught and lifted her primaries. Her head darted here and there, checking her bearings, senses coming alive. Then, with a final look at Harper as her primeval instincts kicked in, she took to the air while all around us time stood still. She soared magnificently on wind and thermal, ever higher. We looked at each other, our faces a contradiction of elated and anxious, and for the next ten minutes we snatched and fought over the only pair of binoculars we had as we excitedly tracked her journey high above the moor.

At the right moment, Harper cast a drop lure, and she came in arcs and swoops, finally homing in like an Exocet onto the carcase of the fresh sparrow he had shot that morning. With satisfied grins and immense pride, we backslapped each other as we watched her tear her reward to pieces with talon and beak. It was the climax to what had been a crazy, eventful year. A year that had seen me finally grow up; a year that had seen Harper stay out of any major trouble. We were kids light years apart. We were kids with a common bond. In hindsight it was probably our happiest time.

§

It was the last week of our last year at middle school. In September I would be starting the city grammar and Harper, along with everyone else, would be heading for the local comprehensive. I couldn't wait to get out of that place; just two more days to go. In class it was mayhem. Bored out of my skull, I glanced up at the teacher who by now had relinquished any notion of control. A paper aeroplane landed on the empty seat to my right. The seat had been vacant for three days now – it was Harper's seat. We'd flown the hawk at the weekend, and that had been the last time I had seen him. I had a gut feeling something wasn't right, and as providence would have it, my instincts were about to be proved correct.

It was never a happy experience walking the streets of LS9 on your own, even less so when you were unexpectedly accosted by Armani Kershaw.

'Hey up, Sarvo,' she squawked and cracked her bubble gum loudly in my ear. 'What you doin' round these parts? Where you off to?'

'I'm looking for Harper,' I replied, settling back into my skin that immediately started to crawl at this chance encounter.

Armani was the first girl to talk to me the day I started middle school, she was the one who took pity on me after Briggsy had whacked me in the face, and on this, the day that school finally broke up for good, sod's law said she had to be the last.

'Why are yer allus knockin' about wi' that loser?'

PRECESSION

'He's no more a loser than anybody else at school.'

She tutted and displayed that familiar curling lip of contempt. 'You're weird, you.' She looked me up and down, the sneer stuck to her face.

'And you're normal, are you?' I asked while observing the lank, greasy hair, the effect the sudden surge of adolescent oestrogen was having on her complexion, the gravy stain down her sweatshirt, a souvenir from her last middle school free meal, and the extra two and a half stone in weight she had piled on since our first meet. I quickened my pace, but undeterred she clung to my side like a limpet, snapping her gum at regular intervals while probing me with inane questions. Then, without warning and totally out of the blue she changed tack.

'I've got tits yer know,' she announced by standing directly in front of me, halting my progress and sticking out her gravy-stained chest.

'I'm very pleased for you,' I said applying a touch of fancy footwork in order to sidestep her. She back-pedalled, expertly countering my efforts of avoidance.

'I know a place we can go,' she husked conspiratorially. 'Yer can finger-fuck me if yer like, an' I'll give yer a hand job.'

'You what?'

'Toss yer off, give yer a wank.'

I don't know if it was the embarrassment, the feeling of disgust or the sheer incredulity of it that stopped me dead in my tracks, but as I stood there and coloured up while she blew bubbles with her gum, patiently waiting for a response, I realised I hadn't exorcised half the naivety I thought I had. I was gobsmacked; we were only twelve for Christ's sake.

'Piss off,' I managed to splutter before barging my way past and moving at a pace that didn't entirely look like I was running away.

'I wun't tell anybody; it'd be our secret. . .' She pursued me with words of persuasion for a few hundred yards down the street until she realised I was having none of it.

'Sod off, will you – I wouldn't touch you with a friggin' barge pole.'

The rebuff quickly turned her tune to taunt and ridicule. '. . . Anyway, I allus knew you were a babber-stabber.'

'Eh?'

'You're a bum-bandit you, Andrew Sarvent. You an' Harper are a right pair o' queers. That's why you're off to find him, so yer can bum each other, innit?'

'No.'

'It is, cos yer gay – You're gay, you are. Gay boy, gay boy.'

I laughed at her and just shook my head. Her accusations were so puerile and not worth defending myself against. I let the tirade of vitriol wash over me until I finally reached the sanctuary of Harper's house. From behind the knackered garden gate, I watched her out of sight, still chuntering and chelping away.

'Have a nice life, Armani – yer slag,' I muttered to myself, thankful in the knowledge that our paths were unlikely ever to cross again.

That was the first time sex, in any shape or form, or the mere mention of it had ever appeared on my horizon. If I hadn't been even a little curious about it up to that point, I certainly wasn't after Armani's come-on. It wasn't until I got to university that I felt any serious awakening or real interest in the opposite sex. Thankfully my encounter with Armani Kershaw (according to Harper her two younger twin brothers were called Dolce and Gabbana and I'm sure he wasn't joking) hadn't left me scarred in any way, although perversely the gravy stain stayed with me for quite some time. And I had been damned certain that I wasn't gay.

Harper wasn't home, so I raced straight down to the allotments making sure I wasn't being pursued by any ex-classmates wanting to be finger-fucked.

There was something in the air. I could sense it. I could smell it, long before I got there. Not even the stench of cauliflower and cabbage reeking away in regimented rows was enough to mask the pungent aroma of charred wood and *cannabis indica,* a smell I was slowly getting used to. The whole place stank like a dope smokers' convention on November the fifth. Faint feathery wisps of blue smoke drifted and dissipated into the air above the hawthorne bushes as I cautiously approached. All around was eerily quiet.

Harper was sat on the upturned bath usually occupied by his granddad. His head was bowed, and he held a cigarette in his hand, which oddly enough surprised me more than the scene of total devastation that surrounded him. The greenhouse and its contents had been razed to the ground; only its low, red brick, now blackened, walled base remained. Exploded panes of glass lay soot-smeared, shattered and haphazard amongst the toasted tangle of what remained

PRECESSION

of Frankie Harper's cash crop. There was nothing left of the aviary, just a pile of ash and dying embers. There was no sign of the bird. I feared the worst.

I inadvertently kicked the empty whiskey bottle that lay on the ground half buried by burnt debris, not certain if it had been emptied by Harper or the old man. Alongside it, sat a discarded empty petrol can.

'What happened?' I hardly dared utter the words. Harper took a deep pull on his ciggie like a seasoned pro, like he'd been smoking for years; he might have for all I knew. I'd just been used to him chewing on blackjacks, that's all. He slowly lifted his head to acknowledge me. The sight made me gasp. Besides having the appearance of a Victorian chimney sweep, behind the soot his face was swollen black and blue. One of his eyes was almost closed shut, the cheek below it proud, hard and as shiny as a billiard ball. A bust lip had started to scab and crisp over. He took another puff from the side of his mouth that didn't look so raw and tender. Unable to pout in order to exhale, the smoke fell from his mouth ragged and grotesquely awkward.

'He killed the hawk.'

The statement came out linear and without emotion, yet full of resignation.

'Who did?'

'Our Frankie.'

I guess I already knew it, but the revelation still brought that cold, sinking feeling with it, like a millstone had dropped through my body and settled in the pit of my guts. The parallels with what had become his favourite film were chillingly prophetic – Harper plays Billy Casper; Frankie Harper plays Jud.

'Did he do that to your face?'

Harper gave a vague nod of the head and then bowed it as if he were ashamed of the fact. Once more I took in the seemingly senseless scene of destruction not knowing what to make of it all. My arms flopped frustratingly helpless against my sides. – 'Why?'

In desperate need of a fix, Harper's elder sister Shirley had taken a screwdriver to the piece of floorboard in Frankie's room beneath which he kept his stash of drug money. Amongst the plastic bags of dried weed waiting for distribution to the Gipton masses she found a rolled-up donkey choker from which she feverishly peeled off five twenty-pound notes.

PISCES

Harper got the blame, and he took it, certain in the knowledge that if Frankie ever found out who the real culprit was there was no way she would ever survive a bout of her brother's wrath. From her filthy armchair, with the proceeds of her ill-gotten gains coursing through her veins, Shirley Connett watched impassively with a self-centred indifference, totally without guilt or remorse as Harper was kicked and punched black and blue around the room, the frightened screams from his mother and baby nephew doing nothing to assuage the relentless assault. In his final pique of misplaced revenge, with a show of pure evil, Frankie Harper stormed out to the allotment, decapitated the hawk and nailed the headless body to her post perch.

Harper was used to such horrors; he'd seen enough of them in his thirteen eventful years; there wasn't a lot left that could faze him. He simply placed himself inside the numb zone, shut down the emotions and reverted to primeval Gipton instinct. He sourced a can of petrol and in a zombie like state, emptied the contents throughout the greenhouse and aviary. Before he tossed a lighted match to the lot, he carefully removed the crucified bird, wrapped her in an old towel and placed the carcase on the blood-stained dresser. He stared at it for a few moments, but that's all. He didn't fully comprehend the concept of prayer, but he knew all about hate, something he lived with daily yet very rarely directed at others. On that late afternoon, as the petrol fumes stung his eyes and the tears rolled down his grimy face, hate began to consume him just as the flames started to consume the best part of a grand's worth of the finest strain of sinsemilla in West Yorkshire. The hate he felt wasn't for Shirley; he made allowances for her. She was a smackhead; he knew what people like her resorted to; they were to be pitied more than anything. That's why he'd kept shtum. He didn't care that his sister had kept her junkie mouth shut when she could have fessed up and prevented him from taking a pounding. He didn't analyse it; the human beings in his life came with all sorts of frailties and failings. His unconscious act of altruism was down to instinct again, never expecting reward or favour for it. And he'd have taken a thousand mashings from Frankie, if only he'd left the bird alone, but his bastard brother knew where to really hurt, and some. Save knifing him in his sleep, this was the only way he knew how to hurt him back.

In the gathering dusk the flames highlighted the bruises and the swelling about his face. The heat began to pop the panes, and along with the smoke a pungent aroma wafted over and above Gipton rooftops. He watched it go up, all the hate inside him reserved for Frankie alone, oblivious to the consequences and further ramification his actions might bring upon him. He didn't care.

As far as I know, Harper never did grass up his sister. I thought he was crazy. I couldn't get my head around this peculiar Rogues' code of honour, especially after the way she'd wronged him. In the end it turned out to be a futile gesture anyway. Inside twelve months she'd be dead from a massive overdose. It was the first time I thought I understood the concept of cause and effect. Pity, sadness, hate and indifference: I never did fathom what Harper really felt about his heroin-addicted sibling. He had kept his mouth shut for Shirley then and refused to talk about her after she died, although I did notice he seemed to grieve more for the hawk than he ever did for her. He didn't even go to the funeral, probably more out of fear of crossing paths with Frankie after that costly and revengeful act of arson more than anything else.

We sort of took him in after his pyrotechnic performance, unofficially adopted him I suppose. By we, I mean mum and dad of course, who spent many an agonising evening debating whether or not to go to social services over the whole matter. Harper was having none of it and aggressively dismissed the notion out of hand. He'd been taken into care once before, as a nipper, and was having nothing to do with SS. He'd run away first, he assured us, and no one would bother to come looking for him except maybe their Frankie who'd be less likely to forgive and forget, especially over the loss of a thousand pounds worth of ganja.

Despite their benevolence, Mum and Dad made it clear that his stay could only be a temporary measure and stressed that once things had calmed down at home he would be expected to return. I remember Harper and I exchanging glances at that one – they had no idea. It was never going to be a cosy arrangement anyway. Harper couldn't get his head around the routines and disciplines of a regular family way of life. He grew impatient and restless while waiting for me to finish my chores after tea and homework after school. All he wanted to do was spend his time with the birds in the new aviary the three of us had built in our back garden. In reality, Harper wasn't staying with us at all. He was only ever in the house for his meals and his bed, and he'd have happily slept with the birds if Mum had let him. Inevitably he outstayed his welcome and mum's philanthropy began to wear thin. In truth she had never gotten used to

PISCES

his feral persona. Her mood always seemed to be one of nervous agitation whenever he was around, and she took to a manic cleaning around the house; dusting and polishing bordering on obsession, a routine I had some empathy with as he always had the knack of making the place look untidy. It all came to head around ten months into the "temporary arrangement" when he brought our newly acquired kestrel into the lounge. Mum's shrill cry of - "get that bloody thing out of here" - spooked the young raptor and the ensuing stramash of raised voices, flailing arms and flying feathers culminated in one of her best Lladro ornaments in pieces and bird shit peppering her three-piece suite and newly laid Axminster. Around the same time, brother Frankie was being handed down a three stretch in Armley as his black market and other nefarious exploits finally caught up with him. The timing couldn't have been better.

As the Sarvent household breathed a collective sigh of relief, I gave him his bus fare and watched him on his way. He wore my jeans, my sweatshirt and my trainers, and he had that slightly bow-legged gait that I guess was a legacy from his formative years when calcium and vital vitamins were at a premium. But he was no longer the wiry, raggy-arsed kid I had originally befriended. Adolescence was already kicking in. Hormones were starting to fly around inside that hyper body of his and you could see he had started to fill out, due, in no small part, I surmised to mum's regular hot dinners that barely ever touched the sides, (although he still refused to go near the broccoli). He was a junior meathead in the making, a true son of Gipton. Physically he was destined to inherit the genetic makeup of his sibling brothers, and as I watched him saunter down our garden path, I silently prayed he wouldn't be taking a trip down theirs as well.

PRECESSION

1997 – 2001

In all honesty, not a lot changed. Harper no longer bunked up in the spare room, but apart from that he was never away. Our back garden and the birds were his sanctuary; his escape from the shitty hand life had dealt him. I would step off the bus from school and head up our road knowing he'd already be there, and I began to wonder if he ever went to his own school or just waited until we were all out of the house before skiving off in our back garden all day. It was almost like we had our very own hermit.

Sometimes I felt sorry for him, but increasingly, and I feel ashamed to admit it now, I began to resent his persistent presence and his constant demands on my time and attention. I had started to move on. Although I still had an interest in the birds, by this time my horizons had broadened; they were no longer, and in truth, never really had been the be-all and end-all in my life. My thirst for knowledge grew stronger by the day. I couldn't get enough of biology, chemistry, physics and history. In short, I had become a nerd and a swot, and my studies had begun to take up most of my spare time. I found myself making up constant excuses for not being around him and the hawks, citing homework and school projects with deadlines for the self-imposed exile to my room. Occasionally while chewing on a pencil as I worked out some mathematical equation or other, my gaze would go to the window and invariably I would see him there with a bird on his arm looking back up at me in a sulk, a look that would over time turn to one of resentment.

I might have fully morphed into the annoyingly studious person I was always destined to be, but over the years I had kept up with my martial arts, and by the time I'd turned fourteen my Taekwondo club had started entering me into nationwide competitions. I did well, started to win a few, and so increasingly Dad and I could be found trawling up and down the country at weekends. Trouble was Saturdays and Sundays were when we flew the birds out on the moors. It was the only time and place Harper could truly be in his element. Now, more often than not, and much to his frustration, the birds stayed in the aviary. We did our best to involve him, said he was welcome to tag along, tried to get him interested in the sport. But

PISCES

Taekwondo was my thing, not his. He'd seen me in action and was bored out of his skull. – *Why the fuck would he want to watch me play Bruce Lee?* – is how I remember his reaction at the time. That unlikeliest of friendships was at last beginning to sour – and it got worse.

In 1999 I won gold in the tournament that made me national champion at my age, weight and class, and a first ever national junior title for my club. I came home on that late Sunday afternoon proudly wearing my medal and triumphantly clutching the gleaming trophy that said I was the best in the whole of Britain. After briefly showing it all off to Mum I ran out into the back garden brandishing my prizes, eager to flash them in front of my mate. I found him in his usual place and marched towards him, flashing the gold, grinning from ear to ear. He strode out to meet me and all in one swift movement, without breaking stride, he "dropped the nut" – head butted me straight between the eyes. The bridge of my nose split apart as easy as a peapod and I relived a sensation that wasn't too unfamiliar although it hadn't happened to me in years. I relinquished my grip on the trophy that fell to the floor with a dull ring. I was catching claret in the palms of my hands long before the lights had stopped flashing, and the sound of ringing bells had subsided. Through watering eyes, I watched Harper striding off down the side off the house with his Mersey tunnel gait. He never said a word.

I could have chased after him. In hindsight I probably should have done, but at the time I didn't care about his rhyme or reason. He'd just stolen my thunder, shit on my parade, taken away my moment of glory and I didn't give a stuff if I never saw him again.

When I came home from school the next day he was there, as ever, waiting for me. I cast him a quick look of contempt before turning to put my key in the door.

'How's yer neb, chor?'

I let out some noise, a cross between a snort and a sarcastic laugh. He approached and pulled a face of regret, something as close to an apology as I was ever likely to get.

'What the fuck was all that about, Harper?' I demanded.

'I had a bad day,' he muttered, bowing his head, talking to the floor.

'Yeah? – Well, I had a spectacularly brilliant one, thanks very much; up until seeing you that is. I thought we were supposed to be best mates?'

PRECESSION

'We are.'

'No Harper. Wrong. Your best mate doesn't come up and drop t'nut on you for no good reason.'

He lifted his head and looked at me with that indescribable expression on his face, like *he* was really the injured party in all this, like everything that happened yesterday was all *my* fault and how could I be so stupid as not to see it.

He'd taken it upon himself to fly the young kestrel all on his own. He'd walked with her on his arm all the way up to Halton Moor. It would have been an unsettling journey for her all that way without a hood; plus the fact it had been a sweltering day; too hot to fly. Halton Moor was semi-urban, too many distractions. She'd never been flown there before; the place was alien to her. Harper had foolishly released the bird, and it had failed to come back. He'd swung a lure all day, looking forlornly up into the sky until he thought his arm would drop off. And that evening he'd trooped back to ours to wait for me, angry. Angry at his stupidity and even angrier at my absence, ready to assuage his guilt against what he saw as my betrayal.

I shook my head at him, determined not to be suckered by his manipulating, self-pitying show of hurt, but he dragged me back to the moor anyway, convinced that we could find the bird and somehow redeem a friendship, didn't even give me chance to get out of my school uniform, no tea; bugger all. Up hills and across fields, swinging a lure; calling for a bird that didn't have a bloody name.

As the shadows lengthened, I followed in his wake, listening to the lure beat the air in giant whooshing arcs, watching it scatter the ritual hover of woodland midges. The kestrel was long gone, but he wouldn't listen. It was pointless trying to explain to him the futility of what he was doing; he didn't even know the meaning of the word, so I shut up, partly at his insistence and let him get on with it; better that than give him reason to have a go at my face again. I had already seen and felt the bubbling propensity to violence manifest, so, from a safe distance I watched him expertly light a fag with one hand while his other continued to doggedly spin the lure. I guess in his irrational way he was working off that bit of guilt he hadn't already dumped on me, and at that moment I felt my best mate become a stranger. We had both begun to change. In teenage tides of testosterone, we were settling into our respective skins, yielding to the inevitable. Harper was seeing who I really was, and he couldn't come to terms with it, while he had morphed, no doubt inevitably, into that person he was destined to become, someone at that moment in my life I didn't care to know. The mischief and the laughter that had been the cement in our friendship had started to crumble. Harper, the cheeky, loveable rogue didn't wash any more, and I couldn't even raise a snigger at that appropriate choice of phrase.

I started to look back at the last seven years. Me and him: misfits. Oddballs. The unlikely lads. Chalk and cheese. Despite all, somehow our friendship had worked. We defied the dissenters and had enjoyed a spectacular time growing up together. Unfortunately, it seemed that the growing up part was our Achilles heel. In my mind I knew it was over, but I was unsure how to let it go without displaying more of the devious creep I could sometimes be or the out and out selfish bastard Harper thought I was.

What happened next, I could have put down to tiredness, over-study, or simply the fact that my stomach thought my throat had been cut, but at that moment and without warning I came over dizzy and slightly nauseous. Surroundings went in and out of focus and sounds came in waves of distant echoes and over-amplification. Trees bent and swayed at impossible angles. I heard the wind in the leaves as giant waves crashing onto rocks. The whooshing sweep of the lure turned into a terrific drone as if armies of bees were in flight. The rolling common land of Halton Moor opened up in front of me and I peered into open fissures of canyon-like proportions. Then, fighting its way through the nausea came a pervading sense of elsewhere; like a time-shift; alien in a sense of not belonging yet all too familiar but almost impossible to describe; close to what people call *déjà vu* but more than fleeting and a thousand times more real. I wasn't dreaming. It was happening here, but it didn't feel like now. I felt my knees buckle and I set down to touch grass that reassuringly felt like grass. To take away that reassurance, a boulder happened at my back from nowhere and offered support. I looked up to see they were everywhere, bold, statuesque, like they'd stood for millennia. There were no boulders like this on Halton Moor.

I didn't fancy being sick on an empty stomach, so I took in slow, deep breaths and once again my senses swam with scents and perceptions that were cognitive yet at the same time unknown to me. It was like nostalgia turned inside out. I sat and I breathed. The oxygen I took in felt warm and unfulfilling like I was sat in the tropics. All around me I saw colours change subtly yet perceptibly. The sky, the hills, and the trees all seemed correct but not as they should be. I could hear a river. I could almost taste it, but there wasn't a river within three miles of here. But I knew that river. I had known it for most of my life.

I have no idea for how long I remained in that state. It can't have been more than minutes, but it felt like hours. And the strange thing is, once the nausea subsided, I didn't mind being wherever it was I thought I was. A mix of feelings: disconcerting but not scary; strange yet familiar.

I came worm-holing back with a sharp kick to the ankle.

'The fuck's up wi you?' Harper stood over me chewing on something, slack-jawed, the lure hanging loosely by his side. He nonchalantly flicked his tab over my head and spat on the floor contemptuously while I tried to compose myself.

I shrugged my shoulders. 'Not sure,' I said eventually, the words coming out weak and shaky. 'I thought I were gonna throw up back there.'

He continued to chew and spit, all the while regarding me with a total look of disdain. 'Why don't you just piss off home, Sarvo? You're about as much use as a chocolate teapot.'

No sympathy there then, not that I was looking for any; I was just trying to fathom out what the hell was going on. I looked up at his looming silhouette then at the immediate surroundings that had gone back to normal. Even the boulder that I had felt at my back had disappeared. I struggled to my feet like Bambi on ice and took in a few more deep breaths. 'Y'know summat,' I said, feeling the blood rush back to my extremities. 'I think I'll just do that.' The sun had set behind the hills leaving behind a melancholy gloom that just about mirrored the way I felt. And now, more than ever, I didn't want to be there. Still shaky but determined I brushed past him and stumbled off into the gathering darkness, leaving him alone and open mouthed. With my senses still scrambled, I walked, half expecting some shout of abuse at my departure, some call of derision. If it ever came, I never heard it.

To this day I don't know what created those visions, sensations; call them what you will, except to say I'm certain they weren't imagined. What I experienced on that weird summer evening was real, but how could that be so when my hawk-obsessed mate saw or felt none of it? For that reason, I kept quiet and never spoke of it to anyone, least of all Harper. It wouldn't have been worth the ridicule.

PISCES

§

Early in 2001 Harper's Mum died. Her beleaguered heart simply couldn't cope with the lifestyle anymore. It gave out in the middle of a bag of Monster Munch, a litre of Irn Bru, a half-smoked Lambert & Butler and Coronation Street. It took six paramedics to remove her from the armchair. Before she'd barely gone cold in her Co-op coffin and before the Council had time to board up and re-possess, the broken family Harper home had already been ransacked and stripped of any saleable commodity, in this case not much more than the copper pipe and wiring. The hapless Marie ended up on the game, operating out of a bedsit in Chapeltown. Little Ryan, her son, who by now had developed severe learning difficulties, was taken into care, as was a sixteen-year-old bitter, resentful Darren Harper.

It was around this time that he started to fulfil what I had hoped wouldn't become his destiny. Unbeknown to any of us, Harper had already left school and had been getting into trouble. Without qualifications or job prospects he had railed against the stigma and slack regime of care and had gravitated towards the open arms of the black-market underworld; familiar territory where he knew he'd be given at least a sink or swim hand. Everyone else had failed him, including us, the Sarvents, who could have, and to my eternal shame, should have offered ourselves as fosterers.

For the first time ever, he failed to show; no sign of him, no contact and no evidence of him being around during the week. I was so busy with my A-levels, I unintentionally neglected the birds and inevitably without Harper's presence their welfare suffered. First, the Eagle owl developed an eye infection that a course of antibiotics failed to shift. The bird wasn't happy and reluctantly dad suggested we give her away to a sanctuary. Within weeks we'd lost the goshawk and the buzzard to aspergillosis, a respiratory disease caused by a fungus that can often be introduced on infected bedding. It left me with a solitary bird to look after, a three-year-old Harris hawk I'd named Bomber, an association that would have been totally lost on Harper; he still refused to give them names. Despite my exam workload I belatedly decided to make an effort and take better care of the remaining raptor. It was just as well.

He turned up one day without warning, right out-of-the-blue.

PRECESSION

Watching him step out of the passenger side of an unfamiliar car I knew straight away there was something different about him. First it was his threads: brand new shell-suit and gleaming trainers, still as chavvy as they come, but new, nevertheless. Second, not apparent straight away, but once I'd heard him speak to the driver of the car, was his attitude: cheeky, arrogant, manipulative; all the old traits were there still, but with them now came a hardened nastiness that even took me aback when I heard it.

'Remember, Darren, I won't be able to pick you back up, I'm off duty at nine,' said the woman with the thick rimmed glasses leaning across the passenger seat.

'Somebody'd berra pick me up,' demanded Harper,

'You'll have to get the bus back with the rest of the money I gave you earlier.'

'I aren't gerrin no fuckin' bus,' he said defiantly. 'You or somebody else had berra be here for me or there'll be trouble,' he threatened while jabbing a finger in her general direction.

'Darren. . .' pleaded the woman.

'I'll get yer fuckin' done – I'm tellin' yer.' He took a gleaming white Nike to the open passenger door and kicked it shut in her face. 'Bitch.' He added for good measure before strutting off towards where I stood with my mouth wide open. The woman looked after him, despair written all over her face. Eventually she belted up and slowly drove off.

'Who was that?' I hardly dared enquire.

In response, he used the word *bitch* a lot. He still liked to talk in the cryptic and it did my head in. Seeing I wasn't in the mood for guessing games, he loosed a couple of lurgis onto the pavement and lit a fag. In stages I learned that the woman on the receiving end of his bad-mouth was a support worker, one of a team of care home staff who he seemingly had at his beck and call to freely abuse and take advantage of at will. The chip on his shoulder was making him lopsided. He started to rant about *fuckin' rights* and *fuckin' respect* a lot, but little of what he said made any sense to me. And of course, I got the inevitable bollocking and blame for what had happened to the birds. It left me smirking inwardly to myself. His old home hadn't been fit for a pig to live in, yet here I was receiving a lecture on aviary management.

The "new" Harper had that sinsemilla scent about him, and I quickly did the maths. I understood they got a clothing allowance

PISCES

amongst the spends they received in care, and although Harper's new threads were chav, they certainly weren't cheap. My guess was he'd usurped their Frankie's somewhat abeyant marijuana empire and had started an enterprise of his own, and although the cigs he smoked in front of me never stank of or resembled a spliff, I was certain he had to be indulging as his eyes had begun to resemble piss-holes in the snow. He was already in trouble with the law and I learned he had been up before the beak on more than one occasion, but I never knew the extent of his profligacy; he only ever told me stuff in that vague, half-truth way of his, whenever the mood took him or whenever he felt the need to brag or show off, but he no longer had the ability to bamboozle, shock or impress me, and I no longer felt sorry for him. The only tenuous link left in our lives now was a solitary hawk, and soon our destinies would conspire to sever even that link.

§

I took my A-levels a year early, only the second pupil in my school to have done so successfully. I got straight A's in every subject, and I would have been disappointed if the outcome had been any different. I'm not saying they were easy, far from it, especially the maths and physics, but I had worked bloody hard for them and the brain-graft I applied justified the results. Mum and Dad were, of course, naturally proud and chuffed to bits at having their only son gain a place at university while still only seventeen. I still had my heart set on becoming a doctor and couldn't wait to start my studies in medicine come September.

We had cause for a double celebration in the Sarvent household that late summer. Dad had been asked by his company to run a new engineering plant down in Basildon, all relocation costs to be met by the firm, along with a big salary increase. It would mean leaving Yorkshire for good, not a problem for me as I would be shortly heading off for uni anyway, but it would mean having to get rid of Bomber, unless, that is, Harper was still interested in keeping the bird, but he would have to find a new home for him and I was no longer sure that he still had the inclination.

For passing my exams and gaining a university place Mum and Dad bought me a new phone. I used it for the first time to call Harper. I said I needed to see him. He told me he was too busy to come up to Roundhay, so reluctantly I arranged to meet him on his old stomping ground.

He was late. Impatiently I paced up and down in front of The Delvers. The odd dead-eyed punter leaving or entering the pub looked me up and down suspiciously or staggered by indifferently. I hadn't been on the streets of Gipton for some time, but the feeling of unease hadn't diminished. I didn't fancy getting my new phone out around here, but after another ten minutes of pacing I quickly and discreetly punched in his number. Half a dozen rings later he answered. In the background it sounded like a riot was taking place.

'Harper – where the fuck are you?'

'That you Sarvo? Are yer there? Be wiv yer in five minutes, mush.'

With that the phone went dead. Five minutes later he announced his arrival with a squeal of brakes and a smell of burning rubber. The maroon Ford Escort did a hand-brake pirouette in the middle of the road and Harper fell out of the passenger side to the thumping, chest hurting strains of some techno tune. He swaggered over, fag in gob and can of Red Stripe in hand, pumped full of gangsta attitude and God knows what else. He didn't say anything, but with a flex of the shoulders and an open-armed gesture along with the cocky smile, the insinuation had to be, *"Look at me, aren't I cool – the dog's bollock's or what?"* I didn't say anything either, but what I thought was, *"What a knobhead"* We stood facing each other like that for a while, him grinning, me grimacing, while in the background the Escort with its over revved engine and its three other occupants whooping and hollering took off in a mad wheel spin.

'Who're your mates?' I nodded in the direction of the cloud of blue smoke.

'Ahh, just a bunch o' mad cunts,' he said dismissively. 'So, what's the craic then? – hope yer lookin' after me bird.' He took a swig of his Red Stripe and belched loudly.

'That's what I wanted to talk to you about . . .' I paused to watch his "mad-cunt-mates" pull another handbrake turn at the top of the road. '. . . Mum and Dad have put the house up for sale. They're moving down to Essex soon, and I'm off to uni in a couple of weeks – the hawk's gonna have to go.' I watched his face closely for a reaction. He gave nothing away but blew smoke and nodded slowly. The car came racing back down the street and slewed into a violent three-sixty, leaving a layer of molten rubber on the tarmac. The driver, face half hidden behind the peak of a baseball cap, hung his head out the window and shouted something incomprehensible in our direction. Harper casually turned and gave him the finger. 'Silly born bastard,' he muttered to himself with the smile still on his face.

'Well?' I asked as he turned back to me.

'Well, what?'

'It's your bird as well as mine. Do you still want it? Can you take him?'

Harper finished his drink, crushed the can in his hand and let it fall to the floor. The smile left his face, and he gave me a look of incredulity. 'I live in residence. Where the fuck d'yer think they'll let me keep a bleedin' hawk?'

'Just thought I'd ask,' I shrugged. 'It's your bird as well as mine.'

'Yeah, you said that.'

As the situation dawned, his manner changed. He took an agitated pull on his cigarette while quickly weighing up the options and realising that there weren't any.

'Shall I see if the sanctuary'll take him?'

'What? – yeah, whatever . . . do what you have to.'

Harper's apparent indifference belied his frustration. He was pretending not to care but I could see through him. 'We could take him up the moors at the weekend; fly him one last time if you like.'

He pulled a few faces and stewed on it for a second or two before pride, or something else got the better of him. He shook his head firmly. 'Nah.'

'You sure?'

'Nah, – too busy, – got summat on.' He flicked his tab on the pavement and stood on the sparking stub, all the while avoiding eye contact. I watched his unreasoned stubbornness take hold, and as ever I couldn't help feeling sorry for him.

'That's okay, I understand.'

As far as our mutual love of birds went, that was the end of it I suppose. We never spoke about or flew hawks together ever again.

'So, yer gonna go off an' become a sawbones then?'

I nodded. 'Looks like it.'

'What about the old Bruce Lee shit?' he asked, accompanied by all the actions.

'Yeah, that too,' I laughed, 'If I can find the time.'

We small talked for the next ten minutes or so, and under the realisation that this really was it, the conversation slowly became stilted and awkward. The knobheads in the Escort had ripped it up and down the street spinning doughnuts for the umpteenth time and were now getting bored and impatient. They were yelling abuse at Harper, threatening to leave him behind if he didn't hurry up. It didn't make our goodbye any easier. I suppose it was just as well seeing as neither of us would have been able to say what we wanted anyhow.

'Whose is the motor?' I asked naively.

'Fuck knows,' said Harper with a shrug, 'It weren't me what nicked it.'

I felt a lecture coming on but now was neither the time nor place. I pulled out my phone and punched in a taxi number.

'Who're yer ringin'?'

'Taxi.'

'We'll give yer a lift.'

'I don't think so.'

I ordered my cab then handed over the Nokia at his insistence so he could inspect it. He turned it over in scrutiny a few times before passing it back. He asked how much I paid for it. I explained it was a gift from my parents.

'Should've come to me, charver,' he said in his wheeler-dealer manner, 'I'd have got yer one fer half the price.'

Along with the phone I stuffed my hands in my pockets and tried to breach that awkward distance that had now become a chasm between us. The driver of the stolen motor had now resorted to leaning on the horn for long intervals or tooting along to the thumping rhythms of So Solid Crew as they continued to shake the street. The last thing I wanted to do was preach at my ex-mate as a parting shot, but I found myself doing it anyway. 'You know if you get in that car, you're gonna end up like your Carl.' Of course he didn't want to hear it, and I don't recall his response, it only hastened his departure. 'Do something with your life, Harper – don't waste it,' I found myself calling after him. He never looked back; he just raised a hand in the air and got into the passenger side of the car. Whether it was a gesture of acknowledgement, a sign for me to be silent or just a wave goodbye, I'll never know. As I watched them roar off into the Gipton ghetto with that familiar screech of burning rubber and blue smoke, I realised our lives had finally turned the corner and would never be the same again; neither would the world for that matter. Tomorrow was Monday. The date: September 11th. 2001.

PISCES

Camp Bastion – 2012

'Still at it, Andy? – Do you know what time it is?' I look up to see SMO Naylor peering down at me anxiously, still wearing his theatre cap, mask around his throat; the bloody evidence of a long hard shift still present on his scrub suit. I aim my wrist towards the beam of the angle-poise and see it's almost one a.m. A flying insect scorches itself on the red-hot bulb and drops onto its back, legs writhing in the air. I watch it for a few seconds, briefly pondering the notion of insect pain before brushing it onto the floor with the back of my hand. I look back at my commander through bourbon-soaked eyes.

'It's late, sir, I know. I just wanted to finish my report.'

'Writing reports at this hour isn't conducive to saving lives through there in a few hours' time,' he says nodding towards theatre. 'Get some rest, man; you look as if you need it.'

'All due respect, sir, I could say the same about you.'

'Yes, well; a shower, a quick nightcap, a catch up on CNN, and I'll be hitting the sack sharpish, don't you worry. I suppose you've heard the news coming in from Pakistan?'

'News?'

'Another earthquake, massive one by all accounts. They're expecting casualties in the tens of thousands. Epicentre near Pashawar. Didn't you feel the aftershocks?'

'Can't say I did – or if I did, I probably thought it was insurgents keeping us on our toes.' My gaze falls back to my report. I stare blankly at the papers; all I see is a blur of black and white print. Naylor clocks the almost empty bottle of Jack Daniels and pulls a face. I guess it's supposed to convey sympathy. The revelation about the earthquake barely registered, just another major catastrophe in an unbelievably shitty day.

'Andy,' he says eventually, 'I know you probably don't want to hear this from me right now, and I understand that. I also understand you wanting to numb the emotions like this – I . . .'

'It's a one-off, Peter. I just needed a crutch tonight, a little Dutch courage. I won't be repeating it. I still need to write a letter to his partner.'

'You don't have to do it you know.'

PRECESSION

'No, I want to; I - I don't know, call it a cathartic need or something if you like.' As soon as the words formed and left my lips, I became acutely aware of just how smashed I was. My SO gave up a weary but resigned nod of understanding before bidding me goodnight, and I settled back into the slurry of self-pity my memories and the Jack Daniels had managed to create between them. I was also becoming acutely aware of a growing sense of loathing I had started to cultivate for this world and its stupid ways. I thought of the Pakistan earthquake and all the people that had perished or were suffering. I thought of the tsunamis, the floods, the droughts; one catastrophe after another as 2012 did its best to live up to the predictions, then I look around me, in this now quiet tent, on this piece of desert, in this beleaguered land, and I begin to laugh. I laugh loud and long, releasing all feelings of bitterness and futility into the night. No matter how hard we try to kill, maim and destroy, somehow nature always manages to do it better.

I re-read the letter, not knowing how to finish it. I try my upmost to convey sorrow and sympathy, but the words crawl off the page cold and impersonal. I don't even know who it is I'm writing to. I'm still waiting for personnel to obtain next of kin from his unit, and I guess it won't include any of his illustrious siblings if any of them are still around. At 2 a.m. I give it up as a bad job and fall into my pit exhausted. The alcohol inside me renders me unconscious for a while, but I don't really sleep. Fractured dreams neither nightmarish nor disturbing take me to places abstract and unreal, scenes come and go without pattern or cohesion yet are oddly familiar to me in those waking moments as I writhe and twist under my duvet. At 5.30 a.m. my alarm shatters the surreal, and the paintings of a tired mind pop off into the sub-ether, never to be pondered over or reasoned with again. *Hands off cocks - on socks* I hear Harper paraphrase inside my head as I throw off the cover, and as the harsh and sour taste of stale bourbon becomes apparent inside my Gobi Desert gob, reality hits me hard in the guts.

I shower, shave, tip a litre of water down my throat and head off to do my rounds. I don't eat breakfast, too early for that; the mere thought of food would see me nauseous. Mercifully I'm not needed in theatre, so I head outside to clear my head. The camp is relatively quiet. In the near distance dark silhouettes of Chinooks at rest are just starting to be illuminated by the large cerise orb that is the rising sun emerging from behind the Arghandab peaks heralding a new dawn of

PISCES

death and destruction. A fuel bowser trundles by leaving in its wake the sickly chemical aftermath of its load to swirl up in the dust and assault my nostrils. I walk on through the dissipating noxious cloud and watch as a Hercules cruises in from Brize with its latest cargo of IED fodder. I stroll over to the apron and watch the beast taxi and turn through a rippling heat haze and suffer the noise of its mighty engines on my pounding head.

I play a game: watching them spill out, a long khaki line, kit bags slung over shoulders: combat virgin, combat vet. As they file past, they're easy to spot. It's in the eyes, even the ones who are playing at indifference. And as I peer at the faces I work at the percentages: who won't be walking back onto that transporter in six months' time? I know it's a macabre thing to do but I can't help it. I pick out faces and try and picture wives, girlfriends, sisters, brothers, mothers, fathers, sons and daughters, all clinging on to that blind faith that there *is* a cause, even though the veneer of justification trotted out by the politicians is wearing paper thin, and deep down most of them must know in their hearts there is no cause at all.

I watch the last man off, and under his crisp-clean fatigues I can see he isn't yet a man, just a lad, a combat virgin. He glances nervously in my direction. My face doesn't slip. Welcome to the lottery of life and death.

With my hangover failing to lift I head back. The rest of the camp is beginning to stir, and already the sun is climbing the sky making the mercury soar. I try to visualise this place in two years, when we've all packed up and left. With the standing joke that is the ANA left to pick up the pieces, what will be our legacy? Could I really have been so naive to think that I'd make a difference? I'm a doctor not a politician, but who's kidding who? Since the Americans rumbled a complicit ISI, the blinkers are off. In degrees we're all just pawns in some elaborate game, to what end I can't say I'll ever be sure, I'm not that smart, just some sawbones doing his job, not supposed to ask questions, no point in asking questions. Sure, I've saved lives, I've saved almost as many lives as I've seen deaths, only now I can't help thinking that those lives shouldn't have needed saving in the first place. And the one life I should have saved but couldn't, the one life that would have made it all worthwhile . . .

My glands go into overdrive and my mouth fills with water. I rush over to a nearby compound and throw up against its corrugated metal piling walls. Acid bile and a bourbon aftermath burn up my

PRECESSION

craw. Beads of sweat pop out in force and drip off my forehead to mingle with the contents of my stomach. Once again, I silently curse to hell everything and anyone to do with this war. Before I even begin to stagger on my way, a squadron of blowflies has massed to begin their toxic breakfast.

I reach the relatively cool sanctuary of my office where I shovel down painkillers followed by water and coffee. On the desk lies the envelope from personnel that I've been waiting for.

I know well the feeling of being kicked when you're down. It happened to me a long time ago, on my first day of middle school, yet it all comes readily to mind like it was yesterday, as does the face of the greasy haired girl who kind of came to my rescue that day; and later a proposition and a gravy-stained jumper that could have potentially scarred a sexually naive adolescent for life.

I finish reading the bulletin from 3 Rifles HQ and pull out the brown envelope from my desk drawer. I put my letter of condolence to one side and search for the photograph. Armani Kershaw, of course it was. How could I not have remembered that face? Harper and Armani - who would ever have guessed it?

They weren't married; in fact, they were already estranged before Harper was posted to Afghanistan. She had left Army quarters and had gone back to Leeds with the kids. The bulletin said she'd not left a forwarding address. I gaze at two mischievous faces, the cheeky chav grins, and the number two crops and wonder what would become of them. I don't even know their names.

I think of my mate and the long, lonely trip back to Brize Norton, the faceless, nameless colleagues who'll carry the Union flag draped wooden box from the Hercules, the Army chaplain who'll spout the superlatives, the personnel who'll represent his regiment but who never knew him – and that's it because there'll be no friends, no family, no loved ones. Darren Harper was destined to become nothing more than a statistic - but that wouldn't happen, because I wouldn't let it.

I carefully put the photograph back in the envelope one last time and bring out the sterling silver chain. I kiss the hawk pendant before placing it back also and sealing it shut. In the background a newsflash comes on the radio - The death toll in the Pakistan earthquake now stood at over a quarter million.

Part 2 – Aeon of The Water Bearer

*W*hen the Blue Star Kachina makes its appearance in the heavens the Fifth World shall emerge. This will be the day of purification. It will come when the Saquashuh (blue) Kachina dances in the plaza and removes his mask.

In the final days we will look up in the heavens and we shall witness the return of the two brothers who helped create this world in the birthing time.

The twins will be seen in our north-western skies, and they will come to visit flying in their Patuwvotas (flying shields) to see who have still remembered the original teachings. They will bring many of their star family with them in the final days. The return of the Blue Kachina, who is also known as Na Ga Sohu, will be the forewarning that tells us there will soon be a new day, new way of life and a new world coming.

They will start as fires that shall burn within us, we will burn up with desires and conflict if we do not remember the original teachings and return to a peaceful way of life.

Not far behind will come The Purifier, the Red Kachina who will bring the day of purification. On this day the Earth, her creatures and all life as we know it shall be offered a chance to change forever. There will be messages that precede the coming of the Purifier. They will leave messages to those on Earth that remember the old ways.

The messages will be found on the living stone, through the sacred grains and even the waters. From The Purifier will issue forth a great red light. All things shall change in the manner of being. Every living thing will be given the opportunity to change, from the largest to the smallest living thing.

Those who return to the ways given to us in the original teachings and live in a natural way of life will not be touched by the coming of The Purifier. They will survive and build a new world; only in the ancient teachings will they have the ability to understand the messages to be found. It is important to understand these messages shall be found upon every living thing, even within our bodies, even within a drop of blood.

Many will appear to have lost their souls in the final days. So intense will be the nature of these changes that those who are weak in spirit will go insane, for we are nothing without spirit. Only those who return to the values of the old ways will be able to find peace of mind. For in the Earth, they shall find relief from the madness that

PRECESSION

will be around us. Many people of this time will be empty in spirit for they will have no Sampacu, no life force in their eyes.

As we get close to the time of The Purifier there will be many who walk like ghosts through their cities, through canyons they have constructed in their man-made mountains. Those who walk through these places will be very heavy in their walk, it will appear almost painful as they take each step, for they have become disconnected from their spirit and the Earth. After the arrival of the twins, they begin to vanish before your eyes so much like muck smoke. Others will have great deformities both in their mind and upon their bodies.

There will be those who walk in their body that are not from this reality, for many of the gateways that once protected us shall be opened. There will be much confusion, confusion between the sexes, the children and their elders. Life will get very perverted and there will be little social order in these times. Many will ask for the mountains themselves to fall upon them and end their misery.

Still others will appear untouched by what is occurring. Those who remember the original teachings and have reconnected with their heart and spirit, those who remember their mother and father are The Pahana who left to live in the mountains and forest.

When The Purifier comes, we will see him first as a small red star, which will come very close and sit in our heavens watching us, watching to see how well we have remembered the sacred teachings. This Purifier will show us many miraculous signs in our heavens. In this we shall know that our creator is not a dream. Even those who do not feel their connection to spirit will see the force of The Creator across the sky.

Things unseen will be felt strongly. Many things will begin to occur that will not make sense, for reality will be shifting back. We will receive many warnings allowing us to change our way, from below the Earth as well as above. Then one morning we shall awaken to a red dawn. The sky will be the colour of blood and many things will begin to happen that right now we are not sure of their exact nature, for much of reality will not be as it is now.

The nature of mankind shall seem strange in these times as we walk between worlds, and we house many spirits even within our bodies. After a time, we will again walk with our brothers from the stars and rebuild this Earth, but not until The Purifier has left his mark upon the universe. No living thing will go untouched here or in the heavens. The way through this time is said to be in our hearts and

AQUARIUS

reuniting with our spiritual self. Getting simple and returning to living with and upon this Earth in harmony with her creatures. Remembering we are the caretakers, the fire keepers of the spirit. Our relatives from the stars are coming home to see how well we have fared on our journey.

It is time to reconnect with your spirit and your Earth Mother. Peace and blessings.

Ancient Hopi prophesy.

PRECESSION

Carver Garrison, Essex

. . . *Only those imbued with certain esoteric knowledge knew of what was to come, and that wisdom was known by only an enlightened few, both amongst the malevolent elite and the benevolent resistance. Those who had given portent to the return of Nibiru and the cataclysmic events from the resulting pole shift were largely ignored or labelled conspiracy theorists, a curiously derogatory term coined by agents of the so-called deep state and aimed at anyone uncovering uncomfortable and potentially damaging truths. Although fear was the primary currency of the satanic entities, they knew that revelation worldwide of impending catastrophe would lead to panic and chaos beyond their control. "Who controls the past controls the future. Who controls the present controls the past", a prophet once wrote. Ordo Ab Chao was the motto of the thirty-third degree Masons; order out of chaos. Problem, reaction, solution: manufacture the fear, create the chaos, offer the solution. Now, for the first time in millennia, they were no longer in control. The return of The Destroyer, long prophesied was imminent, and for those who sought to enslave humanity under a New World Order, time was running out. In desperation Agenda 2030 was brought forward. Bluebeam had been the cabal's final gambit, and it had failed. Despite partial victories with the climate hoax, manufactured scarcities and a de-population agenda via bioweapons, plandemics, and proxy wars, The Great Awakening had begun and was now unstoppable. The people's revolution in China had inspired citizens across the world to overthrow the puppet governments of the WEF. The imposition of martial law and NATO troops on foreign soils was a futile act. With overstretched resources, inept leadership and overwhelming resistance the Bluehats capitulated en masse, and the puppeteers along with their cronies began to run to their DUMBS.*

AQUARIUS

Ironically, nearly all of their designs would come to pass, only this time the events in the skies would be real, not CGI, the change to climate would be real, not geo-engineered, scarcities would be real, not manufactured, disease and pathogen would be real, not made in a lab, and sadly, their vision of a mass population cull would be realised, not by proxy wars, the kill shots and the death towers but by the catastrophic events that were about to unfold . . .

With a grunt, engineer Jed 'Spunky' Murphy climbed into the relative warmth of the cab, playfully flicking tiny ice shards from his glove at his young travelling companion, while starting the engine of the APC.

'Child,' Maeve Bradley tutted under her breath as she wiped the now melting particles from the pad she had been writing in.

Outside, great clouds of steam from the vehicle's exhaust had formed, swirling and then vaporising almost instantly in the freezing air.

'Still writing, I see,' said the big man in his ancestral Dublin brogue. 'I hope you're not going to have yer head stuck into that bloody pad all the way down to th' smoke. An' you, Sleepin' Beauty,' he nodded over to his second travelling mate. 'I hope you're not going to be sat there with yer gob open catching flies like yer usually do. It's so fucken rude. I can still get youse both transferred yer know.'

'No, you can't. Don't talk silly,' said Maeve in a tone that belied her youthful appearance and any perceived authority the Irishman might have thought he held.

'Look, guys, all I'm asking is for a nice bit of civil conversation just to alleviate the boredom and make the journey run nice and smooth, is that too much to ask – is it?

'I'm not being funny, Jed,' piped up engineer Navinder Buthar, 'but if your past topics of conversation are anything to go by, I'd rather spend the journey catching up on some shut-eye – no offence.'

Jed sucked at his teeth, raised the angle of the snowplough and drove towards the garrison gates. They slowly opened before them revealing a bleak, grey-white wilderness, where land was indiscernible from sky stretching as far as the eye could see. He breathed a heavy sigh. 'I don't see the point in any of this, I really don't.'

PRECESSION

'Don't see the point in what, Jed?' Maeve asked wearily looking up from her pad.

'All this bollocks. I mean just how many bloody books d'yer think these lot are going to find anyway?' He jabbed a thumb towards the back of the APC that carried the ten-strong team of specialist bibliophiles. 'They'll have been used for fuel by the freezing masses yonks ago.'

'There are secret underground vaults at the London Library. We have the blueprints. Our brief as engineers is to locate, make safe and facilitate the removal of anything we find of value and importance.'

Jed did a double take. 'Oh – engineer now, is it? Is that what yer calling yerself? My God, you've only just learned to clean your own arse, and now you're an engineer.' He did another double take beyond Maeve to Nav, who had pulled his cap down over his face and settled down comfy with his arms folded. 'Engineers – engineers,' he mused the word to himself. 'I've fucken shit 'em. Anyways, that place'll be razed to the ground by now, so it will.'

'Not according to the drones,' stated Maeve.

'I still think this is a futile operation,' Jed persisted. 'I know for a fact that all the books in the world are filed and crystallised at the DSC up in Boston Spa.'

'Not all, apparently, Jed,'

'Well, I...'

'Oh, for fuck's sake, give it a rest will you, Spunky?' pleaded Nav from under his cap. 'Is there any wonder nobody wants to have a conversation with you?'

'I see what you mean,' Maeve concurred.

Silence ensued for a few blissful minutes until Jed started humming an out of tune ditty whilst feigning interest at the stuff that was on Maeve's pad. Annoyed at the sound of his discordant refrain, she donned her earphones.'

'Oh, now, that *is* bloody rude,' he protested.

Exasperated, Maeve removed the phones. 'Ok, Jed; you win. What do you want to talk about?'

'Hmm... Oh, I know, how's about we talk about you?'

'Why? – Why do would you want to talk about me? According to you, I've just come out of nappies.'

'Ooh – I dunno, maybe because I hear you're one of the special ones.' He narrowed his eyes and formed a look of intrigue.

Maeve screwed up her face. 'What? – What does that even

AQUARIUS

mean?' she asked incredulously.

'It means that you're from up there,' he pointed loosely to what used to be north. 'You're from Catterick.'

'Well, so is Nav. So are around a fifth of this garrison. What's your point?'

'I hear you're from one of The Diggers. Word has it you have special lineage and were born an Indigo child.'

Maeve scoffed a laugh. 'Oh, please. An indigo child is an old New Age term. My mother was an Indigo, so was my grandmother. They're just old labels; we don't do them anymore. It simply means souls who come into this world with a higher level of consciousness. It's no longer anything special. And yes, my Great Grandfather was a New Leveller, and yes, he had a part to play in the survival of humanity at the time of The Shift, along with thousands of others.'

'Oh, come now, Miss Bradley, no need for modesty. I hear he was one of the great architects, a pioneer, a founding father of this phenomenal altruistic tribe.' He paused in anticipation of an enlightened response but could see that she was reticent. 'Yer know what the people are callin' us now, don't yer?'

'No, do enlighten us.'

'The Meek. What's the passage there from that old book?'

'You mean The Bible.' - *"Blessed are the meek, for they shall inherit the earth"* – Matthew 5:5', stated Maeve.

'That's the one,' said Jed. 'How d'yer feel being a descendant of someone whose legacy gets that kind of a label?'

'Be careful now, Jed. Another label is all it is, and these second and third hand stories are how myths and legends are born, and most, if any, don't have a grain of truth to them.'

'How about this one then,' announced Nav. *'"When the earth has been ravished and the animals are dying, a tribe of people from all creeds, races and colours will put their faith in deeds, not words to make the land green again. They shall be known as - The Warriors of the Rainbow."'*

'That's an ancient Cree Indian prophecy, if I'm not mistaken,' said Maeve.

'Yeah, well whoever said it, I wish it'd hurry up and come true, cos I can't see much fucken' green around here, can youse?' Jed lowered the plough and smashed it into a drift, cleaving a flurry of snow and ice to one side in their wake. 'So, if what I've heard is just hearsay, let's be having it from the horse's mouth then.'

PRECESSION

Maeve took a deep breath. 'Really?' Nav, now fully awake and engaged sat up and raised his cap. The two engineers nodded in anticipation. 'Very well,' she began somewhat reluctantly. 'My great grandfather was a doctor, an army surgeon. He served his country in a long-forgotten conflict out in the Middle East. On his return from his last call of duty, appalled, ashamed and disillusioned by what he'd witnessed, he began researching the origins of all theatres of war past and present, and what he discovered took him down a rabbit hole that he never really emerged from. He also witnessed first-hand the systematic dismantling and destruction of a National Health Service that had served the public for decades. He saw the Khazarian mafia fuel and fund their brothers-in-arms in the shape of mad scientists and doctors playing God come close to bring about a mass extinction event while paradoxically posing as the saviours of mankind. His was virtually a lone voice of dissent amongst his colleagues and peers towards the perpetrators of this crime. Many were complicit in what was unfolding as a silent genocide. Hospitals and care facilities became killing fields, and for being brave enough to speak out he was disciplined and then warned in no uncertain terms by some shadowy but very powerful people to keep his mouth shut. He refused to be silenced, became a whistle-blower, but was ostracised by his profession, stripped of his army rank and was left out in the cold. He came to realise there was a very sinister agenda at play, not just in his field of health, but in all matters, be it political, military or religious, and it was global. He became an activist and morphed towards an ever-growing network of like-minded scientists, doctors, philosophers and researchers. Through this network he learned of the hierarchical spider's web that had conspired to enslave mankind for thousands of years.'

'Ah,' said Nav, 'so this is the Khazarian mafia of which you speak, the Illuminate and The Cabal. The Demiurge that was made up of secret societies: The Jesuits, Zionists and Freemasons.'

'That is correct, my learned friend,' said Maeve impressed.

'I knew that.' interrupted Jed. 'Everybody knows that.''

'Ok, said Maeve. 'So, what else shall we talk about?'

'No, no, I didn't mean it like that,' apologised the big man. 'Please carry on.'

'You sure?'

Two nodded heads confirmed once more. Maeve didn't really mind imparting this stuff, after all it was tying in with what she was

AQUARIUS

documenting in her journal.

'In the years preceding The Shift,' she continued, 'those in power, let's call them The Establishment for want of a better word, or should I say the entities that controlled The Establishment, knew that their time was at an end. Mankind was entering a new age as had been foretold by all the ancient religions. Some called it the end of the world, but this was largely misinterpreted. It was simply the end of the age of duality, as could be seen by the precession of the equinoxes. The masses, having been held in a perpetual state of unconscious fear and blind servitude for centuries, were finally starting to awaken. A slow but sure mass shift in consciousness was taking place, and the more tyranny that the so-called elite tried to impose, the more people started to see through it. So they ramped up the fear even more, because they knew that they still held sway over a vast majority who had been conditioned to embrace their slavery.'

'Stockholm Syndrome,' said Nav.

'Stockholm Syndrome, what the hell is that?' asked Jed.

'It's a psychological phenomenon whereby an individual or a group of people would acquiesce willingly to any malfeasance imposed on them, outwardly showing a reliance and even reverence to the captor, right, Maeve?'

'Right; and for a while it worked. Their last hope of retaining world dominance came in the form of a plan long in the making. The New World Order was a call for the transformation and centralisation of global society that would manifest under sinister agendas cloaked in philanthropic subtitles such as The Great Reset, Sustainable Development and The Fourth Industrial Revolution. The two blueprints for this Great Global reset were Agenda 21 and Agenda 30, both of which called for, among other things, an end to national sovereignty, abolition of private property, dismantling the family unit, children raised by the state, travel restrictions, mass resettlement, mass surveillance, land confiscation, state-controlled income, and the big one: Mass global depopulation.'

Jed shook his head in disbelief. 'Surely you would've thought the peoples across the world would've cottoned on to all of that.'

'Well, none of it was kept secret, it had been foretold long before its implementation; they even wrote it in stone.'

'How the hell would you enforce such a thing?' asked Jed incredulous.

'Not so difficult if you think about it. The templates were already

PRECESSION

there in Soviet Russia and the CCP. Through what became known as The Totalitarian Tiptoe they mission-crept to realise their agendas by mass deception, regime change, false flag events, the falsification of what was known as *his*tory, and a narrative built on lies. They created fake pandemics, locked people in their homes, ordered everyone to wear masks in the ludicrous assumption that this would deter a pathogen that didn't even exist. They developed poisons as bioweapons that were injected into the body on the lie that it would protect them from the deadly virus, but it killed, maimed and made millions infertile.'

'Now, that bit I do know to be true,' Jed nodded solemnly.

'How so?'

'My own great grandfather was a gonadotroph. His mitochondrial damaged sperm made his wife barren, killed her eventually.'

'So, how come you're here, then?' puzzled Nav.

'He eventually fell for another woman, a pureblood. Her eggs were good, found a donor who didn't demand a fortune for his untainted seed, and a petri dish did the rest. The nickname's a hand-me-down, I guess.'

'Bloody hell, I did wonder where you got that moniker from – well bugger me.'

'Yep, I'm a Murphy in name only.'

'It was a Eugenicists' dream,' said Maeve. 'The perfect depopulation tool; better than any weapon. The seed of life used as an antigen of death at the end of a needle. And to augment it they rolled out a weaponised micropulsed phased array system, disguised as multi generation wireless technology, that made those who had taken the arm spear light up like Christmas trees...'

'Light up like what?'

'It's just an old phrase, Jed,' said Nav. 'Stop interrupting.'

'Their bodies were full of hydrogels and graphene oxide, making them super conductors for the biometrics and AI surveillance technology that was in the offing through genetic corruption and micro-chipped implants. They were well on the way to blanketing the whole Earth with this radioactive smog via thousands of satellites deployed in low-orbit space. In effect they were trying to create the ultimate slave race from those that would survive this holocaust.'

'So how was your great grandfather able to prevent it – or did he?'

'Please don't think of him as some messianic figure saving the world single-handed. He was part of a vast body of dissenting voices amongst professors, doctors and epidemiologists worldwide who weren't under the control of the giant pharmaceutical companies who in turn pulled the strings of governments. No, you're right, they weren't able to save large swathes of a generation who willingly, albeit ignorantly, but obediently queued in line with their sleeves rolled up, but they tried. Instead, they were dismissed as quacks and conspiracy theorists under a deluge of misinformation and propaganda. All dissenters were socially de-platformed, and so eventually they were forced underground. For a while they used a thing called The Dark Web to carry on their campaign against The New World Order, but the CIA, MI5 and Mossad were still able to find and harass them. Many brave souls who refused to lie low were sought out and suicided, most were experts in their respective fields.'

'What is CIA, MI5 and Mossad?' asked Nav.

'They were the so-called security arms of certain governments, secretly controlled by the military industrial complex, tasked to carry out their dirty work.'

'So how did they escape the attention of these organisations?'

'A turning point came when a crack team of dissenting IT specialists from Silicon Valley in California came on board, bringing with them technologies that had been kept under wraps for years, far in advance of anything in the public domain. Undercover, they built a whole new IT framework, a new totally encrypted internet in effect.'

'There must have been a hell of a lot of trust issues there. How did they vet these people?' asked Jed.

'By now they had well organised teams of the most brilliant minds all working in tandem. Luminaries of the esoteric sciences: psychics, remote viewers, synthesisers, people who could accurately read another's true intentions. They were good, they were thorough; they knew that they had to be.'

'So, what was Great Granddaddy's role in all of this?'

'He basically masterminded a coup d'état of the British military, or what was left of it after the Blue Hats took over, but not by an armed insurrection as you might expect.'

'Don't tell me, he used mind control.'

'If you're gonna be facetious, Jed, I'll go back to my scribing,' stated Maeve flatly. Nav fixed him a withering stare.

'Hey, look I'm only teasing,' said Jed holding up his hands. It's banter. Chill out the both of yers.'

PRECESSION

'Ignore the idiot,' said Nav. 'Please continue.'
'Okay, so they knew what was coming, and they planned for it.'
'They?'
'Yes, I told you, he didn't do any of this on his own. The brainstorming must have been phenomenal. Look, I'm referring to them as *they* because they all came from disparate groups and organisations that went by many names until they became the ultimate secret collective I'm describing now. I know they were sometimes known as The New Levellers, or The Diggers, but they rejected any such titles for fear of being labelled a cult or even architects of a doctrine. They were simply humanists who believed they were here for a reason as part of their evolutionary journey – any more questions?'

They both shook their heads in unison.

'Okay, so if it makes you happier, we'll refer to them as the Diggers. They knew what was coming. They also knew that mass non-compliance was the only way to stop the implementation of the so-called New World Order in its tracks, but the acquiescence of the servile, brainwashed masses meant that was never going to happen until it was too late. With all civil liberties eroded, planned pandemics, food shortages and collapse of the financial markets were implemented globally and the portent for mass social unrest and civil war became inevitable. In the West sovereign armies were demobilised and martial law introduced under the auspices of a long-standing sinister organisation known as NATO.'

'These were the Blue Hats, yes?' Nav interjected.

'Correct,' said Maeve. 'It was the litmus test for what was designed to become a One World Army, but it had never been deployed in such widespread international domestic conflicts before. The sheer scale of operations became a logistical nightmare. The chain of command dissolved into a Babel of ineptitude and incompetence; ultimately their so called "Crisis Management Operations" were doomed to fail. A lot of the displaced and disgruntled ex-military hierarchies tried to take advantage of this. There were coups and counter coups. It became a maelstrom of warring factions, and chaos ensued. Across the pond, militias joined forces with expats. In France, top-ranking generals collaborated with a populist anarchic movement previously known as The Gilets Jaunes who openly executed many government officials and politicians.'

AQUARIUS

'Hmm, the Americans and French did have a propensity towards rebellion,' remarked Nav. 'It was part of their story, written into their psyche.'

'Indeed, and to that end our American friends had a distinct advantage.'

'Second amendment?'

'Yes, they had the right to bear arms written into their constitution. Most Americans had access to weapons. Civil war was part of the agenda, but it backfired spectacularly on the cabal. When the subjugation of the American people failed, other western governments and their puppet masters began to panic, China looked on, waiting for the West to tear itself apart, but they took their eye off the ball, and its people, long enslaved by such a tyrannical regime, became emboldened by events unfolding across the world. En masse the people threw off their shackles and the largest standing army in the world disintegrated almost overnight.'

'And yet millions of people in multiple countries still lost their lives,' qualified Nav with a sad shake of the head.

'Unfortunately, so,' Maeve concurred. 'And although many perished upon these shores, The Diggers did their best to make the transition bloodless. The hawks were separated from the doves, homeless veterans from numerous theatres of war were fed, housed and re-mobilised. Patriotic elements from the military were given new roles, and the blueprint for what some termed The Silent Revolution was implemented. When the occupying Blue Hats finally capitulated and were dispersed, the Diggers commandeered all military garrisons and barracks throughout what was known as The United Kingdom. Catterick became the control and nerve centre of operations. Tribunals were set up under Common Law and a reinstated Nuremberg Code. Many of those who were complicit in the imposition and maintenance of a one-world despotic government were tried and convicted.'

'Who exactly?'

'Those who sat in corrupt seats of power and their minions. Politicians, bankers, doctors, military, police, and the judiciary.'

'So, if the lawmakers were on trial, who sat in judgement?' asked Nav.

'The people, of course. The Common Man. Don't forget, so called democracy had long been usurped by now. Governments were merely large corporations operating under Admiralty law and legislation.'

'But what became of the cabal, those at the top of the pyramid, the puppet masters?'

'Ah, that is a very good question. I fear that they may still be among us in some capacity, although their vibrational influence has diminished now that the Schuman Resonance has been reinstated globally.'

'7.83ghz,' stated Nav, once again flexing his knowledge.

'They no longer have the capacity to influence world events,' Maeve continued. 'Some say they retreated into DUMBS that are still located around the world.'

'DUMBS?'

'Deep Underground Military Bases. Others say that they were mostly taken out by The Pleiadians, but that's another story.'

'Why were those convicted only incarcerated when most of the other nations imposed the death penalty?'

'Because that would have left a stain on our legacy from the outset. Story shall always judge us by our deeds. The trans-generational crime syndicates and elite satanic death cults were elevated into their seats of power through a system of paedophilic blackmail, and when the extent of their depravity was unveiled, the wrath of the people knew no bounds, hence the summary executions meted out in other lands.'

'You're forgetting about The Chavs,' said Jed. 'I understand that their vengeance was pretty brutal.'

'Their actions were born out of survival.'

'Survival of the fittest,' countered Jed, 'They didn't care who they slaughtered. Even murdered their own, didn't they?'

'Where did the Chav's get their name from?' asked Nav, changing tack slightly.

'None of my teachers could ever tell me.'

'No one really knows,' answered Maeve. 'Some say it was a derogatory term used to describe a perceived subclass of people during that time.'

'Subclass?'

'Meaning ignorant, uneducated. Lacking intelligence.'

'Do you believe that to be so?'

Maeve shrugged. 'All I know is they were trying to survive, and they became pretty good at it.'

'Through looting, raping and killing,' Jed persisted

AQUARIUS

'Not condoning it, Jed, but it's what pretty much most of the world was engaged in, not just The Chavs. The genes of any organism will program it to do everything it can to negate threats to its survival, especially in humans; terror and starvation are but two of these programs. From the relative safety of the garrisons the Diggers reached out to them, guaranteeing food and shelter if they agreed to relinquish their weapons. They were offered the chance to come and work for the common good and were granted amnesties for the less heinous crimes.'

'And it worked, didn't it?' asked Nav.

'The assimilation took a long time. It was a slow, painful process. Many gangs resisted through a combined mind-set of distrust, greed or power lust. They were fine for a time lording it around the country estates they had plundered, but all the trinkets and material wealth in the world was of no use to them once they ran out of things to eat. They lacked the most basic but important survival skills such as nurturing seed, purifying water and growing food. All that was left to them was Viking style raids on those who had learned to be self-sufficient. It was also hard for those who had become proselytized to at first accept the Diggers' creed of non-violence. They couldn't understand how an organised stronghold with a defunct nation's arsenal at its disposal wouldn't want to take out the remaining Chav armies and help them exact revenge for their families and lost loved ones.'

'I guess the squaddies must've felt the same way,' said Jed.

'I'll say,' said Nav. 'Imagine being tasked to defend the nation's towns and communities from insurgents with a – don't shoot to kill – directive. It sounds insane.'

'It does, doesn't it?' Maeve agreed. 'But as you said yourself – it worked.'

'Just how did it work?' interrupted the Irishman, sceptically.

'You mentioned it earlier, Jed.'

Jed did his now familiar double take. 'What, fucken' mind control?'

Maeve nodded her head and smiled. 'Kind of.'

'Ah, you're pissin' up me back now, so you are.'

'Not at all, my friend. It was easy. They simply used the same methods that the illuminati had used for centuries, a technique known as mass formation, only this time with an altruistic design. The ex-army vets were re-trained using advanced NLP techniques. All captured Chavs were killed with kindness. They were given access to warmth, food and shelter. Communities were encouraged to house and look after them. In time they were allowed to leave, but most didn't want to. They realised there was an alternative, and it slowly morphed into a different mind-set. The Diggers knew that trust would be the game changer, Years of living in fear and being lied to had put up almost impenetrable barriers, and so they came up with the idea of pairing the most hardened Chav warriors with the equally hardened veterans. They devised harsh training programs where trust and reliance on each other was paramount. Once finely honed their combined skills were used out in the field to pacify any resistance. Preserving life, not taking it became their modus operandi. Eventually families of the respective tribes grew together and formed unbreakable bonds.'

'And so the concept of a CM was born,' breathed Nav in a moment of illumination.

'Quite.' said Maeve. 'But the CM phenomenon and subsequent tradition was an unintended consequence of the program.'

'How so?'

'The perceived brawn-brain combination was designed merely as a means to an end, not as a lasting legacy of the struggle.'

'But the Chavs wore minder status as a badge of honour. Still do. Walkabout came into being as homage to their forebears from the following generation.'

'Yes, I know. I suppose many of the old guard, my great grandfather included, saw it differently. It reminded them of times of class and division rather than unity and mutual reliance. Despite its symbolic tradition, I was never assigned a CM, neither were any of my family before me. They wanted nothing to do with such a legacy. Same with the sigil on the side of these vehicles.'

'What, you mean the Flying Hawk?'

'Yes.'

Nav screwed up his face, perplexed. 'But it's our flag, our symbol, our identity. It flies above every garrison. Every UDC displays it. How could they have denied it?'

'Do you know its story?' asked Maeve, 'how it came into being?'

'No, do you?'

'Not entirely, but I think it may have had something to do with this...' Maeve unzipped the top of her tunic and reached behind her thermal, producing a tarnished pendant of a hawk in flight. Her companions leant over to scrutinize.

'I don't understand,' puzzled Nav. 'It's of similar design to what a lot of us wear, me included, only yours looks very old and, dare I say, cheaply produced.'

'Yes, you're right, there is no value to it apart from the knowing that it once belonged to my great grandfather and now it has been passed down to me. Story has it that it was given to him by a life-long friend and that it carries a great sentimental weight. I was told there was a tragedy attached to its significance but that is all. I can offer no other insight except it was said that he would often turn lachrymose and fall into deep moods of introspection whenever questioned about it. Later in life he would often grow irritable and obfuscate when challenged on the matter. Apparently, the gift was reciprocated, but he ultimately took the story of his mysterious friend and the hawk to his grave. At the time of The Shift the symbol was adopted and was used on flags and banners to identify places of sanctuary throughout the land. This emblem and the advent of the CM by all accounts were his only reservations along with the fear that they would be attributed to his legacy, and from what has been verbally handed down to me, I believe this is because both things were somehow deeply connected on a personal level, but whatever that connection was I fear we shall never know.'

'Nevertheless, he was obviously revered by his peers to have had such a legacy bestowed, despite the reluctance,' observed Nav. 'How is it we do not know of his name?'

'Because that is how he wanted it, and that is how it shall remain.'

Jed took a long sideways look at his young colleague. 'Tell me, just how did you become an engineer?'

Maeve smiled. 'I didn't "just become" an engineer, my friend. I am schooled in many disciplines – including learning how to clean my own arse,' she added with a wink.

With a puzzled look and a furrowed brow Jed slewed the APC ninety degrees onto what his navigator told him was the old M11, although there was no discernible junction or demarcation from road, field or river along the grey-white plain on which they travelled except for the occasional barren skeletal outline of a tree or the snow-covered ruins of buildings.

At Hackney Marshes they were intercepted and guided into the old capital by a couple of drones and an AGP that circled the convoy in a show of fancy banks and swoops.

'Is that thing manned or auto?' demanded Jed, sounding slightly agitated.

'Manned,' confirmed Nav. 'It's a prototype. Do you want to speak to her?'

'Her? Fucken' typical. No, I don't – bloody show off,' he added grumpily under his breath.

'Could you not see yourself in one of those, Jed?'

'Absolutely not,' he said sounding offended. 'I'm an engineer, not a skydriver.'

'Looks a better deal than rumbling around in one of these old things.'

'This old thing has never let me down. We've seen plenty of action together.'

'Yeah, but you've got to admit it's kind of vintage; dare I say obsolete.'

Jed observed his passenger through narrowed eyes. 'I ought to make you walk into London for such a statement.'

'Ha, I'd still probably arrive before you.'

'Don't tempt me, Mr Buthar . . .'

Maeve let the two men continue with their banter while she resumed her writing. What she had failed to tell them was that one of her other disciplines was that of a storian. She was part of a team that had been tasked to document mankind's journey from the time of The Shift, and some of that team was travelling with them now, each chosen for their unique backgrounds and insight. It would be a chronicle that, at its inception at least, would be free from bias or influence. No words from winners or losers. Any moral code would be hidden in plain sight, without direction or decree, just a presentation of the truth, open and fluid with the opportunity for future generations of scribes to add to its lustre. Unlike the old religious testaments this work would be incorruptible having been created with an esoteric energy so powerful that even she could barely comprehend its fullness.

AQUARIUS

The City Within a City

Close to their destination, the flashy AGP performed an aerial pirouette that, much to Jed's relief, signalled its silent departure. The two drones flew overhead, navigating the convoy along what used to be the Euston Road. Gazing out of his window, Nav observed the petrified and frozen landscape of ruins that were once the structural heart of the old capital. They were travelling at the very edge of the result of great seismic upheaval that had beset this and other parts of the country. Just a little to the south he could make out the great ice sheet that had been the Thames estuary, now covering much of the old city of London. It was a vast fault that now stretched along the M4 corridor all the way to the recently formed Avon and Severn delta.

The three engineers had now ceased all conversation. Inside the cab everything fell silent save for the continual hum of the hydrogen engine of the APC and the occasional beeps of radio signals. As Nav continued to gaze out impassively at the stark surroundings, Maeve started to get an uneasy feeling in her gut. Despite its inevitable demise and ultimate destruction, they were approaching what was once known as The Square Mile, The Corporation of London, and the city within a city, an enclave that had been ordained as the seat for a global financial empire, acting as the debtor state of the Western World. Exempt from National law, it operated under its own internal legal status, with its own private courts, its own police force and medieval guilds and its curious displays of ritual pomp and pageantry. Within its virtual walls shady bankers and financial handlers for the global elite moved and laundered pirated assets around the world like pawns on a chessboard. Delving into her storian education, Maeve recalled the words of a long-forgotten politician: *"The City of London, a convenient term for a collection of financial interests, is able to assert itself against the government of the country. Those who control money can pursue a policy at home and abroad contrary to that which is being decided by the people."*

Hidden in plain sight, Maeve couldn't yet understand how this and the other two Illuminati bastions of control, namely Washington (military) and The Vatican (spiritual) operated unchallenged by the

PRECESSION

masses for so long.

'We're here.' Nav broke the silence as he received a signal from one of the drones. Jed called the convoy to a halt, and they all peered out at the scene with mounting dubiety.

'Okay,' said the Irishman finally, 'let's see what delights await us – not a lot, if yer ask me.'

After a short debriefing, the thirty-man strong expedition comprising engineers, sappers and book boffins was split into three teams. Guided by drone, they manoeuvred their way on foot over uneven snow- and ice-covered terrain, blanketed ruin, shattered stone and mangled steel. The blueprints for the underground vaults showed access via the now largely flattened St. Pancras station. Maeve followed the route from a virtual map on her pad that showed the building in its original neo gothic splendour. As they entered what used to be the site of its great glass and steel domed roof, she once again sensed that feeling of unease and negativity. She shivered involuntarily; convinced it had nothing to do with the minus twenty-six-degree temperature. To shift her senses away from the bad vibes, Maeve made small talk amongst the book experts who were patiently huddled together in small groups while Jed and Nav consulted maps and directed their engineers who used sonar probes in search of any concealed tunnels or shafts.

When the call eventually came, they arrived at the site to find the sappers had already cleared obstructions and were in the process of exposing what looked like an ornate Victorian archway that had been walled up with red brick. A hubbub of expectation arose amongst the gathered bibliophiles while an engineer attached a device in the centre of the wall. It soon began to emit a blue flashing neon light along with a low resonant hum that slowly began to increase in frequency and pitch. Nav urged the gathered onlookers back a few paces before the blue light turned to red and the brick wall instantly and almost silently disintegrated and fell away to a pile of brown dust before their eyes. From the dark depths of the exposed tunnel came a rush of cold, dank air accompanied by a low moaning sound as the escaping wind spun in a vortex up the hollow shaft.

The engineer picked up his device from atop the pile of dust, brushed it down and packed it away while Jed selected a recce party from the team. Much to her annoyance, Maeve noticed his selections were all men.

'I'm coming too,' she stated flatly. Jed opened his mouth, but quickly shut it when he saw her expression and merely nodded.

They proceeded in cautionary Indian file; head-torches flashing here and there picking out the old glazed tiled walls, steam from their breath and little else. Further in, they encountered another obstacle in the form of a heavy, rusted steel door that set the team a challenge in such a confined space. Maeve was impressed with the skill and efficiency of Jed's men, but she knew of women back there who would have done just as good a job.

Beyond the door the incline became steeper, and the glazed tile had given way to rough cut stone. Giant icicles hung regimented from the roof that when illuminated by a dozen torches gave off a shimmering display.

'Shh! – What's that noise?' someone piped up out of the gloom. 'Do you hear it?' The group stood still, statue like, straining their ears. 'There – there it is again.'

'Yes, yes, I hear it,' said Maeve. To her it sounded like a school of whales in distress, an eerie melancholic dirge, strange and unsettling. It didn't do anything to alleviate the already instinctively bad feeling she had about this place, a vibration so low as to have been rooted here for millennia. Despite having been well versed in it, this was the first time in her life she had felt anything close to what people used to call evil.

'What on earth *is* that?' came a nervous voice near the back.

'It's the ice,' said Nav.

'The ice?'

'We're close to the fault line. It's the sound of the compacted ice moving along the fault.'

'Are we safe?'

Nav guided his torch towards the question and smiled. 'As safe as we're ever going to be, my friend.'

Under torchlight, Jed consulted his pad. 'According to this we should be under the library, let's keep moving.'

They moved, but not much further. The passage began to narrow with every step until, hunched over, almost on their knees, Jed called a halt. 'This is as far as we go, people,' he said shining his light towards what was a dead end. He dug the heel of his boot into the hard floor. 'This has to be the water table. The vaults, if there were any, have flooded and frozen. If there are any more passages like this, they'll all be the same. Project over, guys, let's go home.'

'Wait,' said Maeve, catching his arm. 'I need to stay.'

PRECESSION

'What?'

'I need to stay a while,' she said taking on her role as a geophysicist. 'If this is the water table, I can get some up-to-date analysis on the permafrost. It will mean our journey won't have been entirely wasted.'

Jed shook his head incredulous. 'Really?'

'Just me, Nav, a couple of the guys and a probe – all I ask,' she added with a smile.

'What about your book buddies? They're gonna be awfully disappointed.'

'I'll let you tell them the bad news, I'm sure you'll enjoy that.'

'Don't leave me hanging around up there,' he warned. 'I don't like this place.'

'I understand; the feeling's mutual. I'll be my usual efficient self – promise.'

The small team of four watched the rest of the party retrace their steps, flickering flashes of torchlight slowly fading into the gloom.

'So, what exactly was it they were hoping to find down here?' asked Nav.

'I'm not entirely sure. I was never fully briefed, but I suspect it was some ancient work of esoteric significance. When I asked specific questions, I got ambiguous answers, so I didn't push it. I guess now we shall never know,' she said with a shrug. 'Let's get this probe set up.'

There had been reports of the ice sheet receding in the Pyrenees and widespread flooding across Catalonia. Scientists across the world were correlating evidence of new sunspot activity. It empirically heralded the end of The Grand Solar Minimum, news to be greeted with cautious optimism, but with it the portent for further global cataclysm. Maeve held enough geophysical knowledge to deduce this was an opportunity to gather important data to further analyse the likely outcome from any major shift in temperature. Here was ideal. They were at the water table on the very edge of a great fault. By taking measurements of the current state of the permafrost the scientists at Ruston Parva would have a better understanding around the rate of geological change and likely consequences. Beyond the droning hum of the probe, they could still hear the groaning lament of ice versus land as they fought for dominance under millions of tons of exertion. Maeve knew that any melting of this vast swathe of ice would result in a colossal release of pressure known as isostatic rebound. The earth would be rent upwards. Great parts of Essex and Kent would be under water and the seismic fallout along the already unstable fault catastrophic. On haunches, under torchlight she studied her pad, poring over the information that was being revealed by the probe, ensuring it was being correctly sequenced, stored and encrypted.

'We have to go!' Nav announced suddenly. Immediately three torchlights landed on his face. He was receiving a message in his ear. 'We have to go – now!' he repeated with urgency in his voice.

'What – why?'

'Lazors. The drones have identified Lazors heading towards us,'

'How many?'

'Does it matter? Disengage the probe and let's get out of here.'

'Just a while longer,' Maeve reasoned.

'Now, Maeve,' said Nav, getting agitated. 'Jed's responsible for our VIPs and he's having a meltdown up there.'

'Nearly finished,' she said sounding annoyingly calm. The three engineers looked at each other wide eyed. 'I'll take full responsibility. We need this information.'

'We need to get out of here in one piece is what we need – now, Maeve, please!'

The concept of time, when time held possible consequences, was hardly a concept for Maeve. For Nav, in this moment, time had slowed right down while her level of consciousness kept her firmly in the now, meaning all and any consequences would be dealt with whenever they arose. Nav loved this crazy young woman, this enlightened daughter of The Diggers, but he couldn't always attune or chime with her maverick style. His fight or flight responses were heightened and right now his amygdala was firing off cortisol in all directions.

'Ready when you guys are,' she said finally closing down the app with an almost nonchalant air. Nav gave her a withering look while the two engineers retrieved the probe and had it packed away at lightning speed.

'What the hell took you so long?' hissed Jed as they emerged from the darkness.

'Ask her,' said Nav.

'Where are the book scholars?' asked Maeve.

PRECESSION

'I had them escorted back to the carriers.'

'Where are the Lazors?' Jed showed her the heat map on his pad. 'Have you engaged them?'

'We showed them our pacifiers when they ventured too close.'

'Why did you do that?'

'Are you fucken' kidding me?'

'We could have assisted them.'

'You really are mad, aren't you, girl? Have you ever been up close to a Lazor, I mean really close? No? Well, I have and believe me it's not a pretty sight.'

'They're still human, Jed.'

'Yeah? Well, it's not a description I would use, I ...'

One of the engineers caught him by the arm. 'Look! – They're back.'

Three dark grey hooded figures had appeared at a distance and stood passive and motionless, silhouetted against the stark undulation of frozen ruin.

'Okay, everyone, back to the trucks,' ordered Jed. 'Spivey, Marv and Bonner, rear-guard; let's go.'

'Wait,' said Maeve.

Jed let out a massive, exasperated sigh. 'What now?'

'We should try and communicate.'

'No, fuck that. No! I'll not take responsibility for your stupid crazy acts of pity.'

'No one is asking you to.'

'I won't detail any of the guys to stay, and I certainly shan't leave you here on your own.'

'What will you do?'

'I'll carry you back if I have to, against your will or no. Please don't make me do that.'

Maeve looked at Nav who merely raised his eyebrows. She looked at the rest of the men and could see reluctance in their eyes. 'Very well,' she said eventually. 'Give me your protein packs, all of you – now.'

The gathered looked at each other and then to Jed for guidance. He could see that compromise would be the only solution to the extraneous demands of this young dissident. With another deep sigh, he gave a reluctant nod of the head.

'Anything else?' he asked, once the pouches of provisions had been piled at her feet.

AQUARIUS

'No,' she said after thinking long and hard. She held aloft a handful of the packs so they were in plain sight of the uninvited guests. As the party retreated to the waiting convoy, the three watching figures remained still, unmoved, without sign, sound or acknowledgement.

The journey back to Carver was conspicuous by an atmosphere of awkward silence. It was the Irishman who broke it. "tis a good job the drones were there is all I can say.'

'It was the drones that probably attracted them,' stated Maeve in a tone that belied a little sulkiness.

'They were there to protect us; they did their job.' His voice rose with frustration.

'Protect us from what? How could you have known their intentions?'

'I told yer. I've had dealings with these - these things. They're malevolent, not fucken' benevolent. They are devoid of any kind of human empathy. They'd kill yer as soon as look at yer.'

'Yeah, I've also heard they eat their own babies at birth. Some survival skill, that.'

Jed set the drive of the APC to auto and looked her squarely in the face. 'I've seen the evidence with my own eyes, Maeve. I wouldn't lie to yers. I've seen what they've done to people, good people, families. There is no hope for these creatures, and I don't use that term lightly. You're not the first altruist to have attempted to assimilate Lazors; most have come unstuck, and I wouldn't let that happen to you. I'm just a simple engineer, I'll never have the knowledge or skill sets you were born with, but I've seen things, stuff I wish I'd never had, so please don't come at me with your empty maxims and platitudes, cos I've been there, I know what they're capable of. Yes, they are cannibalistic, they eat their own, why do you think they are dying out? I, for one, welcome their demise, and if that don't fit with your Digger theology, then tough.'

No one really knew the origins of The Lazors, how they came detached from the assimilation of The Chavs or even if their barbaric, some say satanic existence ever had anything to do with the Chav story. Other legend says they were the spawn of the deposed elites, a humiliated bloodline that existed on a vibration of fear and hate that most of humanity had now shaken off. The Earth was no longer their domain, no longer were they able to control and bend its subjects to their will.

PRECESSION

Maeve sat silent and reflected for most of the journey home. Her gifts were sometimes a curse, especially when her ego got in the way. She hadn't intended to come across as superior to Jed in any way even if his old-style army authority, which was obviously a family trait, irked her somewhat. She began to ponder the plight of The Lazors and wondered what horrors her colleague might have witnessed. She had scant knowledge of these people, but recalled her answer to Nav's question: *"What became of the Demiurge?"* Could the theory be true? Are these people the remnants of that demonic bloodline that still walked among us? Do they live deep underground and eat of their own flesh and blood? She had only recently learned of the global child trafficking and the paedophile networks that had been exposed prior to The Shift. Probably for her own young age and sensitivities she had been spared the more gruesome accounts of satanic cult ritual and the adrenochrome harvesting of children carried out by and on behalf of the cabal. It was a major wound to the psyche for an empath to learn of such things, and being a storian also sometimes made her hope that a lot of the tales she read about the time of duality were hyperbolical to the extent of myth, but now, after listening to first–hand accounts, she wasn't so sure. The gut feelings she had felt in that place were real. Her instinct was her primary and overriding sense and it never failed her. If what she'd experienced, that tangible sensation, was tainted with a word she previously only had a notion of, then a layer from her blanket of youthful naivety had finally been lifted. Maybe Jed was right, perhaps there was no assimilation to be had for these beings. Nav had used the word demiurge, a term associated with the Sumerians who had the Anunnaki as their deity pantheon. The Sumerians had given us the notion of linear time, the twenty-four-hour day and the sixty-minute hour, all of which were now defunct, no longer of any use. No longer prisoners of time, no longer slaves of our own destiny, we were now living in the age of reunion, the age of water. Water is fluid; it denies linearity, resists separation. Water with its cycles, ebbs and flows is the antithesis of control. If these ancient correlations are true, the demise of the Lazors is inevitable. Their evolution, which sounded like an oxymoron to her now, was at an end. Despite this realisation, there was still a part of her, an innate yearning coming from deep within that wanted to reach out, to offer solace, love and understanding. *Indigo child – Just another label,* she laughed to herself, while inside her head she started to formulate a grudging

AQUARIUS

apology to the big man.

PRECESSION

It's Grim Up North

'Hey, Bradley, what youse up to?'

Maeve turned to see the Irishman approach her carrying some sort of mechanical part. 'I'm gathering a petition to have the garrison gates removed. Will you sign it?'

'Er, not just now – got me hands full.'

'So I see. What is that?'

'Ah, I knew youse didn't know everything. It's called a manifold. Why would yer want to take away the gates? Wait, no, don't tell me; I don't think I want to know.'

They strolled on together exchanging small talk and banter. 'Oh, by the way,' Maeve remembered, 'I just wanted to say thanks.'

'Fer what?'

'The London expo; for not bringing everything up in your report or mentioning it to council.'

Jed laughed. 'It didn't matter. They seen the drone footage and the cam recordings. They know what went down. Didn't need me to confirm or deny anything. Besides, I think you redeemed yerself with your little geo project. You seem to have impressed a few people with all that data you managed to retrieve.'

'Yeah, well, I guess it has offered me a reprieve of sorts. They want me to present my findings in person up at Ruston Parva.'

'What, you're heading north? Well, that's great news. So am I.'

'Oh?'

'Yeah, they want a team of us up in some old Leeds suburbs, clearance detail for the new geothermal plants. You should travel up with us, Nav is coming, he's gonna be working on the M1 crossing.'

'Hmm, I still need to get across to Ruston.'

'The lines go east, no problem. And you'll get to meet Declan.'

'Declan?'

'Yeah, he's my CM.'

'You have a minder?' Maeve asked surprised.

'Of course; we all do.'

'Why didn't you tell me this before?'

'Because at the time we didn't want you to feel left out, seeing as you don't have one.'

AQUARIUS

'Silly man,' Maeve laughed. 'You know my family's stance on CM's, why do you think I would be any different? - Okay', she said after a short ponder. 'I'd love to meet this Declan. Yes, I'll travel north with you. APC?'

'Afraid so. Now if you'll excuse me, I have to get this thing to the workshop, me arms are killing me.'

§

The further north they travelled, the worse the weather. Driving blizzards heralded their arrival in old Yorkshire. By the time they had departed company with Nav and his team it had become a complete whiteout. Maeve had been intrigued to see the newly built crossing over the northern fault where the old rivers Aire and Calder converged, but once again land and sky had become a stark two-dimensional canvas, hostile and blank, offering no sense of distance or proportion to the eye. She watched the tail end of Nav's team disappear into the swirling maelstrom and offered up affirmations for their good fortune, while they travelled on under the control of magnav to their own destination.

'Spunky! – Ha-harrgh, you made it,' boomed the voice that belonged to the giant silhouette emerging through the eye of the storm. Jed and Declan came together like two long lost bears, hugging the life out of each other in-between wrestling moves and thrown punches that would make any normal man wince. Maeve stood by with a forced smile, hoping she wasn't in for such an intimate welcome.

Inside the bustling hubbub of noise and chatter that was the communal chalet, dry and warm, she was presented with a hot drink from a small, smiling, bright-eyed weathered looking guy called Hamish. Around a roaring fire she sat and watched Jed and Declan catch up on life and stories, heightened conversation interspersed with loud hearty guffaws of laughter. The two men were of similar size and stature, the only real distinction being Declan's fiery red hair and beard that had been covered in ice but was now thawing and dripping pools of water in front of him. Despite the conditions they had to work in, everyone here appeared friendly and happy. Men and women queued in turn to offer their welcome, eager to tell their stories and keen to hear hers. In her head she began stockpiling material for her journal, allowing her subconscious to absorb this experience through all her heightened senses. By the time she retired she felt exhausted but fulfilled. Before sleep she meditated on the manifestation of the aspirations of these good people. Through her pineal she saw an image of someone she had never met but whom she knew so well. His warm smile and gentle nod of the head gave her all the conformation she needed before falling into a fitful slumber.

On waking she peered out the window. What she hoped to see she wasn't sure. Why would it be different from any other scene in this grey-white world? Just another day, but it wasn't even that. Just like the hours and the minutes, days no longer existed, just a transition from black to dark grey to a different shade of grey. Such a transit didn't deserve the word day; she would have to find an alternative to use in her journal, a word that described habituation and repetition. She impulsively rubbed hard at the window, maybe unconsciously trying to summon up a genie with a wish to change the dramaturgy she saw before her.

After breaking their fast, Declan took them into the field where they were introduced to Professor Bryant, The Chief of Staff, who, despite being kitted out in full PP with hard-hat still managed to look unbelievably young for the role. She enthusiastically provided them with a guided tour of one of the new geothermal plants that had just been sunk. Once fully cleared, she revealed, this old district of northeast Leeds would provide heat and energy for what had been the biggest part of the old county of Yorkshire. Maeve was enthralled by the imparted science behind this ambitious, innovative undertaking, but Jed was quickly becoming bored. He was keen to get back to his men and get stuck into what he came here to do. He wouldn't have long to wait as right at that moment Declan received a message.

'Sorry, guys, but I have to go. We've got a problem up in zone eight.'

'Zone eight?' enquired Jed. 'Isn't that the site I'm supposed to be clearing?'

'Yep, old Gipton.'

'Let's go, then.'

'Don't you want to stay and chaperone Maeve?'

'She's a big girl, Dec. Trust me, she can look after herself.'

AQUARIUS

'I'm done, fellas. I've got all the info I need,' she said tapping her pad. 'I'd like to come with you guys if that's okay.' The snow was coming at them in spasmodic flurries now, and she would be grateful for any short respite from the biting, bitter wind that was blowing in from the east. Maeve thanked Prof Bryant for her time and knowledge and headed for the waiting APC.

Driving through the abandoned and virtually flattened districts once known as. Harehills and Gipton, Maeve observed the hive of industry taking place. They wove their way among gangs of workers, some poring over plans, others directing operations. Giant trucks with wheels the height of two men were being filled with demolished ruin and debris while cranes and excavators worked feverishly. To her, it looked like a scene of organised chaos, to Declan and Jed, it showed resolute efficiency. Decaying and abandoned, "smart cities" like Leeds, once paradigms for the old, flawed and ultimately doomed system, were now being erased and transformed. These lands and others like them, when nature would eventually relent and allow, would form the blueprint for the beginnings of a new era. The dawn of The Golden Age was imminent. Aquarius had one last test in store for mankind. The Meek and their brothers and sisters around the world were preparing for it. Esoteric knowledge, once the coveted bastion of the Cabal was now being harnessed with technology that was evolving at an exponential rate. It had to be. It was vital for any survival.

Jed scrutinised the concerned features of his CM as he received updates through his earpiece. 'News?'

'Not good. I'm hearing one of your guys has sustained a head injury.'

'How?' Jed asked concerned.

'Falling debris.'

'Is he okay? Was he wearing his PP?'

'I think so. He's on his way to the MSH. They say he's conscious.'

Jed let out a heavy sigh. This was all he needed on his first shift. He cursed himself for not being there with his men, instead of arseing about accommodating Maeve and her inconsequential little projects. He was beginning to regret inviting her on this trip. The London fiasco should have forewarned him. He didn't really believe in luck, good or bad, but whenever he seemed to be in the company of this precocious young woman things tended to go bad, and he

PRECESSION

wouldn't have to wait much longer for further confirmation of that theory.

Jed had exited the vehicle before the wheels had stopped rolling. He met a small entourage of his men. 'Who is it?'

'Connor Bailey.'

'How bad?'

'Suspected broken skull.'

'What the hell was he doing?'

'He triggered a fall of stone on entering a derelict – Jed, this was no accident; this was done deliberate.'

'Oh, feck, not again,' said Declan.

'What d'yer mean, "not again"?' Jed spun on his minder. 'This has happened before?'

Declan nodded his head in conformation. 'Three of my guys have walked into pre-set traps. Thankfully none of them died.'

'Why didn't you warn us?'

'We've had no incidents in a while. I guess we assumed whoever resented us being here had given up and gone away.'

'Have you ever seen them?'

'Yes, but only fleetingly; he or she is frighteningly fast and elusive, and always out of range from a pacifier.'

'Just the one?'

'I think so, we've only ever seen one at one time.'

'D'yer think it could be a Lazor?'

'Possibly. Whatever it is, it certainly don't want any contact with us.'

'You think they've been living in the old dwellings?'

'Yes, there's been evidence, but I won't let my guys inside to check anymore.'

'So you demolish them without knowing anyone's inside?' asked Maeve aghast.

'We issue multiple verbal warnings before sending in the wrecking crew. I won't risk the lives of my men against anyone or anything that wished them harm,' Declan stated plainly. 'This is the last row standing. If there's anyone still in there, they won't have anywhere to hide for much longer.'

'You can't just knock them down without checking.'

Jed sighed and raised his eyes skyward - *Here we go again* - he thought to himself.

'Jed?' she appealed. 'You can't let that happen.'

AQUARIUS

'This isn't my jurisdiction, Maeve.'

She glared at up him until he had to look away. 'Then I'll go in.'

'Oh, no you won't.'

'Try and stop me.'

Jed turned to Dec and sighed once more. His CM returned a wide-eyed look. 'What d'yer think?'

Declan thought long and hard. He knew he would be up before Council to explain away this latest incident, and any more mishaps however caused would be certain to result in a major inquest he could do without. Jed had already given him the lowdown on this impulsive and often stubborn young woman, and now he could see why. Against his better judgement he was about to put himself out on a limb. 'Okay, two of your men, two of mine, but we go in with pacifiers,' he relented.

'No pa ...' The look the two men gave her stopped her in her tracks. She fell silent knowing it would be best not to push it.

The demolition gang stood idle beside their machines and watched the team of six men and one girl approach the end terrace. They had pleaded for Maeve to stay behind but their petition had fallen on deaf ears. The door where the unfortunate victim had triggered the trap lay half open. As they entered, blood spatters could still be seen on the fallen debris. Leading the crew, Jed and Dec trod cautiously over rubble, eyes darting to every corner of the four walls and crumbling ceiling. With his pacifier at the ready, Declan spoke into his collar mike: *'This notice goes to anyone hiding or taking shelter inside this terrace. These buildings are earmarked for demolition. They will be flattened just like all the others. You have been warned and advised previously of our act of intent and have chosen to ignore these notices. We wish you no harm but warn that any further attempt to cause injury or death by your actions will lead to serious consequences. We give you this final opportunity to give yourself up. We also guarantee you protection, food, warmth and shelter. We are here to help. I repeat, we shall cause you no harm. Show yourself now. If you are armed, lay your weapons down and we shall do the same. If you do not comply and you choose to remain here, I shall have no alternative but to commence the destruction of these buildings. Please show yourself now . . .'* His words echoed and faded against the walls. The group fell silent and strained their ears. There was nothing but the crunch of rubble under booted feet, or the sound of the wind howling through smashed window cavities. Dec sent the men off in pairs to search what was left of the rooms, then up precarious stairs where rotting treads creaked and groaned underfoot. 'Eyes ceiling, eyes floor, watch out for trip wires,' he warned after them.

Drawing a blank, they focused on the attic, gingerly moving aside the hatch with a long pole that triggered another heavy fall of brick and stone. 'Crude, but effective,' Dec muttered after the dust had settled and checking everyone was okay.

In the roof space they found evidence of a fire and the skeletons of several rodents, but more intriguing was the hole in the dividing brick wall that led into the next terrace. There were seven former dwellings on this un-demolished row, and it looked as if access to them all could be had through the walls under the eaves. Splitting into two teams, Declan's men searched the attics while Jed's team with Maeve progressed along the lower floors. Every attic hatch had been loaded with piles of brick ready to be released upon any unsuspecting inquisitor. Shards of glass and sharpened bits of metal had been jammed in and amongst the crumbling masonry along the narrow accesses as deterrents to their progress. In the fifth attic along they discovered a scrap of roof felt that hid a hole in the floor. Carefully removing it and peering down into the room below they saw glass and large nails sticking up from the floorboards below. Crawling through into the next space a fetid stink of ash and faeces assaulted their nostrils, and it felt a degree or two warmer. This hole had been lived in for sure. The way through to the final house had been crudely shorn up with brick and rubble. They crept close to the wall and listened. Silence. *'We're here to help you, not to harm you,'* announced Declan. *'There are three of us here, and four below you. Please come out peacefully now and you shall be looked after. My name is Declan. You can talk to me if you have any concerns.'* Silence. *'If you refuse to speak or cooperate we will have no choice but to come in and have you removed for your own safety. Do I make myself clear?'* Silence. 'You guys ready?' His two men nodded affirmative and primed their pacifiers. Dec talked into his collar: 'We're at the end terrace. Going in now.'

'Copy,' came the reply in his ear.

Declan took the flat of his boot to the barricade and had collapsed it after a few attempts. He tentatively stuck his not inconsiderable head through the aperture only to be met with a barrage of missiles pinging off his face and helmet. An object opened up a cut under his eye and he withdrew wincing in pain. His colleagues desperately tried to remove the collapsed stone and brick to gain access but were met with the same onslaught.

'Report.' Jed's voice came through Dec's earpiece.

'No compliance. Hostile,' said Dec as the blood started to trickle through his fingers and mingle with his whiskers. 'Think they have catapults as weapons. Proceed with caution.'

'Numbers?'

'Unconfirmed but feels like more than one.'

'Copy. On our way up.'

Above their heads Jed's team could hear a muffled commotion. Despite several attempts the loft hatch refused to budge. There was no other access, but also no other means of escape for their adversaries. As the standoff ensued Jed and Dec desperately sought a solution. 'Can't you deploy a pacifier?'

'Negative. Can't get to see who we're aiming at. If you can find and bring us something we can shield with we might have a chance.'

'Okay, I'll send my men.'

'Copy - but get them to tread carefully.'

The commotion ceased momentarily. With eyes fixed to the ceiling above them Jed and Maeve could hear Dec's repeated appeals. There was no response.

'I don't think there's more than one person up there,' said Maeve. There's hardly any movement.'

'Well, if it is only one person, they're doing a hell of a job at keeping three guys at bay.'

'I hope they don't need to use a pacifier.'

'It might be the only option. It won't do any long-term harm.'

'I still see it as a weapon. I long for the now when they are no longer needed.'

Jed understood her sentiment but couldn't get his head around her reasoning, especially in situations like this. It was merely a pacifier, a deterrent to those who would perpetrate violence and harm unto others. As far as he could see, until mankind had totally expunged the notion of malice from the psyche, this was an unfortunate but necessary tool. He admired her noble but somewhat flawed notion of utopia, and if his experiences were anything to go by, then the dream was still a long way off. 'So, just how would *you* deal with someone who went to such lengths to want to kill or maim another human being?'

PRECESSION

'I would first want to find out why. What drove them to such actions? Get to know the cause, instead of just dealing with the symptoms.'

'Sounds reasonable. Ain't gonna work in a life-or-death situation.'

'I'm talking about after the event and the consequences of one's actions – for every action there is an equal and opposite reaction – what made them take that particular action?'

Jed shook his head. He should know better than to get into a philosophical debate with this girl, and why the hell was she was bringing an old Newtonian law of physics into it? He was saved any further discourse on the matter by an incoming message. 'Go ahead, Bonner.'

'Jed, we've had another incident. Staircase collapsed on us; Spivey's broken his leg.'

'Shit! – How are you?'

'I can walk.'

'First building?'

'Yeah.'

'Copy. Coming now.' He turned to Maeve. 'Did you catch that?'

'Yes, shall I come with you?'

'No, stay here and contact me if there's any developments.' He slung the pacifier off his shoulder. 'I'll leave you with this, just in case.'

'I shan't need it.'

He gave her that now familiar look before heading back down the stairs. Two injured men on his first shift and an obstinate woman to deal with was about as much as he could take. He silently prayed for a happy resolution to this little caper, but right now he wasn't feeling too optimistic.

Maeve paced the room attempting to make her tread as quiet as possible while trying to trace footsteps above her. She felt as though whoever was up there was doing the same, almost as if they were mirroring her every move. When she stood still, all motion above her seemed to cease too. An eerie silence descended, making her conscious of just her heartbeat and breath that came in and out in regular misty puffs. She began to get that intuitive twist in her gut, a feeling of impendence that something was about to happen. Every sense sprang to attention and hair stood on end. And then all hell broke loose.

AQUARIUS

After the initial explosion, her first realisation was that she was now covered in black lime, plaster, lath and rotten wood, while emerging from the resulting cloud of dust crouched an apparition of indescribable form. Maeve shot a glance at the gaping hole in the ceiling from whence it had come to the glistening shard of glass wrapped in crude cloth that it was clutching menacingly. Almost black from head to toe, the creature slowly brought itself to a standing position and like a wild animal began to circle its prey. Maeve, with debris still falling from her hair slowly offered up her hands in a show of no resistance, while making sure she was more than a lunge away from the crude weapon. She quickly assessed her adversary, although it was hard to determine gender with its face and head hooded. Similar height but much slender in build is about all she could determine for now. Maybe if she could hear a voice.

'Hey,' she said softly with her hands still in submissive mode. 'It's okay; I'm not going to hurt you. No one's going to hurt you. We just want to make sure you're safe, that's all.' They continued to circle each other. 'I'm here to help you. My name's Maeve,' she said pointing to herself. 'What's yours?'

Hearing a voice seemed to agitate it and with lightning speed it lunged. Maeve's reactions were quick enough to only suffer a slashed sleeve of her topcoat where the thermal inner started to sprout.

'Okay, okay, I understand you're frightened, but there's no need to be. We can work this out if you care to talk to me, we can...'

With a guttural scream it lunged again, this time with hand held aloft intent on stabbing downwards. Maeve caught the stroke with her left hand, quickly shifted her weight and forced the arm behind its back while catching it around the neck with her right arm. She shook the weapon loose and as it hit the floor smashed it to pieces under her boot. Not wanting to apply force, Maeve released her hold. The creature immediately sunk its teeth into her right hand and sprung free snarling and hissing blood. Before she could recover, it launched another attack. Catching her off balance she reeled backwards as it tore at her face. Maeve hit the deck hard landing on stone and rubble, but as her assailant came with her, she was able to use the momentum, bringing her feet up and planting them in its midriff, sending the thing flying over her head. It felt to carry no weight, but it was fast and ferocious. It sprang up instantly and was about to mount another attack when more debris cascaded down from above. Declan's ginger clad face peered down at them. 'Get out the way, Maeve,' he boomed. Let me get a clear shot at it.'

'No,' she shouted, keeping her eyes firmly fixed on her foe. 'You get out of there, Dec. You're gonna have the whole ceiling down on us. All of you get back. I can handle this.'

'Where's Jed?'

'He's not here.' A groaning sound came from above and another section of plaster hit the ground with a loud crump behind her. 'Please, Dec, go back, you're only gonna make this worse.'

The thing in black ran at her and fired itself feet first, aiming for the head. Maeve ducked to one side and deflected the attack with a forearm. It landed shrieking in a heap amongst the fallen debris. The hood had come away and for the first time Maeve could see features. But what she saw still didn't allow her to determine gender. It looked gaunt, deep set sunken eyes that carried no emotion, and thick matted dark hair set in crude dreads. The jaw and nose were angular, the skin covered in grime, and it stank. She sensed it was female. It sounded female. Other than that, there were no feminine traits. Coiled like a spring, it spat and hissed, watching Maeve's every move. Whatever it was it was totally feral. While it remained crouched on its haunches Maeve slowly undid her cumbersome topcoat and let it fall to the floor, allowing her better freedom of movement. Once again she faced her palms outwards in a show of passiveness. 'We don't have to do it like this,' she said, watching the blood drip, drip from her hand. 'We can be friends.' She circled her good hand in front of her tummy. 'Are you hungry? We have food.' She pointed to her mouth. 'Hot food, warm drink. Do you understand me? Are you able to talk?' Her opponent hissed and feigned another lunge. Maeve now realised any verbal reasoning was futile, but she was determined not to show any form of aggression. She remembered the oriental defensive martial art technique that had been passed down to her that she still occasionally used as part of her physical and mental disciplines. She cuffed her bloody nose and took up choom-bi, then formed a poomse, ready to block any further assault. For a moment it served to bewilder and confuse. She smiled confidently, signalling her readiness and certainty she could handle anything that was thrown at her. It came again, raging and shrieking like a banshee, arms and feet flailing in all directions. She dodged, parried and blocked, never once becoming the aggressor, this in turn only served to confuse even more, Its default response to attack. It attacked to the point of sheer exhaustion, while Maeve simply repositioned and rebalanced. Crouched and panting like a dog, with what looked like defeat and desperation in its eyes, it suddenly, yet stealthily produced something from its ragged clothing. In an instant it had loaded, drawn and fired. The small shard of red brick shot from the catapult hit Maeve straight between the eyes. Stunned, she crumpled to the floor. In a daze she felt herself being straddled and her arms pinned to the floor. Close up its odours were tangible and many. Its panting breath was sour, its hair hanging over her, dank and smoky. The rest of it smelled of shit. But as she slowly began to re-focus, what stopped Maeve's struggle if only for a fleeting moment was the object that had fallen from its vile rags and was now dangling from its neck, to-ing and fro-ing in front of her face. Hung from a necklace was a tarnished pendant depicting a hawk in flight. She didn't have time to ponder it any longer as its forehead met hers with such severity that she saw a multitude of flashing lights. Stunned once more, she suffered a flurry of punches to the head and face, frenzied and relentless, despite them thankfully carrying little force. Her own arms now finally free, she desperately grabbed the pair of skinny wrists and hung onto them with enough restraint to finally subdue the flailing fists. With one last effort she thrust up her hips, shifted her weight and reversed the roles. It bucked, it struggled, it wrapped its stick-like legs around her waist, but it was almost spent. Maeve used her weight advantage as sparingly as she dare. With head still ringing, and blood pouring from her face, she shushed and calmed. Her vision was blurred but as she looked into the dark, deep-set eyes that were filled with terror and trauma, she could at last see it was definitely female, a young girl. The negative energy she was giving off was intense. Maeve could feel it in her chest, and it hurt. She didn't profess to be a healer, but this was her role in the here and now. She brought the cold, sharp air deep into her lungs, held it and released it in a steady rhythm, bringing down her heart rate, and resetting the synapses inside her head. She closed her eyes and mentally cleared her chakras, concentrating on her heart in an effort to disperse the negative and the pain. She became aware of the cumulative evil that had befallen this child and the stain it had left behind. It began to restrict her throat, and tears started to fall down her cheeks. She could still feel the fear and the resistance. Fear in her eyes and the resistance from such a wasted and emaciated body that was still somehow determined to fight against anything that represented her own species. How could there be so much mistrust?

PRECESSION

What had she seen and been through?

Maeve knew that while ever she was in this position of dominance, any healing could never effectively take place, and so she prayed. She mentally made herself as light as possible, she lifted herself away from the physical and appealed to the universe. Slowly, the girl's cries and desperate moans, began to fade into the ether, Maeve felt the waves turn theta and as all linear time stood still, she lapsed into a hypnogogic trance like state.

Like emerging from a deep sleep, she became vaguely aware of a presence, warm and powerful. She cautiously opened her eyes until they focused on two floating white orbs, framed by the open aperture of what had been a window. She immediately felt the energy as they moved towards her and the girl in a gentle dance until they stopped and hovered above their heads. She also became aware of heavy footsteps ascending stairs. As the two swirling spheres of electromagnetic energy morphed from white, to turquoise to green, Jed and Declan emerged at the doorway out of breath, and open mouthed at what confronted them. Maeve, still sat astride her would-be killer, turned and calmly, almost messiah like, bade them lower their pacifiers. Whether from the sight of her bloodied face or the strange but mesmeric apparition hovering above her head, or both, they did so in silent compliance. The girl, as if heavily sedated now simply stared upwards as the orbs began to turn pink. Maeve felt any remaining resistance evaporate from the waif-like body. She removed her restraining hands and held them out, palms up, absorbing the multiple positive vibrations that they were now being showered with. As the two men continued to look on completely dumbstruck, the orbs finally turned from pink to gold, the sign of unconditional love. Maeve reached inside her tunic and pulled out her pendant. She saw that hers and the one the girl had around her neck were identical, made from the same cheap silver sterling, tarnished and faded, but definitely identical. She had no idea what this meant, if it meant anything at all. She brought it to her lips and kissed it. She then gently kissed the girl on the forehead, the same forehead that moments ago had been used as a formidable weapon. She smiled down upon her small, tortured features, the girl let out a sigh and her eyes rolled up inside their sockets. Maeve Bradley raised her head, and as the two orbs began to fade away into nothingness, she offered up a silent prayer of gratitude and forgiveness.

As if a spell had suddenly been broken Jed and Declan recovered

AQUARIUS

their senses and rushed into the room.

'Maeve!' Jed shouted.

She got to her feet and fell into his arms, exhausted. They hung on to each other for what seemed like an age. 'Maeve,' he whispered into the debris-strewn mess that was her hair, 'You crazy, crazy girl.'

Declan knelt at the side of the girl and checked her pulse. 'It's breathing,' he announced.

'It's a girl,' corrected Maeve, with her bloodied face still resting on the big man's chest. 'She's a girl.'

PRECESSION

Kersha

Just how much wisdom is imparted when being bestowed a gift? Is it a reward or a curse, or both depending on how you use the gift? Some gifts feel like second nature, innate and taken for granted; others tend to get sprung on you and catch you off guard. It's like, - hang on, did I ask for this? – Well, I guess you must have done somewhere along the line, so deal with it, it's a life lesson; reward or curse; the choice is yours. Maeve, as she often did in times of retrospection, reflected on the words of a wise but long forgotten writer-philosopher: *"We are lightened when our gifts rise from pools we cannot fathom. Then we know they are not a solitary egotism and they are inexhaustible. Anything contained within a boundary must contain as well its own exhaustion."*

She sighed and pondered all of this while attempting to pass a thread through the eye of a needle for the umpteenth time. Her ancestors would have been adept at such a simple task, and yet here she was struggling with the mundane. It put a sobering perspective on the ascent or decline of the species depending on which way you looked at it. All she was attempting to do was sew the head back on the rag doll that one of the guys had found up in the attic of what was left of that bleak terrace building. The fact that her actions and the previously untapped phenomenon she had manifested had almost certainly saved a life was secondary to her now. The restoration of a filthy, flea-bitten child's toy that in her mind must carry some deep emotional significance for its owner was her priority at this moment, and that she was failing in that task left her greatly frustrated.

She put down the needle and cotton, let out a yawn and stretched in her chair, feeling the aching bones in her vertebrae crack and pop. With any movement every muscle in her body seemed to cry out in protest. She'd been sat there all through the night, at her own insistence, getting little if any sleep, observing, monitoring, wondering. Gazing across to the bed where the young girl now lay, she wondered some more. After she'd been cleaned, de-loused and disinfected, she looked more like the child she was, waif-like and completely vulnerable. Apart from the odd cry out or pitiful moans in her dreams, she had remained comatose. The saline and glucose drips had stayed in place. The monitors were showing all her signs vital. Maeve's concern now was the likely reaction to an alien, clinical environment once restored to full consciousness.

With a painful sigh she got to her feet and approached the bed. The raven-coloured hair, still tangled but cleansed, spread across a crisp, white pillow framing gaunt, callow features: eyebrows thick and lashes long juxtaposing sockets sunken and hollow. She failed to comprehend how such a delicate, fragile looking creature could have given her such a run for her money and left her in so much pain and discomfort. Her survival instinct was primal, and she could only imagine what traumas she had endured in her short life to be found all alone battling for what she mistakenly thought was her very existence. For Maeve, apart from the physical reminder, it all felt like a dream to her now.

She remembered leaving her body as the Irishman took her in his arms; two totally spent, lifeless forms being carried out of a crumbling edifice by a pair of giants past a bewildered guard of hi-vis clad demo men, all viewed from somewhere up on high.

She walked to the bathroom and looked in the mirror. Her face was a mass of bruises, reds turning purple. She didn't recall the four stitches being sewn into her forehead, now matted black and crimson. She didn't remember arguing the toss with Jed and the clinician on the wisdom of staying in the same room as her assailant overnight, but she remained mindful of the two orbs, the healing balls of energetic light, that had come to her assistance, as smooth, as real, and as easy as a single thought, although she knew it was more than that. The process and its manifestation had felt natural, inevitable, a gift. And yet her inability to thread a needle still irked her.

Doctor Helen Vaughn was the senior clinician and orthopaedic surgeon at the MSH. Her last shift had been a busy one, and she was back in again doing her rounds.

'How is she?' asked Maeve.

'Well, physically, apart from being malnourished, she's surprisingly fine,' said the physic, checking the drip levels and monitors. 'Mentally, I'm neither qualified nor equipped to say. More importantly, how are you feeling?'

'Tired and aching. Did you put these in?' she asked pointing to the stitches in her head.

'Yes, and you wouldn't let me numb it.'

'I'm sorry, I don't recall.'

'Hmm, I have a daughter just like you at home,' she said in a motherly tone.

'Oh?'

'Stubborn, argumentative, you know, all the adolescent traits.'

'I'm sorry, I…'

'Don't worry, I'm only teasing. I've been hearing all about you and your, shall we call them, holistic methods.'

'Really? Do you not approve?'

'Oh, of course I approve; in fact, I'm fascinated. I would love to know what sort of sedative you have given this girl.'

'Maybe she is simply exhausted,' said Maeve giving nothing away.

'Perhaps,' she agreed, looking questioningly over the top of her glasses. 'Her bloods are back.'

'And?'

'It would appear that during the course of her life she's had almost every disease there is to be had: TB, hepatitis, meningitis just to name some. How she's still alive is a mystery to me, except to say she now has the strongest immune system I've ever come across. She's unique, a medical mystery. It looks like her white blood cells are able to manufacture antibodies and T cells at an astonishing rate. As soon as she's recovered, I propose to send her for further tests.'

'Whoa, wait,' said Maeve, becoming concerned. 'Tests, what tests?'

'We're just a field hospital. I mend bones. She needs to see an Epigen.'

'For?'

'Like I've said, Maeve, her genes appear unique. Sequencing her genome and studying her RNA to see how it's regulating proteins, could prove groundbreaking to better understand how our bodies combat pathogens and disease.'

'You mean use her as a guinea pig?'

'Voluntary, of course.'

'I'm not sure she will be able to consent; I fear she is mute.'

'Ah…'

'Look, Doctor Vaughn, from your standpoint as a clinician I fully understand your eagerness to further explore these anomalies in her physiology, but first and foremost we must try to comprehend the extreme trauma this child has suffered. Where is her family? How long has she been on her own in an area that has been evacuated and abandoned long ago? What abuse has she been through? What atrocities has she witnessed? What I saw in her eyes was abject terror. These marks on my face and body were born out of fear. The techniques I used to pacify her are innate, they come to me intuitively, yet I have never used them before, and I don't yet fully comprehend how they work, but they did. When she opens her eyes what will she see? She will see an alien environment, clean and sterile, strange faces intent on causing her harm.'

'Why would we cause her any harm?'

'Because that is what she will see. It's what her PTSD has programmed her to perceive. No amount of words or deeds will convince her otherwise. She is likely to go off her head and your only course of action would be to restrain her, which would only compound the trauma even more.'

The doctor looked from Maeve with her bruised and battered features to the almost pixie like frame of the patient and did some quick reasoning. Tranquillizing medication was only ever used in extreme circumstances now and it wasn't a route she particularly wanted to go down. As she said herself, she was merely a bonesetter, an allopath albeit a bloody good one. If this remarkable young woman had other solutions to offer, she was intrigued to learn them. 'What would you propose?'

'We get rid of the drips and monitors and holograph the room.'

'Holograph the room.' She slowly repeated the words back to her to confirm she'd heard correctly.

'Yes. Turn this place into a shit hole – virtually, of course, so that when she wakes up her surroundings will appear familiar. I already spent the night uploading the apps and the software; I just need to scour the archive for suitable images.'

'I – I'm afraid I won't be able to sanction that,' said the physic, dubiously. 'It would have to go before council.'

'Not enough time. She could open her eyes at any moment. We have to set it up now.'

'Are you sure this will work?' she asked sceptically.

'No, but unless you have any better ideas, what choice do we have? If it fails, I accept all responsibility. I acted on my own and you had no knowledge of my actions. I shall testify this to council if I have to. You have my word on this.'

'That's quite some responsibility you're placing on your shoulders.'

Maeve shrugged. She knew if she was able to manifest the right vibrational conditions again, then she just might be able to gain the trust of this vulnerable human being. If not, then she was prepared to take the consequences. 'Trust me?'

Doctor Vaughn slowly nodded her head. 'I do. Is there any way I can help?'

Maeve pondered. 'Yes, could you thread a needle for me?'

'What the feck is this?' Jed's large frame filled the doorway. He scanned the hospital room that now looked like a post-shift condemned dwelling interior. Paint and wallpaper appeared to be hanging off walls. Bits of plaster dangled from the ceiling exposing lath and joists. A single broken chair sat in a corner. Even the glass in the window looked cracked and about to fall out. He gazed down to see bare, rough-hewn floorboards. His eyes followed the lines to the bed and the moth-eaten blanket that covered the small frame of what he still suspected to be a Lazor, then to the apparition that was his colleague. She half turned in her chair and smiled. She looked unkempt and tired. The marks on her face and stitches in her head didn't help. Her short-cropped hair stuck out in all directions making her look more like a boy than she usually did. And she was clutching a rag doll. He shook his head at the sight. He stepped into the room, looked around some more and sniffed. It smelled of damp and decay. He was quietly impressed; she had even managed to introduce olfactory sensations into her little scenario, although he was grateful, she had left out the stink of faeces.

'What brings you here, Jed?'

'What brings me here?' He mused the question to himself. 'What brings me here? Hmm... why, it's to see how my little Digger is getting on after her ordeal, isn't it?'

'Is it?' she asked dubiously.

'No, of course it feckin' isn't, you bloody dipstick. I've got two men laid up with broken bodies next door because of you and your stupid games. That's why I'm here.'

'I'm sorry,' she said sheepishly, 'but only one incident was down to me, really – wasn't it?'

AQUARIUS

He sighed and scratched his head in frustration. 'Two casualties in one shift. What the hell do you think Council are going to do?'

'I'll take full responsibility.'

'That's all you ever say. It's your answer to everything. I bet you're taking full responsibility for… for whatever all this is,' he said waving his arms about in exasperation.

'Not now, Jed, please,' she said, turning away disappointed at his reaction.

'Why are you even doing all this for a Lazor?'

'She's not a Lazor.'

'Going by the state of your mush, I'd say it's a Lazor.'

'Well then, I'd say that you know fuck all, Spunky. Just look at her for godssake.'

'Yeah, well, it won't look like that when it comes to, I'll warrant.' He raised a large, calloused hand, passing it through the 3D image of the bare ceiling light bulb socket, and laughed to himself.

'So, what would you do, oh wise one?'

'I would hand it over to a team who knew what they were doing.'

'I know what I'm doing, Jed, and please stop referring to her as "it".'

'I seriously doubt it,' he scoffed, 'but Maeve knows best. Maeve's way or the highway and bugger the consequences.'

The comments poked at her ego and clashed with her intuition, causing a churning inside her stomach. She didn't want to make an enemy of the big fella, and fully understood his standpoint, but now wasn't the time for a blame game or an inquest. The ego was telling her to fight her corner; intuition was saying focus on job in hand. She bit her tongue. 'I'm sorry you feel like this, I suggest you go look to your patients, and I shall tend to mine.'

'Oh, I will, and just in case your magik don't work fer youse this time, just give us a shout; I'll be next door ready with me pacifier.'

'Thanks for your concern, Jed. Don't forget to close the door on your way out.'

She had insisted on doing this alone, promising the doctor that she would use her aircom if she needed any assistance, and now, even more determined to keep him and his bloody pacifier out of the loop no matter what the outcome. She closed her eyes and sighed, his short unannounced visit had sown a small seed of doubt in her designs, but there was a stronger overwhelming sense in her psyche that she was doing the right thing. Intrigued by the holistic phenomena that had been unconsciously summoned to her aid, she was ever more curious to test that latent energy and see if it could be harnessed and used to whatever will or thought she used in her affirmations.

With the big man departed, door locked, and lighting dimmed Maeve set in motion a subliminal rhythm of binaural beats, undetectable to the human ear, but audible to the subconscious, creating an ambiance and an atmosphere that morphed with the virtual scene. She began her visualisations. In her mind's eye she could already see the orbs, but they were distant and vague. She connected with each and every chakra in turn and felt her heart rate slow. She began to sense heaviness as if weights had been attached to the whole of her body pulling her down through her chair. Tiredness started to overwhelm, so she consciously tried to remain aware of every breath, as deep and as slow as it now was. To accompany her projections she added a mantra: *What I feel, I attract – what I imagine, I create,* round and around, dynamo like, creating an energy that slowly transformed the kinaesthetic from heavy to light, weightless and without form, the words now merely white noise, jumbled and incoherent, until at last, a blessed release from consciousness to nothing; a vacuum, devoid of anything humanly tangible, yet somehow sweet in its indescribability. She surrendered…

. . . Wake up – open your eyes, wake up, open your eyes . . . She came back from her bliss with a dawning realisation that the mantra was no longer hers, not her words, not her thoughts, not her voice, a feeling of disappointment and guilt as she came back to the denseness that was her body, then the rude shock of entelechy and the sudden impression that she should obey the command. She opened her eyes.

'Fuck!' Hand to mouth came a microsecond too late to stop Maeve from blurting out the expletive in surprise and shock. The girl was sat bolt upright, dark eyes boring holes in her. She slowly raised an arm and levelled a bony finger at the rag doll that Maeve was still holding in her lap.

'Hey – hi – er…' Maeve, still half-stuck in the twilight zone, was momentarily lost for words. The girl's eyes widened, her mouth set with displeasure. 'Oh, yes, this is yours, I guess,' she began, offering the doll. 'We fixed it for you, I hope...' Before she could finish the waif had reached out and with lightning speed snatched it from her grasp, bringing it close to her chest with both hands. The doll stared back at Maeve with its blank button eyes and fixed inane smile. 'That's okay, that's fine. I, er, I'm sorry I was asleep when you woke. I guess we both needed some sleep, eh?' The girl continued to look daggers. 'Erm, can you hear me?' Maeve began to sign. 'Can you speak? My name is Maeve. What's your name? Do you have a family, mum and dad, brothers, sisters?' Nothing. She tried again with both words and sign. 'Can you hear me?' There was a faint, unsure nod of the head. 'Good, good, that's great,' she said encouragingly. 'Do you understand my words?' Nothing. They continued in this vein for a while until the girl became bored and began to take in her surroundings, leaving Maeve stumped and frustrated. No sign of orbs, but an ineffable sense of peace and calm filled the room. She watched her closely, not certain if the holograph was working or if she could see through it. At least she showed no propensity toward violence at this time, which to her meant progress. 'You must be hungry,' she signed. 'I'm hungry. Let me get us something to eat.' Maeve spoke quietly into her aircom and gave Doctor Vaughn a progress report. She ordered food and drink to be left outside the door, hoping she might have a better chance of opening up a line of communication if she had something in her belly.

The girl eyed her suspiciously as she wheeled the trolley into the room. Maeve took a bowl of broth, sat down in her chair and began to eat. 'Mmm, this is good, really tasty.' She continued to make noises of approval while spooning the soup into her mouth. The girl looked from Maeve to the second bowl that was sat steaming away on the trolley. A guttural sound came from the back of her throat. 'Oh, would you like some – yes?' A short growl came from her by way of reply. Maeve reached for the bowl and offered it. The girl took it cautiously and sniffed, discarded the spoon and then tipped it down her throat in one go. With overspill dripping from her chin and down her gown, she proceeded to lick out the remnants, while Maeve, wide-eyed, looked on in astonishment. 'Here,' she said offering her a protein drink, 'I think you might want to cool your mouth down, but you need to sip it slowly, like this. . .' The demonstration had no effect, and the drink went the same way in one swift action. She finished it off with a resounding burp and then looked on expectantly. 'Still hungry? Let's see . . .' Maeve selected a pear from the trolley and handed it over. 'These are specially grown in a place called Ruston Parva. They're sweet and juicy, and - hey, slow down! You'll give yourself a stomachache; you're meant to chew it, taste it, enjoy it - oh, never mind . . .' By the time she'd finished speaking the piece of fruit had disappeared, core, stalk and all. 'My, oh my girl, what have you been living on? You were starving, weren't you?' Behind those dark, sunken eyes, Maeve thought she could see a sparkle of light. She smiled and watched her lick every last drip of glistening juice from around her mouth. Her lips looked fuller, and colour had started to return to her cheeks. She took in her surroundings once more before throwing off the duvet and easing herself out of bed. In silence, Maeve observed her sniff at the gown she was wearing, and then in turn both the sheet and pillow she had been laying on. She touched them gently, and then, in a dazed wonderment, slowly began to pace the room. A frown had formed, and Maeve wondered if she'd sussed her little deception. She spoke again in the hope of distraction. 'My name is Maeve, what's yours?' The girl glanced at her; features void of any emotion or response. 'Maeve,' she repeated, pointing at her chest and then back at her. 'You . . .?' Nothing.

She persisted, patiently probing, trying to illicit a response without success. Her hearing was fine, but Maeve had gleaned nothing vocal apart from the odd guttural noise or grunt. Without any breakthrough in communication, she began to worry that the four walls of her confinement might soon trigger an unwanted reaction. She desperately tried to form another plan of action in her head, when she noticed over in a corner of the room the girl had begun to pace around in small circles almost animal-like, and then without warning, she lifted her gown, squat and defecated on the floor. Surprised, but neither shocked nor disgusted, Maeve waited till she'd finished and then collected the deposit in a swathe of paper towels. Heading for the bathroom she bid the girl follow her. With a curious look on her face, she watched as Maeve flushed away her waste. 'Gone,' she said as if talking to a small child. 'No more smell,' she indicated by holding her nose and shaking her head. Maeve sighed once more at the absence of any reaction. She turned on a tap and washed her hands, encouraging the girl to do the same. It had no effect. She held out her hands. 'Look, nice and clean.' - *Although the rest of me stinks, I guess* - she thought to herself before hitting on an

AQUARIUS

idea.

Steam from the shower rose above the cubicle as Maeve began to remove her clothes. The girl looked on, her face now a mix of wariness and curiosity that soon turned to anger when Maeve removed her thermal vest to reveal the pendant around her neck. Her eyes widened and that now familiar guttural growl came from her throat, she pointed accusingly.

'Oh, this? No, no; you still have yours, look, feel.' Maeve gestured. The girl reached inside her gown and pulled out the identical object. She stared back and forth, total confusion written all over her face. 'I know, they're the same, crazy, isn't it?' Now conscious of her own nakedness, Maeve smiled, turned and entered the cubicle, allowing the warm, cascading water soothe her weary body. She poured a generous amount of oil over herself and started to wash away the accumulated grime and dust. Aromatic aromas rose on the steam and the girl moved closer, now fascinated. She watched avidly as Maeve moved her hands slowly around her body in a show of sensual cleansing. Part of it was indeed show; an act to entice, but it genuinely did feel good to be clean again and she made all the appropriate noises to go with it. With one eye half open she playfully flicked water at her gawping voyeur, who immediately snapped out of her trance, jumping back shocked at getting wet.

'You want to join me? Come on in, it feels great. Come on, don't be shy; you'll enjoy it.' It took a few more moments of encouragement and persuasion to tip the balance between fear and curiosity before the girl cautiously moved towards Maeve's open armed beckoning. 'No, take it off.' She gestured to remove her soiled nightgown. A thick mound of dark pubic hair appeared looking strangely at odds against the wiry undernourished body where her tiny breasts were almost imperceptible. She entered the shower allowing Maeve to take her by the hands, guiding her under the warm water where she let out an involuntary shudder, her eyes widening at the alien sensations that had started to coarse through her meagre body. 'Good, yes?' Maeve smiled as the girl's breath came in short, sharp excited bursts. She showed her the oil, allowed her to sniff it in order to gain her approval before proceeding to wash her, being careful to retain eye contact at all times, and when they met Maeve could see and sense both confusion and wonder along with the makings of a surrender. A barrier was being dismantled and for the first time, and with relief, Maeve felt vindicated. She was under no illusions; this, whatever it was she had taken on, wouldn't be easy, she knew that, but she now knew to never doubt her intuition.

Maeve tried to encourage her to clean her own private parts, but in the first real show of communication, the girl shook her head and indicated that they should be cleaned for her. 'Oh, okay . . .' said Maeve cautiously. As she moved her hands over her slender buttocks, the girl pointed and poked at Maeve's own pert nipples. She giggled, it was the very first sign of any emotion other than fear or anger. Behind the steam, Maeve began to colour up, but the sensations now flowing through her own body were beginning to confuse. She didn't resist the girl's newfound playfulness, she told herself that would be counterproductive, and she quickly dismissed that other part of her that was saying – *ha!* – *fine excuse* - Maeve had never felt like this around boys, to her they were all infantile, immature. She'd never been in a relationship and the very thought had never even crossed her mind. Even the notion of her sexuality had never entered her paradigm until now.

She found her hands lingering on her butt long after it had been cleaned. The girl's arms, those hands that had so recently wanted to kill her, that had given her the marks and bruises, now gently wrapped around her, their bodies met. The two tarnished pendants depicting hawks in flight had never been in quite such close proximity. Maeve gazed into those deep, dark now smouldering eyes as the water fell from her long, black lashes. 'Who are you?' she whispered. 'What is your name?'

For a moment the girl's attention seemed to drift, off and away to some faraway place until her eyes came back and fixed them on Maeve's. Her full lips parted, and a sound began to form. 'K – Ker – Ker – K – Kersha . . .'

AQUARIUS

Ampleforth

With her head resting against the cold window of the carriage, Maeve gazed out at the flat, frozen unchanging landscape as it rolled by. She tried to envisage the scenery as it had once been or how she would one day hope to see it in her lifetime, applying colours and senses gleaned from images, because these are all she had. She replaced the grey-white tundra with rolling hills and meadows of vibrant greens and fields of golden barley undulating to the tune of a warm summer breeze. Although she had never experienced the seasons, she held within her psyche a kind of yearning coming from neither the past nor the future, neither a memory or a prediction, just an innate knowing of something her soul had once experienced and shall again. It gave her that aching feeling in her gut, an inevitability marred by impatience and longing.

She sighed and observed her travelling companion, lost, as she was in her own little world, chattering away to her rag doll in her own language, making sense to no one but herself. Maeve smiled inwardly; at least she had a language even though it was gobbledygook. It had been a relief to discover she was not entirely mute and a puzzle as to whether she ever had a full command of English or had merely forgotten or had chosen not to speak. Of the half-dozen words she had uttered, "Maeve", "okay", and "eat" had been learned, while "Kersha", "cunt", and "no" had come from her own limited vocabulary. Maeve, thinking back, smiled again as "cunt" had been the first word Kersha had screamed at Jed on seeing the big man once she had been coaxed into leaving the virtual space of the ward she had been in. She had cowered behind her new confidante hissing and growling in her feral way until he had backed off with a bewildered shrug of the shoulders, muttering the words "fuken Lazor" under his breath. Men, it appeared, were a focal point for her fear, trauma and mistrust. Initially, she had even kept a wary distance from females such as Doctor Vaughn, clinging onto Maeve limpet fashion whenever she approached, but on their eventual departure from the field hospital Maeve had been pleased that she had managed to give the good doctor a reciprocal wave goodbye. As she had watched them on their way, Helen Vaughn marvelled at the resolve but wondered if this young woman was fully sentient of the enormity and responsibility she had willingly taken on.

Aware of her newfound friend's attention, Kersha paused from her dolly dialogue and launched into an indecipherable tirade. 'De shfnk ata byou as mines int dersch wit svert is en pshh der cunt – bli ash mnnn a git fre wanna is mines, is mines', she said assertively.

Thinking she could detect Germanic overtones in her speech, Maeve smiled and nodded in agreement. 'I think you're absolutely right.'

'Der isht onis der cunt,' she stated before turning her attention back to the doll.

As they neared the outskirts of old York, Maeve stewed on the cautionary warnings from Doctor Vaughn and the sheer incredulity from Jed at taking on such a task, but once again she erred on the side of her intuition and would allow herself to be guided by her instincts. For their own individual reasons, all four of them, Maeve, Jed, Declan and Doctor Vaughn had conspired to keep any reporting of any incidents away from council, and now that she had the girl in her confidence, Maeve had agreed to consult a renowned Epigen in Ampleforth.

The train slowed as it approached the temporary crossing over the vast tract of ice that had been the river Ouse. Temporary, as it would not be able to withstand the geological upheavals that were still likely to come, despite the innovative engineering feats of people like Jed, Nav and their teams. Maeve looked back at the long snaking convoy of waggons laden with ton upon ton of concrete and steel, the structure beneath her groaning under the sheer weight. They were hauling half of old Leeds behind them, demolished material that would help form the flood barrier being constructed in the Humber estuary and along the East coast. Everywhere, the crumbling edifices of the old world were being put to use, a tarnished legacy at last playing a part in the survival of the species. What part she would be playing now, Maeve was no longer sure. If she ever had a perceived destiny, it had unexpectedly taken a twist. She had been proud and excited at being asked to present her findings in person in Ruston Parva, but now that she had inadvertently managed to manufacture a major distraction for herself the invitation had somehow lost its initial appeal.

Appealing to her now was something else, and there was a part of her scared to admit it, not least because the appeal had come out of the blue, born under a cascade of water and growing by each passing moment, but also because this was new to her; emotions alien yet warm and enticing, and then her left brain logic throwing up guilt and confusion. She stared across in curious wonder at Kersha, sat there still chattering away to herself dressed in a set of Maeve's thermals that fit her perfectly. She had already begun to fill out; a pleasant colour had come to her face and her eyes no longer looked sunken and hollow. The matted dreads on her head now untangled revealing a thick wavy ebony mane that fell down the length of her back. In Maeve's head a suggestion to take scissors to it, quickly dismissed as she ran her fingers through it, liking what she felt. She had allowed her to tie it back for practicality, exposing her high cheekbones that had her transfixed. She had become aware that she might be shaping this girl to her own ideal, taking advantage of her vulnerability and it perturbed her somewhat, but the pull of her emotions was proving stronger, any guilt assuaged for now.

At York they watched the juggernaut slowly pull away from its unscheduled drop to continue its journey east. As it rumbled off into the distance an eerie silence descended. Maeve shivered involuntarily, and not entirely due to the minus twenty-degree temperature. The old station reminded her of St. Pancras, and she was none too keen to hang around. She had signalled ahead their imminent arrival and hoped they would be picked up soon. Kersha had resisted all attempts to get her to wear a topcoat, she was happy in just her borrowed thermals. Apparently, she was oblivious to and unaffected by the cold, but she was happy when Maeve offered her a cuddle and playfully wrapped her close in her own, their unified breath mingling and dissipating into the freezing air.

Presently, the AG-MAGLEV came into view and approached silent and sleek. Kersha tightened her not unsubstantial grip around Maeve's arm as it hovered to a halt a few feet away. *'Welcome – please board now'* announced a disembodied voice. A door slid open, and Kersha pulled back, wide-eyed and fearful.

'It's okay,' said Maeve trying to remove the iron like grip on her arm. 'Nothing to be scared of; you're with me, it's okay.' Her reassurance was blind being that this would also be her maiden voyage in such a machine. She took a seat in the vehicle, intrigued by the absence of a pilot, and encouraged a reluctant Kersha to follow her lead. After some gentle coaxing and with hands held tight, the door slid closed. A screen pinged into life, and the face of a smiling

PRECESSION

woman greeted them.

'Hello, Maeve. I'm professor Donna Channing. I hope the journey into York wasn't too arduous. Thankfully the trip up to Ampleforth will be a short and hopefully pleasant experience. I look forward very much to meeting you both on your arrival. See you soon.'

'Oh, short and sweet,' said Maeve as the screen went blank. Almost immediately the MAGLEV levitated, turned three-sixty and took off as silent and sleek as it had arrived.

'Der fuck's dis?' Kersha exclaimed, still wide-eyed and unsure. She peered warily out the window as they flashed past the ruins of old York, hugging the contours of even older castle relic and city walls now imperceptible under snow and ice.

Maeve circled a hand over her abdomen. 'Exciting, yes?' Kersha returned an unsure grin, revealing teeth that were remarkably white and straight. Her skin had taken on an olive hue that served to enhance the look. Transfixed, Maeve stared back maybe slightly longer than she ought.

'Der sin a betch n foosish,' said Kersha pointing out the window at the fast-moving landscape, semi oblivious to her guardian's attentions. Maeve's sense of guilt was still present, not just from her obvious growing attraction, but from her acquiescence to the tests she was about to subject her to. Kersha's inability to give consent still made her feel uncomfortable.

The rifts and escarpments recently formed by the upshift in land north of the M62 cut came into harsh but spectacular view. Parts of what had been The Vale of York had been re-shaped and elevated up against The North York Moors. The ancient village of Ampleforth now sat majestic on its own plateau and was home to the most advanced healing facility in the land. To the eye the sprawling complex appeared completely tonal with the landscape apart from the green neon -flashing beacon that now guided them in. The MAGLEV descended to a landing that was both silent and soft. A tubular appendage from an adjacent low building extended and attached itself to the side of the vehicle. The door of the Maglev slid open, and Maeve had to do twice the coaxing for Kersha to exit the vehicle than she had for her to enter it.

Inside, Doctor Channing was there to greet them with a broad, welcoming smile. Maeve formally held out her hand only to have it ignored and was surprised, instead, to be met with a warm, heartfelt embrace. The kindly professor smelled fragrantly fresh with tones of what Maeve detected as jasmine and frankincense. As they parted, Maeve took in her features: long, grey hair casually tied back in a ponytail, revealing faint crow-feet lines fanning out to her temples that belied the brightness and vibrancy that shone from her eyes. She appeared slim and toned; in fact, her whole demeanour exuded optimum health and wellbeing. She wore an eye-catching multi-coloured blouse and turquoise pants, a husk of beads around her neck and wrists and nothing on her feet, all of which served to disarm Maeve a little. - *"Serves you right for stereotyping,"* - said a condescending voice inside her head.

'Welcome, welcome,' she said brightly. 'It's so good to meet you at last – and you must be Kersha – I've been hearing so much about you...'

Kersha tucked herself behind her companion and out of the reach of this over-familiar person. 'Cunt,' she muttered with a sneer and curl of the lip.

With increasing curiosity, Maeve began to take in her surroundings. She had never been inside a healing centre of this magnitude, and once again had unconsciously formed a perception inside her head of what one should look like. This place was nothing like the Mobile Surgical Hospital in Leeds with its Spartan walls and clinically sterile ambience. Here, the spaces were filled with exotic looking plants displaying palms and fronds of all shapes and sizes, foliage in a hue of rich greens and purples. The walls were adorned with art: paintings, collages, sculptures and moving holographic scenes and stories. The various scents were heady and ever changing as they slowly walked. Ambient, soft solfeggio tones of ever-changing frequencies seemed to hit them in gentle waves, without a single detectable source. The ground beneath their feet also felt undistinguishable and indescribable, neither hard nor soft as their steps perceptibly became light and effortless. The doctor led them to what appeared to be a lift whose doors slid open as they approached. 'Please . . .' she bid them with an open-handed gesture. Maeve entered the space that now seemed surprisingly large for a lift. Kersha followed her closely, scowling suspiciously at the strange, smiling woman. The door slid shut behind them and the doctor's smile remained fixed, but she didn't speak. Maeve noticed the absence of a panel or any form of floor selector; in fact, the four expansive walls were totally bare, and from that she quickly deduced that unless there were floors below them, the room they were now in couldn't possibly be a lift as the whole complex appeared to be single storey.

Without noise and without any notion of movement, a band of soft turquoise light rippled up the four walls in gentle rolling waves. Maeve observed the phenomenon in silent wonder, while Kersha in her now familiar wary manner clung tightly to her guardian's arm. Donna Channing continued to smile.

Curious, and with a mounting list of questions ready to be asked, Maeve began to speak just as the calming, mesmeric patterns fell away as instantly as they had formed. The doors slid open, and Maeve saw that in fact they hadn't gone anywhere, neither up nor down. They were in the same place.

The doctor tilted her head and smiled once more. 'You were about to say?'

'What? – er, nothing; it'll wait.'

'Good. Refreshments, then, would you like tea?'

'Tea? Yes, thank you.'

'Pine, turmeric, dandelion?'

'Pine would be lovely.'

'And for Kersha?'

'Oh, maybe a juice; she'll drink anything you put in front of her.'

They were led a short walk along a corridor into another larger room. Immediately they were met with an array of coloured patterns and multi-dimensional images that appeared to flow from the walls and circle them in a peculiarly warm welcome before receding before them as they entered.

'This is one of our R & R spaces, please, make yourselves comfortable, I shan't be a moment.' With her infectious smile, Dr. Channing left the room.

'Der fuck,' exclaimed Kersha.

'Der fuck, indeed,' said Maeve.

Soft looking chairs and sofas spread about randomly welcomed them, books, screens and pads were set out at their disposal, the ambient music still drifted in and out from all corners, and the scents in the air were, to Maeve at least, pleasant and uplifting. Over in one corner of the room something had caught Kersha's eye. Three young children, two boys and a girl were playing. Two of them were painting, one at an easel, and the other at a desk. The other boy was making a construction from some brightly coloured interlocking bricks. Kersha relaxed her grip that had been holding on tightly to Maeve's hand and wandered over. Nervously, Maeve followed in quick pursuit.

'Der isht?' said Kersha to no one in particular.

'Der isht?' she repeated, pointing at the picture the young girl was painting.

The three children looked up from their endeavours curiously.

'Would you like to paint?' enquired the young girl. She picked up a paintbrush and offered it. Kersha unceremoniously snatched it from her grasp, an action that visibly shook them all. Maeve quickly intervened and tried to take the brush from her, but the steely stare and determination not to relinquish immediately brought back memories of their first encounter.

'No, Kersha, not like that . . .'

'Ish mines,' she growled, 'Ish mines.'

The bizarre battle for the paintbrush and the bewildered expressions of the three kids met Donna Channing as she re-entered the room with refreshments. 'Hey! – Hey!'

'I'm sorry,' said Maeve, spinning round red faced and flustered. 'She's not used to being around people, especially children.'

'Ha! – Cunt!' screamed Kersha in the background holding up the brush triumphantly.

'It's okay, it's okay – it's fine; would she like to paint? There are plenty of easels . . .'

'So, questions, questions, you must have plenty,' began Doctor Channing while she poured tea.

'What? – Oh, yes,' said Maeve, still distracted by trying to keep one eye on Kersha who was now happily throwing paint about with wild abandon in her newly acquired apron. 'Well, firstly, the tests; what really concerns me is the issue of consent, and . . .'

'They're done,' interrupted the doctor.

'Pardon me?'

'All the tests are done. Complete.'

'But . . .'

'We already have her DNA from the blood samples she gave in Leeds. From that we have also extracted stem cells and a host of other information. We've also just mapped her biometrics and scanned her auric field.'

PRECESSION

'You mean you did all that from the brief moment we were in that other room?'

'That's right,' smiled the doctor, 'Completely non-physical and totally un-invasive. Is that what you were worried about?'

'Well, yes – yes, I suppose it was.'

'And do you think what we've done is unethical? There's been no prodding or poking. Look at her, no added trauma, none-the-wiser.'

Maeve slowly shook her head. 'No – no, I guess not.'

'We'll have a full physical assessment available shortly, In the meantime I would like to study her mental and emotional status.'

'Are you able to do that by pure observation? She can barely communicate.'

'You think so? Look at the way she's throwing that paint around. I'd say she's communicating right now.'

The waif's bright yellow apron was already streaked with splashes of black and grey paint. They watched from a distance as she proceeded to attack paper and easel with a crazed look in her eyes, cursing and spitting in her own clipped dialect while the other kids looked on warily. Maeve was beginning to be reassured by the doctor's hands-off approach, but she was still on edge in relation to Kersha's unpredictability alongside her virtually non-existent social skills.

'What is it exactly that you hope to uncover?' she asked while keeping an ever- present eye on her charge.

'We shan't set goals or expectations, except to try and understand and find ways to heal the trauma she's experienced. Our first task will be to gain her trust.'

Maeve concurred, 'Have you seen many like her before?'

'Yes, but none with such a unique physiology. I shall enjoy working with her.'

'I can't stay long; I have to present a paper in Ruston Parva.'

'I'm sure she will be fine here with us while you're gone.' The doctor read the doubt on her face. 'At some point she will have to broaden her trust; better sooner than later.'

'She hasn't been out of my sight since – since that . . .'

'I understand it was a revelatory experience for you; would you care to talk about it?'

While doctor Channing replenished Kersha with fresh reams of paper, Maeve took sips of tea wondering how she could put into words the experience of their first encounter and the strange phenomena of the orbs that now seemed like a distant dream that only came to the fore in rare waves of spasmodic, yet totally clear insight. Forcing it up from memory didn't quite work, it became foggy and fuddled, and she thought that trying to convey it all in a way that was both cohesive and coherent would be nigh on impossible.

She needn't have worried, Donna knew all about orbs, healing orbs, protective orbs, guiding orbs, cleansing orbs et al. She was totally familiar with the phenomenon and the respective energies that their colours represented, and her understanding made it easier for Maeve to relate her story.

She had welcomed the opportunity to unburden to someone who was both receptive and sympathetic, but when pushed for a more esoteric explanation of her experience, the doctor had remained ambiguous.

'Previous so-called informed schools of thought said that they were vehicles for spiritual entities, angels and other off world beings. 'Some said they were gifts left to us by The Pleiadians.' She had laughed at that.

'Your take?'

'We know that they are concentrated fields of electromagnetic energy, that have the ability to harness and carry thought forms and emotions. They are also able to tune into and amplify whatever frequency either thought or emotion emits. These energy fields or vibrations exist everywhere. How they vibrate and at what frequency they vibrate can determine what shape they take. Orbs make the most efficient shape for the flow of energy, but not all these shapes or fields are visible to the naked eye. It's usually only those whose chakras are fully open and pineal is un-calcified that are able to see orbs. I have no doubt that it was you who manifested these balls of light that came to your assistance. How you did it and how you used that energy to be able to pacify our young friend in a non-physical way is not for me to speculate, but for you to begin to understand and nurture over time what is a unique gift if you choose to do so.' She paused and studied her guest inquisitively.

Maeve, now lost in thought, slowly raised her gaze. 'I'm not sure if I do.'

'Have you found a calling?'

'Not sure that I have,' she said shaking her head. 'I am a trained geologist. I currently work as a geo-engineer. I am also a storian and a scribe tasked to document our times, and to separate the truth from the lies of our past, but I can't say I've found a calling.'

'No, of course, but already so learned for one so young.' Donna Channing nodded and smiled. – *You may not know it yet, but you, my dear, are a born Geomancer* – she thought to herself. 'Your guardians?'

'My father is a mathematician and councillor in Catterick. Mother is a solar physicist. She is currently stationed at CRREAT in The Hebrides. Why do you ask?'

'I'm just curious. An innate gift such as the one you possess is just that, something that is usually passed down through generations.'

'There have been doctors and healers in my family, but this gift you are alluding to, if that is what it is, remains a complete mystery to me aside from the knowledge you have just shared.'

'No matter; I feel, in time, that a better understanding of the esoteric and spiritual energies that permeate the Earth will be shown to you and shall enhance your geological skills. But tell me, how will you reconcile your work with the commitments you have made to our young friend?'

'I don't know. I have yet to cross that bridge.'

'Will you try and seek out family?'

'Where would I start?'

'I could look in the DNA bank, but if she's of Chav extraction, which I'm more or less certain of, then I doubt I'll find anything. At least she's Pureblood, which means any kin would have had a fair chance of survival.'

Maeve let out a sigh. 'Kersha was found in some ruin in the old 'smart city' of Leeds, which means her grandparents must have survived the ravages of The Shift, and whoever brought her into the world, somehow the aftermath, but they can't have been assimilated, they remained ...' she used the word reluctantly, '...Lazors. Their survival up to that point must have been through luck or providence rather than the fact they had untainted blood. I fear she no longer has any kin.'

'She managed to give you her name.'

'I'm not sure if it's her given name or a family name, it's just how it came out and she seems to respond to it.'

As with Doctor Vaughn in Leeds, Donna Channing wondered if Maeve fully appreciated the responsibility she was placing on her shoulders with these commitments while being totally unaware of the emotional bond that was growing between the two of them – for now, anyway.

'Given time and patience, I'm sure we shall find some answers,' she said reassuringly. 'Meanwhile I shall arrange your transport to Ruston Parva.'

Maeve thanked her, but deep down she wasn't too concerned about uncovering Kersha's past and the added trauma that might bring with it. The chances that she had somehow been accidentally separated from a loving family were remote, the odds that she had been abandoned, sold and abused, more likely. All she saw now were new beginnings; she felt them in her heart and in her gut. They were here to heal and move on.

Maeve had risen early, showered, dressed and was now stood gazing fondly at a face, neither soft nor cute, but deeply fascinating with ebony hair spread randomly across the white apparel of a medbed. She leant over, quiet, and planted a gentle kiss on her forehead before reluctantly leaving the room.

Poring over her notes on her pad in preparation for her presentation, Maeve barely noticed the sudden change in course of the MAGLEV as it banked away into a complete three-hundred-and-sixty-degree shift. The screen in front of her pinged into life and the face of a flustered and agitated Donna Channing filled the screen.

'Maeve, I'm sorry but I'm recalling the MAGLEV, I need you back here as soon as possible . . .'

'But . . .' started Maeve, distracted from her revision.

'You'll see why when you get here, I'm sorry, I must go . . .' With that the screen went dead.

Initial puzzlement gave way to a realisation of likely events unfolding back in Ampleforth. Mental pictures began to form in her head, and by the time she had landed, exited the craft and run into the building, those images had manifested into reality – and some.

Staff members, their voices raised in an attempt to rise above the sound of alarms echoing through halls and corridors, were running around aimlessly. Pictures had been torn from walls, plants upturned, and fire sprinklers were showering anything and everything. Maeve dodged and weaved her way through the panicking throng until she

PRECESSION

finally arrived at their dorm. Two medics were crouched tending to a prone nurse who had blood pouring from a head wound. Three other staff members were desperately trying to prevent the locked door from being battered open from within, while Doctor Channing and two other colleagues watched on helplessly.

'What's happened?' shouted Maeve above the din, a stupid question, she thought to herself the moment it left her lips as it was easy to second guess what had gone down.

Donna raced through a précis of events as they had unfolded: Kersha had been discovered tearing through the building naked screaming for Maeve, kicking open doors, rampaging through theatres and assaulting staff in a desperate effort to locate her guardian. No amount of gentle coaxing and reassurances had managed to calm her down. Anyone who dared to confront was met with unbridled violence and resistance, (Maeve had already witnessed one poor soul gingerly scraping excrement from his face and garment) even Doctor Channing had been savaged and spat upon.

Maeve drew a deep breath and urged those guarding the door to step aside. 'Kersha? – Kersha, it's me. It's Maeve – can you hear me?' she shouted through the door. All at once the banging and crashing from inside stopped. Silence ensued. 'I'm coming in, ok? It's ok, I'm here now.' Silence. Maeve and the doctor exchanged looks of cautious optimism. 'I'm coming in now, I'm here for you, just me, no one else, ok?' Silence. With that she slowly turned the key, opened the door ever so slightly and slid inside.

Kersha stood there totally naked, soiled from head to toe in her own faeces and blood, empty fire extinguisher she'd been using as a battering ram raised above her head in anticipation of some deception or other. On seeing Maeve, she let the thing fall to the floor with a dull clung before emitting a sigh of frustration and betrayal, turning her back, folding her arms and finally uttering the word 'cunt' under her breath.

The room was trashed. Any excrement not covering her or Doctor Channing's staff had been daubed around the walls mixed with blood and fire extinguisher foam, it looked similar to one of her art creations. The only thing seemingly untouched was her rag doll that was propped askew grinning inanely in what was left of the medbed.

Taking in a lung full of air and holding her breath for as long as she could Maeve had approached her carefully from behind and slowly wrapped her arms around her, allowing her face to nestle into her now sweaty black locks. 'I'm sorry,' she whispered softly and sincerely. 'I wasn't going to be gone long. I thought you would be happy here for a while – I guess not, eh?' She kissed a shoulder. 'It was stupid of me. You weren't to know where I was. Stupid. It won't ever happen again, I promise. I'll be here for you for as long as you need me. Wherever I go, you go, that's a promise too.' Maeve turned her around to face her trying her best to ignore the smell. 'Do you forgive me?'

'Me thought me lost ya - cunt,' replied Kersha in a sulky tone. 'Stupid cunt.'

Maeve laughed. 'Yeah, I'm a stupid cunt, and you're a smelly cunt. Let's both get showers, eh? – If you haven't trashed them as well,' she added hopefully.

'Still think you're gonna enjoy working with her?' asked Maeve, raising her eyebrows.

'Hmm,' pondered the doctor, now slightly ruing her own underestimation of the case, but with a growing understanding of the unique bond that had quickly developed between the two girls. She removed her glasses and looked Maeve in the face. She smiled inwardly at her flippancy. Doctor Vaughn back in Leeds had been right; this girl was a medical miracle. Kersha was an Epigenesist's dream. Despite the scene of devastation and destruction she had created, Donna Channing was secretly ecstatic with the further anomalous yet revelatory discoveries relating to her physiology that had come to light. Her own scientific reputation was unsurpassed, and working with this young woman would only add kudos to her work. 'Well, all I can say now having received further results is I may have a better insight into the extent of her ordeals.'

'Please elaborate.'

She flicked a finger across her pad to convey the information therein, 'We know almost for certain that Kersha has been pregnant at least three times.'

'Oh.'

'She miscarried twice but possibly gave live birth to one.'

'Chances of survival?'

Donna shrugged and shook her head at the same time. 'She may have used the foetus to survive herself.'

PRECESSION

Maeve looked aghast. 'You mean she . . .'

'It's a possibility; dare I say an inevitability.'

Maeve shuddered involuntarily. She recalled Jed's tales of Lazors and their cannibalistic behaviour while desperately trying to separate ritual satanic sacrifice from a basic human instinct to survive. The revelation went some way to explaining her distrust and apparent hatred of men. 'She must have been raped.'

Donna nodded sadly. 'She has the scars.'

'Have you managed to age her?'

'Yes, we know she's around sixteen, certainly no more than seventeen in old years.'

Maeve couldn't be certain since they stopped counting in old years a long time ago, but she guessed her own juvenescence to be that of Kersha's give or take a few signs. She then began to ruminate on their respective lives thus far and the unlikely confrontation, union and subsequent bond that had morphed from such polarities, and from those musings arose a tangible feeling of what used to be described as déjà vu, a kind of inevitability, strangely familiar, warm and yet tinged with the hollow absence of not being able to grasp what was to come. Now, knowing in her heart they were fated to be together; she urged the doctor to reveal more findings.

Where to begin? It hadn't been quite a eureka moment as she still didn't have all the answers. There were so many anomalies arising from the tests that she had insisted on them being repeated multiple times, but the results had all come back the same. She would have an immense task in compiling a credible paper for her peers yet alone imparting these revelations in layman's terms to one as intelligent as Maeve. Despite the personal legacy brought about by trauma, Kersha had survived against all odds, and Donna Channing was fully aware that the implications this would have for the future of humankind were immeasurable.

'. . . Her blood belongs to an even rarer group of RH negative and carries amazing amounts of DMT. What we have seen through microscopy are some amazing holographic images showing how the pleomorphism in her cells is working perfectly in league with her symbionts to regulate bacteria. The kundalini energy centres in her body as well as her pineal appear to be fully open. Her root and sacral chakras need work but given her experiences there's no surprise there.'

'She sounds like a living yogi,' said Maeve.

AQUARIUS

'Yes, that's a fair comparison, which also provides a caveat for what I said earlier. Yogis are able to access the cosmic energy and life force known as Prana, or Chi, they sustain themselves through this energy and can survive without food or water for long periods. If Kersha has developed any kind of empathy or regard for human life, then I may have made an unintentional prejudgment. Also, the amino acids in our digestive system give off signals whenever diet is altered or restricted in any way, and so the brain's evolutionary alert mechanism fires off warning signs and we adapt accordingly. As we now know, the speed at which evolution occurs is directly related to the degree of urgency manifesting in the species' problem. As I have said, her biome is extraordinarily unique.'

The professor's attempt to tergiversate was well meant but unnecessary in Maeve's eyes. She was under no illusions. 'What about her propensity to violence? You've witnessed it first-hand now.'

'As I've indicated, all her senses are heightened, not least that most ancient and primitive part of the brain called the Reptilian complex that triggers the fight or flight instinctual response via the limbic and neocortex layers. It explains the violent nature of humans against one another. You then see the devastating repercussions due to its constant over-stimulation. The reptilian brain controls the most basic animal functions, including survival and reproduction. It has the same standards of behaviour that characterise the - fight your way out or run - instincts of reptiles and most other animals. It's a survival mechanism that is handled by a – kill or be killed – response. It does not learn from mistakes, and it does not have the capacity for either thinking or feeling. Its only function is to act. When the Reptilian brain is activated, it has total control over the emotional and rational aspects of the brain. It behaves in the neurotic legacy of the super ego, which can prevent some people from adapting and developing. It is therefore cold and rigid. It is territorial, aggressive, hierarchical, obsessive and paranoid. It is most always triggered by fear.'

'Can it be cured?'

'It's not meant to be cured; it's a natural and vital human response. We all need it in times of genuine danger, and no doubt it has served Kersha well. Our job now is to help reduce and calm those hormonal responses that produce excess cortisol and adrenalin.'

'How is that achieved?'

'Until we establish some form of verbal communication, we continue to allow her to express herself through her drawings and paintings, which are extraordinary, I might add.'

'She's so mistrustful of anyone and anything.'

'Think of her as a lone wolf you are attempting to domesticate.'

Maeve looked puzzled.

'All life operates in a morphogenic field,' explained the doctor attempting to describe Kersha's unique mitosis. 'All living cells emit light, from ultraviolet to very low frequency radio waves. Nocturnal animals operate on a frequency that enables them to see in the dark. She has that ability; she sees things, as say, a fox would at night. When we are in bright light, our brains emit more biophotons, which allows us to receive and send even more light. In the absence of any natural light, she still has the capacity to absorb and transmit at certain frequencies because her blood carries more neutrophils, which in turn, creates a higher immune response, hence her extraordinary ability to fight off disease. Why or how this is happening we still don't know except to say that her auric field appears to be in constant harmony with the Earth's circadian rhythm, even as disrupted as that appears to be right now.'

'You mean the Schuman resonance?'

'Yes. This obvious connection between the electrical body of the Earth and her DNA makes me . . .' She brought a fist to her mouth and began to almost well up as the enormity of such a thesis began to develop.

'It's almost as if you've come to a point where poetry meets science, isn't it?' offered Maeve by way of understanding, given some of the geological revelations she had uncovered in her own line of work.

'Yes – yes, exactly that,' she said taking a moment to keep her emotions in check. 'What we are seeing here is both the macrocosm and microcosm at work. Antennas work both ways. The entire electrical body of the Earth is both the sender and receiver of all the vibrations in the entire DNA, in all-living things, over all the aeons that have unfolded within her. Inside us are a trillion antennae that are both the senders and receivers of all the love and wisdom contained in the long body of our Mother Earth. The DNA in one of your cells unrolls to roughly your own height. An organism the size of a person needs an antenna roughly its own size to adequately send and receive all the information required for an entire life, from conception to death.'

'Wow!' said Maeve. 'So just imagine the combined length of *all* the DNA in *all* of your cells.'

'Indeed,' said Donna, pleased that Maeve totally understood the magnitude of her revelations. 'We have within us antennas whose combined length happens to be the right size to resonate with the entire body of the Sun and the planets all the way out to the heliopause; who could conceive such a thing? Yet the connection must be there because the ladder is unbroken. Whether or not any one of us can knowingly receive those signals or is capable of intentionally or otherwise broadcasting over such distances is a very good question and maybe one that Kersha, in time, will allow us to find an answer to.'

'One thing that has struck me about her is how remarkably white and straight her teeth are, almost perfect.'

'Oh, yes, didn't I mention? – She's a polyphyodont.'

'A what?'

'She has the ability to grow more than two sets of teeth, rather like a shark, unlike us mere diphyodonts.'

Maeve was fascinated and awed by most of the doctor's revelations. They conversed at great length, and she would have happily listened for as long as the Epigen, who was now on a roll, was prepared to continue to disclose, but she was acutely aware that she was expected in Ruston Parva some time ago and on this occasion her charge would be by her side.

'You will come back to us, won't you?'

'As long as you can guarantee she won't be the prize exhibit in some freak show,' stated Maeve.

PRECESSION

Ruston Parva

Maeve looked at Kersha, Kersha grinned back at her displaying those unfeasibly straight white teeth, totally unabashed before gazing back out the window of the MAGLEV to watch the grey-white landscape flash by. She couldn't be mad with her for disrupting her schedule, it was impossible, and it oddly reassured their commitment to one another despite the scene of devastation they had both just left behind. She was indeed unique, so unique that Professor Channing almost had to beg them to promise to return. Maeve had begun to see a different kind of uniqueness in Kersha, one that was not to be shared with doctors and scientists, but for her alone. She felt proud to be her one and only trusted companion for now, but there was a part of her that felt it wanted more than blind trust. Trust in others would come in due course, – well, maybe not so much for men – she was sure of that, but she began to wonder if Kersha would ever be able to feel and express anything else. Were there any other emotions redundant or lying dormant that could ever be brought out, shared and reciprocated? They enjoyed holding hands and showering together, but could that merely be a sign of security? She would never be the one to destroy a naivety and innocence or betray such a hard-won trust by taking any kind of advantage. She wouldn't know how to; she'd never been in such a position before.

'Ubishen n boof, Maeve,' said Kersha looking down at her hand that her guardian was now squeezing so tightly as to turn it white.

Snapping out of her musings, she hurriedly released her grip. 'Sorry,' she said while colouring up.

'S'okay,' Kersha grinned casually. That small gesture, for some inexplicable reason made Maeve's heart soar.

They flew low over a vast area of what looked like small but regular and regimented drifts of snow that were actually row upon row of photosynth tunnel for as far as the eye could see. As they neared their destination these gave way to low built, tightly knit structures that made up the thirteen-thousand-acre complex that was Ruston Parva. Way off to the southeast Maeve could just about make out the giant ice sheet that covered the Humber estuary, but what she saw triggered a series of flashing images inside her head, almost subliminal, but real enough to create a real concern, almost like a portent of impending catastrophe. As they banked away to land, the images and feelings left her but had disturbed her enough not to dismiss them outright.

The MAGLEV set them down at a building at the south end of the complex, a structure externally that was not unlike the Healing Centre in Ampleforth. As they entered hand in hand, Maeve recognised a familiar figure waving to them.

'Maeve, sweetheart; we thought you would never get here.'

'Aunt Elena,' exclaimed Maeve, both shocked and surprised. 'Is that you?' They met with a warm, loving embrace that lasted a tad too long for Kersha's liking, but instead of going off on one, she merely stood back, head bowed in a spot of childlike jealousy rather than shyness. Maeve was quick to include. 'So, this is Kersha - Kersha, this is my aunt Elena . . .'

'C . . .'

'No, don't say that word, say hello.'

"lo,' she muttered reluctantly without making eye contact.

'It's so nice to meet you, Kersha.' Elena went for the hug but received the now all too familiar rebuff. She glanced at Maeve questioningly.

'It's nothing personal. I'll tell you all about it when we get a moment; it's quite a story.'

'Hmm – does it involve that?' She pointed to the fresh jagged little scar in the middle of her niece's forehead.

'Yes,' she fingered the wound and smiled reflectively. 'Yes, it does.'

'I'm intrigued. Are you okay?'

'Oh, yes, I'm fine, and how about you?' she said, changing the subject. 'You're looking well; I had no idea you'd be here.'

'Yes, I'm to be your guide and chaperone for the duration of your stay. I've scheduled your talk for later, give you a chance to get acclimatised, prepare and relax if you need. Have you been here before?'

'No, never.'

'Great, let's give you a tour . . .'

The three of them strolled through the spacious foyer arm in arm and hand in hand, Maeve taking great interest in the monotone pictures that adorned the walls, depicting scenes of the old hamlet that was once Ruston Parva with its ancient church, farmsteads,

PRECESSION

windmills and a transcript of its entry in The Doomsday record.

'Have you spoken with Mum?' asked Maeve.

'Yes.'

'Is she well?'

'Still bemoaning the bloody cold, and the fact you haven't been in touch or answered her calls, but terribly excited about the recent sunspot activity.'

'I know, I know; I'm a terrible daughter. So, it's really happening, then; the GSM is completing its cycle?'

'Looks that way. What's even more pleasing for those guys up there is the predictions were spot on; the data's been borne out, which bodes well for moving forward. We just need to see what you and your buddies come up with now. – Nervous?'

'A little.'

'You'll be fine. Just be yourself. From what I've heard, Beresford and his team were mightily impressed with your findings.' She gave Maeve a broad smile that exuded faith and confidence; it was something that ran in the family.

Elena Fortune was older and slightly taller than her sister, apart from that, not much could separate their characters. Born eighteen and twenty old time years after The Shift, they grew up on the Catterick garrison in hard but relatively safe conditions. Theirs was the generation that carried the hope of innovation and development beyond the legacy of sheer survival. Massive responsibilities were heaped on their shoulders and the two sisters, schooled hard, took to their education with an intuitive, inbuilt fervour that created an almost obsessive competitiveness between them. Now innovators in their respective fields, the fervour had diminished but the competitive edge still bubbled under. Maeve wasn't entirely sure what Elena's role was as they didn't assign fixed titles here at Ruston, but she was aware that her aunt was multi skilled and played a vital part in the development and running of this vast complex.

They were led through an ultraviolet shower before entering a large brightly lit space where all manner of plant and vegetation was growing behind tall vertical glass-like walls. In another section hanging from grid-like structures were regimented rows of various greens being reared hydroponically and tended by workers dressed in hemp paper coveralls.

'This is one of our orchards,' stated Elena stepping through a set of giant doors that had opened up before them. A heady scent of fruit and blossom hit them as they entered. Senses that had lain dormant sprung to life as the two girls gazed in wonderment at the vibrant colours and sheer scale of what appeared before them. They boarded a mini-MAGLEV cart that transported them slowly down seemingly endless avenues that were lined with trees and vines. Orange gave way to lemon, to reds and purples, all set against a backdrop of lush, variable green.

Maeve began to get a dose of hopeium, it surged up into her chest and she offered up thanks and gratitude to the visionary botanists who devised and engineered this mammoth undertaking in her great grandfather's day, but she knew that if all this was ever going to prove a vital legacy in the survival of mankind, there were potential problems that needed to be urgently addressed as the time of the great thaw approached, and she prayed that Beresford and his team were on top of the tasks that lay ahead, because she had seen things, things that, if proven correct, would be of great concern.

'Pear!' exclaimed Kersha, pointing excitedly. She leapt from the moving cart and swiftly plucked three pieces of fruit from a tree.

'Oh – I don't think they will be quite ripe yet,' said Elena by the time the girl had taken her third bite.

'It won't matter to her,' stated Maeve flatly. 'Pears are her favourite.' They watched her devour it stalk and all as was her wont, while generously offering up the other two with a broad grin on her face.

On entering one of the many aviaries, Kersha became wide-eyed at the abundance of flying meals on offer. Once again, she was off the cart in a flash. Gathering up a stone from the side of the track, she deftly loaded it into her catapult and was taking deadly aim at two plump wood pigeons perched high on a bough before Maeve hastily intervened.

'Arrggh . . .' she screamed in frustration with animal in her eyes.

'Oh, my,' exclaimed Elena.

Although she now had a full belly, Kersha's survival instinct still held sway, and she wasn't about to pass up an opportunity like this. She'd never seen so much feathered sustenance gathered together in one place. It was at this point that Maeve thought now might be the time to give her aunt the lowdown on this mysterious young woman.

'I know what you're about to ask,' said Maeve to Elena who was now looking slightly nonplussed. And the answer would be the same one given to Donna Channing, Helen Vaughn and all the others who had asked before, in that she simply didn't know how any of this would fit into her life, but she had made a conscious commitment and from that she would let the chips fall where they may.

'And you're still finding time to write your gospel?' enquired Elena in relation to the many undertakings her niece had been tasked with.

'Ha – it's hardly a gospel, but yes, I continue to write.'

'We were all so very proud when you were offered the gig, you know.'

'Hmm, there are many other scribes who have been asked to contribute; my offerings may not even make the final cut,' she said with diffidence.

'Nonsense. You sound just like your father, too much false modesty. I won't hear of it.'

'And you just sound like my mother,' she laughed, remembering the driving force that had helped her attain so many achievements at such a young age.

They moved on to be shown fields of hemp and bamboo in myriad strains and hybrids respective to their purpose, from clothing to construction to food, fuel and medicine; just two of Nature's many abundant gifts to mankind that had been cynically suppressed and abrogated by the old cabal.

Pushing their way through another giant set of doors, they entered a vast hanger-like space where fungi were being cultivated on an industrial scale. Floor to ceiling Archimedes screws trammelled streams of dried mycelium and other binding agents through heating and cooling chambers at rates of four tonnes an hour. Towering stacks of moulds of varying design were wheeled between growth chambers and vast drying racks. The chambers were digitally controlled microclimates where light, humidity, temperature, oxygen and carbon dioxide levels all varied in carefully programmed cycles. As Elena explained, the system had been devised from studying termites and their unique mycological association and reliance on fungi. It was the industrial human equivalent of a Macrotermes termite mound. She went on to show how mycelial materials, all grown on waste, were replacing plastics, brick, concrete and other polluting building methods of the past. Lightweight, water resistant and fire retardant, they were stronger than any other construction material, when subjected to stress, excluding hemp bast and bamboo, and exhibited better insulation values all round. Thousands of square feet of mycelial leather could be grown in less than fifty clicks on material that would otherwise be disposed of, and at the end of its life could be composted and recycled.

'One of the ways fungi are helping save the planet is by restoring the contaminated eco systems,' said Elena, now relishing in her role as tour guide and educator. 'In something called mycoremediation, fungi become collaborators in environmental clean-up operations. They have a remarkable appetite for a range of toxins and pollutants. In here,' she said pointing to an annexed laboratory, 'we're developing ways to break down chemicals and neurotoxins that were left to us as legacies both from our poisoned past and exacerbated by The Shift. Fungi are some of the best qualified organisms for environmental remediation. Mycelium has been fine-tuned over countless aeons of evolution for one primary purpose – that is to consume.'

At the seed bank they donned thermals and entered a vast vault that was kept at a constant temperature of minus twenty degrees and contained over five billion seeds from over fifty thousand plant species from across the world.

'Impressive,' said Maeve. 'How were they all sourced?'

'Most were rescued from the Millennium seed bank in Sussex, some were donated from Svalbard in Norway, others smuggled into the country just before The Shift. This place is key to our survival; it's quake, radiation and flood proof.'

'It's going to need to be.'

'We are well aware that this region will become coastal. It was chosen for its elevation and relative stability, but more importantly for its geophysical properties. It is centred over two intersecting dragon lines. Our data shows we will not be affected by isostatic rebound.'

'It's not rebound that concerns me.'

'Oh?'

Maeve sighed, not really knowing how she would qualify what she was about to say. 'You know how I just described the orb phenomenon and the intellect that seemed to bring about the manifestation?' Elena slowly nodded. 'Well, on our approach earlier I experienced a similar feeling except it came to me this time in like a series of short flashes; images that appeared in my mind's eye as I looked southeast from the MAGLEV, almost as if it were a portent of things to come.'

'And what did you see?'

Maeve sighed once again; not certain she should be imparting unfamiliar visions without hard data backup. 'South of Driffield the Asthenosphere is unstable. After the rebound it will become fluid, and the plate will slip and sink all the way down to the estuary. The incoming water will act like a tsunami. The whole area will form a delta of similar magnitude as the Avon-Severn. I estimate you will permanently lose approximately five thousand acres.' She looked apologetically at her aunt. 'Look, I'm no mage, and I don't know or understand why I'm experiencing any of this, but I was always taught to trust my instinct, and now that instinct is being supplemented with visuals, well – I don't know what else to say. Should I mention it in my presentation? They'll laugh me out of the room without data to back any of this up.'

Elena thought long and hard before replying. 'This site was selected long ago after much research, study and deliberation from people who were renowned in their field of expertise, many of whom are no longer with us . . .' She pondered some more. '. . . If these visions, this intuition of yours has any merit, there may be one person I know who might be able to corroborate or refute your claims with any degree of accuracy without further long-term study.'

'But studies will need to be done.'

'Yes, of course, but if you are right then I want your findings to be announced alongside your scheduled presentation whilst you are here.'

'Beresford and his crew must be losing patience with me already. And ratifying my claims is still going to take time. Who is this person anyway?'

'Her name is Moira Duggan; she was one of the major architects that drew the blueprints for Ruston Parva. She was also one of the most respected Geomancers of her generation. Her work in divining this land and discovering the subtle energies that flowed alongside and through the intersecting dragon lines was key for the collective selection and agreement of this site. Moira is a very old woman now living in quiescence near Aviemore in Grampia. She, more than anyone, will be able to confirm your predictions.'

'But surely there are geomancers among Beresford's team who would be able to conclude one way or the other without imposing on

AQUARIUS

an old lady in her twilight?'

'Yes, maybe, but no one still carries the respect and clout that she does, and I have a feeling that she will be most intrigued to meet and debate you and your discoveries. And as for Beresford, you can leave him to me. He still hasn't been informed of your arrival, and I'm sure I can put him off for a few more clicks.'

Elena Fortune was being clever if not entirely ulterior in her thinking. Maeve's revelations delivered with such insight and assuredness, despite the accompanying diffidence, told her that her young niece had acquired a latent yet burgeoning gift. She had already got members of Beresford's team dropping her name. She could see her star rising, and because Elena came from that ambitious, opportunistic side of the family, she would facilitate that rise at every opportunity. Maeve needed a mentor, and she saw Moira Duggan as that mentor. She would have no qualms persuading the old woman from her recluse all the way back to the object of her vision now manifest in order to meet the remarkable young woman who could potentially take on her mantle.

§

Moira Duggan smiled to herself. Despite her obvious physical frailties, her mind was still as sharp as a tack, and that reflected in the mounting sense of intrigue, almost excitement she was feeling inside right now. She had never flown in a MAGLEV before, and as the silent machine rose majestically above her relatively isolated homestead her smile broadened while she looked down on curious members of her community as they came out from their crofts and dwellings all along the frozen river Spey to follow the unusual contraption in the sky.

She had greeted the request at first with total disinterest and dismissal, but the persuasive methods of Elena Fortune combined with her niece's remarkable story had finally piqued her curiosity. Why the hell not? she had thought. She had become bored to death anyway, whiling away the time in her self-imposed semi reclusiveness; besides it would be good to get what might be a final look at the ongoing development of what was one of her pet projects. Inwardly, she had been surprised but none the less pleased that her name and legacy was still remembered.

PRECESSION

Before the MAGLEV banked old south towards the Cairngorms, Moira saw physically for the first time the results of The Shift on The Great Glen Fault. It brought up a swell of emotions. Gone were the great lochs from Lorn to Moray. The sight of the vast tract of ice sheet that now filled the chasm that separated the North-West Isle from Grampia, both shocked and awed her. It was as she and the teams that came before her had predicted, but to see it first hand from such an elevated position left her both speechless and tearful, a strange mix of validation, unwanted confirmation and benediction.

Crossing over The Highland Boundary Fault, a great divide that would eventually link the Clyde with The Forth, Moira could clearly make out the areas of land that she, as a young woman had dowsed along with her geomancer colleagues that created relatively safe havens from the effects of The Shift and were best placed to provide sanctuary and shelter from any outside influence or insurgents. They now formed well-established communities across the harsh landscape, and as she reflected on her life, long and hard as it had been, she was beginning to draw great comfort for what she now saw as a privilege to behold her life's work in such a manner.

She had been especially curious and excited to see the Humber-Mersey, or M62 cut, as it became known, from up above. The fault was initially believed to extend from the River Mersey into The Trough of Bowland, but it was later found unexpectedly to continue through The Pennines and across Yorkshire. Without the magnitude of the other three divides, it was still an anomaly that had caught all the experts, including her, by surprise. The scale of the subsequent uplift of land from Leeds into what was The Vale of York gifted them a plateau on which they could implement a plan for survival long in the making, a colossal, some said impossible undertaking, given the climate and subsequent lack of resources, but it had worked and continued to work. Ruston Parva became a model; its blueprints shared amongst those bastions of civilization across the world who knew what was coming and had been prepared. A time would come when it would not be needed. It will outlive its purpose once the waters recede. Former farmland in Lincolnshire, Norfolk, Suffolk, and Kent will become largely salt marsh. Above sea level, lush, fertile valleys will replace the once frozen tundra on the newly formed archipelago, becoming the breadbasket for its inhabitants.

Moira had been given verbal control of the MAGLEV and was now quite enjoying herself as it swooped, banked or hovered under her command over the vast site she had helped pioneer but now hardly recognised. She ordered it south over Driffield. Clutching two crystals she produced from a small hemp bag, she closed her eyes and connected to the ether, giving notice of her intent. The crystals soon began to produce heat, and she was guided southwest down towards Tibthorpe, then back northeast past Driffield again, up to Burton Agnes. She chuckled to herself, pleased at the responses she was getting, happy that her abilities hadn't deserted her over time. And sure enough, she soon began to get confirmation that there indeed was asthenospheric instability under the permafrost, a phenomenon that they had failed to discover back in the day. She mapped the area all the way down to the estuary, feeding the coordinates and references into the MAGLEV's computer, thinking how easy things would have been if she'd have had access to this kind of technology back then. But of course, just like the remarkable young woman she was now dying to meet, she possessed a latent gift so precious that no gadget could ever hope to replicate.

Pointing stark and forlorn to the blank grey sky, she circled what remained of the two rusting skeletal supports that once formed part of the old Humber crossing. She detected current deep beneath the ice sheet, slow and barely perceptible, but there was movement, she was sure of it. Moira knew that this time would come, as they all did, but she never would have predicted she'd get to see such geological phenomena begin to manifest in her lifetime. A feeling of trepidation and excitement began to stir within her; something she hadn't felt since she first saw Nibiru appear in the sky as a child. Pointing the MAGLEV back in the direction of Ruston she reflected on a life cursed to witness unspeakable natural disasters and yet blessed with the experiences and tests presented so to withstand, survive and ultimately thrive despite them.

Eager to compare notes with her soon to be protégée, the feeling of trepidation and excitement began to give way to one of renewed energy and vigour. It seemed her life's work was not yet over, and for that she smiled to herself and gave up a silent prayer of gratitude.

Jorge Beresford was somewhat annoyed with Elena Fortune for keeping him out of the loop, but his exacerbation was tempered by the revelation that none other than Moira Duggan, no less, was waiting patiently for an audience with him.

PRECESSION

'Bloody hell, Elena!' he exclaimed feeling honoured privileged, confused and flustered all at once. 'How could you do this to me?'

'Oh, do relax, Jorge,' she said in a slightly supercilious tone. 'This all came to light out of the blue, and I felt that I needed to act on it immediately. I know that you're overextended with the implementation of the new CO_2 generators, and the mere mention of involving Moira Duggan in all of this would have you vacillating all over the place. Anyway, once you see the findings I'm sure you'll agree that time is of the essence.'

'I still would have liked to have been briefed,' he said, failing to let go all his exasperation. 'And how on Earth did you manage to get Moira Duggan all the way down here? I wasn't even sure she was still with us,'

'Oh, she very much is, and on form too, I might add,' Elena said with a cryptic smile knowing this would wind him up some more.

'And Miss Bradley?'

'They've been introduced, comparing notes as we speak.'

Jorge let out a sigh, wishing he could exact a little more speed from the cart they were travelling in as they manoeuvred their way through a forest of willow and hemp.

Moira Duggan and Maeve Bradley had come together like they were long lost buddies, the frail old woman and the boyish young girl beaming smiles of mutual admiration at one another at their introduction. Maeve had been instantly amazed, not only at the sight of her diminutive stature but of the obvious physical fragility she felt in her warm embrace that yet belied a sense of inner strength and fortitude that also shone from her dark, heavily lined eyes. Moira had been as equally shocked to behold such an unassuming youthful creature. With unashamed familiarity she had cupped her head in her hands and gazed into her face, mapping every facet of her features before nodding to herself knowingly.

'It's such a great honour to meet you, Miss Duggan,' said Maeve, colouring up.

'Oh, the honour is all mine, dear,' Moira replied in her soft Highland lilt. I've been hearing so much about you; we're going to have so much fun working together.'

'I do hope so.'

'Hope has nothing to do with it, my dear; I don't state anything

AQUARIUS

without being certain of it . . .'

Jorge Beresford had been a very young and raw scientist when Moira Duggan held sway around these parts. He remembered her as being approachable, but she always carried with her an air of forthrightness that could sometimes be intimidating. Questions had to be carefully thought out because if you posed something to her that she deemed otherwise, she would fix you with a steely stare until you scuttled away to solve the problem yourself. Jorge had been a good student, very thorough in his work, but when you reached a level of competence and expertise in your field that carried responsibility, she would take you to task if you reneged on that responsibility in any way. Jorge was now multi skilled, a renowned geologist, biologist and botanist and an innovative organiser, he was at the top of his game, but an unknown intern had discovered a geological anomaly on his doorstep that he and his team had failed to discover. The teacher was back in the house and the man in charge now felt like that raw nervous student that he was back in the day.

'Moira!' he exclaimed as he burst through the door a little over dramatically. 'If I'd have known you were . . .'

'Ah, Jorge – there you are,' she interrupted, barely glancing up from her notes in acknowledgement. 'It's so good to see you after all this time. How are you? Come and see what we've discovered.'

Jorge opened his mouth to speak but nothing came out. He meekly obeyed her instruction, slightly relieved at least that she remembered who he was.

The sense of intrigue was tangible amongst the chattering hubbub of noise being created by the thirty or so gathered scientists. Some were feverishly working away on their pads trying to gather and assimilate any data they could find in relation to the Chinese whispers that abound. Others simply excited at the prospect of being addressed by none other than Moira Duggan, if the rumours were true.

All noise and any speculation soon gave way to an astonished and respectful silence as Elena Fortune took to the small stage slowly followed by a slightly bent old woman being supported arm in arm by two young girls. As they approached the lectern, one or two of the older scholars rose to their feet in total recognition and began a round of spontaneous applause. The remainder quickly followed suit until the whole theatre was stood clapping in adulation. Meanwhile, Maeve sat Kersha down at the back of the theatre making sure she was equipped with plenty of drawing material to keep her occupied. Moira acknowledged the kind reception with a shaky wave of the hand and a humble bow of the head, before indicating visually that they should all now sit down and shut up.

While Elena made the introductions and gave a small speech, Maeve's nerves began to rack up at the prospect of addressing her peers. Although she had prepared meticulously for her London Library presentation, the other scenario would be a little harder to explain. Even Beresford had shown scepticism in front of Moira at the findings until he was shown their respective slides and data that when overlaid were almost identical. Moira had told her not to worry. This had been Maeve's discovery, and she should be the one to present the findings. Moira had assured her that she would be there to field any awkward questions that might arise. They were on the same page with this, and she would back her all the way.

Maeve cleared her throat and let out a long sigh. She glanced sideways at Moira Duggan who was sat as erect as her aged body would allow, her arms stretched out holding onto the brass topped cane in front of her. She smiled a crinkly smile and gave her young accomplice a confident wink.

'. . . As we saw across that fault and into the Aire valley, the asthenosphere rose lifting the lithosphere with it, elevating large swathes of land to their present positions, at the same time protecting areas like old Leeds from any future catastrophe. What we have here is the same phenomenon, except that the areas marked on SIM 17 on your pads show the extent of the subduction zone that will eventually facilitate the roll back of the asthenosphere taking the lithosphere with it to fill the space it vacated.'

A scientist from the audience raised his hand.

'Yes?'

'Does this mean that all the breakwaters and defences we're laying down in the estuary are futile?'

'I'm afraid so. No matter how much tonnage from however many of the old cities you lay down, it won't be enough to hold back and prevent what is to come. The resulting tsunami will extend its reach to the areas shown on SIM 18. Our calculations show that you are likely to lose up to 35 percent of hemp production, and as you can see, this particular building will be under approximately six feet of water. Will these levels subside? – Yes, but at what rate and timescale has not yet been ascertained . . .'

As she wound up the presentation, Maeve realised she'd been in the zone. Time had stood still, and she had no idea how long she'd been up there, but judging by the round of rapturous applause she was now hearing it had all gone rather well. She glanced down at Moira who was nodding her head proudly and beaming up that crinkly smile. Maeve closed her pad and feeling immense relief now that it was all over, allowed herself to wallow in the appreciation she was receiving. But not everyone present was feeling so approving. They had been starved of attention lately, and it just wouldn't do. But they knew of a sure-fire way of getting that attention back. The sound of applause soon gave way to gasps of shock and incredulity. The gathered throng of scholars began to point wide eyed beyond the now confused looking Maeve, the triumph quickly leaving her features. She slowly turned to see Kersha, who had all this time been sat in the background sketching on her pad, finish defecating openly on the stage while crouched staring at her defiantly and mouthing the now inevitable word – 'Cunt.'

§

'It's not fucking funny, Elena.'

'Oh, yes, it is,' she managed to blurt in between bouts of hysterics, 'and you really shouldn't swear like that in front of your auntie.'

Maeve tutted and shook her head at such a puerile display from somebody who should know better, but it only served to set her off some more.

'Your face – oh my, your face . . .'

'So embarrassing; God knows what Moira must have thought.'

Elena continued to snort and chuckle at the picture now firmly embedded in her mind, so much so that she had to set her cup down in fear of spilling its contents. 'Oh, dear – I've not laughed so much in ages,' she said wiping away tears. 'Such a bizarre image.'

PRECESSION

'It was to be my finest hour,' Maeve lamented. 'You said people would be lining up to offer their approbation and plaudits, now they're passing me by with awkward smiles and faint nods of the head – *There goes the genius with the freak.*'

'Oh, don't worry about them, they'll come around.'

'I can't do this, Elena; I thought I could, but I can't . . .' Maeve unexpectedly burst into tears, taking her aunt totally by surprise. Elena had tried to make light of the whole incident, but for Maeve the family stoicism had finally failed her.

'Hey – hey, what's all this?' said her aunt, falling into her embrace. 'What can't you do?'

Kersha, who had been alerted by her sobbing, had abandoned her drawing and was now attempting her own version of comforting as she joined the huddle. 'Sup, Maeve? – Sup?'

'This – I can't do this,' she replied to Elena with genuine pain in her eyes. She planted a kiss on Kersha's forehead. 'Nothing, babe, It's okay – I'm okay,' she said composing herself. 'Why don't you go make me a drawing, eh? Do a drawing just for me,' she indicated to her with a mix of words and sign.

'Okay, Maeve,' she said, slightly bewildered.

Maeve wiped the tears from her eyes and watched her back to her station with a fond but hopeless look. 'I made a promise to her. I said I'd never leave her alone again – I can't keep that promise, can I?'

'No, you can't,' replied Elena, hoping not to sound harsh.

Moira and Maeve had been asked to oversee the redevelopment of the south-eastern sector of Ruston. They had also been tasked with finding a suitable site for the relocation of the National Library currently housed in Boston Spa. Moreover, a Chronicle summit was fast approaching, and her writing assessment was due. She was a victim of her own success with far too much on her plate. And then there was Kersha – oh, Kersha.

'Have you ever been in love, auntie?' she asked biting her lip while staring into space.

'Erm, I guess I thought I might have been at some point, but then again, I've never had a long-term partner, or children for that matter, so maybe not. Depends on how you define love I suppose. Why do you ask? – Oh, I see,' she said as the penny dropped. 'Are you . . .?'

'I don't know. I – I have these feelings; I'm not sure what they are. I feel so responsible for her. She has no one else. I – I find myself staring at her and I can't communicate. I feel – oh, I don't know what I feel; I'm so confused.'

'Hmm, well now, there's a surprise. I must confess; I didn't see that coming. Has she, erm – y'know, has she given you any signs or . . .'

'This is just it; I don't know, she has no filters; she's unashamed about anything and everything. Until we can communicate properly, I don't know how to deal with these feelings. I just don't want to betray her trust.'

'Bloody hell, girl, you have got yourself into a predicament, haven't you? Okay, let's think about this for a moment. You know you can't be with her twenty-four seven, as they used to say, and she has to understand this.'

'But she doesn't. The last time I left her in Ampleforth she trashed the place.'

'So, we do it with pictures.'

'How do you mean?'

'Apart from a few choice words, her only language is through her drawings, so until such time she learns to vocalise and fully understand what you're saying, you talk through pictures.'

'Ha, I can't draw to save my life.'

'So, we find someone who can.'

'I promised Donna Channing we would return to allow her to continue her analysis and observe Kersha's development. Perhaps she could help.'

'I'll speak with her directly. We'll find a way through all this.' She placed a reassuring hand over Maeve's as Kersha approached with her completed sketch. It was a triptych; the first depicted a sad looking Maeve with tears rolling down her cheeks. The second showed what was obviously Maeve and Kersha in a close embrace, kissing, and the third of a happy, smiling Maeve. Although hastily drawn, the observance in the features was so amazing that both Maeve and Elana gasped in delight. 'Oh, my, that is wonderful, sweetheart.'

'Like this?' Maeve took hold of Kersha around the waist and enacted the middle sketch with a hug and heartfelt kiss on the lips.

'Ah, yes, we'll find a way through all this,' said Elena Fortune looking on.

The relocation and fortification of the south-eastern part of the complex would be a major undertaking in and of itself. Beyond the planning stage, the project would be time prohibitive for Maeve. The blueprints that she and Moira Duggan had drawn up would have to be followed to the letter, and she knew of only one team she could trust to carry out such a task in her absence.

'So, do you think you and your guys are up to it then, Spunky?'

The Irishman reached up and scratched at his whiskers with the fingers of a giant calloused hand. 'Yer not askin' fer feckin' much, are yers, Bradley?' he growled while poring over the plans.

'Keeping half the nation alive could depend on it.'

'Well, seeing as yer put it like that . . .' He gave her a sideways glance through narrowed eyes.

'I shan't be around to oversee,' she said smiling up at him.

'Good!'

Jed Murphy wasn't superstitious in any way, but as soon as he'd gotten the call and been given the brief, his heart had sunk a little. Anything that had the stamp of this young woman on it had the portent for potential disaster written all over it. Against his better judgement he had reluctantly accepted the gig, as a decline to council wouldn't sit well on his CV.

'You'll be working alongside Fortune, Beresford and Duggan, and do try and treat them with a bit of respect; they all know what they're doing.'

'Sure, as long as the old girl doesn't get in me way; looks like she could croak anytime.'

'I'm assured that the old girl is quite fit and formidable. I'm sure she would wipe the floor with you if you got on the wrong side of her.'

'Yeh, whatever,' he said dismissively, closing down the screen and stretching out his large frame. 'I see you've still got yer pet Lazor,' he observed with a nod of the head.

Maeve sighed. 'It's been really great to see you again, Jed, but I have to go now,' she smiled through gritted teeth while ignoring the remark. 'Give my regards to Nav when he gets here.' Maeve sauntered over to Kersha who was tucking into a bowl of strawberries freshly harvested from one of the fruit sheds, she picked one out, placed it between her lips, and with great deliberation invited Kersha to take a bite. As their mouths came together, she made it look as sensual as she dare, all the while making sure the big man had a clear view. As they left the room hand in hand, Maeve looked over, smiled and raised her eyebrows.

Jed, open mouthed, watched them leave. 'The feck . . .' he said under his breath.

§

Maeve made good on her promise to return Kersha to Ampleforth and Dr Channing led them both into the room grinning from ear to ear.

'Oh, my Goodness!' Maeve stood there surveying the scene wide-eyed. Three walls were covered almost top to bottom with Kersha's "artwork".

'We've managed to sequence all her drawings. She's been trying to tell us her story all along,' declared Donna excitedly. 'What do you think?'

'I . . .' Maeve remained wide-eyed and speechless.

Kersha, unannounced launched herself at the epigen and wildly flung her arms around her. Immediately, memories of their last physical encounter came flooding back and for a brief moment the professor had fear in her eyes, but this time it was an immense show of gratitude. The young girl continued to hold onto her tightly, all feelings of past frustration now evaporating. Tentatively returning the embrace, Donna looked to Maeve for signs that everything was okay.

'Well, I'm still not entirely sure as to what you've done here,' said Maeve eventually while scanning the room in bewilderment, 'but you've certainly won her approval.'

'Donna good – not cunt,' stated Kersha, finally relinquishing her hold.

'Why, thank you, Kersha; that's er – very kind of you – I think . . .'

Taken aback by the reaction, Donna continued to look to Maeve for guidance, but she merely smiled and shrugged her shoulders.

Buoyed by the breakthrough, Kersha dragged her newfound ally by the hand and proceeded to move around the gallery using a melange of noise, sign and the odd decipherable word to point out the occasional areas where the storyline had been erroneously misplaced. The pair soon began to build a stilted dialogue between

PRECESSION

them, and a crude understanding of what she had been trying to portray began to emerge. Maeve watched on fascinated as Kersha dipped into her backpack and produced her recent volume of work. Spreading reams of paper across the floor, she excitedly spun her tale while Donna, now on her knees, surrounded by sketches, listened patiently and intently. What to Maeve had first appeared to be the crude, angry scribblings of a child, now seen as a whole, began to take on a cohesiveness, one that was still undeniably dark and cryptic, a saga so obviously full of sadness and touched by evil, but one that now at least could be disentangled and partly understood thanks to the dogged determination and skill sets of this dedicated epigenesist.

'I can't thank you enough,' said Maeve, zipping up her thermal and strapping on her backpack.

'Nonsense,' said Donna, laughing. 'I should be thanking you. After all, you kept your promise and brought her back into our midst.'

'I wouldn't trust her with anyone else, you know that.' They both gazed fondly at the object of their attention who was happily engaged with a group of her newfound younger friends, showing them how to knock down towers of building blocks with balls of paper fired from her catapult.

'Think she'll be okay this time?'

'You kidding? You're her bestie now; I'm definitely playing second fiddle. Anyhow, I've told her I'll be back in twenty sleeps. I think she understands.'

Donna nodded in agreement. 'She's not stupid. We're making great progress. She'll be talking fluently by the time you get back.'

Maeve laughed at her optimism. 'As long as she's toilet trained – is all I ask.'

AQUARIUS

Percival Snodgrass

Dressed in a moth-eaten maroon velvet smoking jacket complete with embroidered hat and resplendent with matching tassel, the rather decrepit looking dude donned his wire-rimmed glasses and randomly selected a playlist from his pad. It was an old school classic hip-hop mix from the nineties. He took a long toke of his spliff as the strains of Heavy Koolaid by Alais Clay filled the reading room. He chuckled to himself as the storical poignancy of the lyrics hit home, quite unintentionally as it happened, but nevertheless it would serve to help him set the tone for the many subjects he would cover in his lecture. He supplemented the hit from the cannabis by skulling a draught of powdered peyote before wiping the residue from his sparse, unkempt beard and letting out a satisfied sigh. Opium and laudanum would have been the more appropriate choice of intoxicants, given his attire and tenuous nod to Carroll and Wilde, but those things weren't so readily available, even the peyote had been hard to come by.

There weren't many adjectives left in the English language to accurately describe Percy Snodgrass. Unconventional? Hardly, seeing as convention hadn't yet re-established itself. Eccentric? Too much of a generalisation now that eccentricity was no longer an anomaly. Genius? Debatable. Mad? Maybe, given the seemingly endless plethora of intoxicants that he happily swallowed or inhaled. Throwback? Only insofar as he had the uncanny ability to present himself from any age, genre or culture that he so wished. In the now, he had adopted a slight Victorian attitude that may or may not morph into something else once the cocktail of drugs had kicked in.

Percival Henry Snodgrass was born on the day the Earth stood still. The only child of John Henry and Clarice Snodgrass, two infamous storians and anthropologists who dared to challenge accepted dominant his-torical narratives, and, who in turn, were subsequently and ironically erased from his-tory, as per the standard modus operandi of the oppressor. He was a studiously gifted boy who quickly took on the mantle of his guardians, absorbing himself in their work, constantly revising and discovering new truths about the past and debunking the lies that were written in a way to justify

PRECESSION

the social, political and economic hegemonies of the day. From an early age he had begun to study all the ancient theologies, the teachings of the Gnostics, the evolved wisdom of the Sumerians and the Mayans. He deciphered and decoded texts and gospels that were often laid out cryptically or shrouded in metaphor, that his forbears had obfuscated on or deliberately ignored, all pertaining to the end time that he had been born into. But he wasn't the first. There had been countless scholars from all sciences who had delved into the esoteric written knowledge of the ancients, who had been ignored, pilloried and condemned as his-torical heretics. To these men and women, he made sure to pay homage and recognition within the pages of his own work. Now, having been recognised as one of the most revered and respected storians of his time, he had been encouraged by his peers to document definitively mankind's struggle from the time biblically known as Armageddon, a time that encompassed the passing of Nibiru and the subsequent magnetic reversal of the Earth's poles. It was to be a New Testament for a new age, scribed initially by a select few, six men and six women, to be edited by himself and a small group of pantologists. Of these select few, Maeve Bradley had been a controversial choice, and Percy had been the prime dissenter.

As a student in the Halls of Learning up in Catterick, Maeve had dazzled her teachers with her prodigious intellect and insight into all things storical. Despite her age, her papers and essays were commended and published to great acclaim, and Percy had been advised to hold a mirror up to himself for that very reason by those who saw the paradox.

'H G Wells - perhaps the most imaginative future-dystopia novelist of his time wrote the book for which he is best known, *The Time Machine*. In an overarching sense, the work was a marvel for several generations of serious sci-fi enthusiasts; but in many ways that reputation lies in it having been the first piece of major literary fiction to take the idea of travelling forward in time . . . and reach both compelling and alarming conclusions about *The Shape of Things to Come* the title of Wells's final novel in 1933.

While Huxley and Orwell had the advantage of having seen the rise of mega-manufacturing capitalism and totalitarian media manipulation, respectively, Wells had been brought up in a period of overwhelming confidence in the British imperial model of - an Empire upon which the sun never sets - Yet astonishingly, he was the only author in the broad set of futurology who achieved the dubious honour of providing a near-perfect description of where we were heading prior to The Shift. The real genius of Wells was to see the species homo sapiens branching off into two separate but equally dangerous branches. The first and immediately visible of these was a childlike, dumbed-down and unaware sort of tamed version of humanity, called the Eloi people. Clearly, they had originally developed a life of everything being done for them automatically: they were about as far from 'natural' as one could imagine - they could not hunt, had little concept of danger and were even unable to discern the difference between one of their number larking about or actually drowning. They waved and smiled in that empty way Hippies had in the late 1960s, and their talk wasn't so much small as sub-atomic. But they were fed by a mysterious species they trusted implicitly - and upon whom they depended totally: whereas the Eloi lived on the surface of the planet, these apparently philanthropic protectors lived underground - presumably because at some point in future history the Earth had been damaged by an unspecified catastrophe that forced them to seek out the dark. Sound familiar? - These were the Morlocks. In reality, they were the diametric opposite of what the gullible Eloi imagined: cunning, brutish and dedicated to cannibalism. They fed the innocent Eloi as our ancestors might have fattened an animal for ritualistic slaughter and consumption. The reality was, the Morlocks were farming and then eating the infantile Surface People. They emerged from their subterranean dwellings during dark when the dangerous sun had set and dragged off what might soon become their next meal. Because of this, the Eloi feared the dark, which was sensible, but had been convinced by the Morlock insistence that they protected them from the dark, which er – wasn't so sensible.

The parallel with what was unfolding up to the final year of twenty-thirty is impossible to ignore. That is to say, a psychopathic, hidden and ethically void gang of inhuman humans posing as protectors feeding upon naive trust and exploiting this in order to survive. At least the Morlock apologist could argue that survival through eating is natural. The hidden élite of the day simply wanted more power and wealth despite being extremely well fed already. But apart from that, the *Time Machine* analogy with the 21st Century

PRECESSION

Great Reset is complete: blind trust in the protective motives of the Reset Alliance - given the IQ of millions who accepted such a ludicrous idea - was based on a chequered past of State government that had, for a century or more dished out welfare to protect from fear. However, along the way the pre-Shift mind-set either forgot or were wilfully ignorant of how all that came about . . .' Professor Percy Snodgrass peered out above his wire-rimmed specs. – 'Any questions thus far?' The twelve strong gathered apostles remained taciturn. 'No? – Good.' Percy lit a cannabis-filled cheroot and took a sip of sherry from a cut crystal glass. He observed his scholars with a look that could have been mistaken for disdain while blowing smoke in their direction. 'I was about to render a potted version of the relationship between state and citizen, but you all look bored to fuck, so I don't think I'll bother . . .'

Maeve took a quick discreet glance around the room to see if there was any reaction in the faces of her eleven colleagues, but there wasn't; whether this was from an insider knowledge of the man's bizarre teaching methods from everyone else present that she wasn't party to, or that they were simply overawed by his formidable intellect, she couldn't say. During a break she had approached one of the older bibliophiles and shown him the hastily scribbled note that had been left at her station, which requested her presence in Snoddy's rooms after the lectures. 'Do you think it's genuine or is someone having a laugh at my expense?' she asked.

'Oh, it's his handwriting, for sure.'

'Why would he want to see me?'

'Have you submitted your work?'

'Yes.'

'Then, my dear, I would say you are either greatly honoured and privileged, or you're in for a dammed good talking to, or dare I say, maybe worse.'

With a feeling of uncertainty and a degree of trepidation, Maeve cleared her throat before knocking on the door. Behind it could be heard the loud rhythmic thumping beat of some old rock tune. She knocked again, louder this time. There was no response. After a few further futile attempts to be heard she dared to turn the handle and cautiously stuck her head around the door. 'Professor Snodgrass?' she called out tentatively. Venturing further into the room she observed the Professor with his back to her reciting scripture from The Book of Enoch loudly in direct competition with the music

AQUARIUS

blasting out from a curious black disc revolving on some kind of platter.

Well I was born in the desert, came on up from New Orleans
Came up on a tornado, sunlight in the sky
I went around all day with the moon sticking in my eye . . .

". . . But in the days of the sinners the years will become shorter, and their seed will be late on their land, and on their fields. And all things on the earth will change and will not appear at their proper time. And the rain will be withheld, and Heaven will retain it . . ."

Got the time to teach ya now, bet you'll learn some too
Got the time to teach ya now, bet you'll learn some too
Sure 'nuff baby, sure 'nuff 'n' yes I do . . .

". . . And in those times the fruits of the earth will be late, and will not grow at their proper time . . ."

'Professor – Professor Snodgrass . . .' Maeve tried again, in vain, to catch his attention.

". . . And the Moon will change its customary practice and will not appear at its proper time. But in those days it will appear in Heaven, come on top of a large chariot in the west, and shine with more than normal brightness . . ."

Hey hey hey all you young girls whatever you do
Hey hey hey all you young girls whatever you do
Well come on by and see me I'll make it worth it to you . . .

". . . And many heads of the stars, in command, will go astray. And these will change their courses and their activities and will not appear at the times that have been prescribed for them . . ."

He turned towards her, still without any acknowledgement of her presence. She now saw he had changed his Victorian garb and was sporting a loose paisley kaftan with matching bandana tied across his forehead. A heady scent of patchouli filled the room, and from the corner of his mouth hung a cheroot at the end of a long, slim onyx cigarette holder, and behind the wire rimmed spectacles his eyes had begun to resemble piss holes in snow. She tried once more to alert him to her ubiety but he continued his recital seemingly oblivious.

". . . And the entire law of the stars will be closed to the sinners, and the thoughts of those who dwell upon the Earth will go astray over them, and they will turn from all their ways and will go astray, and will think them gods. And many evils will overtake them, and punishment will come upon them to destroy them all." With that he slammed the book shut. 'Are you familiar with the passage, Miss

PRECESSION

Bradley?' he asked without looking up.

'The book of Enoch, chapter eighty, verses two to eight – is what I was party to.' she said without hesitation. 'Although I do prefer the Kolbrin version: "When blood drops upon the Earth, the Destroyer will appear, and mountains will open up and belch forth fire and ashes. Trees will be destroyed, and all living things engulfed. Waters will be swallowed up by the land, and seas will boil.

"The Heavens will burn brightly and redly; there will be a copper hue over the face of the land, followed by a day of darkness. A new moon will appear and break up and fall.

"The people will scatter in madness. They will hear the trumpet and battle cry of the Destroyer and will seek refuge within dens in the Earth. Terror will eat away their hearts, and their courage will flow from them like water from a broken pitcher. They will be eaten up in the flames of wrath and consumed by the breath of the Destroyer . . ." Maeve paused waiting for any kind of reaction, but Percy merely stood there with his eyes closed nodding slowly, so she continued.

". . .Thus, it was in the Days of Heavenly Wrath, which have gone, and thus it will be in the Days of Doom when it comes again. The times of its coming and going are known unto the wise. These are the signs and times which shall precede the Destroyer's return. A hundred and ten generations shall pass into the West, and nations will rise and fall. Men will fly in the air as birds and swim in the seas as fishes. Men will talk peace one with another; hypocrisy and deceit shall have their day. Women will be as men and men as women; passion will be a plaything of man.

"A nation of soothsayers shall rise and fall, and their tongue shall be the speech learned. A nation of lawgivers shall rule the Earth and pass away into nothingness. One worship will pass into the four quarters of the Earth, talking peace and bringing war. A nation of the seas will be greater than any other but will be as an apple rotten at the core and will not endure. A nation of traders will destroy men with wonders, and it shall have its day. Then shall the high strive with the low, the North with the South, the East with the West, and the light with the darkness. Men shall be divided by their races, and the children will be born as strangers among them. Brother shall strive with brother and husband with wife. Fathers will no longer instruct their sons, and the sons will be wayward. Women will become the common property of men and will no longer be held in

AQUARIUS

regard and respect . . ." She paused once more, but with eyes still closed as if in some kind of rapture and with a flourish of his hand, Percy silently bid her continue.

". . .Then, men will be ill at ease in their hearts; they will seek they know not what, and uncertainty and doubt will trouble them. They will possess great riches but be poor in spirit. Then will the Heavens tremble and the Earth move; men will quake in fear, and while terror walks with them, the Heralds of Doom will appear. They will come softly, as thieves to the tombs; men will not know them for what they are; men will be deceived; the hour of the Destroyer is at hand . . ." 'Chapter three, The Destroyer, verses four to nine, I do believe,' she finished, clearing her throat.

From behind his unkempt, sparse and greying whiskers, Percy betrayed a wry smile. 'And the music?' He pointed over to the black spinning disk.

'I'm sorry, I don't . . .'

'Don Van Vliet, a.k.a. Captain Beefheart, accompanied by his most able Magic Band,' he said with a smirk, like they'd been scoring points.

'You, er, left me a note; you wanted to see me . . .?'

'Yes, I did, and lo and behold, here you are. Please, sit.' He pointed to a sofa that was fully occupied with a tangled mountain of dressing up garb. He removed the gently undulating stylus from the revolving black disc while Maeve awkwardly created a space for herself. 'Would you care for a brandy?' he asked while pouring himself a generous measure from a cut glass decanter.

'No, I don't . . .'

'No, of course not. Do excuse the mess; where cobwebs are plenty, kisses are scarce. Shall we cut to the chase?'

Cut to the chase? – Maeve hoped this summons wasn't going to be peppered with archaic phrases and cryptic terminology. Percy had a reputation for bamboozling his students thus. She would have to keep her wits about her.

'I didn't want you on this project, but much to my chagrin I was outvoted,' he stated flatly. Maeve, unable to form an adequate response to this, remained silent. 'Democracy for you, eh? – Such a flawed concept.'

'I assume you studied my work in order to reach your opinion?'

'Some of it, yes.'

'And you deemed it unsatisfactory.'

PRECESSION

'Oh, on the contrary, I found most of it highly commendable, thoroughly well researched and stylishly presented. Most satisfactory. It's just, I feared, for this particular undertaking you lacked the necessary experience.'

'Age is no barrier to knowledge; you should know that.'

'No, you're absolutely right; perhaps I'm confusing knowledge with wisdom.' He pulled at his sparse whiskers and stared into nothing. 'I do remember the copper hue.'

'I'm sorry?'

'The skies that burned redly, and the copper hue over the face of the land – chapter three, verse five that you so eloquently recited – I remember them as a boy, I can still smell the sulphur. And of course you are right, The Kolbrin is far more expressive and emotive, which brings me to my point: all those passages were scribed as prophesy from a knowledge and wisdom born from some sort of experience we can only marvel and wonder at. Velikovsky, Sitchin, Cayce, to name but a few; they all drew from these works, but all still failed to get it quite right, wouldn't you agree?'

'Well, yes but I don't ...'

'Chinese whispers, third, fourth, fifth hand, misinterpreted, altered, diluted, corrupted, politically bastardised or demonised, and yet it all came to pass as was originally set down. How shall we in our efforts follow such an ultimately immutable legacy?'

'It should be easy; we aren't in the business of prophecy.'

'Precisely. We are merely chroniclers of events unfolding before us in real time, and yet there is a real danger that we will get it all wrong.'

'How so?'

'By our perceptions. Individual experience will create unique mind maps that don't always square with absolute truth. Take for instance our good friend and oldest colleague Jarod Buchman. He lost his entire family in the great deluge that covered what is now the Avon and Somerset delta after The Shift. Another fleeing family found the young boy and took him to a garrison along with thousands of others who all had their own unique stories and experiences to tell. As you know, Jarod became a truly gifted writer and storian, and the first name to be proposed when the shortlist for our little team was drawn up. If I set you both an assignment to write about the catastrophe and the desperate scramble of the thousands of hapless souls seeking out higher ground, then no doubt through your research

AQUARIUS

and observations you would both come up with an accurate portrayal and version of events, but your perceptions would be different – why? Because he experienced a tiny, localised yet devastating part of the whole event, the subsequent trauma of which we can only guess as to what part that now plays in his psyche and perspective of something that happened long in his past. Whereas all you would have had to go on were archive, testimonies, first-hand accounts such as Jarod's. You had no experience of what you were writing about, and therefore I would expect your account to be storically factual but somewhat impassive – and yet your work is anything but. How do you do that?'

'I, er ...'

'Rhetorical. This theatre, this pantomime you see before you is merely my attempt to capture the essence of the day. If I didn't live through it, I want to at least get as close as my attempts at authenticity will allow. You see Miss Bradley; despite all the plaudits and adulation I feel that my work and that of my esteemed colleagues falls far short of the expectation of the vision. Mere chroniclers and arbiters of the truth is all we are and shall ever be. As noble as you think that may be, it is not enough.'

'Then what? Is it your desire to be seen in the light of Quetzalcoatl, Prometheus, maybe?'

'Oh, my goodness, now there's a thought,' spluttered the old man almost choking on his brandy. 'Osiris and Isis respectively – no, my dear, civilizing heroes we are certainly not, although I do find your assumption quite amusing. No, the point I'm trying to make here is that our story telling must be imbued with space for esoteric expansion. It always must be open-ended. It has to have a longevity that can be added to by future generations of scholars, like adding lustre to a diamond. If we fail at this, then our work shall be seen as a relic of its time, largely factual but stilted in its storical worth. I'm afraid that some of your colleagues have not quite understood this yet. The intellect is unquestionable, but there is something missing, and however you want to describe that missing something, I can see that your writing thankfully has it and it makes me so happy.'

Maeve's jaw dropped. 'Oh, I, erm ...' she managed, totally disarmed.

'I called you here this evening to say I'm sorry for doubting your abilities. This is my feeble attempt at a grovelling apology. It is also an informal request that you take on my mantle when I'm no longer

PRECESSION

around.'

Still open-mouthed, Maeve became ever more speechless. 'But I – I'm sorry, I just don't know what to say,' she said eventually. 'I – I mean you surely just can't make an arbitrary decision like that. It would all have to go before Council, wouldn't it?'

'Of course, like I said, this is an informal request, one that I sincerely hope you will give great consideration to. As for the ultimate decision, I do like to think that my recommendation shall come with a great deal of influence.'

Maeve still felt somewhat perplexed. She had come here this evening half expecting a damning assessment of her work, worse still maybe her removal from the project with the consolation that her workload at least would be lighter, but not this. She had read the works of Buchman and her peers, all competent and flawless in her eyes, so whatever this missing component was that Snodgrass was alluding to remained a mystery to her.

Seeing the confusion writ large across her face, he made an attempt to explain. 'They all use the phrase, Pureblood. I hate that word. It's too parochial, too limited. Our parents, our guardians, all those of us who refused the arm spear, the survivors, did so not just by avoiding the death shot. There were so many other factors at play. Look at me; is my blood pure? Of course not, it is swimming with the uncountable intoxicants I have used in my lifetime, yet I am a product of that epoch. The term is finite. It works only in its given time and place, soon to become meaningless in the grand scheme. I noticed you used the subtitle 'The Book of The Meek' in the margins of one of your essays. Where did that come from, may I ask?'

Maeve shrugged. 'It's only a term that the people are starting to use to describe us, pretty much the same as "Purebloods", I guess.'

'Yes, but Meek carries so much more nuance, don't you think?'

'Nuance or ambiguity?'

Professor Percy Snodgrass peered at her through piggy eyes and the thick-rimmed glass of his spectacles. 'I really do like the cut of your jib, Miss Bradley,' he said with a chesty chuckle.

They debated long into the night; Maeve doing her level best to navigate and decipher Percy's antiquated terminology. She argued that any word or phrase would always be open to interpretation by future generations. The word 'Pureblood' could be used to describe those pure in heart, spirit and soul, as much as the 'Royal' blue bloodline of the old ruling élite, similarly, as The Meek written about

AQUARIUS

in scripture bore no descriptive resemblance to the definition that held sway in the lexicon of the twenty-first century and beyond.

Not long into the waking period, as the candles burned low, Maeve became distracted by the curious artefacts that littered the room and adorned the walls: the Hendrix, Joplin and Grateful Dead posters, the mind-bending works of Escher, and the curious monochrome work of Aubrey Beardsley; curios from bygone eras that held little gravitas in the now, but as the professor cryptically stated: "nostalgia isn't what it used to be – but it will be again, one day . . ."

'Where did you manage to find all of this?' Maeve wondered aloud.

'My mother and father were hoarders, preppers; the ultimate survivalists you might say. We had things stored in underground cells in the most remote and secret locations. Nothing ever got thrown away, even items of little practical or survival value. The rest, I find at the barter markets in Wetherby and Thirsk.'

'I'm amazed that such trivia still exists,' she said while curiously studying a 'God Save The Queen' Sex Pistols poster that was casually leant up against an antique Victorian era baby grandfather clock.

'Trivia or cultural legacy – when does one morph from one to the other – how and why does that happen? The entities that create empires, civilisations and nations ultimately destroy them along with their culture and technologies. The subsequent reset always leaves us with almost total amnesia, until finally, almost when it's too late, we realise that there was so much more . . .'

The professor's philosophies presented as many dichotomies as absolute veracity and she began to realise this was done deliberately in an attempt to keep his students' thought process in a constant state of flux. She studied the sedentary and defunct timepiece and its near arbitrary division and sub-division of numbers that made up its face and wondered if in time, for want of a better phrase, its significance would be as close to the poster in terms of its cultural worth or otherwise now that linear time had taken a sabbatical, almost certain never to return in its previous capacity as a pacemaker for people's lives.

Percy began to slump in his chair, eyes closed, he precariously balanced the empty brandy glass on his chest that started to rise and fall in entrainment to a gentle snore. *'How long have I got you for,*

PRECESSION

you intriguingly strange man?' Maeve thought to herself. She had that curious mix of feelings again. Honoured that someone so esteemed would want to bestow his legacy on her but overwhelmed at being asked to take on such a task. She came to the realisation she now had two true vocations and two of the best mentors to help her develop these callings. For how long either of them would be around given their respective ages and lifestyles, she couldn't say, but she now understood that these unsolicited manifestations had become her destiny, and she would put her heart and soul into the gifts she had been conferred. She carefully removed the empty glass from his bony grasp and set it down next to the equally empty decanter, before extinguishing the remaining candles and exiting the room.

AQUARIUS

The Twelve Apostles

A pair of dark eyes made watery by the cold looked out East above The Aire valley. No other features were visible as Moira's head and all other parts of her face were swaddled tightly with tartan-patterned hemp. Way down in the valley a sea of frozen mist had risen above the permafrost and settled thick and flat like a becalmed grey-white ocean. The phenomenon provided further evidence that atmospheric changes were afoot, and despite Moira's safeguarding of her old bones from the harsh elements, the mercury was predictably rising.

'It's beautiful.' Maeve's breath shimmered in the air as it turned into microscopic particles before falling away.

'Yes, it's also a good benchmark as to how high the waters are likely to rise once the thaw's underway,' stated Moira.

As spectacular as it was, beneath it all lay the abandoned ruin that once was the mill city of Bradford. Looking southwest from this elevated position high on the Queensbury plateau the same phenomena could be observed way down in the Calder valley where the curious sight of Wainhouse Tower, a wealthy mill owner's flight of fancy known as a *folly,* pierced the sea of frozen mist reaching up boldly into the grey sky. The tower, built in the late eighteen hundreds, had somehow managed to survive the tectonic upheavals created by The Shift. During the Chav wars it served as an observation post and a beacon for those seeking higher ground and sanctuary.

This place was the penultimate site on their shortlist. They'd been divining almost non-stop, and although they'd been granted use of a maglev, Moira preferred to dowse on foot. Maeve marvelled at the old girl's stamina, and despite her features being closed to the elements, Maeve could sense she wasn't happy.

'You're not sure about this place, are you Moira?'

'The elevation is perfect, but nothing else is falling into place. The lines are there but there are blockages that go deep, way in the past. They will take too long to clear. Do you not feel it, my dear?'

'Yes – yes, I think I do.'

'Where?'

Maeve circled a hand over her solar plexus. 'Here.'

PRECESSION

Moira nodded. 'Where is it strongest?'

Maeve thought for a moment. 'Over here, in this direction – towards that building.' She pointed to a low-built structure off in the distance. 'What is that place?'

Moira sighed. 'That, my dear, is an old incinerator. It's where they disposed of all the bodies.'

'Aren't they called crematoriums?'

'Only where ceremony is involved. There was no ceremony in these places. Disease was the primary killer after the ravages of The Shift. The rotting cadavers of all species had to be dealt with quickly. They became a common sight across the land.' An image entered her head: stockpiled sacks of calcium oxide – mountains of quicklime shrouds for those who didn't make it. She sighed once more before slowly turning three-sixty as if to confirm her feelings. 'I think we've seen enough, our business is done here,' she said while packing away her trusted willow rods. 'Time to move on.'

They climbed the steep rise past Hangingstone rocks, known colloquially as The Cow and Calf. Behind them to the north, the millstone grit scree fell steeply away into the Wharfe Valley. Beyond the two giant mushroom-shaped outcrops known as The Doubler stones, they came across numerous rock carvings beneath the ice that Moira identified as cup and ring stones, some dating back to the Mesolithic period. Here, in such an ancient and spiritual location Moira was in her element, and despite the inhospitable terrain, she urged her young colleague onwards, yomping over treacherous snow-covered ghyll and moorland. The powerful energy of the ley became their guide and soon they stumbled across an elaborately carved Celtic era Swastika Stone. Brushing ice particles to one side, Moira studied the artefact while holding out a pair of glowing crystals in the palm of a gloved hand. With eyes closed she emitted a series of satisfied grunts, before struggling to her feet with the aid of her stick.

'This way,' she said. 'We still have a lot of ground to cover before it gets dark.'

Breathless, they finally reached the trig on the high plateau of Rombald's Moor. Moira sank to her haunches and leant her weary back against the stone. She produced a hip flask from the depths of her many layers of garments, and took a long, satisfying swig before

AQUARIUS

offering it to her student.

'What is it?'

'Whiskey.'

'Oh, I don't think I ...'

'Och, go ahead; get it down you. It'll warm your innards,' Moira insisted. Maeve took the flask and tentatively held it to her lips. The subsequent choking, coughing and spluttering sent Moira into her own fit of cackling. 'Oh my,' she laughed. 'The good stuff's not for you, my girl, is it?'

'I'll stick to my juice, if you don't mind,' she said offering back the flask while trying to wipe the burning sensation from her lips.

Maeve scanned the three-sixty panoramic view that offered the best part of what was old Yorkshire, from the recently elevated lands and escarpments away to the East to the troughs and canyons now scarring the West where great sections of The Pennies had been torn asunder. Looking North to the Dales and beyond, the high land had been left largely unscathed up to the borders. These were the regions to where large swathes of Northerners had relocated, where new autonomous communities were being formed. Even land such as this ancient moor, with its characteristic peat and heather, now dormant, would soon be at a premium. Where once roaming tribes of Briganti held sway, these exposed heights would inevitably become home to those still remaining on the vulnerable valley slopes.

By now a stealthy westward wind had begun to take shape and seemingly out of nowhere brought with it sharp, stinging sleet and hail being driven horizontal. Maeve helped Moira to her feet. Huddled together they moved perpendicular to the onslaught, guided by rod, crystal and raw intuition. Moira finally brought them to a halt. She held out her hand and pointed into the near whiteout. At first Maeve saw nothing in front of her but the driven snow, then out of the swirling grey maelstrom she began to make out the circular outline of a series of standing stones.

'What are they?'

'The Twelve Apostles.' Moira's shouted words were whipped away by the wind.

'The what?' Maeve leaned in close.

'The Twelve Apostles. They are the remnants of an ancient stone circle dating back to the Bronze Age, although the site itself is much older. There were twenty stones erected here originally, and these remains are no longer placed on the original coordinates.'

PRECESSION

'Of what significance are they to us?'

'None. It's the site itself that is important. Somewhere beneath us is a waterline. It runs in a non-linear fashion in a South-westerly direction and converges with two Michael and Mary lines that meet and cross, I would guess, approximately five to six hundred yards away. When we find it, I do believe we shall have our site.'

'Will the waterline not be frozen?'

'No, it's primary water; the electromagnetic energies keep it flowing. Once you find it, you just have to follow it.'

'You mean me?'

'Yes, my dear, I mean you. You wouldn't have an old lady dowse in these conditions, would you?'

'No – no, of course not; just tell me what I need to do.'

In truth, Moira Duggan would have and indeed had dowsed in any condition. Now was the time for her young charge to show her mettle. 'Just trust in your intuition, my dear,' she said. 'Remember to deliver your intent and ask for the best outcome.'

Maeve allowed herself to be guided to the true epicentre of the stone circle. From here she closed her eyes and began to visualise. Colours soon began to appear from her pineal and dance behind her lids. She set out her intent and repeated her affirmation in a silent mantra, and eventually, fell into what was now becoming a familiar state, where the thought process dissolved into a silent and timeless abyss. In a somnambulistic trance she paced the site, totally unconscious to her bearing or orientation. Moira watched from a distance, paying particular attention to the rods Maeve held in her hands. After a few sweeps of the area, something brought a smile to Moira's face. The rods began to twitch and then spin wildly.

'Eureka!' the old girl exclaimed. 'You've found it.' Maeve immediately stopped in her tracks and opened her eyes. 'You feel it – you feel the energy?' asked Moira excitedly. 'Now, let the rods be your guide ...'

Maeve wove her way carefully across the frozen tundra at the behest of her divining rods, Moira following in her wake beaming from ear to ear. By now the icy storm had melted away as quickly as it had appeared. The sky, normally an unmoving dense, opaque grey had acquired a peculiar dirty pink cast. To the South, ripples in the form of physical scalar waves had formed and a glow was being reflected from the Earth's icy surface. In the near distance, in front of the two women, a kestrel hovered, silhouetted now by the unusual formations in the sky above. There it remained, motionless except for the steadying beat of its wings, seemingly monitoring an invisible prey, until Maeve was directly beneath it. Immediately her rods crossed, the small raptor broke its hover and banked steeply away, flying off into the distance. Maeve, as if emerging from her hypnopompic state, turned with a degree of bewilderment.

Moira, now free and unfettered from her scarf and head coverings, her long silvery hair flowing behind her, approached with that familiar beaming smile. 'Congratulations, my dear, you've found it.'

'These are the dragon lines?'

'Yes, this is where the telluric currents converge; this shall be the site for our new library.'

'Did you see the bird?'

'Yes.' Maeve gave her an inquisitive look, expecting some enlightenment. 'Don't ask me,' Moira shrugged. 'Can only be a good sign, I guess.'

As if more confirmation were needed the sky to the Southwest all at once began to swirl and oscillate. The grey-pink blanket started to break apart and a pale, neutral light emerged through the once impenetrable gloom. The two women stood transfixed as the faint outline of a disc appeared and disappeared beyond the maelstrom of agitated cloud. And then, almost as if a veil had been lifted, a brilliant shaft of light, the like of which, Maeve had never experienced, illuminated the ground they were stood on, followed by another, and another until myriad sunbeams were highlighting localised spots that were being moved and guided by the ever-changing atmosphere.

'What does it mean?' asked Maeve, shielding her eyes.

'What it means, my dear,' said Moira Duggan while staring directly at the prodigal life giver, 'is that the true dawning of the Age of Aquarius is now upon us, and time is of the essence.'

PRECESSION

A Meeting of Minds

Moira schooled her protégée in the ancient and sacred art of divine design. Together they drew up blueprints for the new DSC using esoteric knowledge, once only privy to illuminated priests and master masons. She showed her how life was given to anything and everything, be it spiritual or physical, from inception by pure thought, to realisation through understanding how energy flows and the wondrous vehicles and naturally occurring adjuvants that are pure and free at source. Maeve learned how to harness and amplify the energies and frequencies of the Schuman resonance, the Toroidal field that surrounds everything, and the sacred geometry that aligns the design to the constellations and their stars.

As a team, they worked relentlessly. The plans had been published, and the project was almost ready to be realised. They were now studiously QS'ing, listing materials and building methods that had to be followed to the letter. At Maeve's request, Nav Buthar had been assigned to overlook the work, much to the ire of Jed Murphy who apparently had been pissed when his right-hand man had been taken off the Ruston job.

Maeve rubbed at her tired eyes and stretched up in her ergonomic chair that hadn't done much to relieve her aching back. She hadn't been sleeping much and put it down to constantly thinking about Kersha when she should have been resting. She took a glance sideways at Moira who was feverishly working away at her station and wondered how the hell the old girl did it. Out of the corner of a sore eye she saw a familiar figure approaching. Percy was kitted out in full tweed: cap, jacket, waistcoat and breeches tucked into a pair of knee length sage-coloured socks, a pair of shiny brown brogues on his feet and a crimson muffler around his neck. As he got nearer, she could see he had a monocle stuffed into one eye. For whatever bizarre scenario he was playing out in his head, Maeve deduced he was now acting the role of a country squire. She quickly grabbed Moira's attention by discreetly kicking her chair. 'Time to keep your wits about you,' she hissed through gritted teeth.

'Laydeez, laydeez,' he dramatically announced his presence. 'I did so hope to find you both here, and do forgive me for the rude interruption, but I did want to seek you out to say thank you for what you are doing and for what you have already done. I've just seen the finished plans for the new library. I can't tell you how excited I am ...'

'Percy, this is Professor Moira Duggan,' she cut him short. 'Moira, this is Professor Percival Snodgrass; I don't believe either of you have met.'

'Professor.' Moira held out a hand.

'Professor Duggan.' He took it in his own, bowed and kissed it. 'Charmed, I'm sure.'

The two women exchanged discreet but knowing looks. 'May I ask what role it is you play here, professor,' asked Moira while eyeing him up and down in his peculiar garb, 'beyond that of mentoring my young colleague here?'

'Alongside my position as resident anthropologist, I am a senior fellow among a council of thirteen who are responsible for developing and managing the collections, curating and interpreting them. In short, madam, I am also a librarian.'

'I have to apologise for bailing on you like that the other evening,' Maeve interjected in an effort to stymie the awkward silence that could have developed. 'You appeared, I suppose you would like to say – out for the count.'

'No - no need, my dear. My excesses are my excuse, which is no excuse at all. It is I who profoundly apologise to you for being such a terrible and selfish host. And by way of redemption, I cordially invite you two charming ladies to dine with me tonight with the undertaking I am to abstain from any lenitive – apart from the odd draught of the finest cognac.'

Before Maeve had the chance to think of and offer an excuse, Moira had piped up. 'Cognac, you say? Deal – we'll be there.'

'Gilgamesh and Izdubar are one and the same. You must learn to separate the Hebrew and the Ninevite from the Sumerian and Akkadian cuneiform. You must also understand that The Old Testament is not a monotheistic work, Elohim is plural, not singular, they are referring to many Gods, not just one; now go away and do your fucking research!' yelled Percy just as Moira and Maeve announced their arrival. He flung the tablet back at the young browbeaten student who hastily retreated looking all red faced and

PRECESSION

flustered, 'Ah, my honoured guests, good evening,' he said with a three-hundred and sixty reversal in tone. He lifted Moira's bony hand and kissed it. 'Madam, I speak with veracity when I say you look absolutely exquisite this evening.'

'Och, you're a sweet-talking fucker, Percy Snodgrass, I'll give you that,' she said without decorum, while secretly wallowing in the bullshit compliment, given that she still wore the same clothes from earlier in the day apart from the addition of an old Pashmina shawl.

He led them to a table dominated by a large silver candelabra and chivalrously seated them in turn. Moira, impressed by the formal layout shook her folded napkin and placed it over her lap expectantly. 'This is all rather charming,' she said. 'What are we eating this evening?'

'Ah, it's only some vegetable soup I've managed to sequester from the library's canteen, I'm afraid. My culinary skills are sadly lacking.'

'Oh, well, I do hope the brandy is still on the cards, is it?'

'Oh, but of course.' He backed away with a bow and quickly returned with his prized cut glass decanter that he brandished with an elaborate flourish. 'Would madam care for an aperitif?'

Maeve had a little smirk on her face as she witnessed the rather overly acted theatre, but she was quickly getting used to the professor's charming if not slightly annoying foibles and doubted that Moira was ever likely to fall for his faux bonhomie.

After the Spartan dinner he offered cake as a dessert, failing or conveniently forgetting to inform them that it contained herb with a sizeable THC presence as an added ingredient. The debates that followed were at once deep and illuminating if not apt to fly off in tangents at regular intervals. Maeve had never taken anything intoxicating in her life and had been ready to take him to task over his duplicity, whether it was intentional or otherwise, but as the conversation flowed, she became ensnared by the intellectual sparring taking place and finally surrendered to the shift in consciousness that felt similar to her meditative states but with added giggle content.

'. . . In the universe everything is in motion, everything is vibration. Matter, energy, mind, thoughts, emotions, and so on are all vibrations. Nothing rests; everything moves, everything vibrates,' explained Percy.

'Which begs the question: Is the universe happening to me or am

AQUARIUS

I happening to it?' posed Moira.

'Excellent question – The physical universe is not strictly objective as it appears, but rather responds to, and changes as the result of the intent and beliefs of the individual and the collective in accordance with the ruleset of our reality. Belief is not only a powerful lens that deeply colours the reality we see, but it also affects how physical reality actualizes itself to us.'

'Therefore, if we are the microcosm of the universe and not separate from it, then it is not the universe "doing" us, nor are we "doing" the universe, because both are inseparable. It is all happening together as one.'

'Precisely, madam.'

'Tell me, Professor,' enquired Moira curiously, 'Do you believe the state of dharma to be achievable in your lifetime?'

'Oh, my,' said Percy, while topping up her glass. 'I believe any sage of note would laugh at such a preposterous proposition. In that respect I humbly declare to be no more than a mere padawan . . .'

As the evening wore on, Moira, as Maeve had before her, marvelled at the curios that adorned Percy's apartment. 'We used to have a timepiece just like that,' she said clutching her brandy glass. 'It belonged to my grandmother originally.' She sat and stared at the old walnut clock remembering as a child listening to the slow regimented sound of it tick-tocking, and the chime that resounded on the hour.

'When were you born, Moira?' asked Maeve.

'In the year two thousand and five,' she sighed.

'That would make you,' Percy did a quick calculation. 'Somewhere in your mid-nineties.'

'Yes, in old money I suppose you're right, but who's counting these days? Numbers mean nothing.'

Percy concurred. 'Tell me, do you not miss the regularity and order of linear time?'

Moira shook her head. 'Why should I? Of what use is it in the now? What kind of calendar and regime do you suggest I follow?'

'The stars will soon be visible. The sun, I'm told has already made an appearance. Will us humans not require once again some measurement to chart our existence?'

'What do you think?' Moira, sensing the professor was playing devil's advocate, returned the question.

Percy shrugged. 'I only asked because you were born into that paradigm, a world of schedule and observed conformity.'

Moira laughed. 'Then I guess you're asking the wrong person. I was never a one for timetables. I was usually late for everything.'

'So how would you define the word *late* in the now?'

Moira pondered a moment. 'You can't.'

'Precisely!' exclaimed Percy. It only works within a construct, as in linear time. When I invited you here this evening I didn't give you a dictat as to when to arrive because there is no longer a point of reference, and yet you came without prejudice or penalty. How did you know when to come? - Because of the natural dimming of light and the intuitive forces that flow between each and every one of us and the universe. Unfortunately, some of my older students, those that were born before The Shift, but unlike you, can't seem to let go the concept, and it reflects in their writing. Their words will be meaningless to future generations.

'The story of the Tower of Babel is one aspect of the narrow frequency of human communication that has impeded our true nature. When the negative forces intervened within humanity, the resulting consciousness encodings restricted awareness to a level of miscommunication, misperception, and misunderstanding of the egoic mind using symbol and sound within fear-based consciousness.

'Currently, language in the visual and auditory band of the human physical senses within the limited 3D consciousness is only partial. 3D language tools are incapable of communicating full meaning. Thus, at this level, humanity is constantly working under a dark veil of misperception and misinterpretation. As a result, the egoic mind works incessantly to deal with this conflict and creates tremendous background noise and static. In this type of language communication through stepped-down frequencies that do not have the energy to carry precise information, meaning is diluted and distorted. Within this dense frequency band, humanity never has full unimpeded communication. There is always a level of disharmonic friction.

'Let me ask our young, learned friend here, how she would use the word *late* in a phrase or sentence?'

'As you say, within a construct, between a preordained set of events. Consequences, if you like.'

'Example?'

'Er – "If we don't remove these books from this location, it will be too *late* to save them."'

Percy nodded his approval. 'You see, when the means to that

AQUARIUS

construct are no longer there, the construct itself becomes irrelevant. Maeve's train of thought operates without it; it has never been part of her life, and that reflects in *her* writing.'

'No doubt five D consciousness has some bearing on this,' said Moira.

'Of course, it's part of our evolution. We are entering the time of The Sixth Sun; our spiritual and technological capacities are evolving at an exponential rate. Concepts such as linear time will be mere side notes in the annals of story and shall be rightly laughed at or derided by future generations.'

'So, back to your question – Will us humans require some sort of measurement to chart our existence?'

Percy thought for a moment before adjusting his monocle. 'The only clock we should ever need has been with us since the dawn of time. Entrained by the circadian rhythm of life: we know when to rise, we know when to rest. Man will always use the stars to navigate, the sun and the seasons, whatever they turn out to be, to sow and harvest. If burgeoning cultures create calendars, they will be unique to their locale. There will be no standardisation of time. Greenwich is long gone. The moon, as I am told has slipped its orbit and is now but another small bright satellite in the sky, and I for one shall not miss it or its influence.'

'Why is that?' asked Maeve.

'A month was a wholly irrational division of time. It bore no relation to anything in astronomy or human experience.'

'Wasn't it a measure of time corresponding to the length of time required by the moon to revolve once around the Earth?' countered Maeve.

'Are we talking synodic, sidereal or draconian? – Too many aberrations, no, it was an inaccurate and constantly varying measure of time that was a perpetual annoyance, a misleading unit in science, and nothing but an ill-thought-out concept and bad habit – I blame The Babylonians.'

'I have seen images of the seasons,' lamented Maeve. 'I have often wondered if I shall ever experience them in my lifetime.'

'And so you shall, my dear,' reassured Moira, 'but not in the way I remember them.'

'I'll take three out of the old four, but you can keep the blasted winter, for me,' said Percy.

'There are still plenty changes afoot,' warned Moira. 'The

PRECESSION

Maunder Minimum is at an end. The skies are about to break apart, the ice is to melt, and we have yet to settle back into our rightful place in the cosmos. The days and nights shall be longer, our movement around the sun will be slower; there are many upheavals yet to be overcome.'

'And many more will die,' Maeve reflected sadly.

'We have almost come full circle as a species; I believe humanity will survive, albeit in numbers that Gaia can support and sustain. Those that don't heed the warnings and those that don't have the wherewithal shall undoubtedly perish,' Moira conceded. 'I have already witnessed the demise of many; I pray what is to come shan't be as bad.'

'Homo sapiens are appetitive, irrational, and prone to unwarranted fear,' said Percy. 'But when under pressure man is a pack-animal whose success is based much on cooperation between packs as competition within them. The noble way to go extinct will be to evolve naturally to a higher species. Death is merely the end of the physical experience and a lifting of the constraints that consciousness bought into in order to be human. Death is not the end, but in fact is a wonderful transition to higher states of being. Metaphorically, death is like removing a straitjacket and returning to the freedom of what one really is, or as a certain Mr. Zimmerman once alluded to: "I was so much older then, I'm younger than that now."'

'I understand all of that,' said Moira, 'but it's still a hard lesson to witness and live through.'

'Please tell us of your life before The Shift.'

Moira drew a heavy sigh. 'It was a time of chaos,' she began. 'The plandemics had failed to cull people in sufficient numbers despite the relentless promotion of the arm spear. The subjugation and corralling of communities into so called smart cities on the back of the climate change hoax and the ludicrous zero carbon policies had been a disaster for the WEF puppets operating as governments, as was the launch of a Global Digital Currency under a World Government Central Bank. Across the country Diggers and Bladerunners were taking out the 5G death towers. Martial law was implemented but the disorganised blue hats were sent packing, and the organisation known as NATO fell apart. Political leaders across the world were removed or disappeared, and those left clinging to power got ever more desperate. I was an undergraduate geology

AQUARIUS

student at Edinburgh University at the time, but the faculty was fast failing. Uni's had become havens for NGO fed extremists and propagandists. Divisions had been long festering, and it got violent and nasty. There were a few of us who were connected to the old Truth movement who morphed into activists like The Diggers and New Levellers, but we were careful to keep our heads down.'

Maeve had been well schooled in the story, but she was fascinated and keen to hear a first-hand account of the sudden and terrifying effects of The Shift. 'Can you tell us what happened in twenty-thirty?'

'Well, we'd long known what was coming. Nibiru had been observed as early as two thousand and eighteen, so we had a fair time to prepare, we just didn't know what the scale of the impact of its passing would be. All we had to go on were models and the accounts from ancient texts of its previous visit that I am sure you're both familiar with. In the summer of 2030, the weather patterns became strange and unpredictable. We were experiencing hot winds that carried a choking red dust. They tried to explain the phenomenon as freak sandstorms being blown up from the Sahara, but the same was happening in the southern hemisphere with reports of more devastating effects in Australia and Indonesia. Nibiru could be seen quite clearly now in the southern sky, a dirty rust colour with a fiery red tail that some likened to a comet. Others tried to say it was The New World Order psychos trying to resurrect Project Bluebeam, but we knew different. There was increased seismic activity. Earthquakes were being reported on a daily basis. All along The Ring of Fire in The Pacific Ocean, volcanoes were erupting, even some that had lain dormant for decades and even centuries.

'My father was an ex-Staff Sergeant with The Black Watch based at Fort George near Inverness. He had been part of the reformed regiments that went down to Catterick to help oust The Blue Hats. We had spent the summer stocking the fort with supplies, food, medicines and other provisions. Many still considered us mad. Some deniers even resurrected the term conspiracy theorist to throw at us, but they were the ones that came begging for sanctuary after November 11th. 2030.'

'Can you describe it?'

Moira drained her brandy glass and closed her eyes. She went silent for a moment and Maeve wondered if she had done too much probing.

PRECESSION

'It was the wind,' she spoke eventually. 'The sound and strength of the wind. It was like nothing I'd ever experienced or ever want to again. It tore into everything. Everything shook and rattled. I thought my insides would be riven out, and the thick-set granite stones of the fort would be ripped from their foundations.'

'How long did this last?'

Moira shrugged. 'Who knows, there was no longer any distinction between day and night - it seemed like forever. When the worst of it subsided, some of the men ventured outside, but we were told in no uncertain terms to stay underground. When he returned, my father had a haunted look on his face that will stay with me until the day I die. Being the young, defiant and inquisitive kid I was I disobeyed the order to remain put and found my way to an upstairs window that had been blown out by the tempest. I can't adequately describe what I saw. It was Armageddon manifest. The land was strewn with the shredded remains of what used to be rock, vegetation, man and animal alike. Unrecognizable metal, torn and twisted. What were once rolling tree-covered hills had simply disappeared, levelled in the blink of an eye. Giant rifts had opened up in the distant mountains, and a frighteningly ominous rumbling and grating noise could be heard in the bowels of the Earth. What caught my attention more than anything was the angry looking blood red sky and what appeared to be two suns sat motionless behind a screen of fire and ash. They remained like that for what some said were three whole days, where nightfall never came. And then, from what I thought was the south I saw this thick mass of black cloud roll in. I remember looking at my compass, but the needle was going haywire. It appeared to be miles thick, and it quickly enveloped us, turning day into perpetual night. It rained down rock and pumice for weeks on end until the land and the devastation brought by the winds had been totally covered in a blanket of toxic ash three to four feet deep. The smell was incredible, like hell had opened its furnaces and gifted us all of its sulphur. Many succumbed to the deadly gases; many more gave up and took their own lives. We never thought anyone unprepared and without the forethought of adequate protection and shelter would survive, but they did. Over what we were still counting as weeks and months, they came to us in dribs and drabs, some were so badly affected and had untreatable injuries, that we knew there was nothing to be done for them except to try and make them as comfortable as possible in what little time they had left. Our dispensary at that time was fully stocked. We were given iodine and selenium on a regular basis, but we knew our supplies wouldn't last forever. We had managed to remain in contact with most of the other northern garrisons, and the primary plans for our continued survival were put into action.'

'Your testament echoes that of many accounts of this and past cataclysms that have befallen The Earth over the aeons,' stated Percy. 'The similarities in all of them, despite what tongue or translation, are too striking to be dismissed as mere coincidence, fancy or fable. "The Earth's lands were all inundated with raging waters and ravaged by horrendous winds, and the oceans were all dark with mud. And the ill wind thundered over the troubled waters also. And, as the storms abated, sunlight came back to the face of the earth as God intended. And while the cataclysm was abating, once more darkness and sunlight were re-established and distinguishable and it was good. And sunlight was again daytime and darkness again nighttime. Again, God's original design was that there be a sky between the clouds and oceans. And in accordance with God's design the heavens were re-established in that the sky again stood between the clouds and the oceans as the onslaught of the great cataclysm abated ...'

'Genesis one, Naga translation,' snapped Maeve, quickly rescuing Moira from one of Percy's lengthy scriptural monologues.

'That's my girl,' said Percy. 'But what are we to ultimately take from these accounts?' he asked needing to labour his point.

'Hope and redemption?' replied Maeve, feeling a little too stoned to be back in class.

Percy clasped his hands together. 'Oh, what an enlightened apprentice we have in our midst, Miss Duggan.'

'Och, aye, she's all of that and more, that's for sure. But as for the hope and redemption,' she paused while her glass was re-filled once more, 'it's taken a God-awful time to come to pass and we're not out of the woods just yet.' Maybe it was a combination of the cake and the brandy, but dragging up the dark past had made the old woman a little lachrymose, and sad memories long put to bed had been aroused.

'You survived it, Moira. You came through and helped so many people,' said Maeve, sensing a dip in her mood. 'Look at all your achievements, there's not many people can boast a legacy like yours.'

PRECESSION

'Yes, you're right,' she conceded. 'I was given that opportunity, and I did my best. For that I suppose I ought be grateful, but others – they never got that opportunity, at least not long enough for them to make a difference.'

Maeve and Percy exchanged looks. 'You're talking about family?'

The old girl closed her eyes. Her features filled with pain and sadness. Candlelight caught tears. She fumbled for a handkerchief and wiped her nose.

'You know, the sappers were the best,' she said, composing herself. 'They were like Gods to us. We surely would never have survived without them. After The Shift, our main threat was contaminated water. The sappers rebuilt and maintained the sewage and water supply. They collected and burned the bodies, cleared tons of debris and re-opened roads, built shelters for the refugees and fortified the garrison. Angus was a sapper.'

'Angus?'

'My older brother. He was a lovely boy. A strong man. Gentle, but strong. He was a younger version of my father. They doted on each other and I on them.

When the cold came, everything froze, even the generators. After the quakes, the lochs were no longer landlocked. The sea poured in separating us from The North Isle. The Kessock crossing fell into The Firth. Food became scarce; we sheltered and fed as best we could those who came in search of sanctuary and repelled those whose intent was to kill and plunder. Units of squaddies, engineers and sappers were sent out on expeditions to garner intel, materials and provisions with orders to assist any surviving enclaves and communities they came across. They entered the un-policed and lawless cities of Edinburgh and Glasgow, trading and bartering with the less violent and mistrustful cells of The Chavs, even recruiting some of their most hardened soldiers to scout and guide them through inhospitable terrain. Of course, whenever Angus was away I feared for his safety as quite often some of the men never returned. Although there was plenty of work to keep me occupied at the garrison, I became restless and frustrated. I felt I could be of better use out in the field with my brother, but he was horrified at the suggestion. I pestered my father relentlessly, reasoning what better opportunity would there be to put all of my training to some good use. My persistence paid off. Seeing that Duggan inspired steely resolve in my eyes, he eventually capitulated and petitioned the command to allow me to join the recces. This is where I honed my geological and dowsing skills. It also allowed me to stay relatively close to Angus, who for the one and only time in his life had a downer on my father for helping facilitate it.

'They allocated me a Minder, a feisty little red-haired hen from Easterhouse called Bridey. She was proficient in cursing and fighting but little else. Angus was my one and only true Minder; he made sure I was safe; no matter what adversity came our way he was always on the lookout for his little sister. With the increasing drop in temperature and our relatively isolated location, we were considered a low risk from further incursions, and so a number of our garrison, Angus included, were transferred to Catterick, which was the main training hub. I begged to go with him, but this time was denied. They only wanted Alpha males, and for good reason. They were being prepped for expeditions, paired with CM's and sent out on missions that would test their resilience and survival skills to the limit.'

'Walkabout,' stated Maeve.

'Yes, that's what they called it, taken from the Aboriginal rite of passage, a ritual separation from the tribe, where boys would embark on a physical and spiritual test of endurance and come back as men.' She paused, reflected, and bowed her head. 'Only, my man never returned.'

'What happened?' asked Maeve softly.

'He was killed somewhere in Mercia by a gang of Precariats while trying to protect a community who had the temerity to become self-sufficient. There were just six of them in his little unit. Only two of them lived to tell the tale. They called them the Magnificent Six. I'm still not sure what exactly happened to him. They spared me the details at the time. It destroyed my father. He became a bitter and angry old man, not good to be around; no longer the dad I knew.'

'I can't imagine what that must have been like,' sympathised Maeve.

'It made me grow up fast. I couldn't wait to be free of the garrison, and when at last they realised I had a set of skills that could be put to good use, I was out of there like a shot. I put everything into my work, and I suppose it helped to compartmentalise the bad memories. From then on and to this moment I never tended to look back – and so, by your calculations, professor, here I am, roughly seventy years, in old speak, later.'

PRECESSION

The room went quiet. Moira continued to stare at the old clock. Inside her head she could still hear the slow, rhythmic, melancholic sound of time passing.

'I was going to gift it to you,' said Percy, breaking the silence, 'but something tells me that's probably not a good idea.'

Moira forced a smile. 'You're the storian, not I. I have no interest in the past, only the possibilities and potential that lie ahead, and if, in my own small way, I can help smooth that path to the new kalpa, then I shall die happy – but thank you for the kind thought.'

'Madam, I wholeheartedly share your impassioned dream of an Elysian future and am certain that your worldly endeavours and exploits have indeed hastened that dream, soon to become reality.' Percy raised his glass. 'To the future – whatever that is, and to whatever it entails.'

§

'Oh, you are alive then' said Joan Bradley as her daughter's image flickered into view on her pad.

'Hi, Mum; how are you?' Maeve asked wearily.

'I'm fine, not that you'd know or care it seems.'

'I know, and I'm sorry, but please don't be sarcastic, it doesn't become you – "Oh, and how are you, Maeve? I'm fine mum, thanks for asking."'

Joan rolled her eyes and tutted.

'See, it's not very nice, is it?'

'I do wish you'd keep in touch more, Maeve, that's all I'm asking.'

'I know, and I've said I'm sorry – How's Dad?'

'Well, if you'd care to just – he's fine,' she said, checking herself.

Maeve nodded as the conversation ground to a halt. 'Aunt Elena's looking great,' she said eventually.

'Good – good. Yes, she said you'd been working together – so, any news to tell me?'

Maeve slowly shook her head. 'Erm, no, don't think so. Been working hard on a couple of projects; no doubt Elena's given you the lowdown.' Joan cocked her head to one side expectantly. 'What?'

'You know damn well what. Maeve, I'm your mother. Don't treat me like I'm stupid. Tell me all about her.'

Maeve heaved a heavy sigh, exasperated. 'Oh, God, mother, there really is nothing to tell.' She started to colour up and Joan raised her eyebrows.

'That's not what I hear.'

'Fucking aunties,' Maeve hissed under her breath.

'Why so cagey; you're not embarrassed are you?'

'No,' she said while not being entirely sure why she was acting like this. 'Look, I'm just not comfortable talking about Kersha here in this space – like this. Okay?'

'So, do we get to see her in the flesh?'

'Oh, I don't know – maybe, sometime – who knows?'

'I'm coming down to Richmond to see your father. Maybe we could all get together then?'

'Look, Mum, I'm really busy, I …'

'Aren't we all?'

'Okay, I'll do my best.'

'Promise?'

'No promises; I've said I'll do my best; can we please leave it at that?'

'Fine. What do you want to talk about then?'

'I don't know, you buzzed me.' Seeing the pained look on her mum's face, she quickly checked her attitude. 'I'm sorry, Mum – I've seen the sun,' she said, happy to change the subject.

Joan smiled broadly. 'Wonderful, isn't it?'

'Spectacular. I can't wait to see it rising and setting.'

'It shan't be too long, and that is a promise I think I can safely make.'

'You sound optimistic.'

'With good reason. The increase in solar activity is happening at an exponential rate. The photons and plasma currently hitting our upper atmosphere are creating anomalies that haven't been seen since The Carrington Event. We've even witnessed The Aurora Borealis here in the Hebrides, but the phenomenon isn't appearing where we would normally expect. What was magnetic north is still way off to the west.'

'So, if our magnetosphere is still off kilter, won't the CME's and flares cause further problems for us?'

'It all depends on the rate and intensity of further sunspot activity, but we're putting measures in place to counter any major geomagnetic storms.'

PRECESSION

'How?'

'By regulating and controlling the amount of ionisation in the Ionosphere.'

'You have the facility to do this?'

'We're using old HARRP technology.'

'How ironic.'

'Indeed. We've also developed a compound, a decontaminant that removes toxic gases and radiation from the trop and stratosphere. We've already begun to seed the skies and the results are promising; it's why you've been able to catch glimpses of the Sun.'

'What is this compound?'

'Its base is monatomic gold, you know, the stuff your mates The Annunaki are supposed to have used in order to regenerate their own atmosphere.'

'Mother, the whole monatomic gold thing was a thesis put forward by Sitchin, gleaned from cuneiform tablets, and the Annunaki aren't – weren't my mates.'

'Oh, and here's me thinking we were practically family – you know, the whole Enlil, Enki, Marduk, Adam's rib DNA thing?'

Maeve sensed one of those family trait intellectual duels simmering and she wasn't in the mood for one. Academic baiting appeared to be a harmless pastime for her so-called loved ones, an annoying habit that had thankfully passed her by. It was also one of the reasons she shied away from family reunions.

'My hypotheses do not necessarily reflect my beliefs, is that not clear in my writing? And the fact that you just conflated at least three wholly separate texts in two sentences makes this topic of conversation pointless.'

'Well, the compound seems to be working, so good old Mr. Sitchin must have been onto something is all I'm saying.'

'Well, he wasn't entirely wrong about Nibiru, was he? And just where did you guys manage to source your gold – King Solomon's Mines, perhaps?' Maeve returned the sarcasm.

'Monatomic gold is a powder; the stuff they've developed is a semi-synthetic version. I'm a physicist not an alchemist, so I can't give you the specifics, I'm afraid. But if we ever run out of the base metal maybe you could dowse some for us; I hear you're becoming quite the expert in that field.'

Maeve glowered at the screen. Hers was a strange family. She remembered her gran saying to her: "The Sarvents had the intelligence, the Fortunes had the intelligence plus the ego, and the Bradleys had the intelligence and the humility." Maybe this was Mum's way of silencing the ego, she thought. Taking the piss and making light of one's achievements, rather than heaping praise, so one never got too big for their boots. Maeve liked to think she didn't care too much. Her talents came to her naturally, whereas Joan and her sister had to work extra hard to achieve their goals in an environment where resources were scarce, and technology was struggling to regain a foothold. Deep down, she knew her mum was proud, her dad had said as much, as was he, but it would be nice to be told in person, just the once. She made a silent promise that she would never get too big for her boots.

'Sure,' she said. 'It's amazing what you can find with just a couple of old willow sticks.' She had been ready to end the call right there, but then, right out of the blue, a question that had been puzzling her came to mind. 'Mum, while you're on, I've been meaning to ask you something.'

'Oh, you need to ask *me* something? I'm intrigued.'

Maeve unzipped the top of her tunic and reached behind her top. 'What more can you tell me about this?' she said, holding her pendant up to the camera.

'Nothing more than you already know,' she replied, all intrigue evaporating.

'It's not a copy, is it?'

'It's a mass-produced piece of cheap jewellery; who'd want to copy it?'

'So, there weren't any more of these in the family?'

'No, not that I'm aware of. Apparently, your great grandfather disapproved of the symbolism attached to the versions that became popular to wear. Your grandmother kept it to remember him by after he passed, she handed it down to me, and I to you in the same fashion. The clasp has failed a few times, but apart from that it's totally original as far as I know. Why do you ask?'

'I've seen another one just like it.'

Joan shrugged her shoulders. 'Mass produced, what do you expect?'

'Identical.'

'Look, there are hundreds, if not thousands of the bloody things in circulation, the odds against you seeing something you think is identical are not that great. Why the special interest?'

PRECESSION

'Oh, it was just something I remember grandma saying to me when she first saw me wear it,' - She wasn't about to let on it was Kersha who possessed the one she was talking about - 'something about it symbolizing a special bond between two people, a token of lifelong friendship and nothing more. I remember not really understanding what she meant because I didn't know who the two people were supposed to be.'

'I guess one of them must have been your great granddad.'

'Yes, but what about the other person? It can't have been his wife or there would have been another reciprocated token of love, and we would have heard about it.'

'I'm afraid I can't help you with that one, Maeve. It's as much a mystery to me as it is to you. Maybe grandma can shed more light if you're that interested. I can arrange for her to be present when we have our little soiree, if you like.'

Maeve thought for a moment. 'Okay, Mum, you win; I'll make the commitment – I promise.' She ended the call and continued to stare at the blank screen. There was no point in getting upset with Mum and her scheming ways. She couldn't keep Kersha under wraps forever, but in what capacity would she present her: ward, friend – lover? She knew which out of the options she would like, but, as of yet, that was not the reality, and she didn't know if it ever would be. If love was what she was feeling, then that love was growing inside her with every passing moment they were apart, an aching that she wished she could share with someone who understood the emotions that were churning her insides. Should that person be her mother? Not a chance. She'd opened up to her aunt who tried to be as sympathetic and understanding as a Fortune could be, but it wasn't enough. Dilemma. She blew air from her cheeks; it was all conjecture anyhow. Her feelings would have to be reciprocated, and that measure of communication and understanding might be still a way off, but she wouldn't have long now to find out. She was preparing for a reunion and that aching feeling of longing began to mix with one of excitement and apprehension. She kicked back her chair and went off to gather her things with her head in a spin.

AQUARIUS

Reunions

'Hi, I'm Max,' the strikingly good-looking young man grinned, revealing a perfect set of pearly-white teeth. 'I'll be flying you down to Ampleforth.'

'Oh,' said Maeve with a slight frown on her face. 'These things usually fly themselves.'

'Yeah, I know. I have to do some manual checks on it before it goes for a once-over in Doncaster.'

'A once-over?'

'Yeah, it's due its first service, got to make sure it's behaving itself. I'll be performing a set of manoeuvres on the way down, nothing too scary – you okay with that?'

'Sure.'

'Great, hop aboard, let's get under way.'

Maeve settled into her seat, closed her eyes, and at once began to visualise the scenarios that were likely to play out at the end of this short journey. Butterflies began to stir in her stomach.

'Someone seems happy.'

Her eyes snapped open. 'What?'

'Oh, I was just observing the smile on your face. I er, - I'm sorry, I didn't mean to appear intrusive.'

'That's okay,' she said relaxing. 'I'm Maeve, by the way.'

'Very pleased to meet you, Maeve,' said the rather forward and confident young skydriver as the maglev left the ground. 'So, just what kind of VIP am I transporting on this rather brief flight – or is that information classified?'

Maeve laughed out loud. 'Classified? Now that's a word that hasn't been in the lex for a while. And what makes you think I'm a VIP?'

'Well, you don't normally get to ride in one of these unless you're someone of import, given that there are only a handful of them in existence.'

Maeve had been so wrapped in her work she had genuinely never given any thought or credence to the notion of a perceived social standing, if indeed there even was such a thing. Without doubt her stock had risen being that she now rubbed shoulders with such luminaries as Snodgrass and Duggan, but to be seen as someone afforded privileges just because of the work they undertook disturbed her a little. She had to admit that the times spent rumbling around in Spunky's old APC or on trains now seemed distant, but she liked to think such modes of transport, although soon likely to be things of the past, still weren't beneath her. She decided to throw it back at him.

'Only a handful, eh? And yet you get to pilot one of them.'

'Oh, I've piloted all six and will soon be giving the seventh its maiden test flight once I've dropped this thing off.'

Maeve was at once, surprised and impressed. 'You seem very young for such an experienced skydriver.'

Max laughed, once again displaying his brilliant white teeth. 'I don't just fly them, I designed, developed and engineered them.'

Eyebrows raised; Maeve checked his bright features for signs of flippancy while he continued to beam at her. 'Well then, Max,' she said eventually, 'it would appear that your VIP status far outweighs my own, so tell me, what type of preferable treatment comes your way?'

'I am lucky,' he said without too much thought. 'I have people around me who have shared and helped facilitate and manifest my visions. Their belief in me and my dreams are my privileges, for that I am both honoured and grateful – and, of course, I get to do this. …' Without any perceptible instruction, physical or verbal the maglev corkscrewed upwards at an astonishing rate, stopping in an instant to silently hover over the vast, grey-white vista beneath. With great show, Max then performed a series of spectacular manoeuvres designed to put both his machine through its paces and to quietly impress his rather recondite passenger, all the while the broad grin never leaving his face. Still in his element, Maeve couldn't help but notice the curious set of symbols, tribal in design, that had been shaven into his hair at the back of his head.

'Where are you from, Max?' she asked once he'd finished showing off.

'I was born and raised in Crewe. Why do you ask?' he said turning round to see her scrutinising. 'Oh, you mean the marks – okay, my ancestors are from the Shona tribe in Zimbabwe; the symbols pay homage to my great uncle, a man of much standing, wisdom and courage. He invented this.' Max reached into a pocket of his tunic and produced a small metal object that looked to Maeve like a valve of some description.

AQUARIUS

'What is it?'

'It's a microsonic energy device, MED. It turns radio frequencies into free, unlimited energy without waste or pollution. Along with an inertial mass reduction system, one just like it is helping to power this maglev right now. Unfortunately, he never got to see the full potential of his work.'

'What happened to him?'

'He was persecuted, jailed, tortured and discredited, just like Rife, Reich and Tesla before him. The Deep State finally took him out, suicided with two bullets to the back of the head. They tried to reverse engineer his prototypes but failed, declared his work pseudoscience nonsense, because it violated all known thermodynamic laws, but those who worked closely with him knew better. You see he had a unique connection to the ethereal. He was like a musician and his instrument was the cosmos. His legacy was guarded by colleagues and family, and finally handed down to me, and I am proud to now be able to make his visions my own.'

'You have inherited his gift.'

'I have.'

'Where do you think it comes from?'

'The gift? – From the universe, of course. I have had no formal training. My knowledge comes from the same source as the energy I am able to harness - from the waves that form the toroidal field. I ruminate, meditate, pray - however you want to describe the transcendental state, until the schematics form inside my head. With the help of those who have the ability to interpret my blueprints, my designs are realised.'

'Maeve nodded and smiled. 'I, myself am just beginning to understand this concept,' she said.

For the rest of the journey, they swapped their stories where the similarities soon became apparent; two young people, kindred in spirit, and gifted beyond their years. In their short time together, Maeve learned from this youthful genius how to embrace her own latent abilities, to blindly trust in their source, and seldom, if ever, question where they came from. The guy was super-confident, and it shone out of him like a beacon.

'Never doubt yourself, Maeve Bradley. Allow your triumphs to validate who you are and celebrate them without deferment in any way you wish, and whenever disappointment or failure raises its head, as no doubt it sometimes will, heed the lesson that it brings and then tune yourself back to source. It works for me every time.'

Such wisdom from one so young, Maeve thought to herself, not fully realising that is exactly what her mentors thought about her.

As they neared their destination, Maeve looked down upon the landscape, the intricate patterns of snow blown by the winds and frozen into mile upon mile of furrowed waves, and the barely perceptible freshly cleared roads that were being quickly covered by the next flurry of snow, sleet and ice. She tried to visualise the scene once it had all gone, and water became the dominant feature, what use would there be for roads then?

'Do you think the wheel will ever become obsolete, Max?'

'For transport, yes, maybe,' he said picking up on her train of thought, 'But even then, any mode of transport will have some sort of wheel in its design, be it a bearing or a gear. The wheel is the most efficient shape; it is cheap, strong and reliable. Given what you have told me about our future geography, I can see the demise of the rubber version used on roads, but it shall always have a place in any functional design. There are versions of the wheel in this machine, although eighty percent of it is made of bast.'

'What, you mean like hemp?' said Maeve, surprised.

'Yes, an amalgam of hemp, bamboo and mycelium cultivated material structured into a form that is as strong and flexible as any metal. Cheap and easy to grow and so versatile it can be made into most anything.'

'Do you think everyone will have access to machines like these in the near future, and not just us VIPs?'

Max grinned his toothy grin. 'Anything is possible if we care to dream it,' he said.

Buoyed by her encounter with the remarkable young man, Maeve entered the building on air, the sensation of her heart beating in her chest amplified with each light step. And then there she was, the object of her daydreams, the protagonist of her fantasy dramas, stood in suspended anticipation, dressed in black from head to toe. A pause of recognition, then like a shot from the barrel of a gun she was off, hurtling towards her, a mass of ebony hair flowing in her wake. In a giant leap of faith, she flung herself and for a fleeting moment Maeve had a flashback to a derelict building somewhere in old Leeds. This time the connection was totally welcome albeit aggressive in nature.

AQUARIUS

They slammed into each other, Kersha wrapping her legs around hips and clinging on like a magnet. She was heavier than that first confrontation, but Maeve cushioned the force expertly and used the momentum to spin them both round and round in a display of unbridled joy, their faces buried under a tangle of wild black hair. Kersha let out a feral scream of relief that echoed down the corridor where Donna Channing stood with a big smile on her face alongside a couple of kids who looked on totally bewildered.

Amongst all the stramash and rapture of reunion, Kersha's first words were not what Maeve expected to hear. 'You is lying cunt, Maeve.'

Joy evaporating fast, Maeve looked to the doctor for explanation. Donna gave her a reassuring smile. 'Come with me, I'll show you.'

'Remember when you told her you would be back in twenty sleeps?' she said as they viewed time-lapsed birds eye footage of their dorm. 'Well, you've been gone longer than that, and she knew.'

'I'm confused,' said Maeve. 'What exactly is it we're looking at?'

Donna zoomed in on the images. 'She took marbles from the activities room and she's placing one in your bed for every sleep.'

'But how has she learned to count so quickly?'

'The kids have shown her how to add up in multiples of ten on her fingers. She's a fast learner. When she'd placed twenty marbles in your bed, she came to me with an expectant and excited look on her face, but you never came. I managed to pacify her and told her you would be back in five more sleeps.'

'How did you know?'

'I contacted the DSC and got the schedule for the maglev. I didn't want to bother you as I know it would have thrown you into a panic.'

Maeve sighed. 'I was counting down the sleeps; I couldn't wait to get back. I had no idea I had to be so specific. I've misjudged her again.'

'She is learning at an astonishing rate, and for that matter, so am I. Through her drawings, sign, and her vastly improving vocabulary I'm slowly gaining an insight into her past. From our sessions I've discovered she never had or doesn't recall a father figure in her life. What she does remember as a small girl is being given the pendant and the rag doll by a woman who I understand to be her mother. The mother was then taken away, along with what I can gather was an older sister, by some men with a promise she would return but never did …'

'Oh, God,' said Maeve, closing her eyes at the thought.

'Can you imagine the absolute terror and helplessness of that little girl waiting and waiting in vain, in the cold with no one to protect her, no one to feed her, hiding from deviants and predators in the bowels of a ruined city? Is there any wonder her trust issues lie so deep?'

'How on Earth did she survive for so long?' breathed Maeve, shaking her head.

Donna shrugged. 'Let's just be thankful that she did, eh? Her resilience must have been off the scale.'

Maeve's guilt at her failed commitment was partly assuaged when Kersha breezed into the room clutching a small, framed portrait. 'I is done this for you, Maeve,' she said with unconditional forgiveness.

'For me?' said Maeve astonished. 'Oh, my ...' She took the picture and stared at it open-mouthed. Kersha had drawn it from memory. It was an accomplished piece of work, much further advanced in skill and detail than her storytelling sketches that had been a means to an end. 'Oh, you've made me look so pretty,' she said as tears began to stream down her face.

'You no like it?' said Kersha, confused.

'Oh, darling, I love it.'

'Why you cry?'

With words failing her, Maeve brought her close and hugged the life out of her. Saying sorry was becoming a habit, but she now repeated it over and over as she held on tight, never wanting to let go. Although Kersha was now a young woman, she still had that endearing childlike quality, a legacy from her traumatic milieu. She was also a warrior, a survivor, resilient, as the doctor had described her. The many contradictions didn't do anything for Maeve's personal feelings or emotions, she was as confused as ever, but Kersha's swift progress was encouraging. She would have to remain patient, bide her time and keep her council for now. With her head nestling next to hers and the tears still streaking down her cheeks, she closed her eyes and took in the scent of that dark, wild hair.

'Why are there cameras in the dorms?' asked Maeve.

'Some of our boarders are remote viewers, some, especially the younger ones, are also somnambulists,' explained Donna. 'In the unconscious state they can get up to all manner of things while on their travels. We monitor them for their behavioural patterns, but also for their physical safety as they occasionally can put themselves unknowingly in harm's way. Danni, the boy who has taken a shine to Kersha, is one such case. We have had to intervene on many occasions for fear of his safety. I can turn yours off if it concerns you.'

'It's just that I woke at breakfast to find her lying beside me, her eyes fixated. Scared the hell out of me in the instant.' She paused, trying to formulate a way to express her predicament. 'She's very tactile, touchy feely, likes to explore, shall we say. I don't want anyone to think …'

'I quite understand,' said the doctor, saving Maeve from any further embarrassment. 'I'll make sure it's disabled.'

'Thank you.'

Donna smiled and gave her a knowing look. 'I want you to be totally honest with me, now, Maeve – Does Kersha's behaviour actually bother you?'

'Personally, no – ethically, yes,' she replied without hesitation.

'You know there is a psychological aspect to the work I do as an epigen; observing behaviour is part of my remit; I see the burgeoning dynamic between two people, and I believe that dynamic could be sexual in nature; am I right?'

'I think so – yes,' Maeve conceded. 'I also think what I feel is a genuine love, and I don't know how to express it in a way she'll understand. What Kersha might be experiencing could simply be a late adolescent show of sexual curiosity played out on someone she knows she can trust.'

'And you're scared of taking advantage of that trust.'

'Yes.'

'Hmm, I see your dilemma, but what I would say is she is certainly capable of understanding the concept of consent, so that takes care of any ethical issue. What I really see underpinning your hesitancy is fear of rejection in the future.'

God, she's good – thought Maeve feeling grateful to have someone around who understood what she was going through, better still able to dip into her psyche and pull out a few home truths. 'At some point she'll begin to understand and want to express her sexual orientation, won't she?'

'She may have already determined that given the trauma she's gone through and her outward hostility toward grown men.'

'What about Danni? You've already said there's a growing bond between them.'

'He's merely a boy. She doesn't see him as a threat. She's happy to take lessons from him, but in all other aspects, she's definitely in charge.'

'What if she wants children?' asked Maeve, once again baring her insecurities.

'That's never going to happen, I'm afraid, the ordeal of her last pregnancy took care of that.' With that statement Maeve all at once felt a curious mix of sadness and selfish relief. Donna saw the ambivalence still writ across her face. 'It's obvious to me that you have a strong moral compass, Maeve, take heed of it, but don't beat yourself up over the absolute right and wrong of any situation, the only person you'll hurt is you.' She placed a hand over hers and smiled.

'Thank you,' said Maeve, softly.

'Come, let me show you her latest work, it's fascinating.'

§

It hadn't been the easy, comfortable ride they had been used to. The hard packed ice on the old A1 had begun to break up, and the old bus on its regular journey between York and Catterick had to prove its worth as it negotiated the scarred surface and the treacherous potholes that had begun to appear. Apparently, a few feet beneath lay something called tarmac. The maglev was sorely missed, and this painfully rough mode of transport had brought them down to Earth with a bump – literally. VIP status didn't apply on personal journeys no matter who you were. Alighting the bus, Maeve rubbed her sore backside and laughed to herself, thinking if only Max could see her now. With the temperature still slowly rising, the regular modes of transport would soon be found wanting; the old bus wouldn't be negotiating this route for much longer, she guessed.

Before them stood the impressive and ever-expanding sight of Catterick Camp, the fortress garrison that had become a citadel, the nerve centre of operations at the time of The Shift and her home for the best part of her life. The walls and ramparts, still flying the hawk sigil, retained a look of menace and imposition. Having outlived their purpose long ago, the sight served to depress Maeve somewhat. For the same reason she had campaigned to have the gates removed at Carver, she would lobby her councillor father and petition to have these symbolic and redundant defences removed.

There was much activity in and around the garrison. There was a mass exodus underway and new compounds were being built on the higher ground. They passed through Somme Barracks, shored up and semi deserted, places she frequented as a child, almost unrecognisable now. Flood defences had been put in place all around the territory, but Maeve sensed they could prove inadequate once the rivers Swale and Ure began to flow again with the sheer amount of meltwater she predicted would come down from the peaks to the west.

They played games as they walked; Maeve pointing out places of interest and patiently showing Kersha how to construct sentences with them, but when she attempted to teach her spellings, she got frustrated and bored and resorted to firing marbles from her catapult that she had taken from the play area in Ampleforth, aiming at icicles hanging from communication wires.

They passed the vast complex that comprised The Great Halls of Learning where Maeve spent most of her childhood. It had become the centre of excellence for all academia, arts and sciences and had been the brainchild and vision of the group of altruistic architects of survival who were sometimes referred to as The New Levellers. They'd even had the foresight to construct the campus at an elevation above six hundred feet, and Maeve wouldn't have been surprised if a certain Moira Duggan had been involved in the planning.

Leaving the city behind them they climbed up into the foothills of Barden Moor, aiming snowballs at one another. They romped and wrestled in deep drifts, their puerile laughter echoing down the slopes. Maeve was reminded of Kersha's unbridled strength; even at play she rarely applied filters, and on this awkward terrain Maeve found it hard to deploy her martial art skills. In fits of giggles, they found themselves in a familiar position: Maeve astride her assailant, pinning her wrists into yielding snow. Their icy breaths came quick and mingled. Their eyes met; laughter subsided. For a moment uncertainty hung in the cold air. Daringly, and with her heart pounding in her chest, whether from their playful exertions or otherwise she couldn't say or have cared, she moved in closer. Her grip softened. Kersha's breath now came out with a little shudder and their lips met. They had kissed before, at meetings and farewells, but this time it was different. It lingered, just long enough to allow Maeve's emotions out. It felt like she was baring her soul, and that feeling was both scary and liberating at the same time. Like the air around them, time became frozen. The apposition of hot breath and cold skin sent a current of sexual energy through them that was heightened by its capriciousness. As they slowly parted, for Maeve the tingly sensation still coursing through her body was tinged with a feeling of guilty pleasure, the ambition of her fantasy now played out with an inner voice saying – *what have I done?* - For Kersha, a feeling of confusion and excitement that was now written large in her dark eyes, an expression that if she could speak it would say – *I'm not sure what that was, but I'm intrigued and I would like more* – With breath still heavy they stared at each other, anticipating, daring, unsure. Then, with a motion that was swift and predictably animal in nature, Kersha pulled her back down, a hand holding the back of her head forcing their faces together. Instinctively her tongue started to explore, hungrily probing, greedy to find more of these strange, but wonderful sensations. Maeve's eyes widened at the frantic assault on her tonsils and fought to come up for air.

'Woah! – slowly ... slow, like this,' she spoke quietly, coming back down to gently reciprocate with her own tongue before burying her face into the nape of Kersha's neck eliciting groans of pleasure. The wildling thrust up her pelvis and wrapped her legs tightly around Maeve's hips. Bumping and grinding in the snow, they held on tight, Maeve cradling her arse as they romped and rolled.

With her heart soaring, Maeve, without thinking, uttered the immortal line. 'I think I'm in love with you, Kersha.'

'I love you, Maeve,' she responded, but it was delivered in the same way she had said it on many an occasion, without any inflexion or altered emotion, just a phrase she had learned, carried without any real understanding of the word. Although glad, in a way, that a certain barrier had been breached, Maeve wondered if the lustful response to her advances was purely down to a raw sexual awakening, or something that held a more deviant connotation pertaining to her past. She recalled Donna Channing's revelations surrounding her three traumatic pregnancies and shuddered at the thoughts that were now trying to formulate inside her head. Her heart was no longer soaring. Rationale was now back in the driving seat, and so, with a sober head she skilfully returned the watershed

AQUARIUS

moment back to one of playful frolicking.

'Oh, soldier, soldier, won't you marry me with your musket, fife and dru – um ...' Kersha sang happily as they continued their journey, trudging through the soft, yielding snow hand in hand. It was an old ditty that she must have picked up from some of the kids at Ampleforth, although why they would have learned such a curious traditional tale of deceit, Maeve couldn't say, but she laughed along as Kersha occasionally forgot the words and replaced them with her own unique set of lyrics, knowing she wouldn't have a clue what she was singing about anyway.

Kyle Bradley was a quiet, shy, retiring, unassuming gentleman as well as being a brilliant mathematician. He had been instrumental in devising the click system, a way of measuring the passing of time that enabled the synchronisation of necessary scheduling; a click approximating what had been known as one hour. It had brought some semblance of order to what had been organisational chaos previously. Although the people had already begun to move away from the notion of linear time dictating their lives, such a system had been vital to the successful rebuilding of communities post Shift.

Like most academics, Kyle was neither practical nor domesticated as was evident by the snow and soot-fall that had dropped down the chimney as he tried to light a fire in the hearth of the converted barn that was the Bradley home. His willing but awkward attempts to brush dust and sooty cobwebs from ornaments and pictures showed that the place hadn't been lived in for a while. Since his wife had been stationed in the Hebrides, he had spent nearly all of his time in his quarters down in the citadel where his research and position as a councillor kept him busy. Eradicating the aura of neglect and trying to get the place looking and feeling cosy didn't come easy to him, but he would do his best in anticipation of the arrival of his family, as today was a special day – in his eyes, anyway. He washed his hands in the old Belfast sink, wiped the carbon residue from his spectacles, carefully opened the pages of an old recipe book and with great deliberation measured out the ingredients.

Maeve and Kersha marched happily hand in hand through the

chlorophyll-starved pine forest of Thorn Hill. In the near distance, swirling grey-blue smoke rose above the snow-covered dead trees. Tyre tracks led them to a small clearing where Maeve's childhood home came into view. Up the ice-covered drive, in a scene that was almost picture postcard, her father appeared at the door to greet them.

'Dad! – What on Earth. . .?' Maeve exclaimed as they fell into each other's embrace.

Kyle was wearing a blood-spattered apron, one hand bandaged and soaked in red, and two white eyes blinking through a face still caked in soot.

'Ah – er. . . had a little mishap, I'm afraid.'

'I'll say – have you seen your face?' Maeve wiped a finger down his cheek and showed him the black residue.

'Oh, dear, is it that bad? I haven't looked in a mirror.'

'And what happened to your hand?'

'What? Oh, nothing much,' he said, pretending to be shocked at the sight of his poorly applied dressing. 'Slip of the knife, that's all.'

Maeve shook her head in dismay. 'Come on let's get you inside and sort you out. Oh, by the way, this is Kersha. Kersha, this is my dad.'

'Hi, my dad,' said Kersha.

Unsure of what to do next, Kyle offered his bloodied hand then swiftly withdrew it. He awkwardly opened his arms and looked to his daughter for approval. Maeve glanced to the heavens and nodded wearily. He gingerly embraced the waif and patted her on the back with his good hand. 'Er, very pleased to make your acquaintance, Kersha.'

'Hi, my dad,' she repeated deadpan, with her arms straight down by her side.

'Where's Mum?' Maeve sniffed at the curious smell of foist and wood smoke while scrutinising the state of the old place.

'She's crunching numbers in my office downtown. New data's coming in. Looks like the weather patterns are about to get interesting. We may have to buckle up soon, which means she might have to cut our little reunion short. My guess is she'll be needed back at CREATT asap.' Kyle shrugged apologetically.

'No, no – I quite understand,' said Maeve, being well aware of the impending situation. They gave each other a knowing look; no words were needed.

'There's hot water if you guys need a brew. I think I'll go tidy myself up a bit.'

'I think you should,' said Maeve. 'And let me take a look at that hand when you've done.'

'What's that smell?' Joan Bradley had just been introduced to Kersha and was still in the middle of a welcoming embrace with her head in close proximity to the young girl's still damp, unkempt hair, when she screwed up her nose inquisitively.

'Mother! Don't be so fucking rude,' said Maeve horrified.

'Smoke – I smell smoke; something's burning,' said Joan, ignoring her daughter's misjudgement.

'It'll be the fire,' said Kyle. 'I've not long since lit it.'

'No, it's not the fire,' Joan persisted. 'It's coming from over there – have you got something in the oven?'

'Oh, shit – my cake!' exclaimed Kyle.

Smoke bellowed into the room as he opened the oven door. Without thinking, he pulled at the baking tray and in doing so burned the fingers of his good hand. Amongst his yelps of pain, the crozzled cake and metal tray clattered to the floor in front of him.

'What on Earth . . .' said Joan standing over the charred remains while wafting away smoke.

'It was going to be a surprise,' said Kyle looking back over his shoulder from the sink where Maeve was now helping him soothe his seared digits with cold water.

'You attempting to bake a bloody cake, that's the surprise,' said Joan holding a hand over her face.

'What surprise, Dad?' Maeve asked calmly while carefully dabbing his fingers with a wet cloth.

'It's your birthday, sweetheart,' he smiled meekly through the pain. 'You're nineteen in old years. I just thought it would be fun, you know, to celebrate the occasion like they used to do back in the day.'

Maeve and her mum exchanged glances; now they were both surprised.

'But, how – how do you know?'

Kyle shrugged. 'Some of the old electronic clocks and calendars didn't stop working just because everything else did. I occasionally need points of reference for my own calculus with certain aspects of my work.'

PRECESSION

'But even the atomic clocks went haywire, didn't they?'

'Yes, but I don't need those – I simply use this.' He produced a small, black object from his pocket and handed it over. Maeve held it up and scrutinised it with great interest. It was obviously a timepiece of some description, a thing called a watch, now minus the plastic straps that presumably used to keep it in place around the wrist. It had a digitised face with numbers and letters, some of which were constantly changing. Four tiny function buttons were attached to its sides. The words, CASIO ALARM CHRONO <ILLUMINATOR> 100M WATER RESIST were stamped on its front. On the back was a metal plate with serial numbers on it along with, CASIO MADE IN CHINA Maeve was amazed that the tiny cellular battery was still working after all this time and guessed her father must have used it or reverse engineered it to devise his click system as it looked pretty similar to the devices that he had pioneered and were worn by the likes of Jed Murphy and his crews.

'What do all these digits mean?' asked Maeve, handing it back with a shake of the head.

'They mean that it is now 3:49 pm, that's post midday. The day is Sunday, and we are 16 days into the month of May. The year, not shown here, but quite easy to work out is 2100. You were born on Friday the 16th. Of May in the year 2081, according to the Gregorian calendar.'

'So, you've aged me, Dad – how erm, interesting,' said Maeve, not really knowing how to react.

'Oh, c'mon, you're a storian,' Joan interjected. 'You know how these things used to work.'

'Sure,' admitted Maeve, 'but when it's applied to you personally, it all seems rather strange, almost quaint, especially the repetitive acknowledgement of a birth date celebrated with a cake.'

They all took a glance at the smouldering remains of said cake and concurred.

'I eat?' Kersha wondered without prejudice.

'Did you ever have a birthday cake, Martha?' Maeve posed the question to her grandmother who was sat cosy and close to the crackling wood fire that was illuminating her sapient features.

'Of course I did, dear,' she responded as if it were an odd question, while flames from the fire lit up her eyes at the very memory. 'With candles that you blew out and made a wish.'

'A wish?' Maeve looked at her puzzled. 'Why would you do that?'

'I don't know,' she said, searching for an appropriate answer. 'It was just the custom, I suppose.'

'What did you wish for?'

'Oh, usually the things that you hoped you'd get for your birthday but seldom did. I think I used to wish for a pony. Anyway, you weren't supposed to tell anyone what you wished for, or it would never be granted. I never told anyone, but then again, I never got a pony.'

Maeve continued her puzzled look. She could have asked a multitude of questions about this ever so strange custom, like who was it granting or declining these birthday wishes anyway, but she had more pressing questions to ask in this short window together, so she shook her head and smiled and left it there. She glanced across at her mother and father who were working feverishly at their stations. It was rare yet good to see them both together like this. Maeve guessed that the love for their work trumped any affection they might now have for one another. Accepting the forced separation that their vocations demanded of them probably made it so. But when they joined forces, flexing their intellectual prowess and bouncing around theories, they became a formidable pair and looking on she saw that there was something quite endearing about it. None of them would have it any other way.

Kersha was sat at the kitchen table, sketching and happily singing away to herself. Now was as good a time as any to do some digging.

Martha Fortune held the tarnished pendant in her hand and fingered the cheap, sterling silver brooch of a hawk in flight thoughtfully. 'I don't think I ever wore it, certainly not when my father was around, anyway.' she said, casting her mind back. 'It's not the most attractive piece of jewellery, is it?'

'No, but I'm more interested in its significance – beyond that of an adopted symbol of hope after The Shift and the fall of the Cabal, and the now almost idolatry status afforded it by the survivors.'

Martha raised an eyebrow, pursed her lips and stared inquisitively at her granddaughter. 'Now, you have me intrigued, child. Why such interest?'

PRECESSION

Maeve sighed and looked over to her would-be lover, not certain how to explain it. 'Kersha wears the same, and I know that there are many of these things in circulation, but ours are identical, cheap, yes, but unlike any other I've ever come across. When she and I first . . .' Maeve cleared her throat, pausing to formulate her words. '. . . Our first encounter was somewhat confrontational . . .'

'You fought like wild animals, so I'm told.'

'She was scared, traumatised.'

'And you managed to tame her, I'm also told.'

Maeve vehemently shook her head at the third-hand, skewed perception. 'I did no such thing, Grandma. Kersha's pacification came from something outside the both of us, something etheric and yet indescribable.' She closed her eyes, trying to reclaim the moment. 'Besides the blood and the sweat,' she said after the longest pause, 'the only other physical joinder that brought things to that unexpected consummation was the near coming together of those two pieces of cheap silver as I sat astride her. I know it sounds crazy, but I'm certain there's some sort of connection, some kind of link.' She paused once more, unable to explain herself further. 'You once told me it represented a token of lifelong friendship and nothing more.'

'Yes, that's what I remember my father telling me when he caught me rummaging around in an old chest of his. He'd stopped wearing it when it became something other than that, and I never questioned him on it any further because I sensed he didn't want to talk about it. To be honest, I was more intrigued with the collection of martial arts trophies that I found, and so he promised to teach me the ancient practice of Tae-kwon-do amongst his busy schedules. I think he saw it as an important defensive skill given what we were living through. Thankfully, I never needed to put it to use apart from competition with others in the garrison.'

'So, he never told you anything about this lifelong friendship?'

Martha shook her head and sighed. 'No, he took that story to his grave, I'm afraid. I only remember my mother warning me not to probe too much as it had some sort of personal tragedy attached to it. I don't know what else to tell you, my dear,' she said handing back the pendant. 'I'm not sure if he would've approved, but passing it down, like we do is just something I started on a whim, seeing as it became de rigeuer to wear one, same as I encouraged you all to take up Tae-kwon-do.' Martha saw the disappointment and frustration written across her granddaughter's face. 'You know, despite the unwanted Indigo label, all the women in the family were born pragmatists – except for you,' she added curiously. 'Me, Joan, Elena, and even my mother, would try to offer a scientific explanation for your experiences, and simply put the hawk thing down to mere coincidence, but now, by the simple light of the fire, I see more and more of my father in you. It was his intuition, his insight that drove him to do great things. His ability to see and predict events long before they happened elevated his status amongst the old military guard and servicemen. Also, being such a skilled surgeon at the very top of his field and in much demand afforded him great reverence and respect amongst his peers. Some say it was the cheap looking chain that he wore around his neck that somehow became the inspiration and eventually the talisman for hope inside the garrisons and beyond. For him, it became an unforeseen and unwanted legacy, and so he distanced himself from it thereafter.' The old lady leant in close and placed a hand over Maeve's. 'You do remind me so much of him, you know. That thirst for truth and knowledge, that intuitive mind . . .' She paused and gazed into her eyes. ' . . . He must have had his reasons for not wanting to share his secret, and we must respect that. Maybe it was something just too painful for him to talk about. And whatever the phenomenon was that you two experienced in that moment shall remain uniquely personal, and so it should. Quite often, over-analysing and trying to pick things apart can lead you up blind alleys, dead ends, throwing up questions to which there are no ready-made answers, leaving you all-the-more frustrated. If it was nothing more than a token of a lifelong friendship, then allow it to be just that. No doubt, the one that Kersha wears has its own story, its own journey. If there is some kind of connection like the one you're alluding to, maybe it will come apparent – if it's meant to be. Otherwise simply allow these simple trinkets to be symbols of your love for each other – you do love her, don't you?' Martha posed it as a question, but the inflection in her voice said she knew it was a given.

'Is it that obvious?' Maeve replied in a half-whisper, hoping that she was out of earshot from Mum and Dad, while her blushing was only partially disguised by the glowing fire reflecting off her features.

Martha chuckled and crinkled up her nose. 'Oh, I still like to think I have some of that old Indigo insight left in me – she does love

PRECESSION

you back, you know.'

'How can you tell?'

'It's just a feeling I get. You may not think the love is being reciprocated in the same way, but it will, once her ability to express such things grows beyond her artwork and the confused physicality.'

'Her drawings are amazing, aren't they?'

Martha nodded. 'Art is one of the oldest forms of expressing love, as well as portraying the failings of mankind.'

'Did you get that same feeling when Mum and Dad got together?'

Martha chuckled again. 'Theirs was more of a love for their mutual intellect, rather than the, shall we say, more nuanced notion of love – but hey, here you are, so who am I to judge? And I do know that they love you to bits, it's just that their phylogenesis sometimes means it's hard for them to express such feelings.'

Maeve nodded. She understood. It was as if her grandma could read her thoughts. She was finely tuned to her late adolescent doubts and insecurities regarding her own physiology and the occasionally awkward relationship with parents that frustrated her so. Without the archaic timelines that birthdays marked, she was increasingly aware she was no longer a child – hadn't been, it seemed for an age. She often felt her own burgeoning intellect to be a curse, and this new, ineffable thing known as love was tearing her apart, as there was no one close enough to explain it to her. This and the phenomena she had faced in that old Leeds terrace were never explained or taught in The Great Hall of Learning where she carried the burden of her family legacy, and as a result, despite all the fulfilled expectations, she had found herself growing up too quick.

Then, of course, there was Maeve the hypocrite. Wasn't it her who had shut her mum down when she had first enquired, albeit in her own clumsy way, about Kersha when she had the opportunity to bare her soul? Maybe she had inherited some of that stoic pragmatism after all.

Martha saw the contradictions writ large on her granddaughter's face. 'You know, I went through something similar when I was about your age.'

'How so?'

'Not long after The Shift, I became the youngest member in a team of alchemists who had a major breakthrough in the development of the synthetic vitamin D that we all now use regularly. Up to then we had only been able to produce D2 from yeast and plant sources; it wasn't enough, and people became sick and ever more deficient because of the lack of sunlight. We had been unable to produce D3 because of the sea and land contaminants to fish and livestock until a team discovered a flock of feral sheep in the Scottish Highlands. The lanolin they produced was thankfully untainted and from it we were able to splice together a lab grown form of cholecalciferol. The development proved to be a life saver, me and my team were lauded for our work, and eventually we were able to produce sufficient quantities to distribute throughout the land. In the middle of all of this I had met and fallen in love with a guy called Billy Fortune – your grandad, God bless him – he was a young anaesthetist working in the infirmary, and, just like me he was part of a team that was faced with seemingly unsurmountable problems, namely the production, storage and delivery of the gases N_2O, entonox and heliox, along with the short supply of VIEs used in the processing of liquid oxygen. Desperately seeking solutions, Billy rediscovered a practice known as Noesitherapy, originally and regularly performed by a Dr. Escudero . . .'

'You mean NT,' interrupted Maeve, 'the method of pain control by inducing a parasympathetic state in the patient without the use of anaesthetics.'

'Yes – yes, I know the practice is standard now, but back then its rediscovery was groundbreaking, and my Billy was instrumental in developing the understanding and use of the technique.'

'I didn't know that.'

Martha smiled and nodded proudly. 'Anyway, back to my point – any spare moments we had together, which were rare, were spent excitedly swapping notes on our respective lines of research and discovery. Being so absorbed in our work didn't stymie our growing affection for one another, despite Mother's undisguised disapproval of our relationship once she found out about us.'

'Do you think Mum disapproves of Kersha and my sexuality?'

'Oh, my God, no,' laughed Martha. 'She's not that primitive in her attitudes. My mother's exception to us being together didn't stem from any personal dislike of Billy, it was more the fear of any adolescent romantic dalliance becoming a distraction to our work, the pressure and importance of which was enormous back then. Of course, through it all I became angry, frustrated and confused, but I like to think I never allowed those youthful emotions to affect my other duties.'

PRECESSION

'How did your father react to all this?'

'He largely stayed out of it,' Martha shrugged. 'He would give me a warm, loving hug and ask me how I was whenever our paths crossed, which wasn't very often as he was so engrossed with his own workload.'

Maeve glanced across the room at her old man, head bowed, working away on his pad. She smiled as the image of his failed attempts at baking a cake for her came to the fore and drew in the parallels.

'I guess it's who we are, Maeve,' Martha reflected. 'Our circumstances serve to shape us. For good or bad, never forget, our aims and causes have always been altruistic. In our own small way, we've all helped to get us to where we are in the now. . .'

'For you, Grandma . . .' Kersha presented her latest pencil drawing and retreated to sit on the rug in front of the fire close to Maeve.

'Oh – oh, my goodness,' said Martha in genuine amazement from behind the square of paper. She peered wide-eyed over the top at the pair of them sat opposite, then back to the sketch, almost in disbelief. 'Extraordinary,' she managed to utter after further perusal. 'Come to me, my child.' She summoned Kersha to her side while passing over the drawing for Maeve to see. Kersha happily obeyed and fell into Martha's arms as she heaped praise on her endeavours. She appeared totally relaxed with the affection and attention, resting her head on the old woman's bosom contentedly, and with a large smile on her face.

Her work, as Maeve observed, was getting ever more intricate and detailed. The depth and spatial awareness she managed to achieve belied the simple pencil monochrome that was her only tool. She had captured the moment of grandmother and daughter deep in conversation. The wisdom in the old woman's eyes and features illuminated by the fire and juxtaposed with the ever-changing shadows had been brought to life with every mark and stroke, lifting the scene off the page with the qualities of a hologram. Within the work was an undeniable story, unique to the observer, profound yet ambiguous, for Maeve almost a mirror into her own soul. She shook her head in wonder. How did she do it? What was it that allowed her to capture that moment, freeze myriad thoughts and emotions onto

AQUARIUS

one scrap of paper?

Maeve looked up from the drawing to the old woman and child as they continued to form a bond. She smiled inwardly as a warm glow began to take hold in the pit of her stomach and a new, uncomplicated notion of 'family' began to form in her head. There'd be no more over-analysing, picking things apart and walking up blind alleys from now on.

Joan Bradley gently shook her daughter awake. From the depths of a contented slumber, Maeve became slowly aware of her mother's features looming large over her and of the mycelium-like tangle of limbs that were holding her and Kersha together limpet fashion. For Joan, it was final confirmation of what, up to now, had gone unspoken.

'Get up, I have something to show you.' Despite no discernible tone of judgement in her mother's voice, Maeve couldn't help but colour up as she slowly prised herself away from the soundly snoring Kersha.

'What is it?' asked Maeve still half-asleep

'Just put some clothes on,' said Joan leaving the room. 'You don't want to miss this.'

Intrigued, Maeve hurriedly dressed and entered the kitchen where her mum was already in deep conversation with her colleagues up in The Hebrides. Outside, on the veranda, Martha sat on an old rocking chair wrapped in blankets, holding on to a steaming brew. Out in the grounds, Kyle was fiddling with instruments on tripods that looked like sensors of some kind that had been strategically placed in the snow and pointing to the sky. Despite her grandmother's protection, it felt unusually warm. Looking across the valley, there was a low mist, not unlike the one she had witnessed up in Queensbury with Moira Duggan, where only peaks of pine pierced the flat, milky haze. Although Maeve sensed it was still early, the sky above had taken on a lighter shade of grey. Looking out over the valley to the east, a herringbone pattern of scalar cloud was beginning to form. All around was an eerie silence, save for the sound of boots in snow as her dad traced a path from station to station.

'What's happening, Martha?'

'Wait and see, my dear,' she said with a knowing smile that only added to the intrigue.

PRECESSION

Maeve wasn't entirely in the dark. She knew that great atmospheric changes were taking place in the northern hemisphere, and the once rare, but now more common formation of these beautiful colloids, meant that the changes were happening at an ever-increasing rate. She now sensed that an even rarer event was about to unfold, and if she'd have taken a guess, she wouldn't have been wide of the mark as to what that event was.

'Good morning,' said Kyle as he bounded up the veranda steps with a broad smile on his face.

'Now that's a phrase I haven't heard in an age – good morning to you,' said Martha.

It was a greeting that Maeve had neither heard nor had reason to use before, so her father got the usual hug and peck on the cheek. 'Is this what I think it is, Dad?'

'That all depends on what you think it is,' he raised an eyebrow and smiled, before going inside. 'Anyone fancy a brew?'

'Be patient – let them have their fun,' thought Maeve.

Her patience would soon be rewarded as they all watched the rippled cloud ceiling to the south-east begin to change colour. The heavily shadowed blanket of variable greys was now morphing ever so slowly and subtly until they took on a deep purple cast. On the very edges, close to the horizon, the purple gave way to a line of maroon and then crimson. A light, still yet unseen began to usher in something called dawn. The silence had now been broken by rare birdsong as the random call of a kind grew into a full-blown chorus of many. Imperceptibly the cloud in its form and colour had changed again, now edged in gold and silver.

Kyle applied filters to his binoculars and scanned the horizon. He then passed them to his daughter and guided her vision. Between land and sky appeared a small arc of the deepest crimson. Through distant haze it shimmered and grew until a flaming ball finally filled her scope, taking her breath away. With shaking hands she passed on the binos and watched as the life-giver put in its long-awaited appearance. From red to blood-orange to gold, melting away any random cloud that got in its way. With it came a natural light and a warmth that was totally alien to her. For the first time in her life, she saw the real depth of blue that was the sky as any remaining cloud began to dissipate.

AQUARIUS

'I think we all should wear these,' said Joan handing out shades, while they bathed in the sun's shimmering glory as it rose ever higher. The tink, tink, tink of melting ice falling from the surrounding trees grew into a shimmering crescendo ringing throughout the forest as the rapidly rising temperature heralded the start of the long thaw.

Kersha, who had woken to wonder what all the fuss was about, was now sat by Martha's side refusing to wear the eye protection. She was simply staring directly and curiously at the strange object in the sky without a frown, scowl or blink.

'How on Earth is she doing that?' asked Joan, worried for her eyesight.

'I'm not sure,' replied Maeve. 'She does many things that leave me speechless.'

'Warm,' said Kersha.

'Yes, warm.' said Maeve. 'It's called The Sun – you like?'

'I touch?'

'No, silly; it's too far away, but because you can feel its warmth means that the Sun is touching you.'

Kersha averted her eyes and gave Maeve a puzzled look, trying to wrap her head around that one, before declaring she was hungry and going back indoors to see what she could find to eat.

'What are you getting from the probes, Dad?' Maeve enquired.

'Trajectory, among other things,' said Kyle. The sun's analemma, new data on the tilt, wobble, spin.'

'Any Earth-shattering findings?'

'Oh, you are funny, girl. I don't know where or who you get it from.' Kyle removed his glasses and pinched the top of his nose between his eyes. He looked tired now despite his earlier exuberance. He and Joan hadn't managed much sleep in preparation for this unique event, and the amount of correlating and analysing that lay ahead meant they were unlikely to get any rest soon.

Maeve knew she would have to be getting back to her own projects at Ruston and Ilkley imminently, but right now she was determined to experience what her grandma had described as "to-day". This was daytime, a phenomenon that shone with a light so bright it still hurt her eyes whenever she removed her shades to experience its full splendour. The dirty white blanket that covered the Earth's surface now sparkled with a brilliance that was blinding, as if trillions of jewels were being reflected by the dazzling white orb in the sky. Even the air she was taking deep into her lungs felt different, it was as if her whole body was being flooded with an unseen energy. Maybe it was the instant infusion of natural vitamin D she was experiencing, or perhaps the adrenalin rush afforded by what she had only seen in pictures now manifest.

At its zenith, the sun's rays, perhaps aided by the heat from the chimney breast, caused a snowslide on the southern part of the roof, a mini avalanche that slid and dumped its load with a low, menacing rumble, revealing the old black slate that hadn't seen light in an age. Maeve looked at her parents and they at each other in turn, all with a knowing look that this was a show in microcosm of what was to come.

As the day wore on and the sun arced its way over and behind the forest peaks, the quartet set off up the slopes of Barden Moor to gain a better view of it setting, leaving Martha to reminisce and compare today's experience with those she remembered as a young girl.

The event, although not as spectacular as what they witnessed at dawn, was still worth the long climb up the moor. A fluffy, cotton wool type covering of cloud was now visible in the north-west of the sky where the weakening orb dipped behind turning its shroud a cerise to pink colour. Without the need for visual protection, they watched the azure sky above them morph to lilac, mauve, and as the sun finally dipped below the horizon, to the deepest cobalt, while the clouds changed colour once more to a noctilucent electric blue, a phenomenon caused by ice crystals forming in the lower atmosphere.

'Bye, sun,' said Kersha, offering up a childlike wave.

Kyle produced his pad and started bringing up data. 'So, let's see what Earth-shattering findings we have here,' he said while giving his daughter a hard look over the top of his specs.

'I'm sorry, Dad,' she said sounding earnest while trying to keep a wry smile off her face. 'I didn't mean to sound facetious, it was just an unfortunate choice of phrase, that's all.'

'Hmm - still funny though,' he admitted with a wink. 'Okay, according to this, we've just had twenty-one clicks of daylight dawn to dusk, which in old speak equates to eighteen point three-eight hours, approximately four hours longer than a day should be at this time of year pre-Shift.'

'This confirms our findings that the Earth's spin has slowed,' said Joan. 'Exacerbated, of course, by the moon slipping its orbit.'

'What about our rotation around the sun?' asked Maeve.

'That's a little more complex. As you know Nibiru's passing

slowed us down due to its immense gravitational pull. As it moves away its effect on us becomes weaker, but even so, at the perihelion it slows us down, then as we move away to the aphelion, we speed up again.'

'So, we are unlikely to experience seasons as grandma knew them?'

'That's right. While the solar cycles remain in flux the seasons will be arbitrary until such time as the cosmos settles back into its circadian rhythm. How long that will take remains unknown, as does what it will look like because we no longer have any fixed points of reference.'

'The tilt is no longer at twenty-three point four degrees to the axis,' added Kyle. 'Also, the wobble has become erratic, due in part to the moon drifting away from us, meaning the precession of the equinoxes will alter accordingly.'

Maeve reflected on Percy's repudiation of what was the Gregorian calendar and wondered what he would make of these revelations. 'So, even though we shall eventually be able to determine night and day simply by our observations, any notion of linear time or calendars shall still be totally useless to us.'

'Precisely,' said Kyle. 'Trying to unify or standardise any transitory system would be pointless.'

'You managed to bring order out of chaos with your click code.'

'Yes,' her father smiled,' but it only works within a construct of predetermined rules unique to locale and participation. Beyond that and making handy comparisons with our past, it could never work universally for obvious reasons.'

As they trudged back down the moor, off to the new north could be seen the faint, shimmering turquoise glow of the Aurora Borealis. The night air had cooled and the melting snow and ice beneath their feet had begun to crystallise again. Puffs of breath appeared illuminated by torchlight in front of their faces. The call of a nearby owl echoed around the otherwise silent wood, and Kersha's eyes seemed to glow in the dark. They came to a small clearing and Joan told them to turn off their torches. Pointing up to the now ink-black sky she showed them the constellation of Orion, as sharp and clear as Maeve had observed in books and images.

'The bright star off to the left, is that Sirius?'

'Yes, the binary star known as 'The Dog' in Canis Major,' confirmed Joan.

PRECESSION

Maeve half-expected some sarcastic quip about the mythological warring Gods, demigods and reptilian entities along with Aryan Queens and Wolfen Kings that supposedly came from the outer reaches of star systems such as Sirius and Betelgeuse to shape the destiny of the cosmos including the slave species here on Earth, but it never came.

'Can we see Nibiru now?'

'No, Nibiru is a brown dwarf, long invisible to the naked eye despite its size. It's heading back out towards Neptune and the Kuiper belt.

'What about the North star?'

'You mean Polaris? Well, it's somewhere behind and beyond that hill, but it's no longer the North star I'm afraid,' said Kyle. 'It's more than thirteen degrees off the celestial pole right now. According to my calculations, Gamma Cephei in the Cepheus constellation will eventually replace Polaris as our North star, around about the time we transition from Aquarius to Capricorn, so we'll all be long gone before that occurs.'

Maeve continued to gaze in wonder at the depths of the heavens and thought on how many times the stars had been named and re-named across aeons, shaping the belief systems of countless cultures, who raised pantheons in honour to their Gods. Percy Snodgrass believed the Universe to be merely what us humans perceived without representing any kind of true reality, and yet cosmic changes by design or accident continue to unfold and ultimately steer our destiny here on Earth. She pondered the conundrums and contradictions while marvelling at the twinkling celestial tapestry above her head, neither caring if what she was witnessing was real or some holographic illusion. Yes, she was fully cognizant that her visual reality was governed by the electro-magnetic spectrum and what her current five senses would allow, and seeing what she saw now for the first time only made her realise that there was so much more left unseen. What was more evidently clear to her at this moment were the all too real tasks that lay ahead, and she silently formed and sent out a message of gratitude to whatever creative power it was out there that had granted her this experience and for being born into this time.

From behind, Maeve felt the rare warmth of a maternal embrace. As if sensing the poignancy of the moment, Joan softly spoke in her daughter's ear. 'I'm truly sorry I haven't been able to spend as much time with you and Kersha as I wanted.'

'That's okay.'

'No – I'm really sorry, Maeve, I …'

'That's okay, Mum,' said Maeve, turning to face her, although in the dark they couldn't really see each other, which was probably just as well. 'I understand, honestly; there's no need to apologise.'

'I have to get back to Lewis as soon as possible. There's a plane leaving Dishforth in fifteen clicks, I …'

'Why don't you say morning, mum? No disrespect to Dad, but - there's a plane leaving in the morning - sounds better, don't you think?'

'Not all the days, if that's what you prefer to call them, that lie ahead are going to be like this one.'

'I know that. I'm fully aware of what's to come. I'm a geologist, remember?'

'I know, I'm sorry. It's just sometimes I'm so wrapped up in my work I forget, I …'

'Please stop saying you're sorry. The work you and Dad have been doing has helped facilitate what manifested to-day, and we were here to share it with you guys. What we witnessed was incredible.'

'It was, wasn't it?'

All the high expectations Joan Bradley had ever hoped for her only daughter had been met, and some. She was immensely proud, of course, but even as the word formed, she baulked and for some reason was unable to utter it, despite the cover of dark. Maybe it was the underlying feeling of guilt of being an absent mother during her formative years and beyond that would make such a statement of fact seem disingenuous, or maybe it was just how she was wired that made her feel uncomfortable in these situations. Having been bold enough to make the embrace, she still felt the slightest of shock in her daughter's reaction at the tenuous show of affection she had managed to muster. Commitment to their respective callings took precedent over most things, and often that included family. Maeve was no different in her outlook as both her parents, and their combined attempts at playing happy families made such attempts glaringly awkward. It was her failed quest to satisfy her curiosity in relation to the hawks that had brought them together like this and would probably never have materialised otherwise, but she had been genuinely thrilled at them all being together to witness the day's events. 'Day' – it was a word she was looking forward to adding to

PRECESSION

her vocabulary.

Good Vibrations

'**H**e's a bit brusque, isn't he, your Irish friend?'

'That's one way of putting it,' Maeve concurred. 'Gets the job done though,' she said while being impressed with the progress his team was making at the south-east section of the site.

'He wasn't too pleased at you sequestering the services of his Indian colleague,' said Elena. 'The air was blue, had a go at Moira too.'

'I don't suppose it fazed her one bit.'

'True. She matched him with her own repertoire of colourful language, which managed to shut him up for a bit.'

'Yeah, I know he can be a bit of an annoying prick, but his bark is worse than his bite, and I have to say he's good at what he does.' Maeve looked out at the recently cleared land and beyond to a vista that would soon be coastal, and then up to the sky that had turned familiar grey, now laden with moisture due to the returning cycle of precipitation created by the rising temperatures and subsequent warming of the Earth. A light but persistent acidic rain fell on her upturned face, and she offered up a silent prayer that the faith she put in Jed's skill sets would be borne out by completing the project in time, ahead of the inevitable deluge that was to come.

Her attempts to engage with the big lump in order to heap praise on his efforts proved futile. He was obviously still pissed off and his petulance reflected in his refusal to parlay, citing his overburdened work schedule that in his eyes she had created in the first place. He had now been tasked with relocating the vast complex of fish farms and sea-life nurseries, a job he deemed unnecessary as in his words - *'the bloody things live in water, don't they?'* - Having explained to him the rising sea levels would still be irradiated and likely to bring unknown levels of contaminants failed to quell his asperity. Maeve shrugged, she was used to his irascible tendencies, and it didn't prevent her from filing a glowing progress report for him and his team to Council. Acres upon acres of hemp and bamboo production had now been moved to new silos and hangers to the north, and the laboratories and lecture hall in which she'd given her infamous presentation had gone, leaving behind nothing but bare foundations

PRECESSION

waiting to be reclaimed by the impending flood.

§

'I'm so glad you made it, my dear,' said Moira Duggan by way of greeting. 'Come with me, you're not going to want to miss this.' She waved her stick in the air and led them to where a gathering consisting of engineers, builders, selected bibliophiles from Boston Spa and a delegation of councillors were grouped at the entrance to the site. Engineer Navinder Buthar, who was the dual focus of attention at this invited audience, was knelt at the foot of the foundation stone on a plump, emerald green velvet cushion adorned with gold braid and tassels. Quoting from the Vedas in Sanskrit, he was performing a ritual blessing of the site in time honoured tradition akin to those performed in ancient eastern ceremonies and of the master freemasons who built the great Tartarian empire. Hovering close by and meticulously following the sacrament and Brahmanas with his own copy of the Rigveda, stood Professor Percival Snodgrass resplendent from head to foot in a curious, but no less colourful mix of traditional Indian garb. On top he wore a Dastaar turban emblazoned with a Chand Tora brooch depicting a double-edged sword and crescent, complete with a golden-red Banarasi brocade Sherwani and a pair of white silk Churidars. Despite the cultural and religious contradictions, which to Maeve were obvious, she couldn't help but smile and silently applaud his efforts at authenticity given the resources at his disposal. There had been dissenting voices from certain members of council at the theological nature of such a ceremony, but Percy had quieted and schooled them on the ascetic tenets of Indo-Aryan philosophy that encompassed the Vedic texts, that had in turn captured the imagination and inspired two of his great philosopher mentors, in Kant and Schopenhauer. Councillors, no matter their standing, were no match for the professor's intellectual verve and acts of persuasion.

After the ceremony, Maeve was introduced to the thirteen PK's, seven women and six men renowned for their psychokinetic abilities, who had been selected for the task of constructing the facility under the instruction of Nav Buthar. Giant shaped blocks of smooth, shiny bast that had been brought to site using maglev technology were now waiting to be put into place and erected with pioneering telekinetic

AQUARIUS

energy using an array of vibrational frequencies once privy only to the ancients. It was an ambitious, if not as some doubters would have it, impossible undertaking that Duggan and Bradley had devised and presented to Council, a project designed to be constructed and completed with minimal mechanical effort. Although the materials being used were no way near as heavy as the great stone blocks used to build the Giza pyramids, it would still be a mammoth and untested assignment that when completed would shine as bright and resplendent as the Taj Mahal.

'I never got chance to thank you,' said Nav.

'For what?'

'Recommending me for the gig.'

'That's okay,' said Maeve.' I had every faith in you, and that faith has been borne out, you're doing a great job; it should be me thanking you.'

'Spunky wasn't happy.'

'I know, and I'm sorry for splitting you guys up like that.'

'Don't be - I'm glad to be away from him and his downers for a while. You've given me a great responsibility here, and I'm grateful for the challenge, so thanks once again.' They hugged, and Maeve felt vindicated with her decisions. She knew Jed was happy being his cynical old self and would have been totally the wrong choice to oversee this project with its esoteric and ethereal vibe, and what he would have made of Percy Snodgrass who was now busy schooling any councillors who cared to listen by regaling them with Nicola Tesla quotes, would be anyone's guess.

The resident PKs had already been successful in constructing a scaled down version of the blueprints and were now busy calculating the vibrational amplification and frequencies required to realise the real thing. At a predetermined signal the thirteen psychokinetics formed a circle of alternate genders. With outstretched arms and hands, they connected as one. With heads bowed they fell silent, and the gathered crowd were hushed. Soon, a low resonant hum arose from the small amplification device that was placed at the centre of the circle. As the volume slowly increased an additional tonal wave of ambient sound started to pulse softly, yet rhythmically over it. On top of that and without any perceptible initiation, the PKs began to emit a collective sound, not unlike a chant, but more choral, without any perceptible pause for breath, and deeply resonant.

'417Hz,' whispered Percy. 'Clearing away any negative energy.'

PRECESSION

'Shh!' Moira admonished.

A small change in pitch - 528Hz - according to Percy, and the further annoyance of Moira, became audible, and although the pulsating rhythmic wave remained constant, the depth and resonance seemed to increase. Breaking rank, the PKs now formed a large semi-circle in front of the object of their attention. On the ground lay a metre thick by five metres wide section of bast curtain wall that when erect stood ten metres high. Four acoustic devices were placed at each corner that when activated added to the ever-changing modulation. Dual frequencies now came into play, which, happily for Moira, not even Percy could detect. Maeve began to feel the vibrations permeate every cell in her body, and a few of the councillors present had to turn away with hands over their ears. One or two others, ultra-sensitive to the constantly altering frequencies, threw up on the spot. The pitch rose ever higher until Maeve's ears popped and rang as if a tuning fork had been placed inside her head. The persistent resonant tone finally dissipated into the aether until it became imperceptible to the untrained human ear. Only the thirteen PKs remained highly tuned and entrained to the subtle but ever present cosmic vibrational energy that was now spiralling down an invisible vortex to link in harmony with the created nutational wavelength. It now felt as if the whole area of their collective presence was placed inside a vacuum where all elements normally recognised by the five senses were now absent, except that is, to the ocular phenomena that all present were witnessing. The highly polished rectangular slab slowly rose from its resting place to hover unsteadily around three metres from the ground. Looks of disbelief could be seen on the faces of those now recovered, but no sound could be heard. High above seven red kites soared in an anti-clockwise motion as if outlining and riding on the etheric energy being produced, and the giant slab of wall, under the guidance of a PK holding a frequency modulator, agonisingly shifted itself to a vertical position. It was then guided onto seven pyramid shaped housing pins that stood erect from the foundation. With uncanny accuracy the giant section dropped slowly and silently into place. Nothing then happened for what seemed like an eternity, until, at last the inertia created by the vacuity relented, senses were released from their suspension but didn't come readily into play for many who were still left in quiet astonishment at what they had just witnessed. Nav Buthar and his team of engineers, who had been waiting impatiently were now given the green light to inspect the build. Lasers flashed across the gleaming structure, measuring, checking levels, testing load. Nav personally scrutinised every centimetre of the construction where the wall met its foundation and reported back to Maeve, Moira and Percy beaming from ear to ear.

'Well?' said Moira.

Nav shook his head. 'You won't get a razor blade in there,' he said happily. 'It's perfect.'

'Beshak, mere dost,' exclaimed Percy, flexing Hindi. 'If you want to find the secrets of the universe, you only have to think in terms of energy, frequency and vibration. They do not lift. They do not force. They tune the field until matter forgets how to resist.' he added, feeling the need to paraphrase some more.

Maeve returned Moira's confidently delivered victorious wink with a broad smile that belied an immense sense of relief now that the first phase of their audacious design had been successfully realised. They linked arms and Maeve guided the old girl, at her own steady pace to where the thirteen PKs were now gathered in a subdued but self-congratulatory huddle. Despite the elation, they both knew there would be no time to sit on triumphant laurels. Speed of construction without compromising the already set standards of precision was uppermost in their thoughts, as was the relatively untested and unknown mental and physical capacities of these brilliant Kinetics to collectively bring this project to completion.

PRECESSION

Healing The Past

As the glaciers and ice-sheets to the north began to shift and melt, tectonic adjustments further south created scenarios that were devastating, but not entirely unexpected. Earthquakes created landslides, floods and tsunamis. Vast tracts of land disappeared beneath the waves and many inland towns and cities became coastal. Volcanoes laying semi dormant after The Shift became active again. The effects were felt worldwide, but the northern hemisphere bore the brunt of those seismic changes, and many who were left unprepared or unable to reach high ground perished. On these Isles, the four major fault lines that had been exposed during The Shift were subjected to enormous pressures due to the shifting and melting of ice. As prognosticated by Maeve and Moira, sections of the lithosphere gave way to these pressures and in short order the waters rushed in to fill the vacated land. From this upheaval five main islands were created forming the archipelago. Neither a topographer nor a cartographer, nevertheless, Maeve was tasked with re-mapping what was once known as The British Isles from the air. A lot of this was done remotely with drone technology, but whenever the opportunity arose she and Moira would sequester a maglev and take to the skies with Kersha as a giddy passenger to marvel and wonder at the ever-changing landscape morphing from bland grey-white to vibrant green as nature began to slowly emerge from its long imposed hibernation.

 Maeve had been thankful that Moira had lived long enough to re-live the sights and sounds of her early childhood, glad that her teacher had been able to show her the geographical beauty and wonder of places that made up these isles that had been so long hidden from view, that were now in many places unrecognizable. Her apprenticeship under the tutelage of the old woman had been a tough but rewarding experience. She had absorbed lessons and accumulated knowledge like a sponge, and at the end of the great thaw, when nature resumed its spectacular yet irregular display of seasons, Maeve's innate abilities came to the fore. Ruston Parva and The National Library were her seminal projects and Moira's swan songs, brought to completion with much laudation for their innovation in

AQUARIUS

both design and structure. They were times of great change and uncertainty, but those times now belonged to the past.

Moira Duggan often came to Maeve in her dreams, even long after she'd passed. The dreams were always metaphorical, sometimes cryptic. Far off in the distance, ankle deep in a lush green meadow with her dowsing wands in her hand as a gentle breeze wafted her wild grey hair across her smiling face, Maeve would fall awake almost always with a nagging problem solved or the means to fix firmly in her head, and she would religiously create time and space in her daily meditations to offer up love, thanks and gratitude to her one-time mentor.

Moira was laid to rest amongst the ancient trees of Rothiemurchus Forest in the Cairngorms, near to her Aviemore birthplace, where Maeve had wept openly, not only for the loss of her beloved colleague, but for the sheer beauty of the place. It was a time when the Earth in the northern hemisphere was moving away from the Sun. The natural but transformative cycle was entering sleep mode, and the colours highlighted by the retiring rays of the Life-giver were indescribable. This period, once known as autumn, brought with it a deep sense of melancholy and an aching in the soul at the arrival of the inevitable. A Great Reset was now underway, and not the one envisaged by The Demiurge. Although their design for depopulation had been somewhat realised, and their skewed aims at fulfilling scripture from the book of Revelation had been on course, their *rapture* had been thwarted by the long moral arc and recur of the cosmos that would ultimately bend towards natural law, truth and justice. New and previously hidden technologies were now being developed and put to use as resources came more readily available. International travel and communications had been restored, and virgin nations arose like phoenix from the ashes of the old order to swap tales of survival and resilience.

§

Maeve Bradley learned many languages and became part of a team of ambassadors and advisors who travelled far and wide. They were missionaries without doctrine or prejudice, showing how their fledgling system of small autonomous communities without any form of governance except for councillors who were selected and rotated by the people worked. The corrupted and failed tenets of democracies and republics had been rejected wholesale, along with the tyranny of communism that unelected dictators from global institutions such as the WEF had tried to usher in with the intent of reintroducing feudalism back to the masses. Although far from perfect, and not without problems, the symbiotic system developed by those pioneers who operated out of the garrison stronghold of Catterick in the old United Kingdom had proven itself by the societal advances that their progenies were now showing to the rest of the world. Links were forged and lines of communication opened among the now burgeoning pocket-sized nations that were emerging in old Europe and particularly across what was left of the North American continent.

From the air Maeve was able to witness the cataclysm wrought by the passing of Nibiru and the subsequent effects of The Shift. The movement of The Mid Atlantic Ridge separating the North American and Eurasian plates, and the activation of The New Madrid fault, which in turn had triggered the Ramapo and Hopewell faults, had all but obliterated what was the Eastern seaboard. Lakes Erie and Ontario merged, forming an extended part of the St. Lawrence Bay. Quebec, Montreal and Toronto had disappeared, as had Boston, New York and Washington, while the Appalachian range had been pressured to new heights. On the west coast, California had tumbled into the sea. The vast Cascadia subduction zone had sent P waves to the shores, liquifying land, giving notice in quick succession to the San Andreas, Calaveras and Hayward faults that gave up their positions in long overdue relief.

The destruction of the old USA had been brutal, both geophysically and politically. In shades of the demise of ancient Rome, the psychopathic ruling classes had tried to cling on to the last vestiges of power with a crazed rearguard subjugation of the people even as its cities crumbled, disappeared or burned.

Maeve met with her counterparts, the sons and daughters of the survivors who had crossed state lines from all over the land to shelter, bond, re-generate and ultimately thrive again, swapping tales and drawing parallels with the experiences of The Meek. Despite the accepted abrogation of the notion of heroes, names were dropped; the altruistic feats of those destined to be spoken off in legendary, almost mythical terms had been kept alive across such vast distances even when the means of worldwide communication had been lost. There

AQUARIUS

were many stories to be told. The pre-Shift generation were largely gone, and documenting the bewildering transition from then into the now would be tasked to the vestigial band of scholars and scribes. She visited many small but ever-growing communities that were beginning to thrive and flourish as autonomous domains. Many of these communities had been deliberately sited on old Indian reservations, an irony that was not lost on her. Moira's pioneering peers across the pond had possessed the wisdom and knowledge to seek out lands sacred to the indigenous people, where the ley was mighty powerful despite the rivers of blood that had flowed through them. Maeve inevitably felt that surge of energy course inside her whenever she was warmly invited onto their homesteads, where she would converse at length with her own peers, those skilled in geomancy and the ways of the land, many of whom were descendants of the First Nations. The use of psychedelics such as Ayahuasca, DMT and psilocybin fungi in carefully controlled ceremonies as a means to expand conscious awareness or to treat generational trauma was standard practice in their healing centres (Maeve was certain that Percy would've wholeheartedly given his endorsement). Channelers and remote viewers now formed a global network, providing spiritual guidance as people became ever more percipient. The international exchange of ideas, means, technique and wherewithal were given freely without toll or tariff. Delegates from Ampleforth who worked alongside Donna Channing now passed on their unique knowledge and skill-sets in return. Among their number was a woman known only as Kersha; a character who could allure or repulse in equal measure dependant on the pervading vibe. Indigenous peoples had a natural affinity towards her and she to them, especially the descendants of the Lakota tribes for some unexplainable reason, or maybe it had something to do with the olive complexion, the strong white teeth and the shiny ebony hair that she often wore in long, braided pigtails that made her resemble one of their own. Her persona and body shape had become softer and more relaxed as time had passed, no longer the angular, hard-wired feral creature of her youth, she now exuded a measured calm in her much-rounded features, which belied the still guarded fight or flight, ready to respond to anything mean that lay behind those deep dark eyes. Through her art she had become a healer, a trauma councillor, widely renowned in both vocations. Although now blessed with a full vocabulary, she was a woman of few words, but who still managed to

PRECESSION

swear and curse in excess whenever emphasis was needed. The old concept of fame was no longer a thing; the pseudo intellectualising of art laughable now, but Kersha's work was hung, broadcast and displayed everywhere because of its visual ability to seemingly transcend dimensions in whatever context or paradigm it was presented. It was one of two things she had given to the world anonymously, the other being her stem cells; the discoveries made by Donna Channing and her team through studying the symbionts in her unique Rh-negative blood that were able to create a constant disease preventing aerobiosis in the pleomorphic cycle of her cells.

The advancement of humankind was now happening at an exponential rate in both technological and biological fields, but this quantum leap was being tempered by a universal conscious reunion with nature and Mother Earth. Kersha's empathy with the reorganised North American tribes reflected this. She fell in love with this land and its people. Her travels took her to all points on the compass where both she and Maeve would often spend nights around a campfire under the stars listening to ancient tales and prophecies of their ancestors that had come to manifest. She particularly enjoyed watching the children playing games, aiming at targets with slingshots, their shared laughter vibrant and carefree. It stirred something within her, a far-off distant memory of when she herself had wielded a similar device, not to play with but to hunt, to survive, and of course without the joy now present. The memory was short-lived. It was a different time, almost a different dimension, any attached trauma long healed and put away, but it still made her instinctively reach out to seek her partner's hand, that would be received with a reciprocal crinkled smile showing faint lines around the mouth and eyes gained with age that were illuminated and accentuated by the warm glow of the campfire. Safe. Secure.

Emile Schroeder was a scribe of note and one of Maeve's respected peers. His knowledge and insight into the relatively short story of the corporation previously known as The United States of America was unsurpassed, and, like his late British counterpart Percy Snodgrass, had been tasked to document the rise, demise and rise of his homeland. Their respective briefs were uniquely their own, of course, but both he and Percy's successor would regularly beta read each other's work and enthusiastically critique and debate at length.

AQUARIUS

The climate across much of what was left of the continent was now temperate, and the two friends would gather in the evenings on Emile's porch on the border of what used to be West Virginia and Kentucky, drinking root beer and listening to the nightly chorus of cicadas while testing and flexing their knowledge by reciting famous quotes and asking the other to identify the author: Wilde, Hemingway, Faulkner, Stein, Kerouac, Woolf, Joyce et al, with words of wisdom still apposite and as relevant as ever.

'"The two most important days in your life are the day you were born and the day you find out why."'

'Samuel Langhorne Clemens,' answered Maeve immediately.

'Huh, you're too good for this game,' conceded Emile.

'Well, I have to admit, Twain is one of my favourites.'

'The professor mentored you well.'

'Percy was a wonderful albeit an eccentric teacher,' Maeve admitted, 'but most of this stuff I learned as a child,' she said with a cheeky smile. 'Tell me, who is your absolute favourite?'

'Hmm,' pondered Emile thoughtfully rubbing his chin. 'Well, beyond the obvious ones, there's O'Rourke and Zappa – both of whom had their own unique way of sticking it to the man, but in all honesty, I would probably have to say Carlin.'

Maeve looked surprised. 'You mean George Carlin, the satirist?'

'Sure, I mean if you put most of the satire to one side, as funny and bitingly poignant as it was, he also made some very insightful observations about our species and how we operate inside societal groups that we could well heed in the now.'

Maeve had scant knowledge of the guy or the other two mentioned to form a debate. 'You obviously have a great regard for the man to place him above such other luminaries.'

Emile shrugged. 'He was a flawed and often contradictory human as were a lot of the others. But it seems once he rid himself of his cocaine addiction and had a few near-death experiences, his real awakening to the machinations of those in power was like a bursting dam, the previous confines of his art were torn apart, and he told it like it was to any who would listen. Holding back with a reluctant self-censorship to appease conservative sensibilities had gone out the window. It was as if time had sped up, as if he knew he now had a limited window in which to get his stuff out. He upset a lot of people along the way, and he didn't give a fuck. I think that's why I put him up there.'

PRECESSION

'Hmm. It's funny you should mention the acceleration of time. I've been thinking about it a lot of late. Specifically, how we weave the notion of linear time into our storytelling when neither you nor I have ever experienced the concept of past, present and future, I mean not in the way your friend Mr. Carlin and his compeers experienced it. I have come across many testaments in the lead up to The Shift that describe how it felt time was going faster, how what they knew as minutes and hours seemed to be flying by and the days becoming much shorter, along with feelings that their reality was being squeezed, speeding through an ever narrowing funnel of time, and as the time sped up, so the noise increased and the madness all around reached new levels: sensations heightening, emotions spinning out of control, lies exploding all around and yet the few shreds of truth left somehow transpired to keep the sanity. But ever present in these stories was the urge to do things faster because there was no time, time was fast running out, running away, playing catch-me-if-you-can.'

'What you're describing is the mass shift in consciousness that was taking place around that time. It was a painful process for many. The space-time continuum was being compressed. It drove some to despair, madness and suicide.'

'I know, but you and I were born into that transition. What seemed bewildering to them was normal for us. I grew up at the speed of light. I don't know if it's the same for you but as I grow older it seems as if I must have had prescience when I came into this world, and I've only ever lived in the now. I would never be able to truly understand the concept of nostalgia, let's say. For me, memories are merely mind maps, they serve no purpose. My experiences in life can be strung out in time if you like but why the need when they are for ever present in the now?'

'You're right,' said Emile, slowly nodding in agreement at the conundrum. 'It's the spells we cast through our words that are the problem. As powerful as they are, we are stymied by their limitations that can only be expressed within the inherent rules of linguistics.'

'Professor Snodgrass and I often debated the semantics without coming up with a satisfactory solution.'

'And there won't be one until we all start to communicate as telepaths once again and the written word will become – dare I say – a thing of the past.'

AQUARIUS

Maeve became fascinated with Schroeder's written accounts of the vast underground network of tunnels and DUMBS that were spread across the continent. Ostensibly designed as nuclear shelters to house presidents and high-ranking officials belonging to the military industrial complex in the event of a worldwide cataclysm, their real use had been hidden from the public in shrouds of secrecy and conspiracy. Emile and his own team of storians had documented the exposure of these survival centres in extraordinary detail as the remnants of the so-called elite scrambled for sanctuary while the rest of the nation tore itself apart in the aftermath of The Shift. And to Maeve's surprise and delight, he had offered to show her what was left of them.

They visited the abandoned location of Mount Weather up in the Blue Ridge mountains of Virginia, the Raven Rock site in Pennsylvania and Cheyenne Mountain complex in Colorado. Here, they passed through an entrance carved into and under two thousand feet of solid granite that once housed two blast-proof steel doors each weighing over twenty-five tons and two metres thick. Its internal highly sophisticated defence systems ran for miles in a series of high-tech modules also built with blast-proof capabilities. Equipped with every need from birth to death, it had been designed and engineered with comprehensive life support systems including its own internal reservoir and water treatment plant, food and growing facilities that could last years.

They wandered through the now abandoned and ransacked labyrinth of tunnels, the giant halls where hundreds of generators lay rusting, its looted and pillaged infirmary, and the command and nerve centre of operations with its smashed state-of-the-art IT capabilities that had ultimately failed.

'This place must have been impenetrable,' Maeve wondered aloud, her voice echoing around the cold, dank chamber.

'Yes, you would think so,' said Emile with a wry smile on his face. 'But they never reckoned on a people who saw a flaw in their grand design.'

'Who?'

'The clue is in the name they chose to give to this place.'

'The Cheyenne?'

Emile nodded. 'It's their ancestral home, they have lived on this land for generations and they know it like the back of their hand.

Secret waterways led to the outside from deep within these bunkers. They were to be used as emergency escape routes if the need ever arose, but they were also a means to enter the complex and the Cheyenne people knew of them.'

'But surely the external defence operations wouldn't have allowed anyone remotely near this place,' countered Maeve.

'True,' said Emile. 'But when the militias mobilised in sufficient numbers and besieged the area, the grunts who had been tasked to defend these bases soon came to the realisation that they had been left outside on their own. They ultimately weren't part of the survival plan, meant only for the chosen few. The jig was up. Some, the bewildered and brainwashed few made a futile stand, but they were soon overcome, and the remainder joined forces with the militias and turned on their masters.'

Maeve closed her eyes and stood in silence, save for the regular sound of drips of mountain water that had leeched through rock and was dripping in regular patterns from a dilapidated ceiling. Witnessing the scale of these operations first hand, the immense feats of engineering with technologies so far advanced yet subverted from public scrutiny managed to put into sharp perspective anything she had ever heard or read about. She allowed her imagination to take her so far, but even her heightened sensibilities couldn't prepare her for what she would experience next. Although she lacked the capacity to feel nostalgia, her percipient faculties were now honed and finely tuned, a gift that sometimes felt like a curse.

Hidden under the Archuleta Mesa on the New Mexico Columbia border lies the most sinister of what were known as Deep Underground Military Bases. The Dulce base, long being the subject of dark conspiracy and official government denial, was the centre for research and development of highly classified technologies, especially those from antediluvian or non-human origin. Also to conduct controversial experimentation, especially relating to behavioural modification, genetic engineering and human cybernetics.

As they travelled along the scrub and desert to their destination, Emile pointed out mile upon regimented ruined mile of FEMA camps that had been earmarked for the millions of expected dissidents who were to be detained during the Cabal's Great Reset.

AQUARIUS

Again, it brought home to Maeve the sheer scale of depravity and human enslavement the psychopathic shadow rulers were planning before the Earth and its orbiting neighbour said NO!

As with all the other sites they had visited, Maeve got that all-pervading sense of dread and foreboding inside her stomach, but on entering this particular complex the feeling soon became overwhelming, tainted with a raw impression of an evil presence, similar to the one she had experienced as a young geological engineer in the ruined heart of old London. If anyone else in their small group were sensing this, they weren't showing it but the rapid change in atmosphere and temperature was tangible to all as they ventured deeper. Illuminated by their torches, Maeve marvelled at the shiny smooth glass like condition of the perfectly round tunnel walls built by nuclear powered boring machines known as subterrenes. Due to the advanced technology employed in these machines, exceptionally large tunnels were constructed at incredible speeds without generating residual debris in a process using charged particle beams that melted solid rock in a vitrifying process leaving a neat and hardened glass-lined tube in its wake.

'This is what the VHSTs ran on,' said Emile, pointing out the still intact monorail track.

'VHSTs?'

'Very High-Speed Transit System, or probably better known to you as a Maglev train. They were suspended above the rail on an electromagnetic wave and travelled through a frictionless vacuum at speeds in excess of Mach 2, which meant they could have traversed coast to coast, Los Angeles to New York in less than a click.'

Maeve wondered at the sheer scale of this ultra clandestine undertaking and then thought about the persecution of Max's great uncle and other pioneering geniuses of his ilk whose work was stolen and used for nefarious ends. 'Do you think the tech know-how came from compromised humans or off-world sources?'

'I would suggest maybe an amalgam of both,' said Emile. 'And it's not as recent as you may think. The blueprints and templates for a VHST were developed by the Rand Corporation as early as the nineteen seventies, presented to the military Industrial complex and later realised by what became known as DARPA, funded with clandestine black budget projects, but I wouldn't rule out a big input from our ET friends, if not in the actual construction but certainly in design and savvy. There are over two hundred of these bases across the land, all of which were interconnected in a vast network one time. This, the one in Los Alamos and area fifty-one are supposed to be where the alien Greys hung out. Stories of abductions, human and animal experimentation and even the presence of portals into other dimensions are rife among the locals.'

'You mention the existence of what you refer to as repros in your writing. Your description of these often malevolent yet recondite creatures mirrors what were known as lazors in my homeland. Many myths have grown up around them. Do you still hold that they were the result of experimentation and hybridisation?'

'This is what first-hand accounts say. There is overwhelming evidence of DNA splicing and gene manipulation as well as advanced human to AI cybernetics. There were many confrontations with entities that couldn't be described as human when the DUMBS were exposed and liberated. A lot of the testimonies came from the thousands of children who had been abducted, trafficked and primed for ritual slaughter in satanic ceremonies. They became a production line for the extraction of adrenochrome, a product of the adrenal gland when the victim was exposed to abject terror that was like a life-extending ambrosia to the Greys and so revered among the paedophiles in Hollywood.'

Maeve shuddered at the thought. 'Do you think they are still among us – the repros, I mean?'

'Well, I've never had the misfortune of confronting one, but who knows? The shafts and chambers go deep, the tunnels here are said to go down ten miles into the Earth. Many collapsed with the seismic effects of The Shift, others were blasted or sealed by the militias that uncovered them. Of course, stories of sightings and encounters persist, but – hey, are you okay?'

Maeve dropped her torch and staggered backwards. With lightning reactions Kersha caught her from behind as her legs buckled. Taking the dead weight, she expertly eased her into a sitting position against the tunnel wall.

'Is she okay?' said Emile, shocked and surprised. 'What just happened?'

Maeve's head slumped onto her chest, her breath coming in rapid bursts.

'She's having a vision,' said Kersha. 'Just give her some space.' All at once Maeve drew in a mighty gulp of air and raised her head to the heavens as she exhaled, while her eyes rolled up revealing the whites as if possessed. 'She does this a lot,' explained her partner calmly.

'Oh – okay,' said Emile, genuine concern still evident on his face.

Maeve's psychic abilities had burgeoned over time. They were never sought after but developed organically, and she used the insights gained as an adjunct to her work as a geomancer. Now, her aura was being bombarded with what seemed like hundreds of disembodied entities attempting to gear down and enter her vibrational space. For an immeasurable time, it felt as though her head would explode, until, at last she was lifted up and out of herself where a calm, soothing voice ushered out the noise and spoke softly to her.

'Greetings, my friend.'

All at once the blunt, dense vibration of the Earthly plane was lifted, her five senses became redundant, and her cosmic awareness opened like a flower.

'We are sorry for the inelegant intrusion. There are many souls who wish to communicate,' the voice continued.

'What do you want of me – why can't I see you?' Maeve found herself asking.

'A visual representation of who I am is not so important now and would likely cause an unnecessary burden on your physical being. What is important is the message we bring to you, and the undertaking we would humbly ask of you.'

The peace and serenity Maeve now felt that seemed to permeate every cell and atom of her being was indescribable, but in the far corners of what she perceived to be her consciousness was a darkness that she instinctively knew had to be addressed. No words were needed. Her understanding of the message and acceptance of the task were sent and received telepathically. She awaited instructions.

'Many, many souls are pleased you are here. You and your companion were guided to this place by the appetence of the guardians of this land; as such your presence and purpose will be two-fold.'

'Who are you?'

'My given name on Earth was Vera. I was a small child when I was taken from my parents and brought here. I belong to a group of older light beings who volunteered to experience this short, unpleasant experience on this planet. We were assigned to chaperone and comfort the many who passed so violently, to ease their passage back to the spirit world. Many were new souls, and the residual trauma left on their essence was so great that their journey back to the Godhead was curtailed in a negative and low vibration that kept them in the ethereal. Even we were not prepared for the extent of man's depraved capabilities. And so the dark energy that blights this land has affected the patrons who have strived for generations to live in harmony with her. Beyond Earth's cataclysm their survival has been further hampered by bad water, poisoned land, failing crops, and infertility between both genders. They believe they are cursed, but, as handed down in their long verbal story, they also believe a saviour to be at hand, and they feel that time is now. Cause and effect, or what you would describe as Karma, is the result of man's limited free will, a process in which we are not allowed to interfere, however, a certain amount of guidance is permitted, and we shall endeavour to facilitate whatever positive reparation you shall bring to bear. I know you are sensitive to the accumulated pain, you feel it in every part of your being, and though you may not fully understand on your return to your conscious self, know now that you chose this path, and walking it won't be easy, but also know that every injured spirit, young or old that came to greet you this day is filled with eternal gratitude for what you have done and are about to do.'

'How will I know I have chosen the right path?'

'As always allow your instinct to be your guide. Your sensibilities are finely tuned and will show you where any bad energies lie. You will be gifted signs and symbols. The three shall be replaced by the four. The three points of the triangle will become the four points of the diamond; thus, the energies will shift, the vibrations shall lift and the waters will flow as they were intended. The caretakers of this land are good people; they have a strong connection with the universal force they know as The Great White Spirit. Know them as your friends and helpers. On this plane there are many who wish to send their eternal love – may God bless you on your journey . . .'

Maeve slowly felt the denseness return to her body. As full consciousness took hold, the kinaesthetic sensations of cold, damp and dis-ease became percipient and a big part of her wished herself back to the unburdened, all-knowing space she'd just vacated.

Kersha's close familiar smiling features were the first thing to come into focus, followed by Emile who was stood close by still not totally sure what had just gone down.

'You're back,' said Kersha, gently wiping away the unforced

tears that were streaming down her lover's face.

'Are you okay?' asked Emile, not really knowing how to react.

Maeve formed a smile, took in a deep breath and slowly nodded her head while not being entirely cognizant of the word "okay" in the now.

'We should get you out of here.'

'Just give her a moment,' said Kersha, holding her water bottle to Maeve's lips.

She had been channelled and gifted visions many times, but none so powerful, enlightening and revelatory as this. In perceived time she hadn't been gone that long, but the experience had taken it out on her physically, and she felt unsteady as she was helped to her feet, although the nausea and foreboding she had felt earlier had now gone. The exact words of the old child spirit were now vague, but her mission had been set and inside her head an immovable resolve was beginning to form.

Coming into light, they were met at the entrance by a fifty strong gathering. Shielding their eyes against the harsh, bright background, the three of them paused uncertain as the silhouettes began to shift.

'Wait there,' instructed Emile, while he cautiously moved toward the welcoming party.

A figure detached from the crowd and came to meet him. 'Yaat eeh,' said a deep booming voice. The tall figure stopped and held out its arm by way of greeting. 'Shil go oneo.'

'Yaat eeh,' said Emile.

'Chin hia, shi nei?'

They shook hands and began a conversation in a language that was alien to both Maeve and Kersha who now stepped further into the light, relieved that they weren't about to encounter a gang of repros. All at once an excited chatter arose from the gathered and fingers began pointing at them.

'What's going on, Emile?' shouted Maeve, still feeling slightly wary.

'He says they have been waiting a long time for the coming of the two hawks,' said Emile, turning back with a big grin on his face. 'He says it has been written in the stars and in the smoke that this time would be now. He also says that the hawks would come in female form and would perform feats of great healing across our troubled lands and waters and chase away the evil spirits.'

'Fuck, I think he means us,' whispered Kersha.

PRECESSION

Totally bemused and bewildered, they were welcomed with open arms amid much rejoicing and ceremony. An overwhelming pungent scent of smudged sage permeated the air as they were feted with music, dance and food. Just as Vera the spirit guide had shepherded the many inquisitive lost souls, so Jon Silvertree, an elder and spokesman for the Jicarilla people of the Apache Nation, was now holding court and bringing order to his tribe who were eager to see and hear the two hawks.

'How did you know we were here?' asked Maeve while chewing on a piece of corn bread.

'This is Molly Ravenstone,' said Jon Silvertree, introducing a diminutive old lady with a serene demeanour and watery eyes filled with wisdom and intrigue set into her careworn features. She bowed humbly before the two women and allowed the elder to continue. 'In her dreams she sees what has been, what is happening and what is to come. As a child she saw the coming of Marduk the Destroyer, the demise of the interlopers and the dawning of the new age. More recently she foretold of the arrival of the two hawks who would finally put an end to the cursed evil that had stained our sacred land for too long.'

'What was it you saw in your dreams, Molly?' asked Maeve.

Jon gave the old lady a discreet nod of the head, she reached into a hemp satchel and produced a bundle of rolled up papers. She untied one and spread it out in front of her. It was a drawing of two birds in flight heading towards what looked like a sunrise, while the foreground depicted figures in a scrawled state of purgatory. The drawing was charcoal crude, not unlike one of Kersha's early pieces. She unrolled the remaining scrolls that all portrayed a similar scene, waited for a reaction.

Maeve turned to Kersha, who was not given to alarm or emotion, but the return look spoke volumes. Without a word she rose, left the small circle and made her way back to where they had left their vehicle. Emile gave Maeve a questioning look, but she simply shrugged her shoulders. In a flash Kersha was back to satisfy the intrigue. She opened the large sketch pad she was carrying under her arm and placed it next to the other drawings.

There weren't any looks of disbelief, just a mutual sense of affirmation and a growing awareness of inevitability. They weren't identical, of course. Kersha's piece was far more detailed and polished, but everything else was there.

AQUARIUS

'I saw you many times in my dreams. I knew you would come,' Molly whispered in Kersha's ear as they embraced.

'When did . . .' began Maeve.

'Only three days ago, after we left Colorado. It came to me while we were on the road. It was constantly in my head and so I sketched it. Don't ask me what it means,' said Kersha.

Jon Silvertree slowly rose to his feet and made himself large. 'It means you have just confirmed that you are our salvation. You and Maeve are the two hawks who are to deliver us from the evil of the past and guide us to the bright new dawn of the future,' he said by way of proclamation.

In order to attune and assimilate herself to the collective psyche of these people, Maeve became absorbed in their story, from a pre-colonial vibrant, organised society, through invasion, suppression and the struggles that remained like an all-pervading stain that had become a living chronicle.

She learned that such a society bore complex social structures that intricately organised their members from birth to death. There were leaders and council members, warriors and healers, craftspeople and storytellers, each with roles as important as the next in maintaining the equilibrium of their communities. Fundamental to their existence was their relationship with the land. It was not merely a backdrop for their lives but a central theme in their unfolding tales. They knew the songs of the rivers and the whispers of the wind through the plains. They understood the subtle language of the earth and responded with reverence. Their respect for nature was born out of a profound awareness that their lives were deeply connected with the world around them. In this way they lived not as mere occupants of a geographical space but as participants in a grand ecological dialogue that they understood had been going on long before their time and would continue long after. For the Jicarilla Apache each day was another verse in a song as old as the mountains, a song that sang of belonging to a world far richer and more beautiful than any one individual could claim or own. They believed the land to be alive with spirits, where every rock, tree and stream is imbued with a life-force. Reverence for nature was not just a practice but a way of being. Nature's cycles dictated the rhythm of daily life, and in return, that reverence afforded a profound harmony with the environment.

PRECESSION

Maeve absorbed all this ancient, often forgotten knowledge and wisdom, and would use it all not only in the implementation of the task that lay ahead but to inform and enrich the philosophy in her written work.

Kinship followed the maternal line, painting a picture of a society where relationships and familial ties were traced through mothers and grandmothers. Kersha was instinctively drawn to these elder, matriarchal figures and would almost always form a natural bond. Maeve would discreetly observe the close interaction and often wondered if it had something to do with the forced abandonment and absence of Kersha's birth mother. The issue had always remained unspoken between them, as had the question of procreation and any desire for children of her own. It was as if the counselling she had received from Donna Channing as an adolescent had wrapped up any residual trauma and packed it neatly away forever. If there ever was a Pandora's box waiting to be opened, Maeve would stay well clear of it. Meanwhile, Kersha had thrown herself into the visual arts that were not mere decoration, but stories etched in stone, woven into baskets, painted on hide and drawn on parchment, celebrating living tales accompanied by the beat of the drum and rise of song that gave the stories and prayers wings. Her artwork drew an uncanny resemblance to that of her Jicarilla contemporaries, and she automatically understood their significance, power and meaning. She took clinics and through her artistry healed many in a language often beyond words, a communication of the soul's journey, honed by her experience in Ampleforth where she had learned to discover who she was.

Kersha and her growing band of Jicarilla child followers were guided to spots where they were instructed to look out for and collect diamond shaped pieces of stone that Maeve would later identify as obsidian and moldavite. These rare stones were then shaped into medicine wheels and placed at sites where the swinging pendulum indicated major energy blockages. At these sites Maeve would receive initiation and ceremonial instructions via Molly's spirit guide, an entity known as War Bonnet who it transpired was one of Molly's brothers in a past life. When channelling guidance for prayer and incantation Molly would often blush and disguise laughter behind her hand. She admitted her brother was a cheeky spirit with a twinkle in his eye and she daren't repeat some of the communications she was receiving.

AQUARIUS

'He says his heart is lifted by the coming of the two hawks, and he smokes a pipe in their honour, but he fails to understand why there are no men in their lives.'

Maeve laughed. 'Tell him true love isn't defined by gender.'

'He says you are wise beyond your years, but you don't know what you're missing.'

They worked tirelessly under the stars where two rivers met and at ancient sacred sites where the Earth's energies once flowed freely. With each cleared location, a solitary eagle would appear above their heads to circle and soar on the thermals, until at last, as Mercury slipped into Sagittarius their mission was declared complete, amidst much celebration and rejoicing on multiple planes.

'Let the pain and the suffering be gone and the light flow again,' announced Jon Silvertree to the happy gathering. 'The deer will drink the water, the seed of our sons and daughters shall bear fruit, the children shall laugh, and all will be re-united.' He gifted Maeve a pendant on which hung a small, polished stone, a token of appreciation on behalf of his people. He told her it came from the stars and would protect her as well as heal any emotional stress accrued from her exhaustive endeavours. The children showered Kersha with many gifts, jewellery, trinkets and keepsakes presented in a elaborately decorated medicine bag, all fashioned with genuine love and kindness. Emile was given a magnificent peace-pipe resplendently decorated with an eagle feather for unknowingly being the catalyst and facilitator.

They drank, feasted and celebrated till sunrise, where Maeve, whether through fatigue or outside control lapsed into a somnambulistic state, where she was visited again by the spirit known as Vera.

'Greetings, once more,' said the voice. This time, through a misty haze, the face of a pretty, blond-haired child began to appear but remained unsharp and out of focus. The voice still sounded like that of an adult, and not as though it belonged to the girl. Maeve began to speak but no words came out. The voice spoke again as if reading her thoughts. 'Please don't be confused,' it said. 'I have grown in the spirit world, but to be able to manifest to you as I am now would mean lowering my vibration to your realm and in my capacity that would be too much to bear. What you can see is who I was and how I appeared on your Earth at the time of my passing. You can see this because a part of my soul still lingers on the ethereal level of your plane. I wanted you to know that the little girl known as Vera wishes to thank you and your friends for the important work you have managed to successfully complete. So do the many others, sent with a love that knows no bounds.'

'Are they with you now?' asked Maeve.

'They are singing like birds released from a cage.'

'Where will they go?'

'Most are busy forgiving those that ended their short existence on your world, others are already flying to the Godhead to add lustre to the diamonds that are their souls.'

'Will young Vera join them?'

'She will. We shall join together and travel far from this dense world of matter to embrace whatever else we may choose to encounter and experience.'

'Where will your travels take you?'

'When The Nazarene said – *I have sheep in other folds* – he was speaking through the Great Spirit, meaning there are many realms in the cosmic kingdom to where all creation has the opportunity to develop and evolve. When we finally escape the confines and trammels of your world, we shall seek out a place that no doubt shall offer further tests and triumphs that shall guide us onwards in our evolutionary journey.'

'I wish you Godspeed on that journey.'

'Your wishes are accepted and received with an eternal love from all you have touched and blessed. . .'

The hazy vision of Vera the child cleared for a brief moment. A simple smile brought with it a wave of indescribable peace and rapture. In that instant, Maeve received an all-pervading sense of ultimate freedom; it was as if she was being given a taste, a reward even of what was inevitably to come. Everything was being presented to her in a timeless flash, every colour, every scent, every sight magnified a thousand-fold from anything her earthly senses could comprehend, all displayed with an overwhelming brightness that seemed to confirm her rightful place in the universe. A large part of her never wanted it to end. There was so much more to ask. She opened her mouth to speak but her words were stymied. - *All in good time* - she heard the fading voice say as she reluctantly found herself returning to that all-too-familiar slow, solid state.

'Fuck!' Maeve opened her eyes to see half a dozen young faces giggling over her and her return-to-reality outburst.

AQUARIUS

'I think it's time you got some proper rest,' said Kersha shooing away the kids, while wiping away Maeve's unbridled tears. 'And then I think it's time we went home.'

PRECESSION

The Aquarians

Home for Maeve and Kersha was a houseboat on the small coastal island of Wolds in an area previously known as Lincolnshire. They lived in the sheltered shallows on the west side of the isle in a place called Tealby, the one-time country seat of poet laureate Alfred Tennyson, now home to many displaced peoples who lined the shaley shoreline in their floating abodes. From their vantage they could see the half-submerged and abandoned town of Market Rasen, where past generations were born and raised, now adopted as nurseries and spawning grounds by shoals of herring and mackerel that were finally restocking after almost being wiped out in the irradiated seas and oceans. In the passing of time, Maeve would closely observe and document the resurgent and resilient ways of nature as all forms of wildlife returned and adapted to the ever-evolving ecological landscape. She witnessed the burgeoning colonies of gulls of all varieties, kittiwakes, cormorants, terns, gannets and guillemots all staking a claim to new, abundant feeding grounds. The fertile lands above water were now teaming with life in a climate that had begun to settle, not so much into a regular pattern, but where the winds were warmer, the rains often welcome, and the seas almost always becalmed in the absence of any notable tidal influence save that of the sun. They were entering a period of Eunomia – good order, where the grandchildren of those visionaries and independent thinkers who helped shape the common mindset and societal norms during a time of great change, now used that legacy of innovative individuality to inform and value the collective egalitarian well-being. Technological, philosophical and spiritual advancements were combined as complementary and inclusive bedfellows, as opposed to the dividing, destructive tools that were often used in the past. This nascent creed had, of course, long been prophesied and had been entered into the great tome of work now imbued with the working title – *Chronicle of The Meek* – documenting how the children of The Water-bearer would survive and thrive during this new epoch.

For Maeve, this work of a lifetime was almost at an end. The brief, formulated by Snodgrass, realised and painstakingly recorded

AQUARIUS

by a band of dedicated scribes, who in line with its essence - free from ego - would remain nameless. Essence, particularly that of the Late Professor Percival Snodgrass, was still very much present in his former residency. On his demise, and at his behest, he was neither buried nor interned but his earthly remains were processed into a piezo crystal that was installed in the mainframe of the digital AI system that now ran the main archive at the magnificent People's Library up in Ilkley.

"*'Every little helps,' said the old lady when she peed in the sea,*" are reportedly his last words after someone had questioned his dying wish.

Like all the great philosophers, Percy Snodgrass had been way ahead of his time, and as that time began to settle into its tumultuous yet rightful place in the grand scheme, Maeve was able to reflect with a smile at his teaching methods where a stock answer would always be supervened with a host of connected questions, keeping his protégés always on their intellectual toes. When a colleague, totally frustrated by the professor's eccentric ways declared him to be mad, he replied in a flash with a quote from Carroll - "Indeed I am, entirely bonkers. But I will tell you a secret – all the best people are". - Even a mentor from ancient Greece once stated - "There is no great genius without a touch of madness".

'Whatcha doing?'

Maeve peered over the top of the book she was reading to be confronted with Kersha dressed in khaki overalls that were spattered with brown clay in various states of hardening, as evidence of her latest sculpturing endeavours. Her hands, face and wild, tied-up hair that had begun to grey at the sides were also covered in the stuff. 'Just sorting out some things I found in this old chest,' Maeve replied, while never failing to be amazed at how messy her partner managed to get whenever she was engrossed in her work.

'Whatcha got there?'

'Oh, just some old book that belonged to my great grandfather,' she said, setting aside the well-preserved paperback copy of *A Kestrel for a Knave.* 'Look what else I found.' Maeve dipped into the chest and unfolded a detailed drawing of her and her grandmother sitting in front of a log fire. 'We should frame it and hang it somewhere.'

PRECESSION

Intrigued, Kersha went on a rummage and unearthed her old rag doll, still smiling and staring inanely with its glass boss-eyes, her catapult, and some Apache prayer beads and dream catchers that were hanging randomly over some martial arts trophies. 'I miss those people,' she said wistfully. 'We should go back there someday.' She dropped them all back into the chest and started to walk away.

'Where are you going now?'

'Next door to see old Charlie. He can't understand why his vines aren't bearing the same yield as ours.'

'I've already told him, the pH in his soil is wrong; it's too alkaline.'

'Yeah, well he'd like one of us to sort it, so that's where I'm off.'

'Don't forget, Max and his new partner are coming over to visit; I hope you're going to make yourself presentable before they arrive.'

'You know, sometimes I feel you're ashamed to be in my company.'

'Ha! – says the woman who used to shit openly in public.'

With her back to her, Kersha held up a single finger of faux contempt before walking away.

Maeve had a little chuckle to herself. They'd lived a life and some. Born into a world without norms, survived, thrived, stood on the shoulders of giants, and surfed the cosmic waves of change as ice turned to water while watching the age of duality crumble into its ruinous footprint. Maybe it was that elusive sense of nostalgia that she could never get her head around that was now informing the overwhelming sense of contentment she was experiencing as she remembered back to a time and place that was almost like another life, another world. More than anything she felt relieved that neither her nor her generation could be found complicit in mankind's destructive machinations, at least she had The Shift to thank for that. She was glad she was able to share the incredulity of her students as she lectured on times when sovereign human beings danced to the tune of politicians and governments who held sway, driven and dictated by hidden hands. – *True libertarians saw Nineteen Eighty-Four as a warning, those who fondly called themselves progressive saw it as a blueprint* – was often a maxim she used in her classes.

She so missed the intense philosophical debates that she shared with Moira and Percy, burning the midnight oil long into the night and on at last to something they could finally recognise as dawn. And of the things that remained unanswered, namely: did we all come

AQUARIUS

here with a set of intensions and predetermined experiences? A choice of path and purpose, only to be foiled by a kind of collective amnesia. Percy maintained they were living an illusion within an illusion, that the universe was merely what humans perceived without representing any kind of true reality. Maeve thought this to be true only in the sense of manipulated perception and hijacked thought. All fear fades when we finally transcend the illusion of limitation. She knew we are all much more than this experience, so much more than this physical presence, so much more than the labels, so much more than our circumstance. So much more than we can ever begin to understand.

She looked out onto the still warmth of the late afternoon. Behind a hazy sun, midges danced a mazy ritual above the calm waters while dragonflies flitted imperceptibly from space to space in a show of metallic-like iridescence. With a contented sigh, she fingered the sterling silver pendant around her neck, picked up her book and continued to read.

PRECESSION

*British Isles
archipelago post-shift,
excluding Eire*

Part 3 – Aeon of The Goat

Brigantia, North Isle

The old woman carefully slid out the ancient looking volume she'd selected from the ranked rows of the impressive archive and placed it on the table. She gently took a cloth to its worn but sturdy hemp cover, although there were no perceptible traces of dust to be seen. She slowly ran a finger across the raised title written in Old English – *Chronicle of The Meek* – and immediately felt that familiar tangible surge of energy course through her veins. It was confirmation. Today was to be an eventful one. She wasn't even remotely sure of the specifics, the dreams had been at best cryptic, but they nearly always were. Her task would be to work out the lesson and offer it to whoever had sought it or who had been sent. But now she was confident. Today was definitely the day. Ariana sat and placed both her hands over the book. She casually glanced around her to make sure she was quite alone, and she was. Amun would be preparing the animals for the pending solar storm; impossible to predict, but Ariana rarely got it wrong, and he knew he'd be a fool not to heed her predictions. She closed her eyes and took a moment to attune before opening the manuscript. With eyes still shut she brushed her small, bony hands over the randomly selected pages as if she were searching for something. A hint of a self-satisfied smile soon broke across her perceptibly wise and spiritually connected features. 'Ahh. . .' she spoke softly, but with an inflexion that was loaded with intrigue and anticipation. Her eyes, now open, sparkled with the lustre of diamond as they began to scan the words, clear and as clean as the moment they were set down. . .

The following account of this period is not intended to be interpreted as fact or perfect truth. It is merely laid out to provide a symbolic chord to our past, an understanding of our present and a lesson for the future. These words were scribed during the age of The Water Bearer, long after the events described took place, and gleaned from stories around the time of The Great Shift. If this document survives, you may be following the original transcription, or a revised version as seen fit by our beneficiaries. Apropos, the words

PRECESSION

herein are a record peculiar to what the people of this age would have called His-story.

It was in the heart of The Cusp between the ages of The Fish and the coming of The Water Bearer that the genesis of a new order began to emerge. Monotheism was at its dogmatic destructive peak. Global conflict was making a nihilistic swansong, and The Earth stirred to shake off its parasitic tormenters. Futile wars fought for perfidious causes became wars fought for survival. Great cities and their peoples vanished as land became sea. Famine and pestilence brought about by earthquake, flood and drought held sway and the pervading values of ego, money, power and control that were all aspects of the epoch of The Fish were diminished.

In prelude to The Shift, and prior to the seismic events that would create these five separate Isles, this was a land where providence brought together disparate peoples from all parts of the world. Humans with minds and consciousness attuned, conversed and then converged as if as one with the changing magnetism of The Earth. It was during the dying moments of the electronic web known as The Internet, even as the Earth's satellite neighbour, The Moon, increased its distance and man's manufactured beacons of global communication started to tumble from their orbits and the world began to fall silent, that the plan for survival took seed. Unknown in number, these architects of change were often referred to as The Diggers, or The New Levellers, thus named in honour of an even older sect of philanthropic humanists. Among these women and men, scientists, ecologists, botanists, strategists, healers, philosophers and free thinkers, were souls who had access to the ancient esoteric knowledge that had long been privy and exclusive to the prevailing global elite and hidden from the rest of mankind for millennia.

It has been spoke of and written that one man, warrior and healer, without name except in myth and legend, but most often associated with the symbol of the Hawk, kept this alliance together during a period of great pain, suffering and bloodshed, a leader amongst an order without leaders. And as the Earth's vibrations quickened, mankind's illusions of fear, hate, malice, greed and envy slowly dissipated, and soon emerged a tribe, pure in mind and spirit and attuned to the circadian rhythm of the universe. The coming of this tribe had been foreseen and spoken of long ago in ancient

CAPRICORN

scriptures. Their inheritance according to a monotheist God was to be The Earth, thus, as named by others, these people, - our forebears who began these volumes, became known as The Meek . . .

Ariana would have read further but Amun had come indoors sounding as though he'd brought half the animals with him. It served to break the spell. She sighed, carefully closing the heavy pages of the great work. Intrigued yet still none the wiser, she passed a hand over the cover in ritual before replacing it back in its space on the overburdened shelves.

'The air is charged, it's going to be big,' stated Amun, in a voice as hard and smooth as polished granite.

'The animals?'

Amun nodded. 'They sense it. Apart from a few silly lambs most had already sought refuge. They ought be safe.'

Ariana, still deep in thought, poured her partner a vessel of water. He drained it in one. Setting down the empty cup, he drew a calloused hand across his rough beard and observed his woman. 'You look troubled.'

'No, not troubled.' She looked up at his big coarse face and smiled in reassurance. 'I don't have any clear pictures. No pictures at all, just a sense of impendence.' She thought of a section in the passage she had just read and wondered if there was any connection to the image of the hawk that visited her in her dreams of late, a link to the past, maybe. 'Unusual, isn't it?'

Amun stood tall behind his seated wife and placed a giant hand on her slender shoulder. 'For you my dear, yes, that is unusual. . .'

PRECESSION

Down from Catterick

The wulf bounded up the last few feet of the scree. Cresting the ridge, she paused and sniffed at the densely charged air, hot and thick even at this height. A lazy zephyr stirred her grey-flecked fur as she checked the humans' progress. She dropped to her haunches, waiting patiently, tongue lolling in the heat while surveying the fertile lands below as if the domain were her own. High above her, circling on large spiralling thermals, the falcon screeched down a defying challenge to that assumption, its call echoing deep into the valley walls.

With one last exertion Ullyman Spence eased himself up alongside his canine companion, dislodging a few shards of limestone and shale in the process, which went cascading down the rise. From far below he heard the tired but threatening curses of his friend. Ullyman laughed to himself and unwound his water skin from off his shoulder. He poured into his hand and allowed the wulf to lap it up. This he did several times before quenching his own thirst. He rummaged inside his pouch and came up with a handful of seed and berries that he casually tossed into his mouth. Lazily scratching the canine behind an ear and with a slight smirk on his face, he watched Nic labour up the scree towards them, while in the vast deep blue of the sky above, the falcon homed in on an unsuspecting smaller bird, and without a sound took it on the wing.

'Do you ail?' asked Ully in mock concern as his friend finally reached the summit.

With beads of sweat dripping from his brow and his breath coming in short, sharp gasps Nic looked up at his travelling companion with an irked look on his face. 'No,' he replied, indignant at the suggestion. 'Air's too thin – no ozone up here – a bit tired that's all,' he managed before releasing his cumbersome pack and collapsing backwards onto the soft green moss of the plateau.

Ully shrugged, tipped more seed and berries into his mouth and offered Nic his waterskin. Without getting up from his prone position, Nic thankfully poured the water over his face and down his throat. The wulf ambled round and lapped up the residue. Revived via water or wulf, or both, Nic was soon sat up surveying the great fertile plain below them. Glancing at his wrist, he checked to confirm their location.

'The three valleys: Aire, Wharfe, and Calder, and beyond is The Vale of York,' he stated impressed, both at the sight and at their achievement so far. Ully followed his mate's gaze while chewing rhythmically, his features failing to register any sense of achievement or wonder at the sight before him. Nic apped a telephoto to his binos and scanned the far-off terrain. Below him stretched vast ocean-like fields of vivid green hemp, and island-like communes dotted spasmodically, with their patchwork patterns of colourful crop and yield, surrounded and protected with sentinel copse and wood. And beyond, the great fault that divided and defined Brigantes from Coritani and Mercia: the M62 Cut. 'I can make out both crossings,' breathed Nic, 'M1 and A1.'

'Which will we take?' Ully spat seed husk into the warm wind.

'Whichever way the ley guides us; we may have to travel west and take the M6 crossing.'

Ully sniffed at the dense, oxygen-sparse air. 'It might have to wait,' he said.

'You sense something?'

Ully looked down at the wulf that had begun to pace around erratically while emitting the odd whine. The two travelling companions looked at each other.

'A geomag?' asked Nic cautiously.

Ully nodded resignedly. 'It feels like it. It smells like it. She senses it.' He looked back to the wulf who was getting evermore agitated. 'We should seek refuge.'

Nic consulted his wrist once more. 'You're right, the air pressure's wrong for this altitude.' He scanned the panorama but despite a slight increase in the wind there were no signs of atmospheric change. The sun sat in its blue sky and a heat haze shimmered across the land, but instinct always prevailed. 'Let's go,' he said, swinging his heavy pack onto his back. Ullyman shaded his eyes and looked up into the vast empty blue. The falcon was nowhere to be seen.

The two youths and the wulf yomped across the plateau that was filled with a sea of undulating purple heather rolling against their progress in continuous waves as dictated by the wind that had slowly but perceptibly increased in strength. If Ullyman was worried he didn't show it, but Nicobar displayed his anxiousness by continually scanning the terrain with his binos for signs of refuge or shelter. The hazy images of far-off estates that lay in the valley way below were unreachable before nightfall and judging by the rapidly changing conditions that would be too late.

Age and size were no longer used as tools of time and measurement, but a sage versed in such archaic ways would probably ascertain Nicobarius Brooke at around seventeen shars and a shade over three and a half cubits in height. He was Spartan in his physique and prided himself on being supremely fit, yet as they precariously trekked their way off the more exposed sections of the vast heathland, he found himself labouring, slowly falling further behind his mate and the canine. Occasionally Ully would glance behind him, his features showing frustration at his friend's dawdling, but he daren't lose sight of the wulf that seemed even more impatient at the lack of progress as she led them southeast down the scree towards the valley.

They reached a vast mossy, boulder-strewn outcrop, where giant shards of millstone grit strata pierced the earth and reached to the sky. A smattering of deciduous trees offered partial shade, and Ully managed to restrain the wulf with an offering from his water skin. Frustrated as he was, he knew he had a duty of care for his friend. Although ancient and primitive, the custom still held a symbolic significance for certain descended sects of the Meek and their Chav wards. Others openly discouraged the practice, declaring it no more than a youthful trend that dishonoured their legacy. It also reprised the notion of hierarchy which had no place in the now. But for Ullyman Spence his inheritance was that of a Chav Minder, he was proud of it, and this walkabout would be undertaken in time-honoured tradition.

Nic eventually appeared, dishevelled and distraught. Sweat ran off him in torrents, and the straps from his pack were chafing his shoulders raw. He collapsed in a heap against a large boulder. He felt dizzy and nauseous. Ully came and stood over him, his shadow looming large. 'I thought you said you didn't ail?' he questioned without too much sympathy in his voice. Although he had a duty of care, he didn't always show it.

Nico looked up into Ully's silhouette while holding onto his guts that had begun to churn.

'I...' he began, when, without warning, something revelatory washed over him, a massive surge of vibration and energy that

CAPRICORN

almost lifted him off the ground. All at once he felt outside of himself, but this wasn't like astral travel, he was confined to the now, but he was also somewhere else. '. . . Do you hear that?' he managed to utter at last.

'What?' Ully asked, puzzled

'That. . . that rumble - that roar in the distance.'

'You mean the river?'

'Yes. . . that's it - the river. I knew it was here.'

'Well of course it's here; it's the Wharfe. Where else would it be?'

'But don't you see? I've been here before. It wasn't here then.'

'What wasn't?'

'The river, you cloth-head.'

Ullyman sighed. He knew Nico was a Sage in the making. He knew he had the ability to heal. He knew he was able to travel in his dreams. Yes, his friend was gifted and destined for fulfilment but now was neither the moment nor place to go off on one. 'If you've been here before, then show us refuge,' he challenged.

'No – you don't understand. . .' said Nico, pulling dense air into his lungs in an effort to clear his head. '. . . I was here in a different dimension.'

'You mean in your dreams.'

'No - I don't know. . . it was. . .' Nico gestured with his hand. '. . . Back, way back.'

'You mean in the past? No such thing according to you,' stated Ully flippantly.

Nico looked up at his friend through sweat soaked eyes. 'No – you're right,' he said after a long pause. 'Must be the heat. Let's go.' He held out his hand and Ullyman hauled him to his feet.

'Sure you're okay?'

Nico nodded. He knew he had to be. The air was now crackling with static. The geomag could be upon them at any time, and there was no sign of refuge. As he steadied himself and secured his pack, Nic looked around him. Déjà vu was still present, and it was strong. Ully and the wulf were disappearing over a rise. On wobbly legs he quickly followed.

To the north the Aurora was now visible. Shimmering shards of green, turquoise and cerise stood horizon to heaven. Elsewhere the sky morphed from cobalt to effervescent crimson and the world began to turn dayglow.

PRECESSION

They yomped at a pace dictated by the uneven terrain until every muscle and sinew cried out for respite. Ullyman, as supremely fit as he was, had a threshold. 'We're fucked,' he turned and managed to gasp desperately.

'Keep going,' shouted Nic. 'Follow the wulf. There's sanctuary up ahead.'

Ully turned back. In front of the agitated, impatient animal was hill, rock and heather for as far as the eye could see. He shook his head in dismay. 'You're raged. There's nothing out there. We're fucked!'

Nic caught up to his companion and passed him without breaking stride. 'Just follow the wulf,' he said between gritted teeth.

Soon, the wind felt like a furnace at their backs. The oxygen was fast being sucked out of the air. They breathed fire and the weight of atmosphere doubled them over as they walked.

'Nico. . .' Fear filled Ullyman's eyes as he pleaded to his friend for some kind of deliverance.

'The wulf – go to the wulf.' Nic pointed to the canine that had dropped to its haunches in front of a series of randomly placed standing stones. A pitiful howl arose only to be snatched away by the searing wind as they crashed down beside her. They pressed themselves flat into hard earth and rock as the last remnants of oxygen were being ripped from the atmosphere. Ullyman Spence was now certain that their end had come as he breathed fire into his screaming lungs.

'The wulf knows – I know' Nicobarius Brooke thought to himself before lapsing into unconsciousness.

CAPRICORN

Sanctuary

'I think you have a visitor,' pronounced the old man. Ullyman Spence, with reservations, drained his cup of goat's milk and unsteadily got to his feet. With a tilt of the head, Amun bid him follow. At the threshold of the dwelling Ullyman paused, squinting cautiously into bright daylight.

'Is it safe?'

Already outside, the old man breathed in deep while surveying all around him. 'I think so,' he nodded slowly. 'She thinks so.' He nodded again, indicating the falcon perched patiently on a standing stone close by. 'She is yours, I assume.'

On wobbly feet, Ully approached the bird and held out an arm. She took it, her eyes all the while darting here and there in the hope of an appearance of food. 'She's a travelling companion,' said Ully, stroking her feathers while letting her take bubbles of milky spit from his lips.

'You're lucky you didn't lose her in the storm,' said Amun.

'She's not that stupid.'

'Not like you and your friend, eh?'

'Nic... Is he...?'

'He sleeps. He's fine.'

'The wulf?'

'She's by his side. They're both fine.'

Ullyman drew in a lungful of clean, cool air and let it out, relieved. He placed the bird back on its rocky perch and took in the surroundings, the large stone-built dwelling set into a hillside, the trees and stony outcrops, the fowl scratching about in the earth nearby, paying no attention to the raptor, nor she to them. In the near distance, a small orchard: trees laden with colourful fruit of all descriptions, accompanied by rows of cultivated roots, tubers and vegetables. He looked up into a clear, deep blue sky, void of any trace of the geomag; gone as suddenly as it had manifested. He became aware that the old man with the long thick silvery hair and beard was scrutinising him closely and with a great deal of curiosity.

'All this – none of this was here,' said Ully, gesturing with a sweep of an arm.

PRECESSION

Amun raised a thick eyebrow. 'Surely you know that is not so.'

'I...' began the youth, before faltering. Why would the old man assume this, he wondered. Did he think he was a sage?

'Your friend knew what was here, so did the wulf.'

'All we saw was hill and rock.'

'Then may I suggest that you weren't really looking?' The old man scrutinised the lad some more. 'You are of Chav extraction, are you not?'

'I am, and proud of it,' said Ully defensively, while standing tall and sticking out his chest.

Amun simply nodded. 'Your friend?'

'Nicobar is of The Meek. He's a Sage, and I'm his CM.'

Amun laughed to himself, a hoarse, chesty chuckle. 'He's certainly not a Sage.'

Ully took on his defensive tone again. 'He will be one day. He has the healing gift... and he can cure remotely,' he added as an afterthought.

Once again, the old man slowly nodded his acceptance of the youth's statement. 'And you're his Minder, are you?'

Ully responded with a curt, assertive jerk of the head.

'Where are you from?'

'Catterick.'

'Ah, of course, the old garrison.' Amun paused thoughtfully. 'And what brought you here do you think?'

'Walkabout – we're on our way to Glaston for the solstice.'

Amun sat down on a large, smooth boulder and leant on his stick. 'Walkabout.' He muttered the word to himself reflectively, reluctantly shifting his mind back to a significant yet painful moment of his life, long dealt with, hard lessons learned. Guilt was the only human emotion that rarely, if ever, arose in his psyche now, a pointless self-punishment that failed to serve, and yet somehow managed to manifest occasionally and prick the conscience. 'Would it not have been easier to use A1 from Catterick?' asked the old man.

'We're following the Ley.'

Amun pondered some more, his thought process measured. Ullyman simply thought that he was old and slow. As if reading his mind, Amun scowled whilst stroking his whiskers, his bushy brow furrowed. A part of him was impressed that they knew how to find and follow the Ley, but another part couldn't help but think how stupid they were to have been almost caught out by the effects of a

CAPRICORN

CME. He tugged at his beard some more. Perhaps providence had something to do with it.

The ancient and archaic coming of age ritual known as Walkabout had been practiced by successive generations of The Meek and their CMs although it had long since lost its significance. The time-honoured ceremony is believed to have originated after the ravages of the last Shift, and the cessation of the Chav wars, but Amun's insight into all things story knew that its origins lay much further back in Aboriginal and Antipodean culture. It is said that when the Chav armies were defeated and finally assimilated into The New Order, all newborns were paired with children of The Meek. They were schooled, utilizing and relying on each other's inherited skill-sets to survive a new, and yet, still frightening world. Beyond puberty, paired individuals would venture out from the garrisons on long journeys of self-discovery, a shared rite of passage into the unknown and the forgotten; brain and brawn now working together with a common goal: to connect and unite. It is said some were met with hostility and death by surviving tribes, others with curiosity and acceptance. Those who returned imparted experiences and knowledge, and eventually the ways of The Meek were accepted universally through a combination of a massive shift in consciousness as well as a great physical and mental battle with the pervading elements. The architects of all this are now largely unknown, and yet as with all myth and legend there is always a recurring theme be it man, beast or symbol. Among the pages of The Book of The Meek are many cryptic references to a warrior and healer who stood fast against the Chav armies, who instead of destroying them once subdued, gave them food and shelter and brought them into the fold. His name is lost but there are descriptions of a founding father of The Meek often referred to as Asar or Sarv who is closely associated with the symbol of the hawk in numerous ancient texts.

Amun looked over to the falcon still perched on the stone, alive and alert, head darting almost three-sixty in short, sharp movements, taking in the surroundings, its primary feathers stirring in the gentle breeze. A hawk had been present in many of Ariana's dreams and visions of late. She had failed to glean any sense or message from them, which was unusual for her and had left her feeling unduly perturbed. Amun looked from the bird to the boy. Could the sudden appearance of two youths, a wulf and a raptor be of any significance?

PRECESSION

Ariana, eyes closed, deep in trance, ceremoniously held the swinging crystal above the sleeping boy, while the wulf lay beside the bed, head on the floor watching the ritual dispassionately, raising a lazy eyebrow every time light caught the circling quartz sending flashes of brilliance around the room.

A shrill cry, the call of a peregrine falcon filled the air in the near distance and broke the spell. Nicobarius Brooke opened his eyes and spoke.

'Hello.'

'Namaste.' Ariana brought the palms of her hands together over the crystal in greeting.

'I bow to the divine in you also... Do I know you?'

'You may have met me in your dreams.'

'Have I been gone long?'

'Yes, for a while.' On hearing Nic's voice the wulf had sprung to its feet, launched its sizeable front paws onto the bed and proceeded to wash his travelling companion's face excitedly with its rough tongue. 'Someone is pleased to see you open your eyes. Does she have a name?'

'My friend doesn't like to give animals names,' said Nic, roughing up the fur behind her ears. 'We just call her wulf... Ully,' he suddenly remembered. 'Is he...'

'He's well. Your friend is a very strong, resilient young man. You're lucky to have him as your minder.'

A note of condescension flashed across Nic's mind as she spoke, but there were no hints of malice in the old woman's words. He instantly felt a telepathic bond that made him feel wary and yet comforted all at once. As if to test his abilities weren't deceiving him, he ordered the wulf down with a single thought and she obeyed immediately, resuming her prone position on the floor. 'Yes, he is, and you are right, I am,' was his reply.

'Here,' Ariana smiled. 'If you are able to sit up, I would like you to drink this.' She took a vessel from a nearby table and offered it.

'What is it?'

'It's a draught that will negate any radiation inside of you and help you regain your strength.'

He took it, closed his eyes and breathed in its contents. Super charged olfactory senses came into play as well as his medical

CAPRICORN

training. He detected iodine, selenium and cilantro but little else that was familiar to him. He drained it in one and offered back the cup. As their eyes met, Ariana smiled and slowly nodded her head. As she took the empty vessel from him their fingers touched and it was as if a million volts of electricity had just surged through his body, something that no geomag could replicate. His eyes widened, and the old woman nodded her head again knowingly. Nic attempted to get out of the bed, but Ariana stopped him in his tracks with a simple hand gesture. 'No, not yet,' she commanded. 'You need more rest. We will talk again at great length soon, but for now...' Her outstretched wrinkled arm and bony upturned hand motioned him back down and he complied without argument, resting his head and closing his eyes in one slow show of acquiescence.

PRECESSION

An Education

The old couple watched their young guests with unconcealed curiosity as they hungrily ate the broth that had been prepared for them. Nic, aware of the scrutiny, looked up from his bowl. 'It's good, it's very good,' he stated while Ully merely nodded in agreement as he continued to spoon up the much-needed sustenance. Amun patiently allowed them to finish their food before opening his line of questioning.

'Where did you learn how to follow The Ley?'

Nic wiped his mouth and shrugged. 'At home, through study and born intuition,' he stated flatly. Ariana looked sideways at her partner and smiled.

'Why would you undertake such a journey without Faraday suits?' continued Amun.

'We do this as the Ancients did it.'

'The Ancients didn't rely on those.' Amun pointed to the Application Information Device Nic had around his wrist and the Binos that were sat on the table.

'From my learnings, I understand that they did, but maybe not as technologically advanced,' said Nic defiantly.

'Then perhaps we are talking about different Ancients,' stated the old man calmly. 'The Ancients I refer to wouldn't have needed such apparatus, and as for the technology, well, they certainly had it.'

'I talk of the time around The Great Shift; I know little of the pre-story of which you speak.'

'There have been many shifts, all described as great at the time of their occurrence. I assume you are describing the one prior to what we are experiencing now that hasn't been so great?'

'Amun teases you,' interjected Ariana. 'I'm sure that your quest is a noble one, although some might say unwise or even foolish to travel without protection given the Earth's current dalliance with our Sun.'

'Nic assured us there would be havens,' Ully glowered over at his companion.

'Indeed, there are, but not so many in the more remote pathways of the Ley,' said Ariana. 'May I ask what it is you hope to gain through this sojourn?'

'An insight and better understanding of what my forebears experienced and went through in order to gift us our legacy.'

'How shall you achieve all this when you won't face the same perils as did they?' asked Amun.

'I have the ability to feel the past.'

'How?'

'By absorbing the residual vibration left by an experience. The feelings are stronger when I'm over The Ley.'

'Do these feelings manifest emotionally or physically?' probed Ariana.

'Both. I feel the physical more if great trauma is present.'

'And ultimately, what will you do with this newfound wisdom and understanding?'

'I shall use it to heal, of course. This is why I'm here.'

'Who gave you this calling,' asked Amun. 'Was it a mentor?'

Nic laughed. 'No, a mentor is merely a facilitator, someone who helps nurture your abilities. My calling is innate.'

Amun continued to probe and test this would-be sage with what Nic thought were increasingly inane and pointless questions, but the young man understood the old man's game and played along.

'...And what of the souls who refuse the higher level of consciousness that you show them? What about those who are unable or unwilling to alter their vibration?'

'I shall send them love and resist them peacefully. After all they are simply infant souls of the spiritual university. Their time to evolve will come if, and when, they are ready. We all come here to learn, to grow, to experience, and those of us who are near or at the graduation stage should lead by example for those who would follow in our paths when their time is right. The ancient notion of Good and Evil are not opposites; they are simply different expressions of the same universal energy. We are entering the epoch of The Makara, the notion of duality has diminished, and although there will be a small group of humans who remain entrenched in their baseness, the majority of us shall transcend the material realm into an ever-evolving higher consciousness.'

The old woman nodded in agreement, quietly impressed by Nicobar's assertions. 'And what have you to say on all this, Ullyman Spence?' she asked.

Ully blew air from his cheeks and got to his feet. 'I'm here in my capacity as a CM. Nic's welfare is my brief. Aside from that, all I want to do is see flyers and troubadours, give my wingsuit a workout, listen to music and make merry. As long as we're in Glaston for the solstice, I care not about much else. Now, please excuse me but the wulf and I need fresh air and exercise. We shall be back before nightfall.' Ullyman called the hound to heel, and they took their leave.

Ariana collected the empty bowls and gave a discreet nod to Amun before she left the room.

Amun thoughtfully stroked his whiskers before he spoke. 'I have something that I would really like to show you.' Nic, intrigued by the tone of the old man's voice, and thankful that the questions had ceased, making him think he'd just passed some sort of test, nodded ok.

Amun led the way into a room whose walls were lined from ceiling to floor with books and volumes. A peculiar smell emanated from this ancient looking library and Nic's senses were immediately flooded almost to the point of overload by the tangible accumulation of esoteric wisdom and story that filled the chamber. Providing the centrepiece was a large stone table, in the middle of which sat a smooth, flat, circular piece of obsidian. In unconcealed wonderment Nic slowly navigated the tightly packed shelves, a hand carefully and reverently stroking the occasional spine of some mysterious work as he tried to take it all in.

'I have seen images of things such as these,' the young man said in almost a whisper.

'You mean books?'

'And libraries, yes.'

The old man easily picked up Nicobar's train of thought and gruff-chuckled to himself. 'Yes, I can see why you would think that.'

'What?'

Amun gestured with his arms. 'Why keep all this in such an arcane form when it can be stored in one minute crystal.'

'I did, but...'

'But you also felt something when you entered this room that would be absent when perusing all this information through a chip, no?'

'Yes, like... like a...'

'There are no words. Best not even try. Some of these great volumes were scribed by first hand, others by generational and tribal

CAPRICORN

legacy. I have them and use them in this form for the very same reason you cited for your walkabout, to be able to absorb the residual vibration left by an experience, something a chip, will never be able to replicate.'

'Of course,' breathed Nic in perfect understanding, his head now swimming with the accumulative energy he was being bathed in. 'May I?'

Amun produced a pair of delicate silk gloves and offered them. 'Be my guest.'

Nic donned the gloves, closed his eyes and allowed intuition to be his guide, pausing, hovering, moving on until his hand finally and decisively rested on what felt like a predestined selection. He opened his eyes and pulled a heavy bound book from the shelf. – *The Chronicle of The Meek* – The beautifully embossed title disappointed him slightly. It was a work that of course he had studied and referenced all his life, admittedly, not in such a crafted physical format, but he still felt slightly miffed that of all the collected wisdom within the room he had to be guided to this. As he placed the book on the table, Amun merely gave a look of inevitability and encouraged him to select random pages. Nic sat, opened the great volume, breathed in the life from its pages and began to read:

Before the formation of these five isles two main islands sat side by side, known commonly then as The British Isles, as they are still sometimes referred to at the time of writing. They constituted five dominions: Engerland, Scotland, Eire, Northern Ireland and Wales. Four of these dominions came under a crown protectorate known as the United Kingdom. Eire, the fifth dominion was independent of the other four and made up the majority of the smaller stand-alone isle now known as Gael.

It was during the Gregorian year 2030, that great seismic upheaval took place upon these shores. Marduk, the outer most planet of the Brown Dwarf star system, Tyche (The Good Sister) had made its cyclical pass between Mars and Jupiter creating massive electromagnetic forces on our planet that ultimately flipped the poles. This, in turn, caused the oceans to rise and lands to be riven apart. It was then that the Sun began to rise in the west and set in the east, until the Sun finally failed to rise, and day became the longest night. In geographical terms, the changes wrought on Earth and these lands were instant. Man's technological advancements were wiped out. All notion of linear time was lost, and many souls perished.

PRECESSION

It is written that forty shars (years) and up to seventy in more northern latitudes passed before the re-emergence of The Life Giver to the skies, and during that period the British Isles had been pulled apart and shaped into an archipelago of smaller islands that came to be known as: Highlands, Grampia, North Isle, Mid Isle and South Isle. Although still fed by rivers, all the great cuts, Lornmoray, Clydeforth (M8), and Akeman (M4) have all become saline with the exception of the narrowest passage, the Merseyhumber (M62) cut that is still largely fresh water . . .

Nic continued to read, but with little interest to the content. Geography wasn't his calling, and a part of him began to wonder why he had been drawn to this great storical tome written by his forbears or to the passage he selected therein. He acknowledged the current coincidental visitation and passing of Earth's binary star with the description he was reading from long ago. He mentally calculated the peron and eventually came up with an approximation of three thousand six hundred and fifty-seven Earth orbits since this twinned planetary system crossed paths with our own. Failing to read any significance into all this, he turned to Amun to shed some light.

Amun once again intercepted Nic's thought and spoke first. 'You are to ask questions I cannot answer.' Amun shook his head. 'I have no insight, I have no kiness. If there is a lesson here, then it is for you alone. All I sense is that you are on a journey, you are here as part of that journey. Ariana and I shall facilitate where we can and are meant.' He gestured with a sweep of his hand. 'All of this is at your disposal for as long as you decide to stay. What I can say is your mathematics is good if not entirely accurate.' Nic raised an eyebrow. 'I know that none of this is your muse, but you were drawn to these passages for a reason. Maybe we should explore some more.' Amun opened a cabinet and selected one of many drawers. When he opened it the light and energy of a thousand crystals lit up the room. He selected one and held it up. A prism of mauve and turquoise danced along shafts of light. 'This is the one,' the old man said with satisfaction. He carefully placed the crystal in the centre of the obsidian plinth, and with a single deft flick of the wrist, sent it spinning. As it gained momentum the crystal began to glow until a fine mist formed and rose into the air as a spinning cloud. Amun stepped back calmly and waited. Eventually the swirling mist started to dissipate until a complete three-dimensional image appeared. Nic immediately recognised it as a moving representation of the solar system with a fiery ball of plasma at the centre. He wasn't awed by this, he had seen plenty of story holograms in the Halls of Learning back home, but this was the most clear and resonant he had ever witnessed.

'This represents the period as written in the book.' Amun sent a closed palm into a corner of the image and then opened his fingers wide. Another image appeared instantly. 'This is our realm showing the two main islands prior to The Shift.' He stepped back again and studied Nicobar's features. 'Do you feel anything?' Nic shook his head in disappointment. He'd seen all this stuff before, and it did little to stimulate his interest. Why couldn't he be shown things about human physiology, auras and the intricacies of the microbiome and immune system? He didn't want to appear disrespectful of the old man's efforts, and so did his best to stymie his thought process. He turned back to the spinning hologram.

'This is Marduk, the planet we see in the southern sky at dawn as we travel, is it not?' asked Nic pointing to an object passing between Earth and Mars. Amun nodded in agreement. 'Why is it signed here as Nibiru?'

'We are seeing this at the time when it was observed. The planet Marduk was then referred to as Nibiru, The Planet of The Crossing, as named by The Sumerians. Its passing between The Earth and Mars created massive electromagnetic energy that in effect dragged our moon out of its orbit and placed it in its current position. This is the process you are watching now. Nibiru is the seventh orbiting planet around Tyche, shown here as Nemesis, The Destroyer, not the outer as The Meek described it. Two other objects, Zyrus and Gersch are now known to also orbit the Brown Dwarf bringing the total to nine.'

'Will the visitation of this old Sun create the same upheaval as described back then?'

'No, at least not so much in the northern hemisphere. As you may be aware, there are tectonic shifts happening beyond the equator where the magnetic pull is stronger. Our magnetic field is created from Earth's core. Any magnetic disruption causes core flow changes and plasma reactions to occur, hence the extreme plate movements and seismic and volcanic activity. Due to the Moon's current position, the magnetic pull isn't as strong. Our magnetic North didn't reach the forty-degree tilt necessary to create a pole shift this time around. Marduk is now beyond its perihelion and its influence is beginning to wane. As you can see, then the system approached from

PRECESSION

below the ecliptic crossing Earth from directly under the Southern Hemisphere where our South magnetic pole then tried to repel it away, and so as the planet rose, our South Pole followed, causing the fast magnetic reversal and the eventual polar shift.'

'Scholars back home say solar activity will persist and alter Gaia's ecology irreversibly.'

'Yes, that is true, and Gaia will adapt accordingly if we let her, as shall we.'

'I hear many have perished.'

Amun sighed. 'Three dimensional beings shall continue to demise; it is their destiny. As you rightly spoke earlier, those who fail or refuse to raise their frequencies to that of The Mother and her ever changing vibrations will eventually cease to exist.'

'I wonder what their life lessons could be.'

'Some will find out, others won't. Spiritually, some are young; others are old, caught in a seemingly perpetual karmic wheel of their own making.' Amun looked hard at the young man. 'And what about you this time round?'

'I know I am here to heal. Whether or not that is an inherited calling or a karmic debt, I cannot say.'

'A healer is what you are and what you have always been,' said Ariana, entering the room as if from nowhere. 'This gift is your vehicle this time around, not necessarily your life mission.'

'Oh,' said Nic slightly taken aback. 'Are you about to enlighten me?'

The old woman shook her head. 'No, of course not. Even if I could, I wouldn't unless I was guided to do so.' She glided over to the open book and closed her eyes, still for a moment. 'Nothing has been revealed to you here.'

Nic wasn't sure if she was asking the question or making a statement. 'I, er...'

'No matter,' she said, carefully closing the book. 'All shall be revealed in due course.' With a wave of her hand the representation of the old solar system collapsed and vanished.

'You are not telling me much,' said Amun easing himself under his quilt with a grunt.

'There is still nothing much to tell.' Ariana spread a lotion across the aged skin of her arms and into the furrowed creases of her wise old face before getting into her own bed. She let out a heavy sigh, and Amun looked across at her in the half-light searching for her thoughts.

'Do you think he is the one?'

'Yes... yes, he has been the object of my dreams.'

'Still no insight?'

'No; all metaphorical, no decipherable meaning.'

'And the other one?'

'Nothing... except, there is a bond between them, something that goes far beyond an old Meek tradition.'

'Of the soul?'

'Yes.'

'Then we must allow them to fulfil their destinies unhindered. We facilitated their survival. Our role is complete. Once recuperated they can be on their way.'

'Of course.'

'You are not convinced.'

'We did not save their souls. The young man, Nicobarius, he knew we were here. No one without great abilities could have known that. He is special. He saved them both.'

'You make him sound almost messianic.'

'Hmm, what a strange concept that would be for the now. Maybe he has already fulfilled that destiny.'

'So, you think this could be a second coming?'

'No, I don't. I sense he is here for something else.'

'A karmic debt? His words.'

'Perhaps, yet there are no signs in his aura. The band of healing energy surrounding him is phenomenal. He has either been or is about to become a great physician, but his ultimate destiny is clouded, it is not for us to see, and on a conscious level, neither for him.'

'Were it not for your recurring dreams and long held foretelling of this, whatever it may manifest to be, I would be reading scant into any of it.'

'I know. As vague as it is, I shan't continue to knock on a closed door.'

'I pray your reveries will soon shed some light. Goodnight, my dear.'

'Goodnight.' Ariana turned on her side and pulled the quilt over her bony shoulders, anticipating the unconscious stream of undecipherable riddles that lay ahead of her as she closed her eyes.

Ullyman propped himself up on an elbow from his prone position. 'Are you awake?' he asked in a coarse whisper.

'I am now,' came the reply out of the gloom.

'What do you make of them?' Silence. 'The old man made me drink milk from an animal this morning.' Silence. 'A fucking goat, no less.' Silence. 'Milk from a goat… Can you hear me?'

'Yes.'

'Well?'

'Well, what?'

'What do you think?'

'What did it taste like?'

'Strange, weird.'

'Was it unpleasant.'

'No, not exactly.'

'Did your gut react?'

'No.'

'You feel ok?'

'Yes.'

'Then go back to sleep.'

'I can't, my mind is racing.' Silence. 'How did you know this place was here?'

'I saw it.'

'Middle eye, eh?'

'Something like that.'

'I sometimes wish I had that gift.'

'You have; you just haven't exercised it yet.'

Silence resumed once again, and Nic closed his eyes in the hope that the questions had ceased, and his companion would now go to sleep, but they hadn't, and he wouldn't.

'So?'

'So what?' Nic asked exasperated.

'What do you make of them, the old couple?'

'They took us in, provided shelter, food, healing and a bed. What do you want me to say?'

'What tribe do you think they belong to?'

Nic sighed. 'Why do they have to belong to a tribe? They are sovereign.'

CAPRICORN

'Sound like Brigantine Tykes to me.'

'Well, seeing as we are in that old Riding, they probably are. What does it matter?'

'It doesn't. I was just making an observation. They were right about one thing.'

'What?'

'We should have packed Faraday suits.'

'We agreed; we both said we should do this walkabout as authentically as possible.'

'Yeah, but it was never going to be that, was it? I can't ever see us encountering pockets of Chav resisters on our travels.'

'I know. I just wanted the journey to Glaston to be a bit more interesting, that's all.'

'Well. Not packing the suits has already made it that.'

'That's true – anyway, your lot had already been assimilated long before walkabout became a thing.'

'When are we leaving?'

'When I feel fit enough to travel.'

'When will that be?'

'I don't know.'

'I pray it will be soon. I don't want to miss the solstice, and I don't think I can drink any more goat milk.'

'Authenticity, my friend; the ancients drank milk from animals, and ate their flesh too. Maybe we will be served some tomorrow to break our fast.'

'Are you serious?' Ully whispered in horror. 'I shall politely decline and continue my fast if that is the case.'

Nic chuckled to himself but was careful not to tease his mate further. He felt a strong and growing, yet inexplicable affinity to this part of Brigantia, like a pull from a magnet, and he knew he would be reluctant to leave even when he felt fit and able to do so. As for their hosts, they both left him super intrigued. Ariana had already been inside his head, and he had been happy to allow her access. He felt the old woman to be a mage of extraordinary insight and esoteric knowing, and that this fateful encounter to be one of, as yet, unexplained serendipity. To Nic, it seemed that her partner was the gatekeeper of untold wisdom. His library could well be the font of all knowledge, and he had graciously granted him full and free reign to seek out and explore at will. The thought sent a tingle up his spine, and he couldn't wait to get started. He knew that Ully would become

PRECESSION

restless sooner than later, and maybe a little kidology wouldn't go amiss in relation to his rate of recovery, maybe just enough to discover if there was any fate or design behind all of this.

Nic peered into the dark. Ully had gone quiet except for his slow, steady breathing that had become entrained with that of the wulf's as she lay by his side. He allowed the rhythmic noise to enter his own subconscious where he soon fell into a calm, hypnogogic state of his own.

CAPRICORN

Further Education

Under Amun's guidance Nicobar soon became adept at viewing crystals. While Ullyman's explorations with the wulf and falcon grew longer, he spent almost every waking moment in the library cramming his head with the accumulated knowledge of his calling, and when he tired of study he would delve into the vast archive of story and the fascinating ways of his forebears. He was now pleased he had taken the time to learn the ancient art of understanding the written word – reading - as it used to be called. Most of his peers in The Halls of learning had scoffed at him for bothering to acquire such an archaic and pointless skill, but he now took great joy and comfort from the many great tomes of literature that had been put at his disposal that informed and exercised his imagination as the words left the page.

Ullyman burst into the library unceremoniously with the wulf panting hard at his heel. 'Thought I might find you in here - for a change,' he added sarcastically. 'This doesn't look like study,' he observed, taking an interest at the images confronting him. 'What are those things?' he asked wide eyed.

From his seat, Nic studied his friend with calm curiosity. Ullyman's physiology appeared altered. His eyes seemed super focused, and the pupils therein dilated. Nic decided to ask some questions of his own. 'If you're staying send the wulf away, Amun will not take kindly to her being in here.' Ully gave the command and Nic offered him a chair. 'Where is it you go during the rote?'

Ully's attention had become fixated on the images Nic had been watching. 'What? - Here - there…'

'Specifically?'

'Erm… to the village of Denton.'

Nic raised an eyebrow. 'Oh, and what is of interest in the village of Denton?' Nic had to put himself between his minder and the images in order to break the spell.

Ully blew air from his cheeks and scratched his nose. 'Err… nothing in particular.'

Nic raised a hand and the images behind him instantly dissolved. He cocked his head and stared hard at the big lad.

PRECESSION

'Ah, grollops,' he capitulated. 'I'm seeing a hemp farmer's daughter.'

'Oh, exclaimed Nic. 'You been tasting his wares as well?'

'Don't talk daft, he grows commercial hemp.'

Nic adopted his doctor persona and scrutinised his mate some more. 'Psychedelics?' He concluded but posed it as a question.

'Shrooms,' admitted Ully sheepishly. 'Edith cultivates them on cow shit,' he added with an inane grin. Nic leant his head on a hand and shook it. 'Hey, what's with the judgement?' said Ully indignantly. 'You're always banging on about the therapeutic value of psychedelics.'

'It's not the psychedelics, you divot, I'm more concerned about you spreading your seed all over Brigantia and being sworn to a tithe for the rest of your life.'

'Edith takes rutin and wild carrot; we're not stupid. She is a fine girl, and we are in the now. I would like to take her to Glaston with us.'

'No, no, no! – We made the ground rules when we left Catterick. I will not be chaperoning a caravanserai of your conquests all the way down to Glaston.'

'But she…'

'No! And I shall hear no more on it. Now, if you want me to continue with the show, then you are welcome to stay and observe, otherwise take yourself elsewhere and finish your psilocybin adventure.'

'We'll never get to Glaston at this rate,' Ully muttered under his breath. 'And at least I'm not a virgin still.'

Nic ignored the remarks and with a sweep of his hand brought the images back into view in all their three-dimensional splendour. 'These things, in answer to your question, are what were known as motorised vehicles, horseless carriages, or commonly referred to as cars. They are what people used to transport themselves about their rotely business.'

Ully watched the scene in front of him with unconcealed awe. 'Beautiful! – It appears to me as colonies of brightly lit insects, or, or even a snake – look.' He traced the pattern of slow-moving images of vehicles lit up along a multi-lane highway at night. 'I wonder where they are all headed,' he added fascinated.

'Who knows,' said Nic, 'And maybe not so beautiful if we add this.' With another hand gesture he introduced audio and olfactory sensations.

The noise and smell of petroleum fumes assaulted Ully's senses and took him aback. 'What is this stink?'

'It is the exhaustive residue of the energy source they used to power the vehicles. Toxic and carcinogenic.'

'Did they not know this?'

'Oh, yes.'

Ully pulled an incredulous face. 'But…'

'Oh, my friend, I am learning that there are uncountable and unfathomable things to know about our ancestors, way more than the crazy stuff we were taught in the learning halls, and none of it makes any sense to a rational mind until you begin to understand who and what lay behind it all.' Nic beckoned the image towards him, and they were immediately presented with a macro tour of the scene. They watched in intrigued silence.

Eventually Ully shook his head in confusion. 'Most of these what you call cars have only one occupant, and yet it seems the space inside is designed for more people. I am no engineer, but surely there is an inefficiency issue here. Why such a large mode of transportation for one person?'

'That question can only be answered once you understand the collective mind control that the people of this epoch were subjected to by their controlling masters.'

'Their masters must have been all powerful.'

'Only insofar as the people allowed them to be. They acquiesced their own collective power to a tiny controlling elite.'

'How could that happen?'

'It happened over millennia. At the beginning of the era of the Fish, a citizen was a citizen, and a slave was a slave; by the end of the epoch everyone thought of themselves as citizens, but in reality, they were all slaves.'

'I've heard about mighty armies and great wars, but if these rulers were few in number, how did they subjugate all the people of the world? You are right, none of it makes sense…'

'Bread and circuses.'

The two boys turned in unison to see Amun, fresh from his labours in the orchard standing before them. Nic was becoming acutely aware of the sudden and unannounced appearances of their elderly hosts, and it served to unnerve him a little.

"… Already long ago, from when we sold our vote to no man,

PRECESSION

the People have abdicated our duties;"' the old man began to quote. *"'for the People who once upon a time handed out military command, high civil office, legions — everything, now restrains itself and anxiously hopes for just two things: bread and circuses."'*

Ully and Nic both stared at the old man nonplussed. Amun nodded, sat himself down between the pair of them with a grunt, stroked his whiskers as had now become familiar and continued. 'Juvenal.' He stated, looking at the boys in turn as if the name might solicit a response. It didn't. 'Juvenal was a satirical poet in ancient Rome. He originated the phrase to decry the erosion of the original concept of democracy – for the people, by the people. The people in question had begun to neglect their civic duties, the most important of which was to keep elected politicians in check. Thus, the political elite were able to generate public approval, not by excellence in public service or public policy, but by diversion, distraction or by satisfying the most immediate or base requirements of a populace by offering a palliative, for example handouts of food or entertainment– hence the phrase "bread and circuses". The people of this time were born, raised and indoctrinated by a cynically designed system that kept them obedient, compliant and believing in a reality that was carefully constructed and presented to them in a way that kept them reliant on that system. Everything they were taught, shown, allowed to do, say, or think fell into the narrative. This concept was compounded in what was known as the late twentieth century with the advent of cinema and television, the perfect tools by which to pacify, restrain and control.' Amun gestured toward the hologram. 'What you observe here is merely a snippet of the collective madness that occurred during this phase of mankind's existence. Our rationale rails against this gross stupidity because we are no longer asleep, our minds and bodies are no longer poisoned. Our spirits are free to soar to their full potential. We acknowledge our sovereignty. Alas, for the majority of the people on Earth during that period, this was not the case.'

'If I were able to view more of these things, would I come under the spell of bread and circuses?' asked Ullyman turning back to the mesmeric images that still fascinated.

'No, of course not,' chuckled Amun in his gravelly tone. 'What you see here is a true depiction of their reality. This rotely commute from dwelling to place of labour was the result of minds controlled by mass acquiescence of personal sovereignty through the devices that drove bread and circuses. The people became lulled into a state of self-destructive compliance. Instead of selling value, they sold their time. Their sense of worth became external, quantified by universal lies and falsehoods that were drip-fed through such devices.'

'What were these devices you speak of?' asked Ully.

'Visual and audio devices, the like of which I have already mentioned, television, cinema and radio. Collectively known as media, they were used to propagandise or falsify facts and information. Even story could be manipulated and twisted in this way to satisfy an agenda. These things were prophesied and written down in great tomes of work long before they came to pass. You may seek out these books in their original format among these shelves any time you wish if you feel so inclined.'

'And yet I have seen depictions of culture and great works of art that originally came through the devices of which you speak,' countered Nic.

'Oh, of course, and indeed there was a benevolent and evolutionary flow of knowledge, wisdom and advancement of humankind through such technology, don't forget, this was the age of duality, but prior to the coming of the last Shift, truth, wisdom, and all things pertaining to art, imagination and culture were savagely censored and dismissed. Baseness and banality held sway, and the masses in their hypnotic state lapped up the circuses they were fed.'

'Is it possible to view such things?' asked Ully curiously.

Amun let out a grunt of indignation. 'I have never archived such of which you speak. No doubt I would be able to find material of this nature but I'm sure that even you, Ullyman Spence would be totally baffled and bemused by its content.'

Disappointed and without perceiving any tone of condescension in Amun's remark, Ully turned back to the scene that continued to hold him spellbound. – 'However,' said the old man in a tone that instantly re-piqued Ully's intrigue, 'If you would care to join me here after our meal this evening, I would like to show you both something that should be of interest, value and hopefully entertainment also.'

The two youths exchanged looks of further intrigue. Nic spoke for them both. 'Yes, yes, we would very much like that.'

Nic and Ully sat in awe-struck silence, neither of them fully comprehending what it was they had both just experienced, while in the background their old host was slowly and painfully descending his library ladder on ancient, creaking knees, clutching a small book.

'Here it is,' said Amun, carefully wiping his sleeve over the cover and offering it to Nic. 'This is the written story from which the film was made; perhaps you would like to read it also.'

Nic took the paper volume and read the cover: *A Kestrel for a Knave - Barry Hines – Penguin Books* He looked from the book to Amun and back again, not sure what to do with it. It felt ever so delicate.

'I preserved the paper long ago; it should withstand your scrutiny.' Nic reverently leafed the yellowing pages while that overwhelming sense of déjà vu swept over him again. 'It is written in old English, but now that you have seen the film with translation maybe the dialect won't be too hard to follow. The work is fiction, but I understand the location in the film is real, and most of the characters are genuine. Apparently, the filmmaker was renowned for the sense of realism in his work. The original location lies to the South of here, about a rote away on foot. It remains close to the M1, largely farmland cultivating hemp and bamboo. At the time of this work, the inhabitants were mostly miners who dug for coal as an energy source deep underground as is documented in the film and book.'

In the background and without warning Ullyman Spence began to sob. Nic and the old man turned to him to see large tracks of tears rolling down his face. They cast glances at each other not knowing what to do or say. Nic had never seen him in such an emotive state, and he wondered if the shrooms might be still playing a role. For all its dark humour, which in large sections had totally passed them by, the ending had been heart wrenching and distressing to watch. Even Nic was finding it hard to disseminate what he understood to pass as entertainment from its moral message or raw insight into its time and place.

Under scrutiny, and feeling slightly embarrassed for himself, Ully slowly got to his feet and brushed away the salty streaks. 'I – I have to go find the hawk,' he managed to stutter.

'In the dark?'

Ully nodded with a pitiful look.

Nic exchanged the look. 'I understand. Shall I come with you?'

Ullyman shook his head. 'No.' And with a final sniff and cuff of his nose, he left the room. He called the wulf to heel and with face half hidden, brushed passed Ariana and disappeared into the inky black night.

'What appears to have upset our friend?' she asked, entering the library. Amun held up the strange, shimmering disc. 'Ah, the story of the boy and the hawk,' she nodded knowingly. He is aware it is a work of fiction?'

'Yes, said Amun, 'but something has struck a chord.'

'Hmm…' She took the disc from her partner, pondering as she stared at its prismatic qualities.

PRECESSION

Amun's Story

Nic read the book in one sitting. Without having seen the film first, the prose and descriptions would have had little meaning, but now he had pictures to go with the dialogue, and the whole experience began to bring with it a far-off familiarity. Despite his intuitive sensibilities, he failed to bring any recognition or joinder save that of Ully's passion for all things feathered. Maybe Amun had simply chosen this particular work to show them because of their association with the falcon. He closed the delicate paperback and sniffed at it but detected nothing but preservative. He carefully placed the tiny volume back in its place high up on the dusty shelf; in doing so he dislodged a small brass key that went clattering to the floor. Intrigued, he picked it up wondering what it belonged to. Most of the many drawers that lined three walls of the library were left unlocked and at his disposal, and so mischievously he went in search of one that wasn't. It soon became obvious that the key was too small for any of the drawers on show, and so he methodically opened and checked each one until in the far corner he found a tiny drawer within a drawer, and the key fit perfectly. The thing was empty save for a folded piece of paper and a tarnished silver pendant sitting on a bed of green baize. Intrigue evaporating, he lifted it out and up to the light where it unfurled to expose a pendant that looked to take on the shape of a hawk in flight. Slightly disappointed, and before he had chance to put the thing back, Amun entered the room and caught him in the act.

'Oh. . . I erm, I was just. . .'

The old man stood, staring.

In his haste to put it back where he found it, Nic dropped the pendant on the floor. 'The key fell off the shelf when I was putting the book back,' he sputtered. 'And . . .'

'And curiosity got the better of you, did it?' Amun held out his hand. Red faced, Nic stooped to pick up the trinket before shamefully dropping it into the old man's outstretched hand.

'I'm sorry, I . . .'

Amun held out his other hand, palm out bidding him to be silent. 'Come, sit with me; let me tell you a story.' Deep in thought he scrutinized the piece of jewellery before carefully laying it out on the obsidian table beside him. Nic, still embarrassed, sat silent, patiently waiting for the old man to speak.

'Long in the past, when I was a young man,' he began, 'not much older than you are now, I belonged to a specialist team of craftsmen who helped build many of the great structures you will see on your travels. I was a telekinetic engineer, a PK. The A1 crossing was my last and arguably most challenging project. Built entirely from bast, its design, strength and composition made it virtually indestructible. All our team were assigned 'mates', similar to your CMs, I suppose. My 'mate' was a wonderful human being, a small man in stature but a giant in physical and mental strength. His name was Kakarak Kik-kik and he hailed from a far-off small island in the Indonesian archipelago. He became a great friend, and we were inseparable.

'Towards the end of the project we were given some downtime. We were stationed on the south side of the estuary, wondering what to do with ourselves, when I heard about how the receding sea levels to the east of us had started to expose vast tracts of land that contained artefacts from the past. The shallow sea around an area stretching from the Humber down to The Wash had been used to deposit the remains and contents of towns and cities that were devastated at the time of the last Shift in a futile effort to reclaim land. Many excavations, although revealing great finds, ended in disaster as the prevailing shifting mud and sand collapsed digs, resulting in loss of life. The whole region was declared unsafe, and yet we continued to hear stories of teams who defied the warnings discovering amazing things.' Amun let out a reflective sigh. 'Despite the standing of our calling we were young, bold, adventurous, and predictably, but unfortunately, stupid.

'K and I set forth with the warnings of our peers ringing in our deaf ears. If he was ever an unwilling accomplice, I'll never know as I was super arrogant and single minded.

'After three rotes of travel the terrain had become flat and featureless. The plaintive cry of seabirds and curlews on the wind was the only respite from the regimented sound of our footsteps squelching through ever thickening reed and mud. Soon we began to see abandoned excavations and tunnels. We curiously explored a few before realising the innermost workings had collapsed. By the end of the third rote my initial exuberance had diminished somewhat. We had plenty of provisions, but we were cold and wet. We bivouacked in an old cutting for the night that offered some respite from the wind if little else. We lit a fire and allowed the flames to soothe us into a fitful slumber. Sometime later we were startled to our senses by a loud hollow rumbling sound. All around us the working had started to collapse, showering us with debris. The fire went out and we began to choke on the dust and smoke. We found our torches, gathered our stuff and somehow managed to scramble our way to safety. Beneath our feet the ground continued to shake and shift. In the near distance, illuminated by our torches, we could see stretches of land open up and disappear, at first with a menacing growl and then a loud whooomp! We feared we'd be taken along into the abyss, but then as soon as it had begun, the ground stopped moving and the earth fell eerily silent.

'Come dawn we opened our eyes to a vivid orange glow in the east, and a ground mist that swirled about our feet. All remained deathly quiet except for the familiar call of curlews and the odd gust of wind that had begun to disperse the ground fret. As our tired and weary eyes adjusted to the emerging light, we saw at last the effects of our nightmare. The upheaval had brought indescribable objects to the surface, bent broken and jagged, ancient, twisted metal, salt-rusted and yet somehow preserved by the impacting mud-flood.

'I had a zealous curiosity, much like your own, and despite the near-death experience, my burning inquisitiveness got the better of me. K was rightly nervous, the more cautious, and he begged for us to abandon this folly and turn back. But I was having none of it. We had come so far, and I badly wanted to explore what had been thrown up in front of us.

'We waded knee deep in mud that clung and sucked at every bone, muscle and sinew, until we managed to clamber upon wreckage unrecognisable from its original design. I urged my reluctant mate to help dig away at the sludge and the silt until, after a great deal of cursing and sweating, we unearthed what I confidently announced to be the rusting husk of a boat. After reclaiming some energy and sustenance from our provisions we set about exploring further.

'The wooden deck had completely gone, and beyond the skeletal remains of the wheelhouse, the orange crusted remains of the prop shaft, engine and rudder were the only other decipherable working parts. I guessed this wasn't a sea-going vessel; due to its size and shape it looked more as if it had been some kind of houseboat. We dug away some more, hoping to discover some artefact or other we

CAPRICORN

could take back and impress with, but there was nothing of any interest to show for all our hard work. Too exhausted to search elsewhere, we were ready to admit defeat, when I noticed a pointed corner of rust poking out from a drift of silt at the stern of the boat. With one almighty last effort we cleared away the gritty cocoon and exposed a large steel locker with ancient flecks of grey paint still stuck to it. The rusted padlock, hasp and staple came away easy, and the lid, unopened in an age, creaked, groaned and fell apart once exposed to air. Silt had seeped inside, but half buried sat another chest of galvanised metal construction that looked surprisingly well preserved. Before removing the chest, we came across a variety of old metal tools and hammerheads, but little else. The chest was locked, and it proved mighty tough to prise open, but when we did. . .'

'You found the necklace inside.' Nic finally felt bold enough to interject. 'What an interesting story.'

Amun shook his head. 'Not only did we find the necklace, but we also found the book about the boy and the hawk.'

'That's amazing,' said Nic. 'And you managed to preserve it after all that time being buried?'

Amun laughed. 'No, the thing disintegrated in my hands as soon as I picked it up, but not before I made a mental note of the title. The copy you have just read came from what was known as The British Library, as does most of the physical collection you see here.'

'Still a fascinating tale,' insisted Nic. 'But I don't understand, of what value is the chain?'

'None,' stated Amun. 'It's a piece of kitsch.'

'Then why keep it under lock and key?'

Amun shook his head once more. 'Allow me to finish my story . . .'

'. . .The earth had started to tremble again, there was movement beneath our feet, and so we vacated the wreck, carrying the chest between us, but in our haste, we forgot our diggers and K jumped back in to retrieve them. As he did a section of the hull collapsed and he vanished from sight in an instant and without sound except for the gurgling roar of liquid sediment that began to rush in and fill our excavated hole. Before I could react, the remains of the wreck, now broken in two, were quickly reclaimed and taken back below from whence it had emerged. It was the last I saw of him, and it all happened in the blink of an eye, no time to even register the incomprehensible terror that must have been in his eyes . . .' The old man paused, obviously affected by having to relive the nightmare. Nic had many questions but chose to stay silent, giving time for Amun to compose himself. '. . . In a daze, I vaguely remember dragging the chest to safer ground and burying it,' he said eventually.

'What else was in that chest?'

'Another pendant, identical to the other, like a pair. Seven double-terminated rose quartz crystals, a curious looking polished stone and some brass and marble miniature statues that looked like they could have been some sort of trophy or award. There were signs of engraving, but the metal was badly tarnished, and any legend was undecipherable. The crystals and the stone, that I later discovered came from a meteorite, looked to be the only items of any value and so I took them along with one of the pendants before I buried the chest. Don't ask me why I did that; my mind was in a whirl. To this rote I cannot fathom the reasoning of my actions, because there wasn't any. When I finally arrived back at site to relate my tale and face the music, I told it exactly how it happened and accepted full responsibility for what had transpired, but I omitted the part about our findings from my account.'

'What happened to you?'

'I was tried by a jury of my peers, stripped of my status as a PK and branded an outcast, an exlex – a pariah.'

'I'm sorry.'

Amun shook his head again. 'I deserved all the punishment meted out to me and more. They accepted that K was a willing accomplice in our little folly, or no doubt the sentence could have been worse, but I remained distraught for a long time, and the shame and guilt has never left me. He was my good friend, and I was responsible for his death.' The old man hung his head and went reflectively silent.

For a reason Nic couldn't quite put his finger on, Amun's story had hit an unconscious nerve. He felt an overwhelming sympathy with the metaphysical effect of guilt that was emanating from his aged host. In fact, the whole story had triggered something deep within him, like a fading dream or a memory that wasn't his own, but seemed to carry a vague implication that somehow he was attached to it. He felt if only he were able to rationalise it he would be able to see its purpose. He glanced down at the necklace sitting on the table and recognised the worn ancient symbol of The Meek that was still displayed by many of the tribes that inhabited the archipelago, especially those who lived on North Isle and his Catterick home. But any other attachment remained hanging in the far-off halls of his psyche, annoyingly obscure.

'Is there more?'

Amun slowly lifted his head and spoke. 'I travelled for many shars aimlessly, without purpose, and with little meaning to my existence, and then, one rote, and I would like to say purely by chance, but I now know that not to be true, Ariana came into my life and slowly helped me bring back my will to live.'

'You told her your story?'

'I didn't need to; she instinctively knew everything. Once our souls had been re-united there was little need for the spoken word to express ourselves.'

'You are soul mates?'

Amun smiled. 'Apparently we have lived many lives in many realms of existence, fought, suffered, and survived, experiencing many hardships and triumphs along the way, and so yes, I suppose our souls are well acquainted by now.'

'Do you still harbour any regrets over the objects that you took away all those shars ago?'

'Not by way of a curse or bad luck. Ariana showed me the power of the crystals and the stone, and I soon learned how to harness their energy and put them to good use. But as for the necklet. . .' He reached out and thoughtfully ran his fingers over the tangled chain and shook his head. 'Never wore it, never fathomed why I ever took it. Whenever it turned up, I would immediately get an image of K in my head and it served to depress and alter my mood, as it is doing now.'

'I'm sorry,' said Nic. 'Shall we...?'

'No,' stated Amun holding up a hand. 'The time to deal with this is now. It has been suppressed for too long. I feel there could be catharsis at play here. Maybe now you understand why I choose to keep it hidden away under lock and key.'

'Couldn't you have simply discarded it?'

'Ariana wouldn't hear of it. Despite its lack of material worth, she knew it held some sort of esoteric importance and that it belonged with its dual back in that buried chest. It was a task I would readily have undertaken but for my stigma and the impositions served on me. There were times, when I was younger, I would have defied those restrictions to ease that burden and lift the mental anguish, but Ariana warned against it; she always said it would resolve itself as and when the time was right. Oddly enough, providence and circumstance always seemed to step in to prevent me doing something I would regret. And so, I've lived with it for all this time, out of sight and mostly out of mind, that is until you, your friend and the hawk showed up to fulfil the prophetic content of her dreams.'

'Ariana knew of our coming?'

'There's not much she doesn't know; save for the things we're not meant to know. Yes, she knew of your coming, but as to its purport, all we have is images of hawks writ large in her visions, the portent of your arrival, and now this.' Amun spread out an arm in a sweeping gesture.

Nic looked to the object of the old man's angst and then fixed him a look of resolve as a notion formed in his head. 'What's on the piece of paper?' he asked eventually, nodding towards the open drawer.

Amun returned the look, but said nothing, just stared as if delving into the young man's mind. 'Coordinates,' he finally breathed without breaking his stare.

'As and when the time is right – according to Ariana,' said Nic, cryptically.

'I would never wish to place such a burden upon you.'

'Why would you bother to take coordinates when the remnants of the chest were worthless, and why bury it?'

'I took the coordinates for K. I thought they might want to try and retrieve his body as evidence to my testimony, but in light of past tragedies and failed rescue attempts, they considered it too dangerous. I hastily buried the chest out of sight to fall in line with my story.'

'Walkabout was and still is our undertaking,' said Nic. 'Glaston is our destination, beyond this our meanderings are aimless. I am fully recovered from the effects of the geomag. It is time we were on our way. This task shall give us purpose. It shall be a journey of reconciliation and redemption.'

Amun could see the resolve in the young man's eyes, and he began to feel the inevitability of the situation as prophesied by Ariana, immense gratitude to whatever providence had brought these two youthful travellers into their midst, and finally a regret that his aged bones would no longer allow him to accompany them on their

CAPRICORN

sojourn.

'If I was younger, I would . . . '

'I know,' Nic interjected. 'You were once a strong, man, but now I detect your health fading fast.'

'What do you see?'

'There is dis-ease in your aura. Your skin is plagued with melanoma, and they are spreading fast.'

'Yes,' the old man conceded, 'You are astute in your observations.'

'I can treat it, I can . . .'

'No, no,' Amun cut him short. 'My time here is almost done. I have managed to live a good life despite the aberrations of my past. I have no need for your cures and remedies. It is becoming clear that I have held out for this moment. I shall be happy to pass knowing at least an effort was made towards restitution.'

'I detect uncertainty in your conviction.'

'Your journey will be long and arduous. You may still face many concealed dangers.'

'I understand the waters along the east coast have receded and large tracts of terra has been reclaimed.'

Amun nodded. 'Yes, but in that wapentek there are still hidden pockets of saltmarsh and treacherous fen lying in wait on any foolhardy enough to venture near.'

'We shall keep our wits about us.'

Amun regarded the youth long and hard, reflecting once more on his own juvenile acts of misjudgement. 'You will be travelling in wide open spaces with scant choice of refuge,' he warned. 'I suggest you pack Faraday suits.'

Nic slowly nodded his head, absorbing the veiled dig that pointed to the bad decision that had landed them there in the first place.

PRECESSION

Redemption – Deception

Exuberant youth and cautious wisdom stood high on the moor encircled by twelve standing stones. All four of them, to varying degrees, could feel at least a tenuous connection to their location as Ariana, eyes closed, deep in meditation, blessed the journey the two boys were about to commence. By their side sat the wulf, tongue out and to one side, panting patiently, while the falcon hovered high in a clear blue sky waiting to break its fast on an unsuspecting bird. To the east, the oft petulant sun was climbing fast; it was going to be hot. At their backs, in the near distance, the ancient monument that had been The British Library reflected the light from its smooth bast walls as spectacularly as the day it was built.

For the umpteenth time since daybreak Nic checked the inner compartment of his overladen rucksack to check that his tiny cargo was safe inside its hemp purse before heaving it all onto his shoulders.

'Well met and safe journey,' said Amun. A light breeze stirred his long grey beard as he offered the two lads a firm handshake. Nic looked the old man firmly in the eyes knowing their paths would not cross again. Amun gave a faint nod of the head with an understanding that all that needed to be said had been said.

Ullyman Spence, eager at last to resume their adventure, bent low and enveloped Ariana with his meaty arms in an embrace that looked as if it would crush her where she stood.

'You will be walking in unchartered territory,' she whispered in his ear. 'But you will be learning as you go. Every step should make you stronger and wiser. The journey is the life you choose to experience, so make the most of it, even when it may feel scary and dark. Sometimes the most beautiful places are reached through the roughest terrain.' She kissed his forehead and bade him well.

Ariana said her goodbyes to Nic telepathically. The communication was short, and only they knew what amount of counsel was imparted in that time. The young man slowly nodded his head, and they held a long embrace where myriad thought-forms and conscious awareness that would be impossible to describe in words flowed between them.

CAPRICORN

From the trig, high on the plateau, the old couple waved them on their way and watched them off into the distance until they crested a rise and disappeared from sight.

'The more you think you understand life, the more mysterious it becomes . . .' Ariana took her partner's hand and gazed wistfully out over the fertile valleys. Amun looked down at her inquisitively. '. . .We come into this world not remembering who we are for the purpose of experiencing the ride as if it were the first time. But at the same time the purpose of life is also to remember; to find the connection with your eternal essence, with your universal presence, and with the Creator of life itself. - Let's forget in order to remember - seems to be the spirit of the adventure our souls signed up to. Unless, maybe things were not quite meant to work that way? Unless, maybe there was interference with the original plan, a distortion of the purpose of it all?'

'So many questions, no clear answers, only seeking, sensing, feeling and ultimately trusting that you know what you know even though you don't know why you know it.' Amun gave a heavy sigh and joined Ariana's gaze over the world they knew. 'Perhaps the mystery of life is precisely that it must remain a mystery, an exercise of faith, of instinct and intuition. A journey into the unknown, an experimental adventure, an opportunity to find oneself and discover who we are by being acknowledged by others. Is that not what we all seek? To find a mirror soul that knows how to reflect our best version?'

'Can you actually see me? Not the face, not the persona, but the me that was and is and always will be? Can you see with your eyes closed and feel without touching – the soul that I am? Can you understand me without words and know me before you do?'

'I can, because you showed me how . . .' Amun's great calloused hand couched her slight shoulder and pulled her in close. '. . . And for that, my dear I shall be eternally grateful.'

The fault that separated North and Mid Isles at the M1 crossing at Lofthouse was unimpressive and proved a disappointment to Ully who had never ventured this far south before. The cut was deep but narrow, the iron-tinged water below appeared shallow and lifeless, unlike the Humber and Mersey deltas that fed the conduit east and west. He was more taken with the sleek architecture that traversed

PRECESSION

the chasm and appeared to be floating in the air with no visible means of structural support and shone with a clinical brightness much like the old library back in Ilkley. The three bridges arced away in ergonomic size and splendour from the pedestrian way he was stood on to the two hyperlink VHSTs for public and commercial transit, incredibly fast and totally silent.

They reached the Dearne valley just before sundown. The place mythologised in the book formerly known as Barnsley was now named Silkstone after the nearby ancient common. The gentle rolling hills and landscape had always been there, but the gritty mining town with its hard, oft downtrodden working-class inhabitants as depicted in the Billy Casper story had long gone.

They walked along pleasant boulevards lined with sentinel-like cypress trees and passed secluded arbours and estates that contained spacious dwellings, and open fields where the bright sound of laughter from children at play rang out in a cacophony of joyous noise. With scenes from the film that had affected him so still inside his head, Ullyman, who had insisted they make this slight detour, was once again disappointed.

'What was it you expected to see?' asked Nic, slightly incredulous.

'The old man said it was real,' muttered Ully.

'Well, it was – long ago!'

The irony was that if Nic applied himself, he would be able to see how it all was back in the day: the soot, the grime, the hardship. He would have loved to be able to somehow transfer his gift to his mate, but he was too tired to even attempt it in the now.

They arrived at a canteen where locals were sat around eating and drinking and taking in the warm evening air. The wulf met a companion of similar size but with a darker coat than hers who was seated with a couple and their two small children. Beyond many tentative and explorative sniffs, the two canines seemed to get along and after making pleasantries with the guardians the boys went inside to order food.

'Hey up, a couple o' strangers. Nah then, what can I do for you lads?' said the friendly lady with rosy complexion and ample bosom. The boys at once recognised the dialect from the film that at least hadn't altered that much. They ate pumpkin, kale and cayenne pie in exchange for a bag of saffron and six of Amun's giant hen eggs.

'Where you bound then, fellas?' she asked, clearing away the

CAPRICORN

empty plates.

'We're off to . . .'

'To Glaston,' interrupted Nic, giving Ully a sharp glance. 'We're down from Catterick, doing the Walkabout.'

'All that bloody way on foot, and without speedshoes? Rather you than me, lads,' she said walking off with her sizeable derrière swinging from side to side.

They pitched in the grounds at the back of the hostelry. Around a crackling fire they contemplated the sparkling tapestry sewn into the matt black heavens above their heads and watched as the tiny bright satellite known as the Moon traced a slow path across and in front of Orion's belt in the eastern sky.

'So let me get this straight,' said Ully, poking a stick at the fire that sent orange sparks dancing up into the night air. 'we're diverting east to search for a chest that the old man buried many shars ago, that contains nothing of value, in order to return an object that also has no value, as some kind of – what was it you called it – a mission of redemption?'

'Yeh, something like that.'

Ully shook his head, baffled. 'Do you think I could at least maybe see this object?'

Nic untied the hemp purse and carefully tipped its contents into Ullyman's outstretched hand. 'Be careful, it's delicate.'

Ully unfurled the pendant and held it against the glow of the fire. Frowning, he dipped inside his tunic to reveal his own bijou, a jet carving of a hawk in flight fastened with a mycelial leather thong. He compared the two, his frown growing deeper. The secular symbol that had been around for a few thousand shars had long lost its significance beyond that told in story of long ago. It was still worn as an adornment, more so by some of the tribes who inhabited North Isle and those who curiously hung on to their ancient Chav legacy, rather than any antiquated homage to the people known as The Meek.

Ully looked across at his mate, seeking further enlightenment, but Nic merely shrugged his shoulders. He slipped the thing into its bag and handed it back none the wiser.

'I still don't understand why we're doing this.'

'They didn't ask for it from us, I volunteered.'

'But why?'

'Because we owe them a debt, and I thought you'd enjoy the venture.'

PRECESSION

Nic wasn't about to try and explain the hermetic undertones hinted at by Ariana that seemed to tie together their arrival in Ilkley and Amun's story, because even now the thought of some kind of serendipity being at play still seemed somewhat tenuous to him. And yet that ever so vague connection that hung on the old man's tale remained with him, like an itch waiting to be scratched. Dare he put it all down to his youthful curiosity?

They de-camped early and set off at a brisk pace eastward. Resting briefly at the A1 hyperlink south of the subterranean tech centre of Doncaster, they watched Levs come and go in a silent instant along with sky taxis shuttling in and out of Finningley.

They soon found themselves yomping over miles of flat arable land in patchworks of vivid greens and yellows, broken only by the odd hamlet, smallholding, farm, forest or orchard. Always a few strides behind his "minder" who liked to set the pace, Nic watched Ullyman swishing a stick at the ears of golden barley that lined their route as he happily whistled some obscure tune. As he did so he began at once to get that déjà vu vibe again. Ever since his episode high on Rombalds Moor prior to the onset of the geomag, the phenomena had come to him with increasing occurrence and frequency. Without actually disturbing him, it certainly served to confuse his rationale, as none of this ever appeared in his dreams, or OBEs, and if it did, then something must have initiated a memory wipe, because he continually failed to find any connections with his eidetic self.

'You know, speedshoes might have been a good idea,' shouted Ully on the half-turn as the phenomena evaporated.

'Only if you want to dilute the challenge,' returned Nic.

'Or better still, I could have been born a flyer and soared down to Glaston,' Ully muttered to himself. He had grown up envious of the small sub-species that had quickly evolved to harness the gift of flight. They were a curious sect of humanity, that didn't actually fly like birds but had acquired the skill of soaring on thermals at great heights and speed, and over time had learned how to master the skies. They tended not to live as long as their Earth-bound cousins, but in Ully's eyes they were free and unfettered, and he was more than a little covetous of their lifestyle. It is said that their ancestors were born with defects due to the radon gas that had seeped into their environment and irreversibly altered their genes. Their pneumatic bones were hollow and thinner, a downy hair covered most of their bodies and over time they developed and grew cartilage-like appendages that stretched from wrist to hip and knee to groin known as patagium. Their large hands and feet became webbed, and facial features were nearly always streamlined sharp and sleek. Tribally they were insular, protective and some say unsociable, but maybe this was a legacy spawned from early unwanted outside curiosity. Ullyman had flown wingsuits before and he had become proficient within their technological capabilities, but compared to flyers they had many limitations, and you still needed the aid of a chute to be able to land safely. Nevertheless, once he took to the air, and for the all too brief time nature allowed him to stay there, he felt alive, and no amount of selling by his friend on the explorative merits of walkabout would ever compare.

Beyond the old coastal town of Gainsborough, the arable landscape began to transform. The reclaimed land, once the flat and featureless ocean floor-bed that sat beneath the shallow inlets of the North Sea, was now filled as far as the eye could see with countless gleaming four sided bast pyramids, some larger than others, the tallest being around 100 metres. Suspended high in the sky above them in grid formation were giant ring carbon structures, ECRs, otherwise known as quicksilver rings, that harnessed electrical energy from the aether and transferred it through the pyramids that acted as boosters and capacitors. They were passing through Mid Isle's largest power farm and a concentrated electromagnetic field that began to affect Nic's sensibilities, making him feel lightheaded and nauseous. Quickening their pace they eventually cleared the pyramids only to be confronted by a multitude of curious looking funnel-type objects projecting upwards from the ground. Large, beautifully contoured, smooth, light-absorbing dark grey structures, arcing up and out with their yawning opening apertures set at ninety degrees. These were energy horns. Like the ECRs they collected, boosted and converted energy into electricity, but instead of harnessing power from the aether, they captured it thermodynamically from deep within the Earth's electromagnetic core. Whenever the wind passed across them they would emit a resonant melancholic chorus akin to that of hundreds of whales coming together in song.

Leaving the farm behind, the land once again became featureless and began to resemble the salt-marsh tundra that the old man had warned them about, a wapentek of little or no human habitat. After three rotes of travel they were nearing their destination; road became lane, became path and overgrown track until they had to app out a safe route towards Amun's coordinates. Ully applied a multi-element detector now they were entering buried treasure country but came up with little or nothing until he got a significant reading of something not far under their feet.

'What is it?' asked Nic.

'It's saying aluminium, around three metres square, only a metre down,' said Ully reading the data from his device. 'Might be worth a dig.'

They unpacked their spades and began hacking away at the peat-like earth, Ullyman all the time excitedly speculating at what they might discover. They soon heard metal on metal and with curiosity heightened, began to carefully remove the soil. The first thing they saw was what looked like the letter 'u', approximately 50cm high on a flaky fluorescent blue background. They scraped some more, to the left and to the right -'c', 'n', and further to the right, 't'. They both looked at each other, at the word that emerged, and promptly fell about laughing.

'What the hell is this?' said Nic, composing himself and frantically scraping away more dirt. After a period of toil and sweat they had exposed the entire thing – Scunthorpe M180 ½ mile – It read with directional arrows.

'What the hell is it, then?' asked Ully, at once confused and disappointed.

'It appears to be an ancient signpost for travellers,' said Nic, wiping the perspiration from his brow.

'Well, that was a waste of time and effort.'

'Hmm,' concurred Nic. 'I suggest you turn that detector off until we really need it.'

They packed away their spades and abandoned the dig as it was, leaving the wulf to partially backfill with her hind legs until Ully called her to heel. The terrain was much drier and stable than at the time of Amun's ill-fated expedition, although there was still evidence of slip and slide that had turned petrified mud and sand into great wefts and escarpments. According to the map, they were approaching what used to be the coastal shoreline of what used to be the Isle of Wolds. Manoeuvring a mazy route through ancient, twisting, dried up tidal creeks blanketed in rich green samphire and clumps of purple sea aster and lavender, the boys arrived at their destination as indicated by the coordinates, relieved but exhausted.

Straight away, Ully got to work with the detector and soon came up with a signal that indicated metal beneath their feet. They began to dig, without much expectation or excitement this time, merely an idle curiosity and a resignation that this would be a mission accomplished without reward save that of a promise made and kept.

They didn't have far to dig, and the old, galvanised metal chest came up and out of its hole easily. Although there was no lock to it, the lid had welded itself fast over time and took some prising open. As per Amun's word the container was empty save for seven faux bronze statuettes stood atop their marble plinths, and a dull metallic tangled chain and pendant identical to the one Nic had in his possession lying forlorn in a corner.

'What are these?' asked Ully holding up one of the trophies and turning it around in his grubby hand.

'I don't know,' replied Nic while searching for the silver hawk in his rucksack. But there was something or someone somewhere telling him he ought to know. He quickly dismissed the musing and took the chain out of its pouch to compare with the one in the chest. They were indeed identical. He carefully placed the tarnished object into the hemp purse alongside its partner, pulled the drawstring tight and placed it back in the chest with a deep sigh that came out of nowhere, but that brought with it an overwhelming sense of relief. Just then, like his sigh, the falcon appeared from nowhere, perched itself on the handle of one of the spades and began to cackle loudly – kak-kak-kak-kak – like it was laughing at the sight of this bizarre ceremony. The boys looked at each other.

'Seen enough?' Ully asked, placing the statue back where he found it.

Nic got to his feet and nodded. 'You fill the hole; I'm going to see if there are any traces of the boat Amun talked about.'

There wasn't, and Nic wasn't about to resurrect ghosts from the past with his detector. He'd made good on his promise and that was enough for him, but he did feel slightly guilty for dragging Ullyman out on what his mate perceived to be a fruitless detour. They disguised the disturbed earth with vegetation and packed away their kit.

'Happy?'

PRECESSION

Nic nodded and set a course south-west that would only meander to follow the Ley. It would be a long drag all the way down to Glaston, but Nic assured his mate they would arrive before solstice without the assistance of speedshoes. They set off towards the setting sun hoping to get a few miles in before nightfall, wulf by their side and falcon high in front of a sky turning pink.

Picking up the pace, Ullyman Spence discreetly patted the breast pocket of his jacket to make sure the hemp purse and its contents was safe and secure . . .

CAPRICORN

Glaston

They followed the river Trent deep into the Mercian heart of Mid Isle, jobbing, bartering and, in Nic's case, healing as they went. At Ashby-de-la-Zouch Ully proffered his labour while Nic went in search of herbs, potions and tinctures to re-stock his apothecary kit. On his return to the inflatent he found two tall, hooded figures waiting for him.

'Well met,' he approached cautiously. 'How may I help you?'

One of the figures turned slowly to face him. 'You are the healer,' it said, features still half hidden. Unsure if this was a question or a statement, Nic was slow to respond. 'We have come to seek your counsel,' it continued in a tone that was soft and thankfully unthreatening.

Nic, still slightly unsure, looked beyond the one who spoke to his companion who hadn't moved before accepting the request. 'Of course,' he relented. 'Please come in.'

Once inside the tent Nic could see the one who spoke to be almost seven feet in height and his shy mate, not much smaller.

'I am Atalan,' the spokesman said, removing his hood at last, revealing features that took Nic aback. 'This is Rae.' He gestured towards his companion.

'You're Pleiadeans,' said Nic, taking in the shimmering long blond hair, the smooth olive complexion and the piercing slate blue eyes.

Atalan gave the faintest of nods while giving nothing else away. Nic, doing his best to keep the puzzlement off his face, silently wondered why on Earth two other-worldly beings would want or need his counsel.

'So, how can I assist you?'

'Rae has contracted a condition that is normally unique to humans, something I believe you refer to as cellulitis. It is causing great pain, and I fear it is spreading to an area of his body you know as the lymph system.' Atalan proceeded to give his friend a wordless instruction by which he at last removed his hood and cloak and began to undress. Although Rae's features were as striking, his complexion was pale, and his eyes dulled. Across the chest area of his long slender torso an angry looking red welt dominated.

'May I?' Nic ventured close and felt the heat from the infection. 'Your diagnosis is correct, but surely you have the knowledge to treat this condition?'

'We do, but we are neither in the right time or place to call for assistance. I am not a physician, and I do believe time is of the essence.'

Nic looked from Atalan to the hapless Pleiadian. Through his pained blue eyes came hope, trust, gratitude, love, and a host of other emotions that Nic felt flood over him. 'You fear sepsis?'

The taller one nodded. 'Can you help?'

Biological infections such as cellulitis were rare in humans now, and his training in such diseases was scant, but curious to get an insight as to Rae's physiology, Nicobar checked temperature and heart rate, identified the bacterium from a blood sample, then without haste got to work with mortar, pestle and crucible, and in due course a sulphurous odour began to permeate the tent. They sat patiently, scrutinising Nic's every move, unnerving him a little. Along with the ingredients and formula required for the remedy buzzing around his head were a multitude of questions he wanted to fire at his higher dimensional visitors . . .

'How did you know where to find me?' . . . was all that came out.

The two guests looked at each other and smiled. 'We are not familiar with this locale,' said Atalan. 'Like you, we are just travellers with an assignment passing through. We heard of a healer offering his services – we are happy and grateful to have found you.' He shrugged his sculptured shoulders and went back to silently observing. From the stilted exchange Nic thought better to probe any further and got back to the task in hand.

'These need to be changed rotely,' said Nic, carefully applying one of many prepared poultices. I have also made some caps that he will need to take regularly. I take it you are familiar with sound harmonics?'

'Of course.'

'This is the frequency it needs to be at during sleep,' said Nic handing over a small device.

Atalan took it in his long, slender hand and nodded. 'The poison?'

'Aside from the infection the blood appears free from sepsis. For a human, the heart rate is high, but I have no benchmark for. . .'

CAPRICORN

'I understand,' said Atalan, cutting him short. If he somehow knew Nic was merely a medical student, he wasn't letting on. The Pleiadian rose to his majestic height and from behind his cloak magically produced an enormous salmon which he placed on Nic's fold up table amongst his apothecary apparatus with a flourish. 'I hope this will be sufficient to settle the debt.' He spoke it as if there would be no question, and there wasn't as Nic merely stood there open mouthed.

'I, er – really, there is no need – I, er – I was happy to. . .'

Atalan placed his giant hand, which now smelled of fish, onto Nic's shoulder. 'I know you have many questions,' he said in his deep yet tender tone. 'These and many more shall be answered when the sun is at its highest point in the sky. Then, all will be revealed, and you shall become aware that you knew the answers all along. Sometimes we need to forget in order to remember why we make these journeys. Mercifully, your journey this time around will be short. Thank you for all you have done here this day; there are no words in your language we can use to express our gratitude.'

With that, Rae, now fully re-robed came and placed a hand on Nic's other shoulder, his piercing blue eyes already beginning to regain their lustre. Without another word they hooded their heads and silently departed, leaving the young physician stunned and speechless.

With the Pleiadian's cryptic words swimming around his head, Nic composed himself and followed them outside where he bumped into Ullyman returning from a day of labour exchange clutching loaves of bread.

'Who on Earth are they?' he asked watching the mysterious pair on their way.

'You wouldn't believe me if I told you,' said Nic, still bemused.

Just then, Rae half turned, smiled and gave a gentle wave.

'Hang on,' said Ully in a moment of realisation. 'I've seen those two before.'

'What, where?'

'Back in Ilkley.'

'You sure?'

'Yeah – remember that time I'd been to see Edith, and I'd been on the shrooms?'

'Er, yeah.'

'Well, when I got back I saw the old man talking to two hoodie dudes just like them, then when they left, the slightly smaller one, turns, smiles and waves just like that. But you know what was even weirder? - before they left, the taller dude reaches into his cloak and hands over this fucking giant of a fish, and then, even stranger, I glanced up again and they had disappeared into thin air, just like – oh, shit!'

Nic followed Ully's gaze, and the figures had simply vanished without trace.

'Just like that . . .' Ullyman breathed, not daring to believe his eyes for a second time.

Nic sighed, also not wanting to accept what he'd just witnessed and heard. 'You'd better come inside; I've got something to show you.'

Ullyman stood staring at the dead salmon, both he and fish open mouthed. 'And to think that all this time I put it down to the shrooms,' he said shaking his head with incredulity. 'What the hell are we going to do with it?'

'Eat it?'

'We're not pescatarians.'

They both stood there uncertain, while the fish, which was starting to stink the place out, looked up at them with a glassy eye as if urging them to come to a decision.

'Well, we've got the loaves,' said Nic, grinning at his own feeble attempt to be funny.

His mate looked at him blankly – he didn't get it.

In the Black Country Ullyman saw his first squadron of Flyers heading south to Glaston. While he looked up in silent awe and longing Nic shook his head at his mate's obsessive yearning and dogged refusal to accept that his dream could never be physically realised.

Along The Avon they worked the fields, farms and orchards. Nic performed spinal adjustment to a farmer's wife who was suffering from debilitating headaches, and they were granted use of one of the many curious looking summer houses that were utilised by farm workers as refuges from the heat. They were in fact giant hollowed out pumpkins, coated inside and out with a hemp based bast that prevented rot and decay. Even more curious was the sight one evening of Ully returning from the fields covered from head to toe in

CAPRICORN

a cloak of vivid red, black-spotted coccines. There had been an aphid infestation up in one of the orchards, and they had introduced the ladybirds to get rid. Consuming more than fifty times their own body weight, many of the now not-so-tiny beetles had decided to siesta from the banquet on their unsuspecting maître d.

'The little fuckers won't leave me alone,' Ully lamented.

Like an overbearing mother, Nic stood at the threshold of their cool abode refusing him entry until he'd stripped and took a dip in the nearby lake.

'How come it's always me that ends up with the shittiest jobs?' he moaned while removing his garments.

Ullyman emerged from the cool water wet and naked but mercifully free from the gorged insects. Sympathetic to his plight, Nic had to assure him they would be moving on at sunrise.

To keep his mate onside, they travelled further south without detour or distraction, arriving at the ancient spa town of Bath where tribes from all over the archipelago had begun to gather. Here, the elevation of frequency was already tangible as excited groups from all walks mixed, socialised, traded and began to celebrate on the energy that was being generated in anticipation of the ever-nearing solstice. Free now from the burdens of working his passage and seemingly pointless deviations, Ullyman's demeanour began to alter as he revelled in the noise and hubbub of his surroundings, visiting as many watering holes as he could, losing himself in the music of travelling troubadours, gazing in awe and wonder at the skills of illusionists, and tasting the wares of culinary artisans.

Tucked away in a corner of one hostelry minding their own were a couple of characters that immediately caught Ully's attention. It was obvious to him, they were flyers, and with Nic's words of caution falling on his deaf ears, he made a beeline to make their acquaintance.

'Well met, fellas,' he boomed, beaming from ear to ear. 'My name's Ullyman Spence,' he said offering his hand. 'I was wondering . . .'

'No!' said the one with his back to him.

'Fuck off!' said the one facing him.

Undeterred, and totally ignoring their request, he withdrew his proffered hand, pulled up a stool and plonked himself down. 'Aww, c'mon fellas, don't be like that, I was only going to ask for . . .'

'We know what you're going to ask,' said the first guy, turning to face him. 'And the answer is no.'

Ully carefully studied the faces, slightly bemused by the hostility. Flyers tended to all look the same: sharp angular features with a pinched, pointy nose, small mouth, no lips, face and body coated with a fine aerodynamically designed peach fuzz which tended to add to the overall hostile reaction. He wondered if they were all as miserably unfriendly as these two.

'Headed down to Glaston, are we fellas?' Ully persisted

'Is it that obvious?'

'What say we meet up, I show you my wingsuit and you show me any improvement I can make in its design and efficiency, nothing more – I have gold credits?'

'What part of "no" and "fuck off" don't you understand?'

'We've heard it all before from you earthers,' piped up his mate. 'Hints and tips turn into guided flights and lessons, we point out your limitations which you promptly ignore, making manoeuvrers beyond your capabilities, you end up dying and we cop for the fallout and resulting bad karma – no thanks.'

'But I'm a good learner, I would follow your instructions down to the letter.'

'Heard that one too – the answer's still no.'

Pondering his next move, Ully fixed his gaze on the curious webbing between the fingers, while the pair of flyers glowered at him, the short smooth hair on their heads seeming to bristle.

'I hear that your women lay eggs in order to birth their young – is that true?'

With that, the two of them drained their cups, got up and left without a word except for a strange, indignant cawing like sound one of them made from the back of his throat.

'Well?' said Nic approaching the table with a couple of drinks.

Ully blew air from his cheeks. 'Can't fathom why, but I think I upset them.'

Getting ever near to their destination, the routes, highways and skies were packed with humanity on a singular mission. The colour and pageantry on display was something that took Ullyman back to his childhood, where the innocent joy of discovery used to make his heart soar, where he and animals and all things Nature seemed to come together in a mutual understanding, where he and his mate had grown up in an ornithological paradise and their passion for all things feathered seemed the most natural thing in the world, something that went way beyond fortuity, something that felt timeless and without end; at least that's how Ullyman Spence felt, the puerile demeanour now writ large across his face filled with an untainted kind of innocence, maybe tinged with naïvety. Nic observed his friend with a smile, thinking back to when he had helped guide and inform that naïve innocence during their formative years, while deep down acknowledging maybe perhaps there had been a role reversal at some point. It was a feeling that fed into the déjà vu vibe he had been experiencing lately. It still remained with him, bubbling under in the caves of his psyche. But right now he was happy to see his mate, who was fast turning into a man, revel in his infantile state.

At Shepton Mallet they picked up a Mary line that took them all the way into Glaston. There were no official gates or entrances, just a sense they were entering a realm of unbridled euphoria fuelled with ceremony and revelry. Close to three million souls were expected to gather for the solstice, a number not seen in one place since the days when cities were common throughout the land.

Music, that timeless, universal language filled the air, automatically tuning itself to the individual, making it a unique experience to each and every one. The range of beats, rhythm, harmonics and melodies now reaching Ully's ears and bathing his sensibilities with incredible sound were like nothing he'd ever experienced, even his psilocybin adventures couldn't compare. If ever he felt he could fly it was now, and as the notion came into being it immediately manifested and along with dozens of others on his frequency his feet actually left the ground and he began to levitate, not as high as some, but at least a few inches off the ground where a walking motion still moved him along with the ecstatic throng. Nic, still grounded, took it all in with his usual pragmatic smile.

'C'mon, man,' Ully shouted down to his mate with boyish exuberance. 'You of all people can do this.'

He was right, it was time he let go of that strange sense of impendency that had been following him around lately. Although he would never reach the heights of his mate's raptness, the surrounding vibe was intoxicatingly infectious, and he had to be ready to lose any

PRECESSION

remaining inhibitions.

Once Nic had surrendered to the sounds he immediately felt his chakras open like flowers. As if being released from asphyxiation he breathed in his share of accumulated potential. It hit him like a reward long overdue, and in short order had joined his companion tripping the light fantastic, way beyond anything Milton might have had in mind for his *Happy Man*.

A nation without boundaries, the site extended for as far as the eye could see in a kaleidoscope of form and colour, where a section of mankind would come together for a few of the longest rotes in the calendar in the northern hemisphere, where there would be birth alongside death and all things in between in a celebration of the natural order of things.

Way, way in the distance, beyond the sea of heads and flags, the Tor could be seen shimmering through the heat haze. Above it flew wingers in seemingly haphazard patterns, while higher still, keeping well out of the way, flyers soared majestically on the thermals. They were two rotes away from solstice and there'd been rumours that there had been activity on the solar surface and a CME was on its way. Depending on the plasma that hit the atmosphere some geomags lasted longer than others and Ully didn't want to be grounded before he had chance to take to the skies. There was so much to do, so much to see. Despite the euphoria and the magical atmosphere, there was a yearning for that adrenalin rush that came with risk and uncertainty. Impatience was kicking in. He couldn't wait to unpack his wingsuit and fly with the birds.

They set up camp amongst an ocean of tents, marquees and all manner of temporary living accommodation. Nic watched Ully disappear into the multitude, thousands of happy smiling faces, all doing their thing, sharing the love and the joy. It was a good time to be alive, and Nicobar took time to take it all in, absorbing the energy and dynamic that seemed to rise up from the people and flow in waves above their heads. Like auras that weren't always visible to the naked eye, Nic was grateful he'd been blessed with the ability to observe such phenomena, and that he was able to be present and marvel at all the subtle hues that were coming together from the individual to inform and enhance the collective experience.

Outside the inflatent he happily planted a pole atop of which flew an insignia of the staff of Aesculapius to advertise his station, quietly hoping there wouldn't be many needing to seek out his services on

CAPRICORN

this occasion.

PRECESSION

Expecting to Fly

'**H**i . . . '

Bloody hell, that was quick, Nic thought to himself, turning around to be met with a very healthy-looking young woman.

'I er, I'm looking for Ullyman?' she spoke with a rising inflection. 'His tracker said I'd find him here; I'm Edith.'

'Edith? Oh – Edith from. . .' Nic pointed vaguely north.

'From Ilkley, Brigantia, yes,' she said slightly nervously.

The hemp farmer's daughter was a big robust looking girl who seemed to be carrying the weighty looking rucksack on her back with ease. Her shiny dark hair was scraped back tight and tied up in a bun at the top of her head. A fine sheen of sweat stood out on her otherwise bright features as Nic observed in that brief moment of awkward silence.

'Oh – well, you've only just missed him, he's headed off to the Tor to book a skypod.'

'A skypod?'

'Yeah – he needs a drop from altitude in order to stay in the air longer.' Edith looked at him blankly. 'Erm, the Tor's not high enough – You know he's a winger, right?'

She continued to look baffled. 'No.'

'Ah – ok,' said Nic as the awkwardness grew. 'Look, why don't you come inside and take the weight off; that thing looks heavy – So, how was your journey down, did you take the Hyperlink?'

Nic eased the clumsy introduction with small-talk over a cup of aloejuice, all the while trying to detect if there was any resentment in his refusal to allow her to join them on walkabout, luckily there wasn't, and looking at her now as she confidently and casually stroked the back hairs of the wulf who had planted itself down beside her, he quietly conceded that it would have been a mission she would have taken in her stride.

His highly tuned sensibilities were at play again. The girl was glowing, healthy, something you would expect from an outdoor person, she worked on her father's farm after all, but despite the salubrious show Nic detected a nervousness, and it was nothing to do with being bashful at their first meet, she was anything but that. He sensed there was a connection between her blooming presentation and the underlying solicitude. Hormones were thick in the air; he had the uncanny ability to detect estrogen and progesterone, and without venturing too close, the presence of HCG, FSH and prolactin. His innate diagnostic tendencies were kicking in and he decided to follow a line of questioning just to satisfy his hunch.

'So, would you say you guys are kind of serious about each other?'

'I don't know; I'd like to think we are.' She paused reflectively while tracing patterns in the wulf's fur. 'I know we've only been seeing each other for a short while, but . . . '

'He seems smitten from what he's spoken of you.'

'Oh . . .' She coloured up slightly, but the rest of her features seemed pleased to hear that.

Nic paused, weighing up his next line, hoping it wouldn't offend.

'You know I'm a physician, right?'

She seemed visibly taken aback by such a statement from someone so young. 'Oh – no, I didn't, I – Ully never said . . .'

He hasn't told you much, has he? he thought to himself before pressing on. 'Do you mind if I ask a personal question? – from a professional angle, of course.'

Despite her demeanour saying otherwise, she meekly shook her head. 'No.'

'When was the last time you bled?'

Edith bowed her head and gently began to weep, her ample shoulders shuddering with her sobs. Confirmation. Nic guessed she was in the middle or nearing the end of her first trimester. Either the rutin and wild carrot hadn't worked, or they had been careless with their protection. He placed a consoling hand over hers while trying to think of ways he could put a positive slant on the situation.

'Have you seen anyone?'

'No,' she said, wiping away tears and cleaning her nose. 'I haven't told anybody.'

'Have you had any sickness on waking.?'

'Yes, but not so recently.'

'Would you provide a sample and allow me to examine you, just so I can confirm?'

She nodded her head pitifully and started to weep again, in part because any confirmation would realise her fears, but to unburden at last to someone with a sympathetic and professional manner was a relief.

Nic was no paediatrician, but he knew the basics, and Edith began to feel calm and trusting as he listened in at her tummy with his steth. He was thorough, he checked and double checked and then checked some more before lifting away with a heavy sigh. Edith looked at him, dubiety writ large across her face.

'What? - Is there anything wrong?'

'No, nothing wrong; there are two healthy heartbeats in there,' he said while packing away his equipment.

'Y – you mean twins?'

'It very much sounds like it,' he said with a forced smile.

The young girl went through a whole gamut of emotions as she tried to take in the information. Finally, she let her shaking head fall into her hands as the waterworks started up again. 'Oh, shit – what am I gonna do?'

Nic placed a hand on her heaving shoulders. 'You know you have to tell him.'

'I don't want to ruin his life,' she continued to shake her head in her hands. 'This wasn't meant to happen.'

'Maybe it was, you know,' Nic spoke softly. 'Maybe it was.'

The falcon heralded their return, perching itself atop the Aesculapius with its familiar raucous call. 'I think he's back – here, dry your eyes,' said Nic, handing over a wipe. 'It'll be fine.' He went outside to prepare his mate for the surprise.

'Three fucking silver credits for a skypod – I ask you . . .'

'There's someone here to see you,' said Nic, cutting short the gripe.

'Edith?' he quizzed after a short pause. 'Edith!' he exclaimed, his eyes lighting up excitedly. Nic nodded with an unsure smile as Ully darted inside the tent, hoping that the would-be dad's excitement wouldn't be short lived.

They embraced, they hugged, they groped, they kissed in the most unashamed tactile show of love and affection. Even the wulf raised a lazy eyebrow. With her chin clamped over his shoulder, Edith closed her eyes happy at their reunion before opening them to stare over at the man who had sussed her plight. In those eyes he

CAPRICORN

could sense that she wasn't ready to tell him yet – not yet.

The two lovebirds set up nest close by with Nic's blessing, the damage already done after all, and besides it would allow him the space to treat any patients without fear of interruption. Despite his intuitive senses, Nic couldn't or wouldn't second guess what his good friend's potential reaction would be when the news was finally delivered to him. Ullyman was a genuine free spirit but observing him with his rustic girl he could see a melding of two souls taking place, being aided and abetted by the collective energy of their present surroundings. In the moment he was content to be happy for them.

'Good to go, my friend,' said Nic, tapping his mate on the shoulder. He'd given the wingsuit a thorough inspection, checked the 'chute, tested the procam and primed the ankle flare. With a big grin on his face, Ullyman enveloped Edith in his winged arms and they shared an intimate moment. A few feet away the pod pilot and another winger looked on impatiently.

'Be careful up there,' said Edith, doing her best not to sound overly nervous.

'Don't worry, I've done this before.' Ully secured his helmet, the grin never once leaving his face, his overconfidence seemingly outshining any disquiet he might have had.

They watched the pod take to the air, getting ever smaller as it followed its predecessors through the busy colourful sky high up to the drop zone miles away.

'Hungry?' asked Nic by way of distraction. Edith nodded in the affirmative.

'So am I; let's get some food and go watch a band.' With the wulf at their side he led them into the heaving throng of happy, smiling faces, while from high above, Ully watched them absorb into the crowd, like tiny droplets of water being reclaimed by the ocean. The higher he rose over the rich and colourful tapestry of humanity that stretched as far as the eye could see, the more the euphoria rose in his chest. Sat opposite, his companion winger was sharing the euphoria as evident by the big beaming grin on his face that mirrored his own.

'Ullyman Spence – well met brother.' Ully raised his hand, and they slapped palms.

'Pascal – Pascal Beaurie.'

'French?'

'Swiss-French.'

'You sound like a vet.'

Pascal shrugged. 'Close to nine hundred drops. How about you?'

'Not sure; never counted.' Even if he had they would only count in tens, not hundreds. He was impressed.

'You mean you never log your flights?'

Ully shook his head. 'You think I should?'

'Depends on how serious you are. You won't be allowed anywhere near some of the more advanced bases unless you've got a number of registered flights under your belt. There have been too many accidents. Too many have died.'

'Surely the risks are ours to take.'

'That is the rationale most of us would use. The governance came about through the influence of the flyers. Apparently, we're giving them a bad name. I'm surprised the Bare Backers have been granted licence here.'

'Bare Backers – you mean chute-less wingers?'

'Yes – you see those three in formation trailing red smoke at two out the window?' Pascal traced his finger across the glass as they hurtled past. 'They're flying bare back. The drop zone is a net or an inflatable.'

Ully watched them flash by open mouthed. 'You ever done it?'

Pascal gravely shook his head. 'It's how I lost my elder brother. He was more experienced than I, had more flights under his belt, but it was only his third bare back drop. I followed him and two others down from base high up in the Alps. After I deployed, I watched them perform a sequence of flares designed to reduce their velocity before slamming into the net, but Maurice overshot the zone and hit the deck hard. He died instantly.'

'I'm so sorry to hear that, brother – it looks like the experience hasn't put you off.'

'As you say, the risks are ours to take. It took me a while before I strapped on a wingsuit again, but I make sure I pick my drops carefully, and no, after witnessing what I did I wouldn't be brave or stupid enough to fly bare back.'

Ully watched as the trailing red smoke dissipated, and the formation wingers were no more than mere dots in the sky. Despite first hand tales of tragedy, his rash curiosity had already started to get the better of him. The closer he could get to performing like a flyer the happier he would be, age, wisdom and experience were not factors he would apply.

High above The Mendips the pod hovered while the two wingers made their final checks. Agreeing to make the drop together, they tuned their aircoms to the same channel. Visors down, they slapped a high-five, belying the adrenalin-soaked nerves that were coursing through their bodies, Pascal counted them out. 'Three, two, one – let's go...!'

The initial gut-wrenching gravitational lurch was quickly arrested by the wingsuits as they spread their limbs and microcells filled with air. Ully let out a relieved whoop! and remembered to breathe, adjusting his angle of flight so to gain velocity and follow Pascal's line as he watched him shooting off ahead.

The read out on Ully's visor clicked past one hundred and sixty mph, the sounds inside his helmet becoming white noise as he cut through the air. Ignoring the soaring heart rate and all the other stats flashing before his eyes, he took control of the cortisol and serotonin rushes and channelled them into an intense concentration without ever losing the euphoria. He was in his element now, his only regret that his life-long buddy didn't quite share the passion. Nic had flown wingsuit before, but only on a few occasions, and although he'd admitted to enjoying the experience, it hadn't bitten him and become an obsession like it had for himself.

For now, he had a new mate to share the joy with. Below him, Pascal had flipped onto his back, grinning inanely back up at him and he didn't hesitate to follow suit, mirroring his every move. Then, with unbelievable dexterity, the Frenchman performed a three-sixty-barrel roll, circling above and below him. The guy's mastery of his descent was super impressive and Ully was in ecstatic awe. Pascal had served his apprenticeship base jumping in the Alps, he was used to terrain flying close to sheer mountain sides, screes, valleys and gulleys, and so open terrain wingsuiting like this was child's play. Even the Mendips, falling away below them were mere mole hills to him.

In the distance Glaston came into view once again, all too quickly highlighting the limitations of wingsuiting. They had been in the air for no more than twenty par-clicks, and the altimeter was already counting down to chute deployment. For Ullyman the euphoria was too short lived and compounded his frustration at not having the gliding capacity of flyers, while also piquing his curiosity ever more into the bare-back phenomenon.

They deployed their flares, one blue, one yellow, into the wake of the many dissipated trails that had gone before them. Finally, and disappointingly, he watched Pascal's bright yellow canopy unfurl, arresting his fall. Not wanting the buzz to end, he flew past him, ignoring the red visual alarm now flashing on his visor.

'Deploy now you fucking idiot!' yelled the Frenchman over the aircom.

Hypnotised by the patchwork of coloured land flashing by below, he wondered how close he could get to the circling flyers ahead of him as the Tor came into view. High above, Pascal continued to scream into his helmet, finally snapping him out of his daze. At last, he flared and pulled the cord, looking on with envy over to his right as flyers soared with ease on the thermals, while to his left, a pair of bare-backers shot past executing a series of flares that slowed their velocity en route to the landing net. Although their touchdown wasn't as dignified as his, theirs was at least one less cumbersome aid towards his dream.

He gathered in his canopy wondering how he could bypass the regulators so that he could jump chute-less, then readied himself for the rollocking the fast-approaching Frenchman was about to unleash on the crazy Englishman for pulling such a deathly stunt.

'You have succumbed to The Influence of the Stars, otherwise known as influenza,' said Nic preparing a draft. 'You're the third Ptero I've seen with it so far since we arrived.' The hapless flyer sat looking sorry for himself, with sore looking red-rimmed eyes and nose standing out from a general grey looking demeanour.

'Is it contagious?' asked his slightly healthier looking companion.

'No, it's not something that's transmissible.'

'Then why are you seeing so many cases?'

'It's due to something called the parasympathetic response that is triggered by the autonomic nervous system when a disease or pathogen is present; it gives warning that the body needs to detox. Our bodies communicate with each other, so if a detox is due, the same symptoms will be seen in others.'

'So, will it affect me?'

CAPRICORN

'Only if your body decides it needs to detox. If you're one hundred percent healthy, then no, you should stay that way.'

'And this is all due to the sun?'

'Yes, the amount of plasma and electromagnetism hitting the Earth at this time affects all of us, more so the birds and Pteros like yourself. Your physiology makes you more susceptible I'm afraid. So, I would advise taking it easy for a while, give the flying a rest.' said Nic turning back to his miserable patient.

'I don't feel like walking, let alone flying,' he grumbled.

'It won't matter,' consoled his mate. 'there's a geomag on its way, so we shan't be taking any chances. I've already seen them doling out Faraday suits for those that need. We've heard rumour all flights are to be grounded anyway.'

'That's going to upset a few people, no doubt,' said Nic with Ully in mind. 'Especially as it's solstice . . .'

'Hey, can you check the wulf out?' said the man in question, entering the tent with his usual bluster. 'She been sick a couple of times, I – oh, sorry, didn't know you had someone in . . .'

'Oh, fuck, not you again.' The healthy flyer spoke on recognition.

The guy with the flu looked up in dismay. 'Agh, now I do feel like shit.'

'Well, well, now look who it is,' said Ullyman with a smile. 'Good to see you again, boys,' he grinned, happy to have captured them on his own turf so to speak.

'Oh, so you three have met?' Nic looked to each expecting an introduction.

'Yeah – unfortunately.'

'Right,' said Nic in a moment of realisation. 'These are the guys you were pestering back in Bath.'

'Just seeking a piece of friendly advice is all,' said Ully.

The two flyers looked at each other, awkward in the moment. Nic looked on expectantly.

'I'm Dido,' said the healthy one resignedly reluctant. 'This here's Icky,' he nodded over to his ailing friend.

'Well, no doubt Nic's introduced himself, and you already know who I am,' said Ully mischievously.

'Yeah, well we conveniently forgot,' muttered Dido.

'Ully, Ullyman Spence,' he announced cheerily, offering his hand. 'Well met, once again, lads.'

Dido observed the skeevy look in Ullyman's eye and knew what was coming. 'Look, we're here and willing to disburse for a service your friend is offering. We offer no such service, and no amount of remuneration you wave in front of us will change that.'

Ully held up his hand defensively. 'Hey, of course, I understand, but remember, barter is our currency, and I'm sure Nicobar here is willing to forgo any professional fee in exchange for a few pointers.' He looked over at him and flashed a wink.

Nic raised his eyes to the heavens. 'The ball is in your court, gentlemen,' he said, throwing open his arms in a reluctant acceptance of Ully's cheeky presumptions.

Dido let out a big sigh. 'Just what is it you want from us?'

'I want to be able to land without a chute.'

'You can, your colleagues are doing it all the time.'

Ully vigorously shook his head. 'Nah, not into a net, it's too undignified. I want to fall and land with style, in full control like I do with a chute – but without the chute.'

Icky let out a raspy laugh. 'Don't be absurd.'

'Your body is too dense,' said Dido. 'The only reason you stay in the air as long as you do is because of the velocity you create. The chute-less wingers slow their velocity by executing a series of flares, but as soon as you lose that airspeed you will automatically drop out of the sky – hence the net, and most of you haven't even mastered that technique yet. There have already been two fatalities during these festivities.'

Ully was undeterred. 'There has to be an adaption I can make to the wingsuit that will allow me to flare to a controlled landing like you guys.'

'Use a maglev unit like the hoverboarders do,' suggested Icky.

Ully shook his head and pulled a face again. 'It's just another prop, like a chute – I want to be more like you, the less aids, the better.'

Dido looked across at Nic with a face that said – please talk some sense into this guy – Exasperated, he sat on a stool and spread his expansive limbs, the claw-like toes of his large, webbed feet spread wide. Between his legs and from ankle to wrist he unfurled his otherwise unnoticeable patagia. He demonstrated the versatility of his detachable wrists, the extra finger and cartilage spurs that helped maximise the efficiency of the patagia and manage direction in flight. Ully had never seen a flyer fully deployed like this so close up. He stared voyeur-like, fascinated, while the fine downy hair that covered most of Dido's body opened and closed like the ailerons on an aircraft that helped to control flight dynamics.

'Unless you can find someone who can replicate what you see here onto a wingsuit, and compensate for body and bone density, you will never achieve what I suggest is an impossible dream. You people call us flyers; we are nothing of the sort. We are Pteros, no more than flying squirrels in semi-human form. We do not fly like the birds; we glide at the behest and whim of the thermals other than that which our evolution has allowed us to master. I suggest you thank the stars for your own enhanced disease-resistant physiology and your longevity, things we Pteros do not possess, and stop trying to become something you were never meant to be – you'll live longer that way.' He retracted his appendages and got to his feet. 'What is the debt?' he asked turning to Nic who held up his hands and shook his head. 'C'mon, let's out of here.'

Icky got to his feet and followed his mate, emitting a battery of high-pitched raw sounding coughs. 'The guy's tilting at windmills,' he spluttered as they left the tent.

'He'll kill himself for sure,' was Dido's parting refrain.

'That went well.'

Ullyman sucked at his teeth in answer to Nico's obvious sarcasm.

Nic shrugged his shoulders. 'You asked for counsel and they gave it; I'd heed their advice if I were you.' He saw the far off look in Ully's eyes, the schematics were already at work inside his head; once he'd set his stall out, it would be like trying to shift a barnacle off the bottom of a boat. He began to worry for both him, Edith and the rest. 'Please don't be getting any crazy ideas.'

'I'm still a bare-back virgin,' lamented Ully. 'There're guys making drops all day long out there, and apparently I can't join them 'cos I don't have the creds.'

'Those guys are at the top of their game, they've made hundreds of drops, and as Dido said, even the elite are coming unstuck – anyway, he says all flights are to be grounded for the solstice.'

'They can't do that,' said Ully indignantly.

'Maybe not for the flyers, but even they wouldn't be so stupid to take to the skies with a geomag on its way.'

Ully wasn't listening. 'First they say I can't fly bare-back, then they say I can't fly at all – whatever happened to liberty?'

'Look at the size of this place,' Nic reasoned. 'Liberty has to accommodate responsibility where lives are at stake.'

PRECESSION

'Meh – don't forget to take a look at the wulf; I'll see you later.'

Nico hated it when his mate was this way out. Despite mentoring him for most of his life, when the ego took hold and the three poisons – desire, anger and ignorance came to the surface it was nearly always impossible to get him to show reason. Maybe once he knew he was about to be the father of twins he might start to show some humility and a touch of personal responsibility. Nic hoped it wouldn't be too long before Edith found the courage to break the news. He went outside and called the wulf.

Ullyman Spence wasn't entirely oblivious to his own obduracy; borne out of frustration and a genuine desire to achieve, he longed to have at least a fraction of the cogitative intellection that seemed to come to Nic so readily. He thought back to the euphoric curtain raiser that heralded their arrival, that other worldly collective energy that allowed him to leave the ground for those few short ecstatic moments. Why couldn't he harness that power and multiply it a thousand-fold? *No worries,* spoke his ego, *we have a plan, let's put it into action.*

'There you are,' said Edith. 'Where have you been? I thought we were going out; I was beginning to get worried.'

'Sorry,' said Ullyman, giving her an apologetic hug. 'Just had to make some arrangements.'

'Arrangements for what?'

'Oh, I'll tell you later,' he deferred. 'You look amazing; shall we go have some fun?'

'Is Nic coming?'

'Nah. He's sitting the wulf; she's a bit off colour.'

'Nothing serious, I hope.'

Ully shrugged. 'Probably just the environment; she's not used to such big crowds. Don't worry, he'll make sure she's fine.'

The wulf looked up at Nicobar with doleful eyes as he palpated her. 'Oh, bugger; what have you gone and done you sneaky girl?' Providence strikes again – he thought to himself at the prospect of having two litters on the way at the same time.

CAPRICORN

They laughed and danced and dallied with holograms, partying long into the evening as the collective vibes built and fell into a unified entrainment of hypnotic rhythms, her energy and stamina outmatching that of the legion of contemporaries that revelled alongside her, while she caught the infectious, unbridled joy of her partner who seemingly no longer had a care in the world now that his machinations had been put in place. She had made up her mind; tonight would be the time to tell him. If his professed love for her was genuine, then everything would work out fine. She leaned in close, their lips met and in his strong arms he whirled her around in wave after wave of dizzying abandon, totally unaware of her condition.

Away from the sights and sounds she persuaded him to take a long walk. They strolled hand in hand to the perimeter of the site until they were well clear of people and distractions. They found a secluded soft spot by the banks of a small lake and made love. - And then she told him . . .

'Twins,' he breathed finally, after spending an age trying to unwrap what he'd just been told. 'How? - I mean, I . . .'

'I shan't hold you to a tithe, I promise,' blurted Edith, still unsure if Ully's reactions were good or bad.

He lay on the bank gazing up at the sparkling display on show in the heavens. 'Twins.' He mouthed the word again, still not quite believing, while another part of him was haphazardly weighing up the implications. He looked at her in the dim light. 'Are you happy?'

'I – I think I am - I am if you are,' she answered unsure. 'Are you?'

He thought about it ever so briefly, then the reality hit him. 'I'm going to be a dad – I'm going to be a bloody dad! I'll show you happy; come here . . .' He pulled her back on top and they rejoiced the news like they did best, Edith's passion matching his own now that any doubts had been lifted.

'We have to get back, tell Nic,' said Ully, spent but excited.

'He already knows.'

'What - he knew before me?' He looked indignant.

'What can I say? - He knew, somehow, he just knew.'

'Of course he did – he's Nic.'

'Look at that.' Edith pointed toward the citadel encampment as they strolled back arm in arm. The sea of tents was covered in an iridescent wavy blue light, that made the whole site look even more like a moving ocean. 'What is it?'

'I think it's some sort of Faraday shield; looks like they're laying down protection.'

'From the geomag?'

'Yeah – look, if you watch you can see the white light from the stages and the beams coming off the lasers, bouncing back off the sky, they're building a solar dome as well by the look of it.'

'They must be expecting a big hit.'

'Ah, it's all overkill if you ask me. They're just being cautious. There's a good chance it won't even touch us; might have passed us by already,' he silently hoped. 'Geomags are so unpredictable.'

It was late - or early depending on which way you saw it - when they got back. Already small pockets of folk were heading out to The Stones regaled in their Faraday suits in anticipation of sunrise a few clicks from now. A geomag forecast at solstice was a rare event, and no one knew what kind of a light show from space to expect. The intrigue was palpable.

Edith crashed as soon as she hit the sack. Ully spooned her until he heard the steady rhythm of her slumbered breathing before laying on his back to contemplate the events unfolded and those about to happen. He wouldn't sleep.

Shadow and silhouette flitted randomly around the tent and the wulf gave notice of warning with a low, menacing growl. In his bed-bag Nic groaned and tossed himself comfortable as he slept. The shadow loomed large, and the wulf went into full blown guard status. Nic shot bolt upright and two lights flashed on simultaneously.

'Edith!' he exclaimed in shock. 'What the hell – are you alright?'

'I'm sorry, I didn't mean to shit you up like that, I . . .'

'What is it – what's wrong?'

'It's – it's Ully,' she stuttered. 'He's gone.'

'What do you mean? - Gone where?'

'I don't know,' she spoke in a whiney voice. 'He's just gone, and I think he's taken his wingsuit and helmet with him.'

'Why would he do that?' Nic thought out loud. 'He knows there's to be no flying today.'

'I told him about us last night,' she said, circling a hand over her tummy. 'He seemed so happy – said he was going to celebrate in style; I didn't know what he meant. Oh, Nic, I'm ever so worried.'

CAPRICORN

'Go grab your Faraday suit, I'll be out straight away.'

It wasn't quite yet dawn, but already the shimmering green and mauve undulations of the aurora could be seen to the north, a sure sign there was some electromagnetic disturbance on its way. They hurried towards The Tor encountering ever larger crowds of folk passing them in the opposite direction on their way to witness sunrise. Due to the shielding in place everything and everyone had taken on a shimmery blue cast that seemed to ripple gently over every contour it met, the multitude of bobbing heads equating to a choppy sea. Inside his own head Nic was trying to work out likely scenarios, and knowing what he thought Ullyman might be up to had gotten him as worried as Edith, but he tried not to show it.

Not too far away, two tall, hooded figures passed by like two pieces of floating flotsam and jetsam, causing Nic to do a hasty double-take. As if in a recurring dream, the smaller of the figures turned and revealed his face with Nic expecting a knowing smile as he was sure had been scripted. This time the young Pleiadian simply stared unmoving until the relentless wave upon wave of revellers obscured them from sight and they became one with the crowd again. Nic hastily composed himself and dismissed the uncanny reoccurrence as a coincidence.

They hurried past row upon grounded row of skypods, copterpacks, flyboards, jetpacks and all other manner of flight hire sitting forlornly in their compounds, while in the near distance, The Tor, unmolested for once, sat silent and eerie under its protective shroud and a skirt of low-lying mist. All the marquees and kiosks were closed, no sign of any activity, all stations empty and unmanned – all but one, that is. They made a beeline for the kiosk showing subdued lighting beyond its exterior and went inside.

The one guy present shut down the image he was looking at with a deft sweep of the hand. 'Sorry, my friend, we're closed,' he announced, quickly jumping to his feet.

'Where is he right now?' demanded Nic.

'Who?' asked the bloke nervously.

Nicobar didn't do angry, but a rush of emotion surged through his body. He moved menacingly towards the skypod vendor, who backed off defensively.

'Hey, he made me an offer I couldn't refuse,' he said holding up his hands. 'Who am I to sit and judge if the guy's got a death wish?'

Edith groaned audibly.

PRECESSION

'Call the pilot, get him back here,' demanded Nic.
'There's no pilot, I'm flying him remote.'
'Let me speak to him.'
'You can't, I've got him cloaked, no comms.'
'I get it; out of sight, out of sound, no comeback you defied the flight ban. Get him back down here now.'

The guy brought up his radar imaging. 'It's too late,' he stated, tracing a tiny blip with a finger. 'He's dropped.'
'Without a chute?'
'Yeah, he's on the bare-back route.'

Nic looked at all the wingsuits stood up in racks waiting to be hired. 'Get me up there,' he demanded.
'Without a chute?'
'No, with a chute, you divot.'
'Not sure about that.'
'How much did he pay you?'

The man looked on, unwilling to divulge, until Nic gave him another look with menaces. 'Fifteen gold credits,' he muttered.
'I'll give you twenty-five and a promise not to cite you – which I fucking ought to anyway,' he added for good measure.
'You're crazy,' he said while checking the straps on the canopy. What you going to do when you get up there?'
'I've not thought that part through yet,' he confided while out of earshot of his mate's fiancé. 'Just get me up there quick.'

Edith, by now totally panicked and bewildered, had a thousand questions, but time was of the essence. Delivered with all the confidence he could muster, Nic gave her a hug and told her not to worry.

He passed out and up beyond the protection of the dome, failing to appreciate the morphing of the south-easterly sky, the retreating fiery red-tailed blip of Marduk The Destroyer being swallowed by the dawning light of the longest day, and the shepherd's pie rippled puffs of cloud being constantly given a coloured makeover. Partly for Edith's sake, he had kept any nerves in check while on the ground, but now he was up there without a clear plan and a novice's experience of wingsuiting, he didn't mind admitting to himself that he was shitting it. It was hot in the pod, and he could feel the trickles of sweat running down the inside of his unfamiliar garb. What he couldn't feel or see as the Earth fell away beneath him was the ultraviolet and X-ray radiation as it shot through the ionosphere ionising billions of atoms and molecules to generate an immense electromagnetic field on the surface. Apart from the searing heat, winds and vortices created by the CME, a geomag was largely invisible, but from his experience he could sense that any oxygen was already being sucked out of the atmosphere at this altitude. Billions of unseen plasma particles were now shooting past as was evident by the sudden juddering halt of the skypod and the instant outage on the display in front of him.

'What the fuck just happened?' he screamed into his mic.

'I don't – ve – los – trols . . .' came the indecipherable static filled response from the ground.

'Can you hear me? - Can you hear me? Come in . . . '

'I can't – ou – yo – ing up . . .'

The pod began to slowly spin on its axis while emitting a low hum. The only thing keeping him in the air right now was the magnetron core that was still operational. He desperately punched buttons, but all circuits were dead. He was becoming acutely aware that he was now stuck in an aerial tomb with no means of escape, and as the inert sky vehicle lazily rotated, he saw the first deep crimson arc of the sun making a show above the horizon, come to gloat in all its deadly life-giving magnificence.

'Are you – ay – up there – an – y – hear me?'

'Yes – yes, I can hear you.' The connection was scratchy, but he was just about able to make sense. 'Can you hear me.?'

'Ye – but not good.'

'How do I get out of this thing?'

There's a manue – over – de in a panel – ve the do . . .'

Nic quickly located the manual override in a panel above the door and began to frantically wind a handle. The door started to open agonisingly slow. 'Do you still have visual on him?'

'Yes, he's fas – roaching, he'll be on you – nently.'

'Coordinates?'

'Sixty degrees nor-wes -.'

As the pod slowly rotated, so did Nic's compass and there was no way to know if it was being affected by the electromagnetism in the atmosphere. His timing would have to be both precise and lucky. With the door now open just enough for him to perform a drop, Nic donned his goggles and scanned the now turbulent sky each time it came around to the flight path. He tried to app his binos but they didn't work. Then he saw the dot in the sky hurtling towards him at an astonishing rate. By the time the pod had completed another three-sixty, the out of control tumbling body was upon him. It was now or never.

He exited the pod and spread his limbs. The wingsuit snapped itself into flight mode and he made a beeline for his target that had just hurtled past. The chemical rush that now coursed throughout Nic's body was present for multiple reasons. He was already entering an altered state that had been prepared long ago. All his senses were on fully automatic, and all the other revelatory pictures now being shown to him as some kind of bizarre side-show would soon, ever so soon, start to give him full disclosure.

Unable to control his descent to match that of the approaching speeds, he slammed into Ullyman's torpid body, the force of which almost knocked him out. Winded, he managed to grab a handful of fabric with one hand while desperately trying to locate his rip cord with the other. Below, the ground was fast coming up to meet them with the peak of the Tor central in a spinning vortex.

Amidst the physical exertion in trying to release his canopy, a resignation came over him. It was peaceful, as if he were in a dream that he would soon awake from. He stopped struggling, and in that moment his hand found the toggle and with one last effort he pulled on it. The arrest on the descent wasn't enough. As soon as the canopy caught air, they slammed into the ground hard. Ironically the net used by the bare backers was only a few yards away. Nic had landed on his back, cushioning the impact of his unconscious mate.

Edith, the wulf and a gaggle of eyewitnesses rushed towards what looked like a bundle of discarded rags. As she approached the lifeless tangle of limbs she feared the worst. Her heart was thumping inside her chest fit to burst. She dropped to her knees calling out his name, the wulf began pacing in circles emitting a pitiful whine.

'Don't move them,' warned a voice.

Edith gently placed a hand on Ullyman's upturned back and felt a faint but definite rise and fall. 'He's breathing!' she exclaimed. 'Help me, someone, please.'

Two hooded figures appeared as if from nowhere, looming large over the scene. The small group of onlookers instinctively moved back as they calmly took charge. One of them ever so gently prised the distraught young woman away, then with one at the head and one at the feet, and without any perceptible physical effort they lifted Ullyman off the prone body of his mate and laid him on his back.

CAPRICORN

Rae then carefully removed Ully's helmet, at which his girl came rushing back to comfort.

'Give him time,' the Pleiadian spoke softly, restraining her with his arm.

Atalan removed Nicobar's head protection. Blood seeped from every facial orifice. His spine was shattered, and he had suffered multiple internal injuries. He felt the side of his neck and detected a faint pulse.

The wulf forced her way to Ully's side and began to revive him by licking his face. Miraculously he had only suffered a broken wrist and a couple of cracked ribs. Mercifully, his ego had seen sense and allowed him to wear a Faraday suit under his wingsuit; alongside Nic's actions it probably saved his life. With his face glistening from canine saliva, he blinked open his eyes. Edith was on him in a smothering shot.

'Arrgh!' he winced in pain.

'Ully, are you alright?' She looked up to the two hooded benefactors. 'Is he going to be okay?'

'Edith?' he croaked. 'Is that you? What happened? Where am I?'

She broke down in fits of relieved sobs, smothering him with tears and kisses. 'You're gonna be okay – you're gonna be okay,' she mantra'd. 'Tell me where it hurts, babe.'

'He's going to be fine,' suggested Rae, gently removing her once more. 'Just give him time to come round.'

'You,' said Ully, managing to raise and point a finger with his good hand. 'I've seen you before. You were in Brigantia – Nic treat you in Mercia.'

'Yes,' replied the Pleiadian calmly. 'He also saved your life just now.'

'Nic?' he asked confused. 'Where is he?'

Rae simply directed his gaze to the supine body still strapped in its harness amidst a tangle of fabric and suspension lines.

At once Ully recognised the fish dude who was knelt over his mate. It didn't do anything to remove the confusion. 'Nic? - Nic?' he called out while painfully trying to get to his knees. The wulf was doing her revival thing, whining pitifully while smearing the escaping blood across Nic's sedate features with her tongue. Atalan got to his feet to allow access as Ully crawled to his side. With every breath he took the pain shot across his torso and his wrist throbbed puffed and swollen.

PRECESSION

'Nic – Nicobar – talk to me, brother,' he said panicked at the sight of his friend and the sky-blue canopy that lay on the ground beyond. Soon the realisation of what had gone down slowly dawned. 'Nic – Nic, wake up, man – please – don't do this to me – please.' He looked up to the skies from where they'd both come and then to the giant Pleiadian who looked on impassively.

'I was there for you *this* time, wasn't I, you divot?' Barely conscious, Nic had managed to open his eyes and bring the frantic features of his friend into some sort of focus.

'Nic! - What was that? He spoke. Did you hear him? What's he saying? He's delirious. He's going to be okay, isn't he?' He looked up to those around him and got no response. 'You're gonna be okay, brother, aren't you?'

Nicobar managed a weak smile and slowly shook his head. 'I heard the good news,' he whispered. 'You're going to be a family. This time you're going to be with them till the end.' He reached out to the stressing wulf who was still in attendance and managed to stroke her fur. 'More than a few young ones to look after for a while,' he said cryptically.

Ully didn't understand. He looked around again for some sort of translation. 'You're gonna be okay – please say you're gonna be okay.'

Nic managed another smile as his bleeding eyes started to dim out. 'I'm okay,' he reassured. 'You make sure you look after them – and make sure you look after yourself, yeah? – Hands off cocks – on socks . . .'

Nicobarius Brooke closed his eyes for the last time, just as the rising sun shone its splendour through the arched gate of St. Michaels Tower atop the Tor. The falcon rode its illuminated rays towards the young healer's resting place, sounding an agonising, echoing call across the Somerset levels.

Ullyman Spence fell into his lover's arms, now oblivious to his own physical pain, but wracked with an emotional painful mix of grief and guilt that no amount of comfort could assuage. A sunbeam caught the solitary teardrop that fell from Ullyman's cheek and hung suspended in mid-air. It contained in microcosm a galaxy of mankind's lessons, follies, hopes, dreams and achievements. It then fell into an oblivion of its own.

CAPRICORN

The Hawks Fly Home

After the passing of the geomag came the rain. It fell virtually unabated for almost thirty rotes, sometimes in short-lived but violent cloudbursts, or else in persistent, monotonous drizzle that was hailed as a blessing by some and a curse for others. Ullyman Spence sat on his rolled up inflatent in a vast, almost deserted field that had now turned into a quagmire, staring blankly at nothing as the rain fell into puddles in front of him. In the near distance, Edith was squeezing the last of her gear into her sizeable backpack, with the wulf, who now very rarely left her side, in close attendance.

Nicobar had been laid to rest in the shadow of the Tor, his grave marked by a solitary silver birch sapling, and given full approbation by his guardians, an enlightened couple who had both looked at each other with a feeling of disquietude when their only son had announced his intention to go walkabout. It had come with a resignation that he had no doubt come into this world with a singular mission, as was evident at birth when he opened his eyes, took his first gulp of air, and let everyone know he didn't want to be here. During his formative years, his wisdom often left them speechless. He even claimed to have chosen them as his parents. His understanding of the human condition amazed them, sometimes feeling as though he was raising them instead. They knew he had been here before, and always got the sense that he was back, somewhat reluctantly, for unfinished business. Always happy in his studious solitude, he rarely enjoyed the friendship of children his own age, apart from, that is, one kid who shared his passion for ornithology. As the most unlikely pair, they had grown up in Catterick, flying hawks high up on Barden Moor. Inseparable until now, the Brookes received the devastating news from a distraught, often incomprehensible Ullyman who found it hard to impart his story amidst the mix of sorrow, shame and guilt he was still living through. They refused to apportion blame for the loss of their son on the young man who had been ardently devoted to his lifelong friend. To them Ully was almost a second son, a funny, larger-than-life, if often headstrong young individual, who was forever on their doorstep eating them out of house and home; a perfect foil for their own flesh and blood who often made them feel like they were all just a means to an end. Whether or not he had managed to fulfil his destiny they would never know, but they both shared a humility that would make them eternally privileged and proud to have been his custodians for the short time he was with them.

Atalan and Rae sat on the Council and were part of the inquest that dealt with the aftermath of The Gathering of the Tribes Festival that witnessed seven births, seven deaths, and an outbreak of avian flu amongst the near three million gathered.

In the case of Nicobarius Brooke, they were both deposed as eyewitnesses to the tragic event that led to his death. They presented their testimonies in a manner that showed both he and Ullyman Spence being fully aware of the flight ban had acted under their own free will as sovereign individuals and found no cause to lay blame on one or the other. As for the skypod vendor, he was ordered to pay back the gold credits and banned from operating for a period of two shars.

After the hearing, still wrapped up in his grief and guilt, Ully sought out the two magnanimous Pleiadians but couldn't locate them anywhere. He went to all the other council members in turn, but no one could tell him of their whereabouts; they had simply disappeared without trace as was now becoming a common theme with the mysterious pair. Keen to thank them for their part in his exoneration, he also wanted answers. Was their spontaneous presence a mere coincidence, or as he was now beginning to suspect were all these happenings preordained? Could they shed some light on Nic's last words that, at the time, had seemed like delirious ramblings? What had he meant by – *being there for him this time - This time you're going to be with them till the end -?* He didn't have the sagacity to work it all out, but he guessed that they did. They were sentient to all this esoteric stuff, and deep down he was beginning to realise that his own belligerence wasn't the sole cause of Nic's demise. He searched the now near deserted site high and low for the two tall stand-out hooded figures until Edith and the wulf dragged him out of the torrential downpour offering comfort and solace.

'You know, my grandmother used to say - "There are things known, and things unknown, and in between are doors."'

'What does that even mean?' asked Ully in a miserable tone.

'I think it means: If we are meant to know something, then that door shall open for us, if not, it will remain closed – maybe you're

CAPRICORN

not meant to go through that door yet.'

Ullyman tried his best to make sense of these words. He remembered back to Ariana's parting advice, as cryptic as it was, and wondered why women appeared wiser than men. He gazed at Edith's rain-soaked features, her hair plastered to her head, then cupped her face in his hands and kissed away a drop at the end of her nose. 'I love you,' he said.

He suggested they take the Hyperlink home, but she said they should complete walkabout in honour of Nic's memory, thinking it might lend time for her man to deal with the trauma.

They left the site during a short respite from the rain, under the arches of three separate rainbows, Ullyman's wingsuit laying discarded in a puddle waiting to be collected by the clean-up gangs.

§

Ralph Wainwright was a dour Brigantine. Stocky in stature with a round, weathered face, and a balding head that he kept hidden under an equally weathered flat cap. A farmer all his life, as were generations of his family before him, he had accumulated most of the traits associated with his ancient Yorkshire ancestry: sharp tongued, irascible, naturally suspicious of outsiders, not one to suffer fools, all tempered with a subtle dry sense of humour. He now stood in front of this weary band of travellers, hands on hips, chewing thoughtfully on a sprig of hawthorn that hung from the side of his mouth wondering what to make of his round bellied only daughter, the hapless looking youth who had made it so and the wulf with its noisy litter of five cubs.

'Well, Dad, aren't you going to say something?' ventured Edith.

He chewed and thought some more. 'What'll be the dowry?' he finally asked.

'Dowry?' repeated his daughter with a touch of incredulity. 'What bloody age are you still living in, Dad?'

'Er – you're welcome to take some of the cubs if you like,' said Ully.

'Are you trying to be funny, lad?' said Ralph spitting out his sprig of hawthorn. 'Is he trying to be funny?'

'He's only trying to be helpful.'

'So, is that all my daughter's worth to you, a couple of runty mutts that'll likely grow into killers?'

'You're an arable farmer, Dad; you don't have any livestock.'

'No, but some of my neighbours do.'

'They're domesticated animals, Mr. Wainwright, they'd have no interest in preying on others unless they were starving. They make great companions and are loving and loyal – see.'

By now, two of the cubs had started fussing and playing around the farmer's legs, pawing up at him with doleful eyes begging for attention. Ralph's hard exterior at once began to soften. He lifted them up in his chunky hands and they immediately assaulted his facial whiskers with their tongues.

'Alright you buggers – enough!' He set them back down with glistening chops and a resignation that he was about to lose the only woman left in his life since his missus had upped and gone off with one of his workers a few shars ago. 'Well, it's not the best deal I've ever made, but I'll take those two off your hands, and no more.'

In a rare show of affection, Edith planted a kiss on her old man's forehead and gave him a hug. 'Thanks, Dad. I need you to know how happy I am. I'm really in love with Ully; I'm going to have his children, and you're going to be a granddad; I hope you can be happy for us too.'

In such an uncomfortable setting for him, Ralph mumbled his approval. As part of his parsimonious make up, he was acutely aware that he was not only losing a daughter, but also a farm hand who knew how to graft when needed.

'He looks the handy type,' he whispered in her ear. 'I hope you've got a couple of handy ones in there too,' he said nodding to her tummy. 'I'm not getting any younger. This place will always be here for you and yours if you ever decide to come back to these parts. Now go on, bugger off and live your life.'

Ully had one more port of call to make before he took his family north to Catterick. They crossed the river Wharfe and started the long ascent high up onto Rombalds Moor. He was now ready to unburden himself of all the bad choices made, undaunted at the prospect of shedding his personal agendas, ready to seek counsel, prepared to listen, keen to learn. Nic should have been here with him for all those things, but he wasn't. He did his best to quell the selfishness that arose in him when his ego tried to put the blame on his good friend for abandoning him like that. It was an ancient sensibility that he knew deep down had been a part of his own make up for a long, long time, and only now was he beginning to be fully aware of its presence. Ullyman had always played the warrior to Nic's sage, but now there was a chink of light that was beginning to evolve his sense of perception, revealing that enlightenment was not a fixed end or goal but a way of accepting the natural order of things and being able to flow with the universal stream. But there were still these strange anomalies in the physical that persisted and irked him somewhat.

He tapped the breast pocket of his jacket with one hand while helping his pregnant girl over an outcrop of boulders with the other. He had a confession to make, and he was still trying to work out the rhyme or reason for his actions that day, save for a fleeting notion that he might have made a gift of something that wasn't his to give and keep the other one for himself.

They finally reached what he thought was their destination. Ully leant on a standing stone and looked all around him; there was nothing to be seen but hill and rock and heather and the valley they had just climbed way below. Confusion was writ large across his face, along with the memory of himself, his late companion and the wulf trying to escape the wrath of a geomag.

'Is it much further?' asked Edith, breathing heavily.

'We're here - I think,' said Ully turning three-sixty, trying to get his bearings. He slapped the top of the standing stone. 'No, we're definitely here – this is the place, I'm certain.'

He moved over the ground where the stone-built house should have been with its quirky rooms and its wondrous library; no trace of it, not even a foundation. He walked down the dip where Amun kept his goats and chickens, looked for the small fruit orchard that was nowhere to be seen – nothing but moorland. He turned back exasperated. Was he going mad? Then he remembered those final moments when the air was being ripped from his lungs, and he thought his time had come. Nic knew there was sanctuary, but he had seen bugger all.

Edith sat on the ground to rest her legs with her back against the standing stone 'What's going on Ulls, why are we here?'

With his mind in a whirl, he sat down beside her. Immediately the three remaining wulf cubs were all over him, chewing at his hands with their needle-like teeth. 'It was here – and now it isn't,' he said shaking his head while batting away the fussing pups.

PRECESSION

'What was?'

'The place I told you about with the old man and woman who took us in after the geomag. It was here, in this very spot – and now it isn't.'

'You sure this is the place?'

He banged the back of his head repeatedly against the millstone grit obelisk, as if trying to knock some sense into it. 'This stone stood in the yard directly outside the front door which was just over there; it's the only thing that's left. I know I'm in the right place.'

Edith looked at him with a tinge of pity that didn't help the situation.

'You don't believe me,' he said, catching the look.

She shook her head while looking around trying to will something to appear. 'I don't disbelieve you, but what else can I say?'

Ully trawled his memory back to that time when none of it seemed real anyway. He recalled telling the old man that all he saw was hill and rock the moment before he lapsed into unconsciousness, then he remembered Amun suggesting to him that he might not have been really looking. It was all so vague, like a deep dream, vivid in the moment, but that often fades on awakening. If it was real, where had they gone, where had it all gone? If all this was part of him evolving his sense of perception, he guessed his psyche wasn't doing such a good job of it.

Edith saw the brain hurt in her lover's tormented features and instinctively stroked his arm. 'You remember when we talked about doors?' He looked at her anticipating some imparted wisdom that he was sure he would struggle to get his head around. 'Maybe you're trying to force open a door that's locked to you right now. No doubt there is an answer to all this out there, but for now why not allow it to be the mystery that it is. Nic's gone, the old couple and the house are no longer here, but we are. We should be all that matters to you now.' She placed a hand over her growing tummy and looked deep into his eyes. In that moment the kaleidoscopic preconditioned, preconceived notions that Ullyman's ego saw as reality were shattered into a thousand pieces, and its illusory world was gone forever.

He leant over and kissed her long and passionately, then bent down to kiss the swollen maw protecting the growing lives that would now shape his own.

CAPRICORN

He had only wanted to tell them about Nic and fess up about taking the necklets with a commitment to make the journey east again and lay them in their rightful place as was their sworn promise, but now he saw no point, that method of assuaging his guilt was a futile act. Learn the lesson and move on. He removed the hemp purse from his breast pocket and tipped the tangle of ancient, tainted metal into the palm of his hand. He gazed at the two tiny cast hawks and wondered what their story was. Why had he been pulled in and made to behave like a magpie in taking those not so shiny ancient artefacts, was it for the same reason they had lured Amun to act in the same way? His rationale could only poke at something oracular and tenuously related to events long ago that had no bearing or influence in the now. With Edith's closed-door analogy fresh in his head, he was able to quell any lingering curiosity as to their significance.

'What are those?' she asked curiously.

'Relics of the past, I guess.'

'Why do you have them?'

'I thought one of them was mine – for a short while.'

She looked at him inquisitively.

'I'll tell you all about it. Come on, it's time we were on our way, get a few miles in before nightfall.'

He untangled the mass of chain and laid each necklet carefully over the top of the standing stone. Out of nowhere the falcon appeared and perched itself atop the stone, its head darting in all directions and its raucous call seemingly approving of Ullyman's actions.

To the west the sun cast its long shadow over the moor before dipping behind a peak. Arm in arm, with the wulf and her playful brood at their side, they set a course north to start their new life together.

Acknowledgements

Sources: Laura Aboli, Timothy Alberino, Mauro Biglino, Harvey, Adam & Josh Bigelsen, Claude Bernard, Antoine Béchamp, George Carlin, Michael Clarage Phd., Ahote Cooper (American Indian.coc.org), Mark Elkin, Arthur Firstenberg, Five Times August, Foster & Kimberly Gamble, Viktor Grebennikov, Charles Hapgood, Suzanne Humphries MD, Lewis Hyde, David & Gareth Icke, Brendan Murphy, Terence Mckenna, Robert L. Moore, Milutin Milankovitch, Lucien Mars, Mark Passio, Royal Raymond Rife, Christian Sundberg, Merlin Sheldrake, Arthur Schopenhauer, Zecharia Sitchin, Anne Tucker, Chan Thomas, Wal Thornhill, Michael Tsarion, Immanuel Velikovsky, John Ward.

About the author

Derryl Flynn grew up in a northern coal mining town in England during the fifties and sixties. He studied Film, Theatre & TV at Bradford College of Art in the early seventies where he developed a passion for writing drama for screenplay and radio. His two previous novels, *The Albion* and *Scrapyard Blues* were both published by Grinning Bandit Books.

Derryl lives with his wife, on the edge of the moors and just a spit away from Bronte country (not a good idea if the wind's in the wrong direction). He is currently working on a screenplay version of *Scrapyard Blues*.

Precession - Pisces: Finalist in the 2014 Exeter Novel Prize for unpublished work.

GRINNING BANDIT BOOKS

Grinning Bandit Books is an independent publisher that publishes mostly humorous books, including fiction, travel memoirs, and children's book. We currently have 30 books available on Amazon (see below).

Website: http://grinningbandit.webnode.com.

Our books

Fiction
Mrs Maginnes is Dead – Maeve Sleibhin
Five madcap sisters hunt for a dead woman's hidden legacy while having to deal with the police, gypsies, and the old lady's troublesome goat.

Weekend in Weighton – Terry Murphy
First-time private investigator Eddie Greene is having a bad weekend. It's about to get worse.

Scrapyard Blues – Derryl Flynn
Sex, drugs, and rock 'n' roll. How did one crazy night of excess end up with 25 years behind bars?

The Albion – Derryl Flynn
Fast approaching forty, angry, disillusioned and sickened by the mindless violence all around him, Terry Gallagher decides to make good.

The Girl from Ithaca – Cherry Gregory
Neomene of Ithaca, younger sister of Odysseus, reveals what Homer

never knew: a woman's view of the Trojan War.

The Walls of Troy – Cherry Gregory
It is seven years into the siege at Troy, and Neomene finds herself defending the Greek camp against fever and Trojan attack. Soon she is embroiled in the destiny of Achilles and the fate of Troy itself.

Flashman and the Sea Wolf – Robert Brightwell
This first book in the Thomas Flashman series covers his adventures with Thomas Cochrane, one of the most extraordinary naval commanders of all time.

Flashman and the Cobra – Robert Brightwell
This book takes Thomas to territory familiar to readers of his nephew's adventures: India, during the second Mahratta war. It also includes an illuminating visit to Paris during the Peace of Amiens in 1802.

Flashman in the Peninsula – Robert Brightwell
Flashman's memoirs offer a unique perspective on the Peninsular War, including new accounts of famous battles as well as incredible incidents and characters almost forgotten by history.

Flashman's Escape – Robert Brightwell
This book covers the second half of Thomas Flashman's experiences in the Peninsular War and follows on from *Flashman in the Peninsula*.

Short Tails of Cats and other Curious Creatures – Frank Kusy
Fat Buddhists, insomniac cats, wide-boy whales, headless horsemen, Polish plumbers, little piggy home-owners, and partially-sighted mice – something for everyone in this short tale anthology of the absurd.

Science Fiction
Sci-Fi Shorts – Mark Roman & Corben Duke
From The Man Who Saved the World (kind of) to the unluckiest man

on Earth. A collection of nineteen amusing SF stories.

Sci-Fi Shorts II – Mark Roman
Ten humorous science fiction stories telling of the retired scientist who invents an antidote to Murphy's Law, a hen party in space, a train journey into a parallel world, and more.

Fresh Meat – Maeve Sleibhin
When Lola visits Old San Juan, Puerto Rico she discovers that her blood is irresistible to both the mosquitos and the vampires that plague the island.

Prime: The Summons – Maeve Sleibhin
Despised by her own kind and exiled on a space base, Xai must somehow return home to fulfil her destiny.

Mother and Other Short Science Fiction Stories – Maeve Sleibhin
A collection of science fiction short stories told largely from a female point of view, and range from comic irony to horror.

The Ultimate Inferior Beings – Mark Roman
An ill-chosen spaceship crew encounter a race of loopy aliens and find that the fate of the Universe rests in their less-than-capable hands. Sci-fi comedy.

Travel/humour
Kevin and I in India – Frank Kusy
Two barmy British backpackers take on India in this true story of adventure and misadventure. All Kevin wants is a cheese sandwich...

Rupee Millionaires – Frank Kusy
Want to make a million? Be careful what you wish for ...

Off the Beaten Track – Frank Kusy
What did Frank do to escape the crazy Polish biker chick? He went

off the beaten track…

Too Young to be Old – Frank Kusy
When Frank starts working with old people, he rediscovers a young dream. And sets out to India to make it come true.

Dial and Talk Foreign at Once – Frank Kusy
Can Frank cover India for a travel guide in 66 days? Or will he crash and burn?

The Reckless Years: A Marriage made in Chemical Heaven – Frank Kusy
The true story of two people who tried and failed to destroy each other. And fell in love. Again.

Life before Frank: from Cradle to Kibbutz – Frank Kusy
With the young Frank's antics and dodgy dealings driving his poor mother to despair, he vows that one day he will make her proud of him. It is a vow he will find difficult to keep.

The Clueless Companion: My Diaries with Dennis – Frank Kusy
Frank has a problem. He wants to retire, but his wife won't let him. Over the course of the next 16 months, Frank is busier than he's ever been.

Going Batty: The Lockdown Chronicles, Part One – Frank Kusy
Known for his travel memoirs, Frank Kusy is used to going places at the drop of a hat. But this time, with the UK in lockdown due to Covid-19, he is going nowhere.

Going Batty: The Lockdown Chronicles, Part two – Frank Kusy
Just when Frank thought lockdown couldn't happen again. It did. Twice.

After the Fire – Frank Kusy
Following a freak house fire, Frank is forced to travel once more – to darkest Sunbury.

Children's Books

Ginger the Gangster Cat – Frank Kusy
Ginger returns from the dead - to carry out the most cunning cat crime of the century. In Barcelona.

Ginger the Buddha Cat – Frank Kusy
Ginger is facing a tough decision. Sausages or enlightenment?

Warwick the Wanderer – Terry Murphy
Rock n' roll: it's the future!

Percy the High-Flying Pig – Cherry Gregory
When Percy the pig decides life on the farm is too boring, he escapes with Sam the sheep dog.

Printed in Dunstable, United Kingdom